WHEN YOU COME BACK

DEBRA WEBB

WHEN YOU COME BACK

A Novel

Debra Webb

PINK HOUSE PRESS
WebbWorks, LLC, Madison, Alabama
First Edition June 2019

ACKNOWLEDGMENTS

I grew up in Alabama. The community was a small one with a k-12 school and the same big old yellow school buses I describe in this story. Though Jackson Falls, Alabama, only exists in this story, it is very much based on the area in which I lived as a child. Like Emma, I loved nothing better than exploring the woods and digging up treasures. Also like Emma, I wasn't exactly Miss Popular and I always sat right behind the driver on the school bus. I loved creating Emma's world and this story. I hope you will love it as well!

This book is dedicated to my precious baby girl, Melissa Bailey. Thank you for always being my sunshine, for the laughter and for always being you.

1

THURSDAY, MAY 10

EMMA

WHY IS it that some people disappear never to be seen again while others come back? Is it fate or karma or just plain old dumb luck?

These two questions occur to me as I enter Madden County, Alabama. My destination is the small town of Jackson Falls shoehorned between Huntsville and Decatur. The Rocket City and the River City. *RC. RC.* Funny, I never noticed the initial thing before. It's late, almost eleven. I've been driving since this time last night. Perhaps I am suffering from white line fever or I'm merely slaphappy. Either way, the questions nag at me as if the invisible umbilical cord of home is now force-feeding regret and nostalgia in equal measures to my brain.

I don't know why I came back and the others didn't.

I doubt I will ever know.

It was early April, the year my world changed. I remember the fallow fields in the valley had gone from drab winter brown to a fresh spring green. Henbit and Purple Deadnettle blossoms had cut a swath of color through the lush sea of green. Pretty to look at but my dad explained that this was not such good news for the farmers. The mild winter had allowed what looked like flowers to me but were actually weeds a head start before planting time, making the intruders far harder to control once the crops were in the ground.

At only eight years old I shouldn't have been too concerned and yet somehow I was. I always had my head in one book or another. I learned to read by the time I was four. So after a bit of investigating at the school library, I promptly told Dad that those so-called weeds were an important food source for pollinators in early spring. My announcement earned me one of his deep belly laughs. When he'd caught his breath he gave me a nod and said, "You've got me there, Emma."

I loved my dad so very much. He was the kindest man in the world and he always had time for me. Unlike my mother. She was always far too busy with Natalie.

Natalie.

Despite the passing of a quarter century, an ache pierces my heart.

Natalie was my sister—older by seven years. Dad always said Natalie and Mother were like two peas in a pod. *Like us*, he would assure me with a big grin and a wink. He was the reason it never really bothered me that the rest of the world— even my own mother—loved Natalie more than me. Natalie was prettier and far more talented. She was on the dance competition team, a cheerleader, straight A student. Natalie was perfect. And I...I was *me*.

Emma Graves, the girl who came back.

I still find it odd that even after my world changed so dramatically at the ripe old age of eight, I didn't. I'm certain I didn't know how or I'm sure I would have made an attempt at least to be a better daughter. To look prettier. Be smarter. More talented.

Some small effort to fill the enormous void left by Natalie.

It was only a day or two after the weed versus food source debate when it happened. It was a Tuesday and it started like any other ordinary day in third grade. At school and everywhere else I was the absolute opposite of my popular sister. She had the long blond hair and bright blue eyes while my hair is dark brown and my eyes are equally dark. To add insult to injury my nearsightedness kept me in overly large glasses until my teenage years when I discovered the convenience of contacts and then later the miracle of Lasik surgery.

The other kids enjoyed many laughs at my expense. I was the homely sister, the four-eyed kid with Coke bottle lenses who loved digging in the dirt behind the old houses my dad restored. Sam, our big old Lab, was generally at my side. Digging for my treasures ensured my nails were perpetually chipped and in desperate need of a manicure. That part hasn't changed either. The fact of the matter is a girl could find all sorts of relics exploring that way. Timeworn spoons. Vintage ink and apothecary bottles. Coins. And even the occasional pile of bones where the family dog or cat, maybe a bird, was buried. I loved it. Sadly, finding those bones really made me a freak in the other kids' eyes.

Never really bothered me…until *that day*.

Like the rest of the kids in Jackson Falls, my sister and I rode a big yellow bus to school. Sam waited on the porch every day for us to come home. We lived on a farm Dad had inherited from his father and the place was several miles outside the town limits. Half a dozen other children lived along that route, including my only friend who was home sick that day, but Natalie and I were the final stop.

Natalie and her best friend Stacy Yarbrough, older and far too sophisticated to sit near me, always claimed the very back seat on the bus. Stacy came home with us at least twice a week for dance or cheerleader practice. The two always giggled and acted silly, whispered about boys and all their other secrets I was too immature and unimportant to understand.

As far as they were concerned I didn't exist. Didn't matter really. I sat behind the driver, Mr. Lincoln Russell. I liked watching him shift the gears and operate the door to let kids on and off the bus. Sometimes he even allowed me to control the door. In my eight-year-old experience no one else had ever been permitted to operate the door. Pulling that lever made me feel quite important.

At the time I considered Mr. Russell pretty old, older than my parents for sure. Later, at his funeral, I heard someone say he was sixty-eight. Most folks whispered that it was his bad heart. It made him a ticking time bomb and finally the bomb exploded and his ticker gave out. Others nodded sagely and said it was just his time to go. Confused, I asked Dad and he explained that it was a heart attack that took him off to heaven to be with his wife.

When the trouble began, on that long stretch of road where there was nothing save fields and mountains, I didn't understand. I only knew that something was wrong with Mr. Russell. If the sky had fallen Natalie and Stacy would have been too busy twittering and whispering to notice. That day I didn't have a lot of room to talk, my attention was totally transfixed on the purple "flowers" in the unplowed fields. I wondered if I picked a bunch and took them home to my mother would she like me better. Or at least as much as she did Natalie. In all probability she would have recognized they were weeds and scolded me for doing something so foolish. No doubt she would have broken out in hives and told Dad I tried to kill her. After all, she would say as she had so many times before that I very nearly killed her when I came into this world.

That was always the way of things between my mother and me. We never saw eye to eye. She was busy with Natalie and I tagged along with Dad. When the three of us—Mother,

Natalie and I—were together I appeared to get on their nerves more than anything else. I was too young to understand, I was too this or that. I actually heard my mother say once to some of her lunch lady friends that she frequently wondered if she brought the wrong baby home from the hospital because, God knew, I was nothing like her or my sister.

As unfortunate as some parts of my childhood were the adult me is, thankfully, no longer the butt of jokes. And though I'm still nothing like my popular sister was, the prickly relationship with my mother has changed to some degree for the better.

Frankly, I rarely allow myself to ponder life before the bus accident. It makes me feel far too guilty. Survivor's guilt, that's what the shrinks call it. Whatever it's called, I would gladly trade any and all attention from my mother for the rest of my life if I could change what happened *that day*.

We were still miles from our house when Mr. Russell started gasping and wheezing. The bus weaved and swayed on the road. My stomach churned with dread. He tried to control the bus. I watched him struggle with the steering wheel, but then he grabbed at his chest and the bus careened off the pavement, bumping along the shoulder like a bucking horse determined to throw its rider.

Terrified, I scrambled under the seat to hide from whatever awful thing was about to happen. Natalie and Stacy screamed at the tops of their lungs, as if auditioning for a bit part in a bad slasher movie. I imagined them clinging to each other, eyes open wide in mind-boggling horror.

The bus toppled into the ditch with a bone-jarring crash, landing on its side. I banged hard against the underside of the seat and ended up slung into the aisle between the two rows. For a minute after the bus stopped, I didn't move. I felt rattled, like a bag of potatoes that had been shaken and then pitched across the produce department at the supermarket.

A single moment of silence throbbed in the air before

Natalie and Stacy began to wail and sob. Poor Mr. Russell lay motionless in the step well. His eyes still open, he continued to gasp for air, but not as hard or as often as before. A trickle of blood slid down his forehead. This was bad and I was really scared but I didn't have a clue what to do.

Natalie shouted at Stacy to hurry. I managed to sit up, right my glasses and peer back at them as they struggled with the emergency door's release. Both carried on as if they were fatally injured. Judging by the way they looked I didn't believe they were really hurt very badly at all.

Probably only scared, like me.

The door flew open and while Stacy jumped out, Natalie turned and ordered me to stay on the bus. They were going to find help. I remember her face—the fear and uncertainty there—as she caught and held my gaze for one endless second.

In those days most kids didn't have cell phones, at least none I knew anyway. They were far too expensive. My parents didn't even have cell phones and there wasn't a phone or a radio on the bus. The next term every school bus in the county had radios installed, but on *that day* there wasn't one.

My head hurt and I felt a little sick to my stomach but I couldn't just sit there. I needed to do something besides wait. I scrambled over to where Mr. Russell lay crumpled in a sad heap. I asked him if he was okay but he only looked at me and made those wheezy, choking sounds. I held his hand and tried to smile, to reassure him. I swiped my face, thought I was bleeding, too, but it was only tears. I suppose some part of me comprehended that he was dying. I pushed my glasses up my nose and stretched my neck to see out the fractured windshield. Natalie and Stacy walked along the road, moving farther and farther from the bus. I'm pretty sure the next house was a couple of miles. Walking might take a while. Maybe they didn't feel like running.

I would have run.

I held Mr. Russell's hand for a very long time but no one came to help. I gazed out at the road in hope of spotting my dad's truck, but the road was deserted for as far as I could see. It cut through the fields and flanked the trees like a long black snake slithering off into the mountains. "That's the good thing about living outside town," Dad always said. "You might go all day without a single car passing on the road."

That afternoon it was not a good thing.

Mr. Russell had stopped gasping for breath and he wasn't blinking anymore. Looking at him gave me a bad feeling in my chest and my head still hurt. I tried valiantly not to cry anymore but those awful hiccupping sobs got the better of me, and the tears wouldn't stop flowing down my heated cheeks.

Finally, I decided that maybe the girls had forgotten about Mr. Russell and me. I wouldn't put it past them. So I promised him I would be right back and I made my way across the seats to the other end of the bus, then climbed out the emergency door and jumped into the knee deep grass. The sun had nested on the treetops sending shadows across the road, but I had some time before it got dark so I started to run. Running made my head hurt worse but I kept going.

The wind whispered through the trees on my right and I could have sworn something moved in the tall weeds. Probably only a rabbit. Maybe a fox.

Could be a coyote.

Not scared, I told myself. *Not scared.*

I shivered as the brisk air cut right through my pink sweater. Pink was not really my color but my mother loved it. She and Natalie always wore something pink. Even the little ballerina slippers on my sister's silver necklace were pink.

I decided that if I kept going as fast as I could I might catch up with Natalie and Stacy. Maybe I would even beat them to our house. Taking the shortcut I'd found once when I was walking in the woods seemed like the right thing to do. I did that a lot back then, walk in the woods with our dog Sam. Something else the other kids made fun of.

Who walks in the creepy old woods? Emma Graves. The girl who digs up bones.

Taking the shortcut might have actually been a reasonably good idea except I wasn't mature enough to comprehend that I had a concussion and that I was merely a child who was rattled and not thinking clearly.

Instead of finding my way home, I ended up lost. Night came and I was all alone and so very terrified. I walked in the darkness until I could walk no farther. Finally, I curled up under a tree. At some point that night I felt Sam's nose nudge me but I was too cold and too exhausted to move. I couldn't even open my eyes. Instinctively understanding the danger of the falling temperature, the big animal curled around me, warming my body like an electric blanket. Later, I learned the temperature dropped just below freezing that night. Dogwood winter, they called it.

The whole community turned out to look for us, prowling the woods and fields all night. The first pale red streaks of dawn variegated the sky before one of the search teams found me, but it was Sam's barking that woke me. He heard their voices and their tromping around well before they reached us and began to bark, the sound booming through the woods like thunder. I was colder than I had ever been in my life and I hurt all over, especially my head. I will never forget how my mother cried and how tightly she held me when she drew me into her arms. My dad, too. Most of the people who had been looking for me were crying as well.

On that cold, weary morning I represented a fragile thread of hope.

That day, twenty-five years ago, they found me, alive if a little cold and banged up. But the others—my big sister and her friend who always sat in the very back seat of Madden

County School bus number 9—were never seen or heard from again.

Mother and Dad were so sad for so long that I worried they would never smile again. Nothing was the same. As much and as often as I resented Natalie's perfectness and the way she drew all Mother's love and attention like the moon drawing the tide, I missed her so much. Every night when I went to bed I cried and prayed it wasn't my fault that she was gone. God knew I'd wished her away a million times.

As the months and years marched on folks still mentioned the missing girls from time to time, especially at reunions, weddings and funerals. I became the little girl who was found while the others were lost. Stacy's father wanted to know why I came back and not the others. The police, the reporters—they all wanted to know what really happened but I couldn't tell them because I didn't remember then any more than what I recall today. Natalie and Stacy walked away from the bus—just the two of them. I didn't see anyone else. There was no other car or truck, just the school bus lying like a wounded animal in the ditch.

Mother and Dad became overprotective of me. I couldn't go anywhere, not even into the yard without one of them hovering near me. I never rode a school bus again. Didn't spend the night at a friend's house until I was a senior and Mother finally stopped fighting me on the issue.

If I was a weirdo, a freak before what happened, *that day* became a whole new way to torture me. *Emma Graves is a witch. Emma Graves is the devil's child. God took the other girls to heaven but not Emma. He left her in the woods to die.*

Nothing promises a screwed up adulthood like a crappy childhood.

Pushing those old memories aside I exhale a big, fatigued breath as I roll along the dark streets of Jackson Falls proper. A good daughter would think how nice it is to be home. A good daughter would look forward to seeing her mother after

9

all this time. But I have never been a particularly good daughter in my mother's eyes. Or maybe the right phrase is "as good as Natalie was." Oh, she loves me. I have no doubts. With Natalie gone and then Dad's passing four years ago, we are the only family we have left. Still, we get along far better with a thousand or so miles between us.

Fully aware of our tendency to grate on each other's nerves, I don't come home often. I make the obligatory call to her once each month—well most months anyway. I tell her about work. She tells me about senior yoga and Bunco and art classes at the community center. We rarely speak of Natalie. It's too painful for her even now. At some point, maybe when I was about twelve or thirteen, Mother started to act as if our lives began after *that day*. I suppose it was her way of coping with the loss.

As often and as hard as I had wished for Mother to love me more, I quickly learned that being the center of her universe was no easy task for me. I was no Natalie. Having passed the thirty mark three years ago, I'm no longer wounded when she never misses an opportunity to mention who has recently gotten married or had a baby, which is, of course, a dig at my single, barren status. All of this I endure without a scathing rebuttal because on his dying bed Dad made me promise to always be kind to Mother and never to ignore her.

"She's lost one daughter," he said. "Don't take another one from her."

"Thanks a lot, Dad," I grumble.

In a reluctant attempt to be the good daughter Dad wanted me to be, I called Mother a couple of weeks ago. She and her trio of besties were readying for their annual cruise. By now they had departed Mobile headed for the Panama Canal, Costa Rica, Mahogany Bay, Isla Roatan and Cozumel. With ten nights on the ship and another two visiting friends in Mobile, they will be gone for nearly two weeks.

Which is why I decided completely out of the blue and utterly uncharacteristically to come back to Alabama.

I need a break from my life but I'm not ready to share the ugly details with my mother. She already believes I have a drinking problem—like Dad's sister Vivian, God rest her soul. She's certain I failed to commit to enough therapy after the last tragedy to plague my life. When she learns the latest Emma Graves debacle she will only look at me and announce, "I told you so."

I can't take it.

Cannot take it.

If that makes me a bad daughter, then so be it.

I need some time to think away from Boston and my work there—assuming I still have a job. Terms like breakdown, PTSD and alcohol induced hallucinations were bandied about at the hospital during my forty-eight-hour mandatory stay—another something my mother will never, ever know about.

The trouble is, I can't go back to Boston until I figure this out. I'm trapped between a rock and a hard place and I simply cannot see a way to squeeze out of or around that tight, suffocating spot.

All those years of hard work. A Master's in Forensic Anthropology from Cal State. A Ph.D., for Christ's sake, from Emory. Two years in Iraq exhuming remains from mass graves as well as surviving a terrorist attack and I have to go and lose my shit in a classroom full of snooty sophomores at Boston University. How screwed up is that?

"Seriously screwed up."

So here I am, slinking home in the dead of night to hide and lick my wounds.

2

Towering Oak and Maple trees line Tulip Lane, one of the oldest streets in Jackson Falls. Each spring a river of tulips fills the space between the sidewalks and the street. The first week of May the Chamber of Commerce places a prestigious marker in the yard of the homeowner whose careful attention provides the most colorful and lushest display of the spring-blooming perennials. It's an all-out war my mother has won for years.

I slow and turn into the driveway of my childhood home. Like sentinels, more ancient oaks surround the Victorian style three-story. Even with nothing more than the light of the moon and a lone street lamp I can see that Mother has already supervised the planting of the spring annuals. Pink impatiens and white geraniums sit amid the ivy and creeping Jenny cascading over the sides of pots. More impatiens mixed with begonias lie in mounds around the mulched bases of rich green shrubs and blooming red Azaleas. Though the Hydrangeas haven't bloomed yet, there are pink ones and white ones. In the middle of it all stands the Chamber of Commerce's spring beautification award.

I sigh. Nothing ever changes here.

This house—the one Dad so loving restored that stands a mere three blocks from the school I attended growing up— became home a few months after *that day*. *That day*. Everyone still calls it *that day*. I imagine until something worse happens it will continue to be referred to in such a way. Then again, what could be worse than two children—teenagers, but children nonetheless—disappearing?

No bodies, no remains, no evidence...not one clue was ever discovered.

For years after Natalie disappeared, Sam lay on the front porch of the old farmhouse waiting for the school bus to bring her home. Each time it passed without stopping, he dropped his head to his paws and waited for the next time. Dad brought him to the new house over and over but he always trotted back to the farm to watch for Natalie. We visited him, fed and watered him every day. The last time, I knew as soon as we turned into the driveway that Sam was gone. He wasn't on the porch to stand up and wag his tail in greeting. Mother explained that he'd gone to heaven and Dad buried him in the front yard under the Dogwood tree. We buried Natalie's favorite teddy bear with him. From that moment I understood that my parents had decided Natalie was never coming back.

It was the second worst day of my life.

Now and again over the years a new detective or deputy who came on board with one of the local law enforcement departments opened the cold case and poked around. I ultimately received a call and I patiently repeated the same statements I made twenty-five years ago. Once in a while a hungry reporter looking for a story that pulls on the heartstrings noses into the case. To date nothing has ever come of the well-intended efforts.

I wonder if the call I received just last month from a reporter putting together an anniversary piece somehow prompted my little meltdown in the classroom? Panic and anxiety hadn't gotten the better of me like that since grad school. I stood in that lecture hall looking across the sea of faces and suddenly my hands started to shake and I couldn't catch my breath. Rather than the slides from one of my better-known digs appearing on the massive screen, I saw my sister's face...I saw the bus lying in the ditch. I felt the cold and the blackness of those dark, dark woods swallowing me up. Abject terror had me shrinking behind my desk, alternately shouting for help and sobbing like a child. The next thing I knew I was in a hospital with a light shining in my eyes and questions being fired at me like the rat-a-tat of a machine gun.

I have no idea how I've fallen so far so fast in the past few months.

Admit it, Emma, you are just screwed up, that's all. Totally, completely screwed up.

So travel weary I can hardly blink, I stare up at the grand house. The interior as far as I can see is dark save for the small lamp in the entry hall. That lamp has remained on at night for as long as I can remember. I'm not sure which of us is more afraid of the dark, Mother or me, but even now I keep a light on at night in my apartment. I'm certain the therapist I am supposed to be seeing again this week would exude copious reasons for this behavior. Dad used to say leaving the lamp on was for Natalie...in case she came home in the middle of the night.

But she never did and eventually he stopped mentioning it.

Dad didn't show his grief the way Mother did, but he hurt just as badly. We all did. Natalie's disappearance left a hole—a wide, gaping hole—that nothing or no one can ever fill. Life forced us to learn to walk around that hole. All of us but Sam. Dad brought that pup home to Natalie when she was three. Until he slipped away in his sleep at seventeen, he waited and watched for her to come back to him.

We never had another dog after Sam.

Still trying to work up the energy to get out of the car, I

push the sad memories away and soak up the details of the wide, gracious porch that wraps the entire perimeter of the house. A small upper porch nestles against the turret where the spiral stairs lead up to the third floor that was once nothing more than a storage attic. My gaze rests on the window looking out onto the street from the space that became my private refuge. Though that window, too, is dark, I don't need the light to know the dream catcher I hung there all those years ago still dangles behind the wavy glass just above my bed. Dad transformed the entire third floor into a place just for me. I think he understood even then that Mother and I needed a little distance between us.

A lump swells in my throat but I ignore it. Just because I've come home under less than desirable circumstances doesn't mean I've somehow failed myself, or the hopes and dreams my parents had for me. Recent events do not in any way define me or quantify the value of my work. Who doesn't need a break occasionally? Two weeks is plenty of time to pull myself together. I can do this. Then I'll figure out where I go from here. I've never been one to give up.

I'm not about to start now.

Emerging from my dusty car I inhale deeply. The air is thick with lingering humidity from the unseasonably warm Alabama day. I've been driving for twenty-four hours without stopping for anything beyond the necessary bathroom breaks and the inevitable road construction. My singular goal was to get here and hide. To that end, I turned off my cell phone and drove like a mad woman.

"Not funny, Emma." Most of the people in Boston who know me are no doubt fairly convinced that I am mad—as in the mentally unstable definition.

I laugh at the irony of my dilemma. As fast and as far as I ran to escape my Natalie-less life in this little town, I guess I'm never going to outrun who I am: Emma Graves, the girl who likes digging in the dirt and prefers being surrounded by the dead more than the living. The one who came back when no one else did. A burst of air pushes from my lungs. A woman who is haunted by a past she cannot fully remember and yet cannot escape.

I reach for my duffel bag in the backseat. Before I crash I'll come out and hide my car around back of the house. I certainly don't want any of the neighbors to spot my Prius with its Massachusetts license plates. The whole block would be wondering if Helen's odd daughter was in for a rare visit. The widow Josephine Elders lives right across the street. Her only child, a son a year older than me, is a Baptist preacher. In the widow Elders' eyes my family being Catholic condemns us to the fire and brimstone her son hails from his pulpit every Sunday. Then again, she feels the same way about most of our neighbors whatever their religious beliefs.

Two doors down are the Noble sisters, old maids who are older than God and certainly wiser, in their opinions. The last time a new reverend at their Methodist church attempted to counsel them, they told him as much. There are other eccentric neighbors, but those are the most judgmental. I can hear them now. How long has it been since that peculiar girl came home? Three, four years? Not since her daddy's funeral. The whole lot will want to be the first to catch a glimpse of the curious Graves child all grown up and too busy to visit her mama like a proper daughter should.

Natalie would never have been so negligent.

I have no desire to see anyone. People in small towns ask questions. They suffer from what my dad called nose trouble. After all these years, I absolutely refuse to become the latest hot gossip. Besides, they will only make up what they really want to say anyway. The truth is rarely as exciting as the industrious imaginations of those who populate the Jackson Falls grapevine.

I climb the steps and cross the porch. The cushions on the swing beckon me. I consider collapsing onto the swing and calling it a night. But then any number of neighbors would come skulking around to see who is sleeping on Helen's porch. The truth is, they won't even need to see my car or me. They will sense the shift in the atmosphere, smell the scent of an interloper—the prodigal daughter returns. People do that in the south. Look out for their neighbors. And get into their business.

Really get into their business.

Deep in the bottom of my shoulder bag my fingers finally locate and clutch the house key. I shove it into the lock and twist. Wilting faster than one of my mother's Hydrangeas in the hot afternoon sun, I suddenly realize exactly how tired I am. Forget the car, forget the neighbors, I need to lie down.

I open the door and step across the threshold to see...my mother standing in the entry hall with my dad's twelve gauge aimed at me.

I blink, certain I'm experiencing another hallucination. She isn't supposed to be here. The cruise...nearly fourteen days of solitude.

"Emma, what're you doing here?"

The barrel lowers to the floor and Mother stares at me as if she, too, is struggling with the concept of delirium. The pink gown draping her slim body is edged in lace and looks completely incongruent next to the black steel of the shotgun. A couple of the pink foam rollers she has used for as long as I can remember dangle precariously from her white hair. In the background I hear Elizabeth Taylor's voice. *Cat on a Hot Tin Roof* is playing on the television in the living room. *You can be young without money, but you can't be old without it.*

"Well, I..." cannot under any circumstances tell my mother the truth—not right now. I am exhausted and over-whelmed and confused.

"Oh my God." Mother's left hand flies to her throat. "Letty called you about the missing girls." Her shoulders sag. "I should have called you myself, but—"

"What're you talking about?"

Though the words are mine, my voice sounds like a stranger's. Ice has filled my veins and my knees are suddenly unreasonably weak. From first grade through high school graduation Oletta "Letty" Cotton was my best friend, my only friend really. I grew up and ran as far from home as possible; Letty grew up and became the county sheriff. We're still friends in that long-distance-remember-when way but we haven't talked in ages.

"What missing girls?" I press when Mother still hesitates.

The fleeting image of Natalie and Stacy disappearing into the distance brushes my senses. Have the girls been found after all these years? Maybe Letty did call. My cell is still turned off. Wait, that makes no sense. If Natalie had been found, Mother would have called. Either way, obviously I should have kept my cell turned on.

"Patricia Shepherd's girl and Naomi Baldwin's oldest," she explains, though the names don't ring any bells for me. "They left school on their bikes yesterday afternoon and no one has seen or heard from either one since. Every able man and woman in the tri-county area's looking for them. You haven't heard?" A frown furrows its way across her forehead. "I think it was on the national news last night. Surely you saw the endangered child alerts."

Totally absorbed in my own misery, I haven't watched or listened to the news in days. Ignoring the tightening in my chest, I ask, "Are the police sure the girls didn't just run away?"

Kids do that now more so than when I was growing up. The Internet makes the world seem like such a small place. Running away should be easy, right? God knows I have worked incredibly hard to accomplish that feat. At some point, I outgrew the ability to believe the concept of running away could actually work.

But today's kids are a different story. What they can find

on the World Wide Web all on their own is bad enough, add to that the sheer number of disgusting pervs skulking around cyberspace in search of naïve prey and you have a recipe for disaster. Parents should be more terrified than ever. Another perfectly good reason not to have children.

No one can take from you what you don't have.

My mother shakes her head, the loose pink rollers swaying adamantly. "Their bikes were found in the ditch on the side of the road. Someone took them, Emma. The whole town is scared to death it'll be just like last time…"

Her voice trails off. She needn't say the rest. I am well aware of what happened last time.

It was as if Natalie and Stacy climbed off the bus that day and simply vanished.

But people don't vanish…there is always something left behind. It's the finding that something that often proves infinitely elusive.

Truth is, even those who are found are never completely whole again.

Here I stand, living proof of that very conclusion.

"Is that why you didn't go on your cruise?" I can only imagine how stunned the whole town must be. Having something like that happen once in such a small community is horrible enough, but again…now…after all these years?

Mother carefully props the shotgun against the wall. "I planned to go. God knows it would have been nice to get away."

Wait, I do the math and realize that the ship she and her friends were scheduled to board actually left port the day *before* the girls went missing. My instincts go on point. Something else is wrong. "Are you all right?" The idea that she looks more frail, maybe thinner, certainly paler slams into me. "Have you been ill?"

She pats her rollers as if she only just realized a couple are loose, then her gaze catches mine. "I had a heart attack, Emma."

I blink, certain I heard her wrong but her eyes warn that I heard right. The duffel bag drops to the floor. "What?" Images of my dad, the cancer sucking the very life out of him, swim in front of my eyes. *I can't lose her, too.* "When did this happen?"

"It was only a mild one," she assures me as she comes nearer, pats me on the cheek as if I'm a child though I tower over her by at least four inches. "The doctor ran endless tests. He says I'll be fine. I just have to take a baby aspirin every day and one of those newfangled cholesterol drugs. That's all. No surgery. No big deal."

No big deal? My mother—the only family I have left in this world—has a heart attack and it's no big deal?

On top of that it happened at least three days ago and she didn't call her only daughter?

Maybe we're more alike than I realized.

3

HELEN

"I KNOW IT'S LATE." I clutch the phone to my ear as I glance toward the stairs.

Emma cannot hear this conversation. When I am certain she has reached the third floor I can finally breathe deeply once more.

"It's okay." My friend's voice draws my attention back to the phone. "Is everything all right?"

I close my eyes, reach for calm. "Emma's home."

I am so very happy that my daughter is home and at the same time I am terrified. As strong as she wants me to believe she is there is a part of her that is very, very fragile. I worry so about her. With those poor girls missing darkness looms over this town...just like before. This is not a good time for Emma to be home.

Misery swells inside me. *Please, God, don't let it be like before.*

"Oh that's good. That's real good," Ginny says, excitement chasing away the sleepiness in her voice. "You need Emma here."

Ginny Cotton loves Emma. Her daughter Letty and Emma have been best friends their whole lives. But Ginny doesn't understand how this could turn out for Emma. I love my dear friend, but I can't tell her everything. Emma wouldn't want anyone else to know…she doesn't even want me to know. The only reason I do is because the university listed me as her next of kin when she was admitted to the hospital scarcely two weeks ago. I flew to Boston immediately to see her but the doctor told me how Emma didn't want anyone to know what happened—especially me. So I came back home and waited to hear from her.

She never called.

I was stunned when she showed up tonight. Stunned…and grateful, despite my fears.

"She said Letty didn't call her about the girls."

A moment of silence echoes in my ear. "She mentioned she might call," Ginny explains, "but I put a bug in her ear about waiting until she discovered something concrete before she bothered Emma way up in Boston."

The air shudders into my lungs and I feel a pain deep in my chest. Lord, I do not want to die. Not yet. I want to live long enough to see Emma happy. Really happy. I don't want this burden Ginny and I carry to one day belong to our daughters and yet I see no realistic way around it.

For the first time in more than twenty years I fear our lies —our awful sin—will find us out.

"Well," I remind myself how late it is, "I just thought I'd let you know she's here."

"We'll get through this, Helen. Just like before. We don't have a choice."

"You're right. We will," I agree. "Good night, Ginny."

I hang up the phone and hug my arms around my cold body. As hard as I try I cannot block the memories of *that day*. I will go to my grave wondering if God was punishing me for what I did…if he's still punishing me.

That day, twenty-five years ago, I waved to the girls as they climbed onto the bus to go to school. I had never been so worried and terrified in my life but I knew I was doing the right thing. I knew it deep in my heart.

If I knew this, why have I spent all these years doubting the decision? Andrew and I made the decision together. It was the right thing to do for our family. But maybe if I hadn't gone to Birmingham things would have turned out differently.

As soon as the girls were off to school that cold April morning, Ginny picked me up. I insisted that Andrew stay home and work as if it was just another day. Besides, someone needed to be close to home in case one of the girls needed us. The house Andrew was restoring was in town. It was best that he stay. Ginny was free to take me. Mildred Potter and both her sons had the flu so Ginny couldn't clean the Potter house that day. I offered to pay her for taking me—I knew she needed the money—but Ginny refused to take my money.

"What are friends for?" she'd insisted.

We drove the ninety miles to Birmingham, arrived at the clinic with half an hour to spare. Waiting in the car, I started to cry. Ginny held my hand and cried with me. She understood how difficult this was. She wasn't Catholic so birth control had been a part of her daily regimen since she brought Letty home from the hospital. I, on the other hand, had never taken a birth control pill in my life. After we had Natalie, I thought we were never going to be blessed with children again. Suddenly seven years later we had Emma. It was a change, we'd adapted to the idea of having only one. But Emma was such a blessing.

Who would have thought eight years after Emma's birth it would happen again? I was almost forty but that didn't matter. We would have adjusted...except something was wrong. Andrew and I were convinced it was just a faulty test result, but we needed an amniocentesis to be sure, to be prepared for whatever was coming.

Maybe we should have simply trusted God.

But we didn't. God knew this as well. Why else would we have bothered with the test?

The procedure wasn't so awful. Once it was over Ginny drove me to a nice restaurant and insisted I eat. We prayed that all would turn out well. After all the fear and emotional drama, somehow in that moment I felt at peace. I sensed that everything would be okay with the baby. It was a wonderful feeling of calm—as if God were giving me a message to trust Him.

I made up my mind then and there that I would put all my faith in Him rather than the foolish test that had brought me to Birmingham in the first place.

We should have been home before five but a multi-car pileup on the interstate put us behind. Neither of us had cell phones so we couldn't call anyone. Andrew would take care of the girls. James, Ginny's husband, was home with Letty who, like the Potter boys, had the flu. There was no need to worry.

It was almost six by the time we turned onto Long Hollow Road. I was mentally exhausted and cramping a bit, both common symptoms. Nothing to worry about. The doctor had assured me all I needed to do was rest and put the worries out of my mind.

"I'll wait until I get you settled at home before checking on Letty," Ginny insisted as she drove past her own house. "You're too tired to be waiting around on me."

I started to argue, I knew she was worried about Letty, but she was right. I was exhausted and I just wanted to go home.

Two and a half miles beyond her house we saw the overturned school bus.

At first it didn't occur to me that it was Emma and Natalie's bus. I don't know why, denial I suppose. Then I spotted the number nine.

I was screaming my daughters' names and trying to get out of the car before Ginny pulled to the side of the road. I ran toward the half a dozen older women crowded around the bus. I looked from face to face and demanded to know where my girls were.

No one could tell me what I wanted to know. Lincoln Russell was dead and Emma, Natalie and Stacy Yarbrough were missing. Andrew, James and every other able bodied man and woman in the surrounding area had joined the search teams assembled by the Sheriff and the Chief of Police. The older women had volunteered to wait for Ginny and me. One had gone to the Cotton home to stay with Letty. They knew we would drive upon the scene of the accident and they wanted to be here to help.

As I stood staring in shock at the women from my parish —women I had known my entire life—a tow truck arrived to take the bus away.

I grabbed Ginny by the arm and begged her to help me find my babies.

We tramped through those woods all night. At some point we came upon other members of a search team. And eventually Andrew found me. He tried to talk me into going home, considering what I'd been through that day. I refused so we carried on together, both of us terrified.

"Sam is out here looking," he said to me. "I told him to find them and I know he will."

I could only nod. Sam was a good dog. Smart. He loved the girls. I told myself he would find our babies.

We had walked for miles calling the girls names and poking into bushes and stumbling over logs by the time the sun lazily hauled itself above the horizon the next morning. Defeat tugged at me. I hurt all over and the cramping was worse...but how could I go home?

Suddenly Sam's deep, thunderous barks echoed through the dark woods, through my soul and I knew he had found our girls. We moved faster, rushing toward the sound of his barks.

Sure enough there was Emma. I drew her into my arms and almost fainted with relief.

But where was Natalie?

I collapsed then. Couldn't move, could only hug my baby girl and cry. Andrew kissed us both and sent us out of the woods with the paramedics. He promised me he wouldn't stop until he found Natalie.

Only he couldn't find our sweet Natalie and that same night I lost the baby we had worried for weeks might have Downs Syndrome.

Ten days later the amniocentesis results came back normal. The baby, a boy, would have been fine.

Except there was no baby…and there was no Natalie.

And I don't think God has ever forgiven me for doubting Him.

4

FRIDAY, MAY 11

EMMA

THE NEXT MORNING I lie in the bed. Have no desire to get up. The ceiling fan turns too slowly to actually move the oppressive air. Though a new central heat and air system was one of the first upgrades Dad supervised when we moved into this one-hundred-thirty-year-old house, retrofitted duct work in a house this age never really operates as efficiently as the neatly designed systems installed in new builds. Combine that with the mostly nonexistent insulation and the thin wavy glass of historic windows and the result is an icebox downstairs and a hotbox up. It's the curse of renovating old homes while attempting to salvage historic elements like original clapboard siding and mint condition horsehair plaster. To achieve one, the other is inevitably sacrificed.

Sometimes I feel like an old house. I don't fit well with change and I rarely function efficiently unless I'm deep in the dirt unearthing bones. Today I feel particularly unfit. My brain has operated on Eastern Time for nearly a year, which explains why I forced my fatigued body from the bed an hour ago. I showered and then promptly crawled back into the waded linens that smell exactly like a lavender field. The sheets are freshly laundered and one hundred percent cotton —Helen Graves would have it no other way. I know the scent and feel of them as well as I know that of my own skin.

How on earth will she take care of this enormous house? The yard? I push the endless questions away. Don't want to think about that right now. The good news is the doctor says she'll be okay and for the first time in weeks I didn't dream last night. For the past month or so I've relived that bus crash in my dreams nearly every night. The dream ultimately morphs into that hole in the Iraqi desert, then I wake up sweating and crying out for help. Maybe I was simply too dead tired to dream last night.

Whatever the case, I'm grateful for that small measure of relief.

Framed Science and Math awards line the walls of my room. Dear God, the faded X-Files poster still hangs between the two windows on the other side of the room. A school banner hangs over the shelves burdened with all the books I loved growing up. Ray Bradbury and R.L. Stine and too many others to name. White walls, white bedspread. As desperately as my mother tried with all the frilly dresses and cute sweaters, I was never really a *pink* girl. Natalie was the girly one. Didn't have my first kiss until I was seventeen. Only one boyfriend in school. Natalie would be married by now with children for Mother to gush over. I close my eyes, blocking the ancient history determined to roll through my brain like a tidal wave stirring up all manner of unsettling memories.

Beyond lying here, the other option is going downstairs and that means facing my mother and explaining my sudden appearance. Last night we let the subject be in deference to the hour. Besides, she couldn't exactly complain. She has been keeping one hell of a secret from me, which is in all likelihood the only reason she didn't give me the third degree the moment I walked through the door. But there would be no avoiding an explanation this morning. Mother is, after all, part bloodhound. My dad always said she could dig up the dirt no matter how far it had been swept under a rug.

Maybe if I just lie here she'll feel sorry for her travel-weary daughter and go on about her daily routine. Except that isn't possible. Helen Graves, the sixty-four-year-old workout queen and health foodie of Jackson Falls had a heart attack three days ago. She swears my unexpected middle of the night arrival almost gave her another one. I squeeze my eyes shut and roll my head from side to side.

Why didn't she call me? I ask myself this, feel completely neglected, all the while knowing that I did not call her when I had my meltdown and was carted off to the hospital for a psychiatric evaluation. But I have a legitimate excuse: I did not want to worry her. As it turns out, I was right to be concerned.

How can this be? Mother is as healthy as the proverbial horse. She participates in the annual spring five-kilometer breast cancer run every year in honor of a friend she lost a decade ago to the horrible disease. Notably, this year she came home with her best finish time ever. Regrettably, an hour later she was in the throes of a cardiac event and on her way to the ER. The cardiologist refused to release her for travel until after considerable testing, forcing her to wave au revoir to her friends as they left her hospital bedside headed to Mobile for their annual cruise.

A truly unpleasant and frightening reality for her, and a sheer disaster for me. As harsh as that sounds, her presence disrupts my entire plan of sorting out my life—the life that is going sideways far too quickly. Add to that the undeniable wake-up call that my mother is not invincible and my suffocating anxiety escalates. I love my mother. No matter that I don't call or visit the way a good daughter should, I cannot imagine life without her.

I think maybe we both need a break from the realities of our lives at the moment.

The news she relayed about the two girls who disappeared day before yesterday echoes through me. Both had just turned fifteen years old. Honor students, soccer players, and Beta Club members. The similarities to Natalie and Stacy are indisputable.

I watch the three wooden blades turn overhead, listen to the whir of the antiquated motor in an attempt to tune out this unexpected reality. I focus on the mundane, review the ordinary all the while ignoring the mounting anxiety. The fans came with the house, as did the twelve-foot ceilings, creaky wood floors and horsehair plaster walls. While Dad renovated the place I found dozens of marbles, old photos, and plenty of newspapers—all tucked into the walls he'd been forced to open for plumbing or electrical upgrades. Stacked on a shelf downstairs I found an entire series of local newspapers that recounted the ongoing search and investigation details of the first month after *that day*. I'm not sure if they were in the house before or if my parents brought them. Eventually they ended up in my room.

I think they're still in my closet.

Hard as I might try, I cannot stop thinking about those two girls. I drove all this way to escape the nightmares haunting me only to crash headlong into history repeating itself. Based on the details that Mother told me, some folks around town have already jumped to the illogical conclusion of a connection to twenty-five years ago. This latest disappearance can't possibly be related to what happened to Natalie and Stacy. Theirs was a crime of opportunity. The bus accident wasn't planned or triggered by some outside factor. And if a sick pervert didn't take them, then they went into the woods for some reason—maybe the same reason I did—and were lost. There are sinkholes in northern Alabama. There are coyotes and wolves. Bears. I tell myself that Sam would have picked up their scent if they had been lost in the woods or dragged to some den or cave. I squeeze my eyes shut to block the images. I don't want Natalie to have suffered. Even now I can't bear to imagine her death.

These girls, the ones whose bicycles were found on the side of the road, were most likely being watched. Their stalker no doubt learned their routines and waited for the perfect moment to snatch them. He had a plan he followed. The act was not spontaneous. The local news channels are probably buzzing with constant updates. Reporters will compare the disappearances, then and now, in every imaginable way. That sort of reporting will only draw critical attention away from the search for the girls who might very well still be alive.

Dread roils inside me at the idea that if anyone learns I'm here, I will become part of the circus. Not that I mind if my participation can in any way help but nothing I remember, nothing I know can help find those little girls any more than I helped find Natalie and Stacy. I chew at my lip. I suppose it couldn't hurt to review the newspaper articles from that first month after my sister disappeared. In all this time I've never looked at them. Maybe if I read the daily reports something long buried will bob to the surface. My therapist seems to believe there are more memories about that day locked away in my head.

My gaze shifts toward the closet door. Maybe later. I look away.

I can just imagine what else is in there and under the bed. I was quite the collector—hoarder, Mother would say—when I lived at home. College dorms, city apartments and long assignments in tents at digs in the middle of nowhere taught me to pare down to the bare essentials and most beloved of keepsakes. The constant traveling—at least until eleven months and thirteen days ago—guaranteed no dependent pets, not even a goldfish, found their way into my life. As a kid there were a couple of cats and there was Sam.

Natalie loved Sam, the cats not so much. Since college the one possession to which I am most attached is my duffel bag. The thick canvas bag lies on the floor where I tossed it last night. More often than not my world is crammed into that bag.

I draw in a big breath, my olfactory instantly reacting to the scent of frying bacon and browning biscuits wafting through the thin walls and narrow cracks around the closed door. My mouth waters. Mother loves to cook so Dad took special care with renovating the kitchen. He ensured the stained glass in the door leading onto the porch and the glass cabinetry that lined the walls of the small butler's pantry were restored rather than replaced. New cabinetry was blended carefully with the old elsewhere. The kitchen is Mother's favorite room in the house. I hope she's not going to too much trouble. I rarely bother with breakfast. Maybe the nurse is here and cooking. She did mention having one who pops in a couple of times a day.

Because she had a heart attack and didn't call me. I could have come. I could be the one helping her.

Frustrated, I go through the motions of preparing for the day, dragging on a favored pair of worn soft jeans—the straight leg kind that keep dig site critters from crawling up a pant leg. This has happened to colleagues and to me far too often. Over my head I pull a BU tee given to me as a welcoming gift by a fellow faculty member at the beginning of the semester. Considering my current standing, she might want it back.

To further delay my departure, I brush and braid my hair and even make the bed. At that I point I run out of excuses to linger in my room. I descend the staircase that lines the turret walls in a wide circle, my hand sliding down the smooth wood rail. Small windows along the journey allow morning light to spike into the round room. A few steps along the hall on the second story, wood floors creaking, and I reach the main staircase. This one flows down to the first floor, landing right in the center of the front entry hall.

Every room on the first floor begins in that hall. From the front door, French doors on either side open into large twin parlors. The one on the west is the living room and the dining room is on the east. Move straight ahead, beyond the staircase with the coat closet tucked beneath it, and the front hall empties into a small, narrow back hall. A discreetly tucked door where the entry hall and back hall meet leads to a powder room that once served as a hiding place for confederate soldiers. On the west side of that little hall is my dad's study.

Straight ahead is the kitchen that occupies most of the back of the house and opens onto the wrap around porch. Both the front rooms do as well. Between the massive windows and all the French doors there is enough glass in the house to keep Windex flying off the shelves at the local Piggly Wiggly.

In the kitchen the petite woman placing the covered basket of biscuits on the table alongside the plate of bacon, bowl of fluffy scrambled eggs and boat of gravy looks vaguely familiar. Her red hair is shot through with gray and smoothed into an efficient bun. The purple scrubs lead me to believe she is indeed a nurse. Though I doubt this morning's menu is on any health conscious diet plans—particularly not Mother's—this was my dad's favorite breakfast. Mine, too—when I was growing up.

On the table in front of my mother sits a small bowl of creamy white stuff, that is no doubt yogurt, surrounded by raspberries and blueberries. A tall, sweating glass of ice water flanks her cup of hot tea. I sigh. I would die if forced to eat that way. To her credit, she has always gone out of her way to serve more palatable meals when I visit. No tofu or chia seeds.

I'm the one who should be worried about heart attacks.

"Well look who's finally up." Mother smiles. "Tricia, you remember my daughter Emma." She gestures to the woman in the scrubs. "Emma, I'm certain you haven't forgotten Tricia Hayes from Dr. Collins's office. She gave you and Natalie all your vaccinations growing up. When I came home from the hospital the other day I was very fortunate she was available to take care of me."

I do remember Ms. Hayes. My butt cheeks automatically clench. "I'm so glad you're here," I confess. "Lord knows she would never listen to anything I say."

"Oh my gracious, Helen," Tricia says, looking from me to my mother, "she is just like you at her age."

For a moment I am taken aback. Folks always say I look like my father. I have his dark hair and eyes. Most of the time I keep it braided as it is now or in a French twist. It's so thick and long that it's more in the way than anything. I've threatened to cut it a thousand times but the stylist always talks me out of the idea. I also have Dad's tall, thin stature. Mother, on the other hand, stands barely four inches over five feet and has the lush curves in the family. Her once blond hair is mostly white now and her blue eyes are still far too seeing. Natalie was the one who looked like her...who shared her many talents.

Not me. Never me.

"Well," Mother laughs, "I'm sure Emma would argue that she looks very much like her father and nothing like me."

Tricia shrugs. "True enough but she carries herself the same way you always did. I guess that's why she reminds me of you."

"If you mean arrogant and bossy," Mother muses, "you might be right."

I force my lips into a smile. "Coffee." I might survive this clashing of hormones and meshing of personalities if the coffee is strong and hot enough.

I circle the large round table that functions as both in-kitchen dining and as an island and grab the mug on the counter next to the Bunn coffeemaker. I'm reasonably confident the Bunn is nearly as old as me. I sip the rich black brew and thank God Mother obviously instructed her friend on how to make coffee in addition to breakfast. No matter where I've traveled, I'm yet to find anyone who makes coffee the way my mother does. Or biscuits, for that matter. Neither of which ever crosses her rosy lips. She is a tea drinker, both hot and cold. The closest thing to a biscuit she consumes is the occasional scone.

"They're expanding the search." Tricia stares at the reporter on the screen of the small television that holds court on the counter near the fridge. "I've got a mighty bad feeling about what happened to those girls."

She and Mother begin a conversation in earnest about the missing children. In Tricia's opinion the few similarities in the two cases, of course, make this latest shocking disappearance identical to the one that occurred twenty-five years ago. Helen argues that the idea is simply not possible. Whoever took Natalie from us, and Stacy from her father, would probably be too old or maybe even dead by now. Helen has never said as much but I know she hopes if that person is dead that he died a slow, painful death. Unlike many of the neighbors Mother has never believed that James Cotton took Natalie and Stacy. My dad never did either.

I know he didn't. Letty's father would never have hurt any of us.

The choking sensation that tightens the muscles of my throat holds the far too familiar pain deep inside my chest. The cold from that long ago night invades my bones as if I was back in those woods and I feel the scratch of the underbrush against my skin as I run faster and faster through the darkness.

I am lost.

I was lost then and I'm lost now right here in the kitchen of my childhood home. How ironic is that?

Stop. I blink away the glimpses of memory. "I have to go into the city."

Both women stare at me. Maybe because I spoke rather loudly, otherwise they certainly wouldn't have torn their attention away from the television reporter. I don't want to hear the words or see the images. I want to go...anywhere but here. The city will work. It isn't necessary for me to specify that I'm going to Huntsville. Whenever folks who live in Jackson Falls say they're going into the city, it's Huntsville. If they mean Decatur, which is the second largest metropolitan area nearby, they say Decatur.

"But you just got here," Mother argues. "What do you need in the city?"

Again, two sets of eyes analyze me, waiting for an appropriately humbled response to my mother's not so subtle rebuke.

To buy time for coming up with an acceptable excuse I sip my coffee. I feel fifteen again. Mother always interrogated me even when my only goal was to meet Letty at the movie theater or the bowling alley. She never trusted me. It wasn't about Letty or her purportedly crazy ex-military white daddy who killed himself when folks pointed fingers at him after Natalie and Stacy went missing. Or her depressed mother who should have married a black man since she was black and maybe her life wouldn't have gone to hell. Not at all. For my parents and most everyone we knew, those attitudes had been tossed out a long ago along with wingtip shoes and bullet bras.

No, it wasn't anyone else's crazy that worried my mother. Helen Graves's concerns were always about my actions, *my* craziness. Or maybe she simply never recovered from what I'd put her through getting lost in those woods and not being able to tell her what happened to Natalie. After all, everyone knew I'd almost killed her coming into the world in the first place.

Even at age eight I think I understood her reasons for holding so tightly to me. If she let go I might vanish, too. I can only imagine how scared she must have been when the heart attack happened, and I suddenly want to hold onto her just as tightly as she held on to me for all those years.

"My check engine light came on." Giving myself a pat on the back for fabricating such a clever excuse I down the rest of my coffee. Need the caffeine in my veins and the heat in my icy bones. Then I deposit my cup into the sink. "I'm worried there's an issue. You know those hybrids, they're finicky."

Mother sniffs and I can read her mind as clearly as if the words are written across her forehead. She drives a Cadillac SUV. Anything that plugs in—even if it also operates on gas—is either an appliance or a garden tool, not an automobile, in her opinion.

"Oh." Mother frowns, most likely because my excuse is too reasonable for her to refute without sufficient notice for composing a logical rebuttal. "Be careful then. Let me know if you won't be home in time for lunch."

Huntsville is half an hour away via interstate 565 but I intend to make a good half day of my outing. I need time to figure out how to lever myself out of this untenable situation. As if fate noticed my panic and wanted to amp up my misery another breaking news story about the missing girls interrupts Mother's favorite morning show.

Photos flash on the screen and my stomach sinks to the classic linoleum floor. Young, pretty. Big bright smiles. Oh, Jesus.

"You have to eat first," Tricia insists before I can drag my attention from the screen and exit the room. "Why you're practically skin and bone and your momma had me make your favorite breakfast."

Rather than argue, I smile as she prepares a bacon and biscuit to go.

5

THE PRESBYTERIAN CHURCH ON THE EAST SIDE OF Huntsville serves as a meeting place for Alcoholics Anonymous at numerous times of the day on several different days of the week. This is one of those days, but it is not one of the scheduled times. Though I adamantly refuse to categorize myself as an alcoholic, I fully realize there's a problem. I drink way too much far too often. I do it in bursts—binges, my therapist would say. I've only blacked out a couple of times—okay, three times. But that's three times too many.

For now, I still have control most of the time and I intend to keep it that way, which is why I'm here. Between the missing girls—their innocent faces posted on trees, street lamps, in storefront windows and splattered across the news—and worries about my mother's heart I'm desperate. I cannot risk another meltdown—particularly not one that occurs in the state of Alabama. Not anywhere near my mother. She doesn't need the stress.

Give me a hole in the ground in an Iraqi desert any day of the week over *this*.

Obviously having sensed my underlying desperation, the

group chairperson agreed to meet me at an unscheduled time for a brief emergency chat.

I find him under the enormous Crape myrtles not yet in bloom lining the west side of the mammoth church. We like big churches in the south. Where I grew up there are more churches than gas stations, supermarkets and traffic signals combined. The different denominations don't mind being located next to each other or even just across the street from one another. It's far easier to keep up with the competition that way. The Methodist ladies can keep up with what the Baptist ladies are wearing this season and vice versa. The men don't usually care, their suits all look alike.

The AA group chairperson is a couple of decades older than me, tall and thin. He wears his hair in a long skinny ponytail and sports a Rolling Stones tee. As I near he taps the fire from the tip of his cigarette, squeezes the end to be sure the heat is extinguished and then tucks the smoke behind his ear for later retrieval. For the first time in ages the urge to savor a smoke assaults me. I've never really been a smoker but occasionally when I'm poised on the edge I indulge some fantasy that the nicotine will somehow makes things better.

This is definitely the edge.

"Marty Griggs." He offers his hand.

I place my hand in his for a brief shake. I need an alias for this and for some reason the only name I can think of is Elizabeth Taylor's because of that movie Mother was watching last night. "Beth Taylor."

I've grown quite adept at lying the past few months. Still, lying in a church parking lot is a new low even for me. I remind myself that I will be here for a couple of weeks and that I have no desire for anyone in my hometown to discover that I'm an on-again-off-again token carrying member of AA.

Better to use an alias. What's the harm?

As if the devil himself wants to prove you can't trust anyone—not even an AA group chairperson standing on hallowed ground—another vehicle pulls into the lot that is empty save for my silver Prius and the green Ford truck belonging to the man whose hand I just shook. The white Malibu rolls up next to the truck and parks.

I turn to Griggs preparing to give him a piece of my mind when he says, "I took the liberty of asking a friend to be your sponsor while you're here. He's happy to do it." Before I can say what he clearly sees in my eyes, he adds, "We both know how important it is to have someone to call."

The fight leeches out of me. Why quibble over the inevitable? Particularly if it's true. This is a good thing. "Thank you."

The man who climbs out of the Malibu is mid-thirties, tall and very handsome...*too* handsome. I order myself to ignore those details. I'm thirty-three years old and completely career focused. I rarely have time for a date much less any sort of courtship ritual. Be that as it may, there is a downside to those hard and fast choices since I am only human. I sometimes drink too much despite my reasonably frequent AA meeting attendance and just as often have physical encounters with strangers I prefer never to see again.

Something else my mother can never know. I have a theme going here. It started around the same time I found it necessary to wear a bra. My mother can't hold against me what she doesn't know. Growing up, being measured by the standard Natalie had set was hard enough.

The man with coal black hair and searing blue eyes walks toward us and I fully comprehend that this is not a good thing after all. "Actually," I say to Griggs, "I don't need a sponsor. I may not be here as long as I thought."

"I hope I'm not late," tall, dark and dangerously handsome announces.

"Absolutely not," Griggs says, already pumping his hand.

Well, hell.

"This is Beth Taylor. She's visiting from New York. Beth, this is Joey Beckett."

The lies regarding my identity sound worse coming from Griggs. Like Griggs, Beckett wears well-worn jeans, but the tee is just plain white and mostly hidden beneath a gray hoodie.

Reluctantly I offer my hand. "Mr. Beckett."

His long fingers wrap around mine and the sizzle of chemistry is immediate and razor sharp.

Damn it.

The flicker in his blue eyes warns that he felt it, too. Damn it, damn it.

"Please, call me Joey."

"Joey," I repeat though he looks about as much like a Joey as I do a Beth.

We chat for a few minutes about the weather and how lucky I am that business brought me here now instead of in July or August. We laugh—I notice that his sounds almost as fake as my own—and then exchange cell numbers. As anticipated the conversation shifts to the missing children and I sink further into myself.

At last, I escape to my Prius and drive away. I'm confident both men wonder why a woman from New York has license plates from Massachusetts.

Secrets and lies. They always come back to bite you in the ass.

"YOU SHOULDN'T BE on that ladder. You might be too young to remember, but Clare Tubbs fell off a ladder trying to paint her house. She was paralyzed from the waist down."

I have no idea who Clare Tubbs is. I glance down at my mother. "I'm perfectly capable of being on this ladder, Helen."

She rolls her eyes. "How many times have I told you not to call me Helen?"

We've argued about this on numerous occasions. In fact, I can't recall a single visit where these very words weren't exchanged. The longer we are together, the more I lean toward using her given name. For the distance, I suppose. Admittedly, arguing with Mother is better than sitting in some bar getting shitfaced which is exactly what I wanted to do after leaving the church. No hard alcohol in Alabama, I remind myself. Too risky. Maybe tonight I'll drive to a motel across the state line and drink myself into oblivion.

The idea crossed my mind as I drove away from Huntsville. I even passed the Jackson Falls exit. Way down deep inside me, I understand that this, whatever it is, is something I cannot outrun so I turned around and came home.

Not to mention, I didn't want to worry my mother and I knew staying gone too long would do exactly that.

Mother—Helen—is saying something else that I don't quite catch but it ends with a dig at my lack of respect. My comeback is the same as always. "You should realize by now that I'm not going to change my position on the matter."

To preserve my unreliable sanity I have decided to do repairs to the house. I continue my inspection of the fascia that bands the roofline of the wrap around porch. This particular portion is in need of replacement as, I suspect, are several other parts. The house should have been painted five or six years ago. I don't say as much since that will only lead to the second most common argument my mother and I have: I don't come home often enough.

"Why are you on that ladder anyway?" she demands from her position on the porch swing. "I haven't seen you in years, we should be catching up."

On the drive back from Huntsville in addition to the revelation that I could not simply run away I came to terms with two necessary steps. One, I need to steadfastly avoid my newly assigned sponsor or risk finding myself involved with him in ways that are not smart. Two, if I don't find a way to busy myself I will lose my mind trying not to upset or stress or worry in any way my mother. I will not risk being the cause of another heart attack. Next time she might not be so lucky.

Besides, I can't move forward, I can't do anything until I've beaten this new demon that's invaded my life since the incident in Iraq.

I am left with one feasible choice—focus on an innocuous project until my life is back under control.

"I'll be here a while. We'll have plenty of time to catch up, *Mother*."

A triumphant smile on her lips, Helen queries yet again, "But why are you on that confounded ladder?"

"When was the last time the house was painted?"

Petulance clouds her expression. "Why when your father painted it, of course." Her gaze narrows. "What are you suggesting?"

"There's some peeling paint on the third floor and this fascia board needs to be replaced." I understand that she likely cannot see these things from the ground. I barely saw them myself.

"You are not painting this house."

"Don't be ridiculous! I helped Dad paint it when I was sixteen." If I remember correctly, Dad painted the house right after I graduated college. He probably would have already painted it again before now except the cancer stole his ability to do much of anything before taking his life.

"That was *before*."

The words are out of Helen's mouth prior to her brain's ability to fully evaluate what she is about to say. The rounding of her eyes and the tightly formed line of her lips tells the tale. She is keenly aware of having treaded into a sensitive area.

There are neighbors. Close neighbors. And her condition, of course. Rather than raise my voice to a sterner level, I descend the ladder and join her on the porch. She looks so Helen in her yellow ankle pants, matching cotton shell and three-quarter-sleeve cardigan. Her love of pink shimmers amid the other colors in the beaded necklace that completes her ensemble. My mother's natural beauty has always been accentuated by her subtle elegance.

Two things I will never be accused of being—subtle or elegant.

"Now you're angry," she says meekly.

"No, I'm not angry," I lie. "It's been a year—"

"Since you survived a terrorist attack," she cut in.

Deep breath. "Yes. But the attack was not aimed at me. My...Dennis and I were in the wrong place at the wrong time and we ended up in the middle of someone else's war."

Dennis Malloy died less than twenty-four hours after the attack. His injuries were far more serious than my own. Since there is always the possibility of becoming trapped or injured in a dig, we were trained to carry food and water and a few medical supplies. That training is why I was able to hold on until we were found. The setting wasn't unique or even particularly dangerous; it was merely bad timing. The situation in that part of the country grew unstable very quickly. We thought we could finish up our work at one particular site and get out in time.

We were wrong. A nearby building was bombed and a collapsed wall trapped us in the dig for days.

Dennis paid the ultimate price. I did all I could for him but he didn't make it. I suffered three fractured vertebrae. It was painful and required a back brace as well as a few months of physical therapy but I was lucky. Very lucky. I wonder if I've already used up my quota for this life.

Somehow I have survived two major tragedies.

But there are scars. Many scars, deep scars.

"I want you to go to Mass with me on Sunday."

The announcement is uttered so softly and so unexpectedly that my mouth must have been hanging open so she repeats the words with a little more bravado.

"You know I don't do church." I haven't been inside a church—any church—since my father's funeral Mass. I don't intend to start now. Church is not my thing.

"We have a new priest. He's young and charming."

Was that supposed to make a difference?

"So you're trying to fix me up with your priest now?"

I almost laugh, can't help myself. This is Alabama. *Small town* Alabama. Mothers over fifty remain convinced their daughters should be married and having children well before they reach the ripe old age of thirty. I am past my prime and there are no photos of grandchildren to show off. Natalie would have married and had children by now. Though Mother never says as much, I am certain the idea crosses her mind. All that aside, I'm confident she has no illusions of my rare beauty and incomparable sweetness luring her new priest from his vows.

"Would it do me a lick of good?" she tosses out.

I shake my head rather than remind her that I have no desire to tie myself down with a man and/or children. I have important work to do. I love my work. Maybe not my most recent position as a professor at BU but that is only temporary. I am ready to get back into the field. I don't need the position at the university. I'm happier in the field...surrounded by the dead.

The dead don't talk back or have particular expectations. The dead don't care if you flip out and have visions of the past dancing in your head that suddenly feel too real.

The taunting from the other kids with whom I'd grown up —even my own sister at times—echoes in my ears. The words don't bother me anymore, they roll off my back. I long ago embraced my weirdness.

"Of course I'm not trying to fix you up with my priest. Don't be ridiculous. I'm only suggesting you might enjoy hearing his sermon." Her expression is so hopeful as she stares up at me that I feel my resistance wavering.

I'm caught off guard by this odd reversal. My mother— the strong, relentless woman who never failed or surrendered —suddenly appears helpless and fragile, needy. Something deep inside me twists with worry and fear. She is literally all I have left in this world. Another heart attack could take her from me.

"I'll think about it," I lie some more. If it makes her happy to believe I'm considering the invitation, then why not? A little well-intentioned white lie never hurt anyone.

Helen smiles as if the weight of the world has lifted from her shoulders.

"Wait until I tell Mary Jo. She told everyone on the parish planning committee you would turn me down."

I should have recognized the trap.

6

MISSING PERSONS FLYERS GREET ME AT THE PIGGLY Wiggly. The two girls could be sisters, their eyes watch me, their faces demand to know how this can happen again... demand to be found.

I can't help you...I couldn't help before.

I hurry through the entrance, lock both hands onto a cart. One of the wheels twists and skids across the tile floor rather than rolls. I grit my teeth and ignore the unbalanced jiggle, pushing onward toward the dairy section.

Milk. Eggs.

Pulling the cap I snagged from the hall tree a little lower on my forehead, I keep my eyes locked straight ahead. I haven't lived here in fifteen years, haven't visited in four—four years, one month and six days—and still I refuse to even glance at any of the faces I meet for fear someone will recognize me.

My last visit is pretty much a blur. We buried my dad on March first. I stayed with Helen for a few days afterward. He would have wanted me to make sure she was okay. And she was. His cancer had been diagnosed the year before. There had been time to prepare, to brace for the inevitable. Most think the advance knowledge makes it easier to let a loved one go. I'm not convinced that's entirely true but I suppose it's slightly more bearable than the sudden death that no one sees coming.

What if my mother had died when she had that heart attack?

I push away the thought and seize upon the list of ways I helped her after my dad died. I took care of the necessary paperwork. It's amazing the red tape involved with dying. She complained about every step of the process. In her opinion the government had no business knowing all those personal facts. Together we tidied Dad's study, then she closed the door and no one has set foot inside that space since.

For once, I was a good daughter.

I stop for a moment and look around the Piggly Wiggly. The dairy section isn't in the far right back corner as it was the last time I visited. Annoyed that I didn't ask or pay better attention, I maneuver my way back through the produce department. The sound of distant thunder rumbles as the gentle mist of water hydrates the mounds of leafy greens. I grab a bag of romaine and a container of spinach. After the burger and fries I scarfed down in Huntsville, a hearty salad is a necessary evil. I may not be the foodie my mother is, but I do try for some sort of balance.

"Em?"

I freeze, the blood in my veins turning instantly to ice. Only one person has ever, *ever* called me Em.

Turning from the mountain of shiny red tomatoes I come face to face with Bradley Turner. The Bradley Turner whose forefathers helped found this town along with the Jacksons and who staked claims on land all over the county. The Bradley Turner who shattered my heart in high school. I want the floor to crack open and swallow me up, he is the next to the last person on this planet I care to see. *Ever.*

"It is you!"

Before I can sputter a word he tosses the bag of apples in his hand back onto a nearby table and grabs me in a bear hug. "Jesus Christ, Em. It's been..." With one last, calculated squeeze of my stiff body, he draws back. "It's been forever."

"Hey, Brad." I prop my lips into a smile. It has been exactly four years, one month and six days. Brad came to Dad's funeral Mass, as did almost everyone else who lived in Jackson Falls at the time. In the south funerals are sacred and as widely attended as celebrity social events. You might miss a wedding or a baby shower but nobody within a fifty-mile radius dares miss a funeral. The only thing worse is blasphemy and most folks actually consider the two equally unforgiveable.

Grinning, he stands back and looks me up and down. Of course this is the day I choose to forego mascara and lip gloss. I braided my hair and threw on a tee still wrinkled like an expired prune from being stuffed in my duffel. Not that I give one flying flip what this arrogant, lying cheat thinks of me but I know that wherever he is *she* will be. His lovely, backstabbing wife will no doubt appear any second.

"You look great."

Somehow I keep my smile in place no matter that his words confirm that he is still a liar who hasn't changed one bit. His blond hair is as thick and shiny as ever. And those eyes. A pale, sky blue that makes you want to stare at them forever. I rarely ate lunch at school. All I could do was sit and stare at him. The classic square jaw, and straight nose. I was so blind and pathetic.

The suit is a perfect reflection of the man as well. He wears one of those skinny fit suits that molds to every muscle, proving beyond a shadow of a doubt that he has maintained the same athletic body he had back in his football days. I imagine him at the gym every day on his lunch break; Bluetooth in his ear keeping him connected to his work.

I stare for a moment at the wedding band on his left hand. "So, how's Heather?"

Heather Beaumont Turner—the *she* in all my references to the very worst of the female species. Her mission in life from kindergarten through junior year was to make me miserable. But then the cutest, most popular boy in school decided I would be his girlfriend. Plain Jane Emma, chipped nails, nerdy t-shirts and all. Bradley Turner had wanted me, not Heather.

All the way until he didn't on graduation night.

He hitches his thumb toward the other side of the store. "At the moment she's giving the manager hell for failing to order her special brand of yogurt." He laughs and shakes his head. "She hasn't changed a bit."

Of course she hasn't.

"Well, it was nice to see you." I back away a little with my cart in tow. "Mother needs milk and eggs."

"I was sure glad to hear your mother is going to be all right. She gave us all a good scare."

Before I can summon a suitable response, he nods toward the other side of the store. "Come with me." He grabs the front of my cart and starts dragging it after him. "They remodeled this place a couple of years ago. It took me forever to find my way around again."

I follow, my chest tight with mounting frustration. My plan had been to hole up in the house and order in anything I might need. Yet here I am in the middle of the damn Piggly Wiggly being led around by Bradley Turner as if it was junior year all over again.

"How long you in for?" He stops in front of the dairy case. "Letty probably has your calendar booked, but if—"

No.

He blinked, startled.

Shit. I said it out loud.

"I mean, yes." I clear my throat. "You know Letty. She's completely monopolized my calendar for the duration."

A line of disappointment forms between his thick brows and his lips droop into a ground-dragging frown. I vividly remember that puppy dog look. "You gotta at least have coffee or a drink with me."

Bradley Turner was my first kiss. My first...*everything*. I will not have coffee much less a drink with him.

I give a little shrug. "I'll try my best."

"Brad!"

The shrill sound plows through my brain like a bullet. Heather Beaumont Turner strolls up in her five-inch heels and a form fitting dress far too short to be worn by a mayor much less the mother of two children. She still looks eighteen. Not a single wrinkle resides on her flawless face. No doubt Botox is heavily involved. Shiny, pristine nails, impeccable hair. With each step she takes that long blond mane bounces around her slender shoulders as if there's a perpetual fan blowing on the supermodel of Jackson Falls. It seems biologically impossible that her amazingly sculpted body ever expanded enough to host not one but two children.

I would be completely jealous except I know without doubt she got exactly what she deserved—Brad. I almost feel sorry for her.

"Look who I found wandering around the Pig."

I'm not at all sure how much longer I can keep this fake smile in place. "Heather, nice to see you."

Her gaze narrows with suspicion. "Did Letty call you about the missing girls?"

Not even a hello. Straight to the potential ulterior motive.

"She did." The slight flare in the other woman's pupils gives me great satisfaction. I shrug. "Who knows more about what happened last time than me?"

Lie, lie, lie. Good thing I don't believe in hell.

"Really." Heather made a disapproving sound. "She didn't mention it in this morning's task force meeting."

Oh, damn. I'll have to warn Letty. I reach for the eggs. "Any news on the search?"

My throat constricts to the point I can hardly draw in a

breath in anticipation of her answer. The faces of those two young girls swim in front of my eyes, the images moving and evolving into the face of my sister and her friend—faces I know as well as my own.

"Are you all right, Emma?" Heather steps back as if she fears I might vomit on her Louboutin shoes. "You look a little pale."

"Milk," Brad says.

I give myself a mental shake and stare at him. "What?"

"You said your mother needed milk, too."

"Right." I suck in a breath. "I should get back to the house. Mother is still recovering, you know."

Mayor Heather Beaumont Turner plunges immediately into politician mode, urging me to let her know if there is anything they can do to help. Of course the whole town already knows about Helen's heart attack. Widow Elders would have started the phone tree the moment the ambulance showed up in Mother's driveway.

People in small southern towns do that.

We exchange parting platitudes and I'm finally on my way out of the store. Thankfully no one else recognizes me as I hurry through the checkout line. I shove the bags into the back seat of my Prius and reach for the driver's side door.

"Emma! Emma Graves!"

I don't recognize the voice so I don't look back. I open my car door and lift my foot to get inside.

"Just one question, Emma, please." The young woman calling out to me bellies up to my door. She is, according to the logo emblazoned across the camera on the broad shoulder of the tall man behind her, a reporter for Huntsville's WHNT News.

Her microphone is in my face before I can maneuver my body into the vehicle. All that stands between us is the slim door that at the same time traps me against the vehicle.

"I'm sorry." I shake my head. "I'm not taking any questions."

"Emma, we're live and our viewers—many of whom grew up with you—want to know your thoughts on the abduction of these two children."

I feel the camera lens zoom in on me, its red light as hypnotic as a swaying serpent's head. Could this get any worse?

"Do you feel these abductions are eerily similar to the ones twenty-five years ago? Natalie was your sister. Surely, your family has considered the horrifying possibility that yet another monster lives in this quiet, paradisiacal community."

My mouth is so dry I can't swallow. I have to say something, I realize this. "You should speak to Sheriff Cotton. She knows the case far better than me."

"But you were the last person to see Natalie and Stacy twenty-five years ago, the only one to return. Now two more girls are missing and you're back in town. Don't you find that oddly ironic?"

Those two words had stalked me all day. "I'm sorry. I can't help you."

Somehow I squeeze into the car and start the engine. My hands shake as I steer through the crowd of shoppers who have suddenly converged in the vicinity of my car.

Voices and images from twenty-five years ago follow me home.

An hour later I stand at the closet door, staring at the wooden panels, my heart thundering. Helen watched the breaking news bulletin filmed outside the Piggly Wiggly. She said she only recognized me because of the cap and, by the way, it was dad's favorite. I glance at the cap that sports the Crimson Tide logo lying on my bedside table. No one had touched it since the last time he hung it on the hall tree. I shouldn't have worn it. Dad wouldn't mind but that isn't the point. The things he left behind are too precious to treat so cavalierly.

Half the town has called to ask when I arrived home and when they can come by to catch up. Every member of St. Mary's, even the twice a year Catholics who only attend Mass on Easter and at Christmas, will find their way to the front door between now and Sunday. My skull throbs relentlessly.

So much for my big plan of holing up and licking my wounds.

Downstairs in the living room there's a liquor cabinet. There would certainly be bourbon and scotch, maybe vodka. To my knowledge Helen never touches the stuff. Wine is her drink of choice when the occasion arises. If I wait until she's in bed I can put myself to sleep with a few shots of vodka or bourbon. Otherwise, the chance of sleep is about zero. I tossed my sleeping pills a week ago. They seemed to make the nightmares worse. I don't want to dream...not about the past. Alcohol doesn't seem to produce that same side effect.

But no. I will not risk it. Maybe a glass of wine. Of course my AA sponsor would tell me that wine is alcohol the same as vodka or bourbon or my personal favorite, tequila, but I take a different view—the one I can live with. A glass of wine now and then isn't an issue...it's the hard stuff that makes me stupid.

My fingers curl and uncurl with the too familiar anxiety and useless anticipation pumping through my system. Is it possible something I saw or heard twenty-five years ago could help the girls who disappeared day before yesterday?

If so, wouldn't Letty call me?

I close my eyes. The television news is all about ratings. I know this. Connecting the two crimes is a way to boost viewer interest. Besides, I couldn't help Natalie and Stacy all those years ago. How could I possibly help the two I've never even met?

Chewing my lip, I consider that whether I think I can or not is irrelevant. I need to try. If there is even the most remote chance, I have to put forth the effort.

I reach for the closet door, open it. When Dad renovated this space for me he made sure I had a nice big closet and I quickly filled it with lots of things not remotely associated with clothing. My rock collection as well as various other collections are boxed up in here on one of the shelves. I would wager I have some unearthed object from the yard of every old house in this town. Not to mention stacks of DVDs and CDs. Boots and hats. Photo albums and rolls of undeveloped shots. When I was ten, Dad bought me a camera. I snapped endless photos of stuff I found in the woods and in the dirt. As a kid I preferred the search for hidden treasures to eating or sleeping or anything else.

The stack of newspapers waits on a shelf in the farthest corner. I take the bundle in my arms, the smell of ink, old paper and dust wafting into my nose. I shuffle to my bed and place the yellowed papers there.

Wishing again for a drink, I climb into the middle of the mattress and pick up the first paper, the one that hit the news-stands the day after the bus crash.

Two Jackson Falls Girls Missing.

Natalie Graves and Stacy Yarbrough, both 15, disappeared after a bus crash…

Whispers and giggles echo in my brain as I read. I smell the diesel fuel from the bus engine. Feel the bumpity bump of the paved road badly in need of resurfacing. We hit a couple of particularly deep ruts left by the icy cold winter. Bounce, bounce. More giggles. Whispers.

I glanced back at my sister and her friend, pushed my glasses up my nose. Hands over mouths, Natalie and Stacy are huddled in their seat whispering, about some boy probably. I can see them as clearly today as I did twenty-five years ago. I felt so alone without Letty.

I remember wishing I had stayed home, too.

I force the images away and imagine the smell of freshly turned fertile earth. The scent is darkly pungent, teaming with life and rich with nutrients. It feels clean and soft in my hands as I plunge my fingers into its depths in search of the secrets it holds. For as far back as I can recall, the feel and smell of dirt has prompted happy memories. It is part of who I am...it is in my blood.

Calmer now, I focus on the newspaper article. So many times during the past twenty-five years those hours and days have played out in my head, in my dreams. But today I'm going to read about them from someone else's perspective. See if I remember something I haven't remembered before.

Experts say that each person remembers events differently based on what they experience from their vantage point. Unfortunately, there was no one else on the bus that day except me, the driver who died and my sister and her friend who disappeared. No other vantage points are available.

One by one, day by day, I scour the newspapers for the entire month after *that day*. I read the articles, flinching when I come to the one about Letty's father. Most folks believed that he had something to do with Natalie and Stacy's disappearance. I didn't believe it and not just because Letty was my best friend, but because I knew Mr. Cotton.

Funny thing is, I know him even better now. I was diagnosed with PTSD after the incident in Iraq. My therapist said I'd likely suffered with a mild form since the bus crash and Natalie's disappearance. Only recently had I lost it the way Letty's father did all too frequently back in those days. The accusations against him had pushed him over the edge. He'd gone into the shed and put a bullet in his head to escape the nightmare.

The idea of putting a bullet in my head hasn't crossed my mind but I can see how he found himself on that tragic path.

The police were at a complete loss for clues or answers of any sort. Volunteers from dozens of surrounding counties had shown up to help with the search. No one could find a single shred of evidence. Not a hair, a fiber or a witness. One agent from the Alabama Bureau of Investigation asked my parents about memory regression therapy. Desperate to find Natalie and Stacy, we tried. The therapist learned nothing and I suffered immensely because of it. My parents refused to allow me to be hypnotized ever again. By the time I was an adult and could make the decision for myself to try again *that day* was so far in the past it no longer seemed relevant.

After the trouble in Iraq I allowed my therapist to try taking me back once more. She learned nothing we didn't already know. In her opinion, if there are any other memories in my head they are locked so deeply they are never coming out.

A rap on my door is followed by, "Emma."

Before I can answer, Mother opens the door and walks in. "Is it okay for you to be climbing all those stairs, Helen?"

Her eyebrows shoot up and I amend, "Mother."

"Moderate exercise won't hurt me. I took my time. Eventually I'll be able to get back to my normal activities."

Jesus. "I could have come down. All you had to do was give me a shout."

"I know how far to push myself, Emma." She frowns, gestures toward the bed. "Why are you putting yourself through that?"

I stare at the papers and wonder the same thing.

"Emma." The mattress shifts as she settles on the bed next to me. "What happened to Natalie and Stacy was not your fault and there is nothing now any more than there was then that you can do to help them. You were just a child. You couldn't be expected to know what to do."

My gaze lingers on the yellowed photos of the girls. "Did I tell you I tried the regression therapy again?"

"You did?" Her eyes grow wider, worry clouds her face. "When?"

"After what happened in Iraq I was in therapy for a while. I figured why not see if there was anything in there—" I tap my head "—that might be useful. But it didn't work any better this time than it did before."

"Have the therapy sessions helped at all?"

A shrug lifts my shoulders. "I suppose."

She reaches for my hand, cradles it in hers. "You're a brilliant young woman, Emma." She shakes her head. "My gracious the things you've done to help others. It's incredible. I hope you know how special you are."

Those sorts of compliments are rare from my mother. "I've already told you I would consider going to Mass with you on Sunday. No need to lay it on so thick."

"Don't be silly. This is not about whether you go to Mass with me or not." Her hand tightens on mine as she searches my eyes, hers far too bright. "You have a guardian angel, Emma. Jake says you have some special purpose in this life and that's why you're still here."

Suspicious, I ask, "This Jake is your new priest?"

"Yes. Jake Barnes." She smiles and nods. "I adore him. He feels like the son I never had. He lets me talk about you and Natalie to my heart's content."

A smile tugs at my lips. I'm beginning to believe my mother has a crush. Maybe I will go to church and check out this guy.

The sound of buzzing like a bee trapped under glass draws my attention to my phone on the bedside table next to Dad's cap. "Sorry about the cap. I wasn't thinking."

Mother leans forward and kisses my cheek before pushing up from the bed. "Your dad would be thrilled to have you wear it. I hope you'll wear it again."

I nod. She's right. Memories of riding on his broad shoulders, of him tugging at my pigtails have me blinking back tears. If I'm completely honest with myself, my resistance to coming home for a visit is more about him being gone than my cantankerous relationship with my mother.

Or the memories of Natalie.

"Get your phone, dear. It might be important."

Newspapers crinkle as I reach toward the bedside table. One missed call appears on my screen. Letty Cotton.

"It was Letty. I should call her back."

Helen gives me a wink. "She's inviting you over for dinner."

I pause, my thumb poised above the screen. "How do you know?"

"She called to make sure we didn't have special plans and that I didn't need you here with me." Mother lingers at the door. "Go. Have fun with your friend. I've got company coming for dinner."

I'm not sure whether to be offended or grateful. "You're certain you don't want me to stay?" Now I'm curious. Maybe it's this new priest. If she wants me to meet him so badly, why not tonight? Unless she does have a crush on him. But she said he was my age. Like that matters anymore.

"You go on with Letty. Howard and I have dinner every Friday night. He's quite the chef."

My eyebrows shoot up. "Howard Kent as in the hardware store guy?"

"That's the one."

She disappears before I can ask anything else.

7

"I CAN'T BELIEVE YOU BOUGHT A HOUSE."

Letty's house is as warm and inviting as she is and gives me the illusion that I can do anything here and be safe, even risk a drink. I clutch my wine glass and wish it was tequila. The voice of Marty Griggs echoes in my ears. *We both know how important it is to have someone to call.* I don't want to need a sponsor. I want to be able to do this myself. To be strong enough, to have enough willpower…

To hell with it. No pity party tonight.

Letty smiles and then sips her wine as elegantly as any sophisticated lady no matter that she wears a gun and chases bad guys for a living. I want to be strong like Letty. Her childhood was even uglier than mine. Her father committed suicide when she was eight. The stigma of having a murderer for a father haunted her even though it was never proven. On top of that she was a bi-racial child—not such a popular gene pool in some segments of the deep south back then.

"I have to live somewhere." Letty sets her glass on the table, pushes her cleaned plate aside and leans back in her chair. "I was tired of throwing my money away on rent. Isn't home ownership the goal of every millennial?"

I down the wine and reach for the bottle. "Speak for yourself."

The red wine splashes into the stemware, sloshing to a point slightly beyond the invisible line everyone recognizes as a proper serving. I plop the empty bottle onto the table and study my gorgeous friend. Her skin is flawless and that perfect golden color that everyone wishes for in the summer—the perfect tan I had to work so hard to attain. Dark twisty curls hug her face. She wears a turquoise ribbed sweater with a bateau neckline that hangs off one shoulder and stretchy, wide-leg brown trousers. She looks sexy and happy and very much at home in her own skin.

I, on the other hand, am still wearing the same wrinkled tee and ragged jeans that started my day.

"Are you in a serious relationship, too?" I lift my glass as her smile widens. "Oh, go ahead. Make me feel like a real loser. You know Helen is already grieving at the notion that she will never have grandchildren."

At one point in my late twenties I suffered through a mourning period in regard to my unattached status. I got over it. I have no permanent domicile. Certainly no serious relationship, not even a steady lover. I have an apartment that I leased barely a year ago and I have encounters with strangers who will never see me again after the first and only time we bump pelvises.

"I am not in a serious relationship," my friend says. "I have no time. As for the house…" Letty glances around her small but utterly charming dining room. "It was time to make it real. We're grownups now, Emma. Barreling toward forty."

"Don't remind me." I sip my wine slowly, knowing I have to drive home eventually.

Home. How is it that no matter how far one roams or how long one stays gone, home is always where you started? As if part of me has always been here—trapped in this place that both molded and damaged me.

Dismissing the self-analysis session, I ask, "So, is the esteemed mayor of Jackson Falls still giving you trouble?"

Heather Beaumont Turner is the Jackson Falls mayor just like her mother before her. And just like her granddaddy before that, and so on as far back as the town's history goes. She is a snob of the highest order—just like her momma—who loves nothing better than looking down her nose at others.

"You mean," Letty asks with a pointed look, "is she the same condescending, racist bitch her mother was when she held the position?"

"That sounds like a yes."

Letty shrugs. "She's more a snob than a racist. She thinks she's better than everyone, not just the folks whose skin is a different color from hers."

I shake my head. This is not the same closed-minded south of long ago except for a few throwbacks, like the Jacksons and the Beaumonts. Letty's point is a good one, though. These days it's not so much about racism as simply considering themselves above everyone else. Of course that mentality is alive and well all over the country.

"I ran into her and *Brad* at the Pig."

"You did not." Letty covers her mouth to hold back the laughter I see in her dark eyes. "Did you just want to punch her in the face? She wouldn't feel it, you know. Too much Botox."

We laugh and I explain how I told Heather that she called me about the case.

"I wondered why she's been blowing up my phone all evening."

We laugh some more, sip our wine. It feels good to be with Letty. Easy. Comfortable. "I heard on the radio that you have a couple of missing cavers, too."

She sighs. "Which is just what I need."

"Does that still happen fairly often?" As a kid I remember

every summer being filled with stories of missing cavers. The smart ones left detailed itineraries about their planned expeditions with friends or family. Those were the ones generally found in a rescue situation rather than their bodies being recovered weeks later.

"People have gotten smarter about being prepared but it still happens far too often. We have our own rescue team now just for the ones who get themselves lost. It's mostly volunteers but they know their shit."

"I guess that takes some of the pressure off your department." I tilt my wine glass, watch the rich burgundy liquid glide around the bowl.

"Yeah." Letty stares at me for a long moment. "How are things going in Boston?"

I meet my friend's gaze. Her eyes tell me how much I've hurt her by shutting her out this past year. We talked more when I was in Iraq than we have since I came back. It isn't fair. She really is the only true friend I have. Of course I have casual friends and acquaintances in all the places I've lived and worked, but none know me as Letty does. Letty is the kind of friend who would follow me anywhere—who would come if I called no matter the time or the reason.

I am ashamed at how I've shut her out.

"The fact that you don't know the answer to that question should tell you." I close my eyes a moment. "Flashbacks, hallucinations. I had a meltdown in the classroom two weeks ago. Totally lost it."

Letty nods. "So that's why you're here."

"Where else would I go except back to the scene of the original crime?"

The graceful line of Letty's jaw hardens. "You know what PTSD did to my dad. How can you ignore the problem? Do you want to end up like him?"

This time I don't bother with a genteel sip, this time I gulp down the remainder of the contents of my glass. I lick my lips and say, "Sometimes I think I'm already there. The night-mares." I exhale, look away.

"So you don't sleep."

"Oh, yeah, I sleep. They make a pill for that. But I dream and the dreams aren't worth the sleep." I sit straighter, shift my butt in the chair. What I really want to do is stand and walk off the agitation. Generalized Anxiety Disorder. I'm a textbook case.

"How long has this been going on?"

"About six months. No matter how hard I work out or how much I drink, the nightmares still come."

I can't believe I'm telling her all this. I love Letty. She's my oldest and dearest friend but we haven't talked like this—shared the most unpleasant secrets—since I left for college. Our lives took different paths. Or maybe I haven't allowed that closeness. Letty has shared plenty with me over the years. I'm the one who shut down. Yet, here and now, I am spilling my guts as if there is no tomorrow. I stare at her stunning face. Her rich cocoa colored eyes that remind me I am safe with her. Letty is beautiful, outside and in. She's caring and loyal.

"While you're visiting let me help you with that," she offers.

I have no doubt that Letty knows as much on the subject of PTSD as any expert. Why not give it a shot?

"Okay." I pick up my fork and start back in on my chicken and rice. It will take food and time to get my blood alcohol level back down in the legal range. I promised myself I would not drink here and risk going too far. So much for good intentions. "How's your mom?"

"She's good. She's the postmistress now."

Happiness floods my chest. "Wow, that's fantastic."

Letty's mother had a hard go when James decided to end his life rather than face another day living with his mental illness and the cloud of suspicion related to Natalie and Stacy's disappearance hanging over him. After years of cleaning rich people's houses—maybe when Letty and I were fifteen or sixteen—her mother landed a spot as a substitute mail carrier. She only got to deliver the mail when someone was sick or needed a vacation, but it was a foot in the door. Letty was home alone more often than not, which was the reason she spent so much time at my house.

Especially after *that day*.

"I'm proud of her." Letty studies me for a moment. "So tell me about the nightmares."

"Same ones as before. I'm in the woods trying to find my way home." I finger the rim of my glass. "Sometimes the forest turns into that sandy hole in Iraq and the dream is one big jumble of me as a child and as an adult. No matter how fast I run or how hard I try, I can't find my way."

"How's the drinking?"

"I'm in AA." I push my empty glass farther away. "Does that answer your question?"

Letty nods to my empty glass. "Not really."

"It's under control," I admit, though possibly the answer is another of my lies to myself. "Barely. I'm careful but I also see the danger in assuming I can handle the situation."

"You seeing a therapist?"

I draw in a big breath. "I stopped a few months back but then I had to start again. You don't spend forty-eight hours in the psych ward at Mass General without a follow-up appointment as part of the terms of your release."

"Maybe that's why you're here."

Letty's gaze presses mine. She's playing bad cop. I recognize the strategy.

"Trying to avoid the shrink."

My friend knows me far too well. "It's possible." I stare longingly at my empty glass. "I need some time to sort out all of this before I bare the full load to a stranger."

"That's going to be a little difficult given what's happening around here. I saw you on the news, by the way. I can try to keep the media off your back but you know they're coming for you, right? Two more missing girls…the twenty-fifth anniversary and all."

"And I wish I could tell them—tell you—something that would help. I even dragged out all the old newspapers and read through the stories from back then to see if any of it would trigger something I'd forgotten."

"Do you believe you forgot something?" A spark of hope flashes in her eyes.

I shrug. "I don't know. It's possible but I sure as hell haven't been able to dig it up." I laugh. "I've spent my whole life digging up things and I can't unearth the unedited, full episode of one day from my memory banks."

"It'll come one day. In the meantime, I have to find those girls." Letty stands and picks up her plate and glass. "It can't be like last time."

I do the same and follow her into the kitchen. She's already told me this was her first night off since the girls went missing. I should leave soon so she can get some sleep. I lean on the counter and admire her kitchen. The place really is so Letty. A neat little bungalow just off the downtown square, it's homey and pleasantly enchanting.

Maybe deep down I'm jealous because she has a real life. My "life" is about constantly moving to some place new. The next town or country. The next dig…the next mystery. As long as I'm moving I don't have to think…to look back. And the past can't catch up to me.

If I don't have to look at it, I don't have to deal with it.

Maybe that's what happened to me in Boston. I stayed still too long.

"Tell me about the case." I know what the news stations are saying but that is rarely the whole story by any stretch of the imagination. The police always keep certain aspects of any investigation out of the media while the media adds their own twist to the facts provided.

"Neither of the girls had issues at home. We've interviewed every damned body close to the family and anyone who has come into contact with them in the past few weeks." She loads her plate and fork into the dishwasher and then reaches for mine. "We've got ABI, FBI, city, county—all on one big joint task force and we have nothing. The bikes were abandoned and the only prints we've found are those of the girls and a couple of their friends and family members."

"So it really is like last time."

She closes the dishwasher door. "In that regard, yes."

"Last time the police believed the disappearance was simply happenstance." I say this well aware that Letty knows. "The theory was that someone just happened to come along and took advantage of the opportunity." The accident occurred on the road where Letty and I lived. Her father's issues and the fact that he walked that road every day, in my opinion, were the two single, flimsy threads used to weave a theory around making him the prime suspect.

He was so convenient and the grieving town so desperately needed answers. James Cotton was the scapegoat.

Letty wipes her hands on a dishtowel. "We believe someone was watching these girls for a while and chose a time to grab them when they were the least likely to get caught. This was a well thought out, well-executed abduction in broad daylight. No evidence left behind. It feels like there should be a ransom demand but it hasn't come."

"Whoever it is, it can't be the same person who took Natalie and Stacy, assuming they were taken by someone," I argue. "Why would a serial offender wait so long between abductions? Have there been similar abductions in the surrounding counties or states?"

"Kids go missing every hour of every day. Many are never found, dead or alive. And there was the Aldridge girl—Jenny Aldridge. She was sixteen when she disappeared twelve years before Natalie and Stacy. Her case was not connected to theirs because of the differences surrounding her disappearance. The biggest being the note the parents found saying she was running away to Los Angeles to be a star. Her family hadn't lived here very long. They moved away not long after she disappeared. I couldn't find any record of her showing up in California or anywhere else later on."

"Jesus." I close my eyes for a moment. I know all of this but, under the circumstances, it's particularly disturbing. I had forgotten about the Aldridge girl. "Unless you get some sort of break, how can you possibly hope to find these girls?"

Letty leans against the counter next to me. "Hope is the one thing I've got. What else can I do but keep looking and refuse to give up hope?"

I take her hand in mine. "The people who're saying it's just like last time, are they the same ones who accused your father?"

Letty laughs. "Oh yeah. They can't look me in the eye now but they know what they did to him. They all know."

It was that handful of people, mostly powerful names in the county, who pressed the theory about Letty's father. Those were the ones who ultimately pushed him over the edge with their witch hunt.

"We always knew he wasn't the one." I put my arms around her and pull her into a tight hug.

Whoever took Natalie and Stacy, that case and this one can't possibly be connected. To agree with that ridiculous theory is to believe the perpetrator has been alive and well right here all this time. So much for the theory that Letty's father was involved. Fools. Every damned one of them.

In the end, whether the person who took these girls is the same one who took Natalie and Stacy is irrelevant. The real question—then and now—is how could people live in a town this small and not recognize a monster?

I know the answer as well as I know my own name: monsters are most often someone you would never suspect.

It could be anyone.

Maybe I'm the real monster. Maybe if I'd watched more closely I would have seen the person or persons who picked up Natalie and Stacy. Maybe if I'd stayed on the bus I would have been there to tell the first person on the scene what happened as soon as the bus was discovered instead of the next morning.

Just more of those what-ifs that haunt my dreams.

8

HELEN

My hands fall away from the work of smearing moisturizer on my face. I stare at my reflection, see the wrinkles and the white hair. In December I'll be sixty-five. I wipe my hands and shut off the bathroom light.

Like every night, I shuffle into the bedroom and climb beneath the covers alone. I miss Andrew so very much. I enjoy Howard's companionship but he can never replace Andrew in my heart or in my bed.

I turn onto my side and stare at the framed photograph I keep on my bedside table. He was thirty-eight at the time and five-year-old Emma sits on his shoulders while twelve-year-old Natalie stands in front of him. Andrew was such a good father. A far better father than I was a mother. If he was still alive, he would deny the assertion. He always made me feel as if I was the perfect wife and mother.

Except I wasn't. Especially after *that day*.

Losing Natalie and the baby damaged me in ways that cannot be undone. Ever. I tried my best to be a good mother for Emma but I'm certain the issues that plague her now are my doing. I should have done better by her.

Eight months after Natalie disappeared we moved into town to this house. It was the most difficult decision I have ever made in my life—other than the one to have that damned test. Once we made the move we worried about Sam. He refused to stay with us in town. Every time Andrew brought him to Tulip Lane he would stay for an hour or so and then walk all the way back to the farm. Sam refused to give up on Natalie. He lay on the porch every day and watched for the bus to pass, hoping it would stop and Natalie would climb off and run to him as she did for all those years before she was lost to us.

He was already an old dog at the time—almost twelve years old. Andrew and I decided it was best to let him live out his life whatever way he wanted. We weren't doing much better. We hung onto the farm, leaving most everything inside just as it was before Natalie vanished. Emma and I went to see Sam every day after school. We ensured he had plenty of food and water. Andrew installed a doggie door so he could go in and out of the house as he pleased. And we left a note on the door for Natalie…just in case.

"Momma, is Natalie ever coming home?"

Natalie had been missing nine months and ten days when Emma asked me this question one afternoon as we visited Sam.

"I sure hope so." We sat on the porch steps and I hugged her close.

Emma peered up at me through her glasses that always seemed to sit crookedly on her sweet little face. "But what if she comes home when we're not here. She might think we forgot about her."

"Daddy and I thought about that." I reached into my purse and pulled out an envelope. "Hold this for me, Buttercup." Andrew and I always called Emma buttercup. She reminded me so of the cute little persistent flowers that sprang up each spring with the promise that winter was almost over. Emma was like that...a promise of better things to come.

I dug a pen and the tape from my purse and set them aside. "Okay. Would you like to read what Daddy and I wrote and then you can add something?"

Emma nodded as she carefully opened the envelope. She unfolded the letter and I had to smile at her dirty little fingernails. How that child loved digging in the dirt.

"Dear Natalie," she read aloud.

My mind drifted to the last time I saw Natalie. I helped her French braid her hair. She was so beautiful. Smiling. Laughing. Happy.

"Daddy and I decided to move Emma closer to school," Emma read. "You know the old Bainbridge house on Tulip Lane. We will be there waiting for you. We have the most beautiful room ready just for you."

That was another thing Andrew and I decided was necessary. We had to prepare a room for Natalie...for when she came home.

Except she never came home.

For five long years after she disappeared, I was angry with God. I refused to pray. I did go to Mass each Sunday but only because of Emma. I sat there, in His house, each Sunday and stared blankly at the priest. I couldn't partake of any of the rituals that had once given me such comfort. God had let me down. I suppose I had let Him down first but I'm only human. He is God. He should have taken care of our Natalie.

"P.S." Emma scribbled at the bottom of the page with the pen I'd given her. "I need you to come home. I miss you. Hugs and kisses, Emma."

She didn't say the rest out loud but I covertly watched over her shoulder as she wrote: P.S.S. Please come home. Momma is very sad without you.

I tried to do better after that. Emma deserved better.

9

SATURDAY, MAY 12

EMMA

I FIND it difficult to believe a Home Depot can be so busy on a Saturday morning. As I watch the swarm of colorful T-shirts, matching cropped pants and flip-flops flitting about in the garden department I wonder how all these people can simply move on with their lives while two little girls are missing.

That part is just like before all over again. People shop, people go to school and to work. Nothing changes...except the number of vacant desks at the local school and the empty beds in homes. Those first few months after Natalie didn't come back, I watched out the window or wandered in the yard, checked her room, rambled through the house... expecting to see her at the next turn.

Each morning I woke up and ran to her room again. No Natalie. Mother talked about *when* Natalie came home all the time. She drove to a different town every day hanging posters about the reward she and Dad were offering. Ten thousand dollars. It was every penny they had in savings. She called the police and the FBI every week for an update. Four or five years later, I can't remember exactly when, she stopped doing all those things. Stopped doing anything. I remember thinking she had become a zombie. Dad took me to school and picked me up every day during that period. Every night as he tucked me in he promised that she would get better soon.

He was right. The zombie period didn't last so long. The next thing I knew Mother was like everyone else, walking through life as if nothing had happened. She hardly ever said Natalie's name anymore. She cooked and made extra special desserts—my favorites, never Natalie's. She shopped and pretended life was exactly as it should be.

Like all these people browsing around in the Home Depot this very morning.

I have no room to judge, I'm here. Shopping as if all is right in my world.

But I'm here because if I don't find a way to occupy myself I will lose my mind. I cannot help those little girls. The newspaper articles failed to prompt any new memories. They did, however, keep me awake most of the night by invading my dreams. Every time I drifted off to sleep I would smell the diesel fuel from the bus, see those faces and the endless sea of green interspersed with purple flowing across the unplowed fields. The woods...so dark I kept running into trees. Bushes scratching at me, pulling at my sweater. Falling to the ground because I simply couldn't take another step. Then my eyes popped open and I paced the floor for half an hour before falling back into the bed so the whole process could start over again.

Eventually I dragged myself downstairs for a hearty break-fast of yogurt, fruit and grains. No Nurse Hayes frying up bacon today.

Mother told the nurse she didn't require her services anymore since I was home.

"You look like hell."

Leave it to Helen to state the obvious as I shuffled into the kitchen this morning in search of coffee like an addict in need of a fix.

"Nightmares?"

She guessed the problem right off the bat. I imagine she heard the floor creaking with my every step as I paced back and forth. She reminded me that I had nightmares as a child for years after *that day*. Like I could forget. I also recall hating myself for a very long time because Natalie didn't come back and I did. Maybe I still do hate myself. As an adult I understood that no amount of wishing when I was a kid that I didn't have to live in my sister's shadow would make her disappear. Some evil piece of shit took her and Stacy Yarbrough or they were just lost some place no one had looked.

It was not my fault.

Even now that statement doesn't quite ring true. It feels like my fault. I know that Helen secretly feels the same way—that Natalie's disappearance was somehow her fault. I heard her crying as she said those very words to Dad countless times in the weeks and months after the bus crash. His deep voice reverberated through the walls. "Now, Helen, you know that isn't true. You were and are the best mother any little girl could ever want. What happened wasn't your fault any more than it was mine. We did the best we could."

The pain of dying with cancer is nothing to compare with knowing you're going to die without finding the truth. Dad said those words to me the day before he died. The misery in his eyes broke my heart.

The drone of the paint shaking machine drags me from the tender thoughts. I take a breath, glance around, and wish I was out of here already. No reporters waited outside the house this morning. A miracle or perhaps a warning from Sheriff Letty Cotton. I wear my dad's Crimson Tide ball cap again today. I doubt anyone will recognize me.

I drove to the Home Depot on the south side of Huntsville, the one farthest from Jackson Falls. The chances of running into anyone who remembers me are slim to none. All I need is the lumber and the paint to get started on the repairs. Dad's tools and brushes are in the storage shed exactly the way he left them. Restoring old houses was close to his heart, he poured himself into restoring the one that became our home—maybe that was his way of coping with the despair—and this is the least I can do while I'm visiting. In the long run Helen will appreciate it as well. Hiring someone to do the work is never as good as doing it yourself as long as you're capable.

"Here you go, ma'am." The guy in the orange vest plops two gallons of well-shaken exterior white paint onto the counter. "Can I help you with anything else?"

"That's it. Thanks." I lug the paint onto my panel cart and head for the lumber aisles.

Today I'll start with three or four one-by's for replacing the damaged fascia. Once I'm satisfied with how those work out I can order enough for the entire project and have them delivered. I was pleasantly surprised Dad's truck fired up as if he'd driven it just yesterday. Helen explained that she asks her friend Howard to drive the truck around the block at least once a week and she keeps the insurance and license plate up to date. I don't know how I feel about *Howard*. Then again, Dad has been gone for four years. Of course Helen is lonely. Dad wouldn't have expected her to ignore her own needs. He wasn't that selfish.

I suppose I shouldn't be either.

Climbing behind the wheel of Dad's truck and backing out of the driveway this morning I experienced a moment of déjà vu. The year I turned fifteen he taught me to drive in this old Chevy the same way he did Natalie those last few months before she disappeared. I'm glad Helen didn't sell the truck after he died. To my knowledge she hasn't sold or given away anything that belonged to him. I haven't looked but I'll bet she still has his favorite shirt hanging on her side of the closet.

I suddenly wonder how my *golden* years will play out. Growing up I assumed that my life would proceed similarly to that of my parents beyond the fact that I would travel the world first. So far the traveling is the only part of that assumption that has come to fruition. Aspects of my life have been fantastic. Far more opportunities, education and occupation wise, were available to me. But my personal life is an entirely different story. At my age Helen had already been married for more than a decade, had Natalie and was pregnant with me.

Not only have I never been married, I have no prospects of entering into wedded bliss in the foreseeable future. I wouldn't be the first old maid in the family. Aunt Vivian never married. No children. She always said her favorite companions were Jack Daniels and the Marlboro Man. She died alone and inebriated in her neat little historic cottage over on Grand Avenue. The house still sits empty. Dad said Aunt Vivian left it to me for when I grow weary of traveling the world.

I don't see that ever happening any more than I do the husband and the kids.

Giving myself a mental kick in the backside for going down that road, I cruise along the aisle until I find the one-by-eight stock boards. This happens whenever I come home. I find myself wondering about my life and the paths I chose not to take. I blame this on Helen—she makes me wonder about things I don't want to consider. Being home makes me second-guess who I am and all I've done in my life.

Exiling the subject, I load four boards on the cart and reverse course, heading for the checkout counter. So far, so good. Not a single face registers in my memory banks. The cashier is quick and I am on my way out the big sliding door in record time.

This might be my lucky day.

Outside the sun beats down on the asphalt and the dozens of cars filling the slots like colorful Lego blocks in neat lines. Dad's truck is a slightly faded blue. Other than the need for a good wax job to return some luster to the paint the body and engine are in mint condition. Even the air conditioning works like a champ. I stow the paint in the passenger side floor-board. The one-by's go in the bed. The nylon rope Dad kept behind the seat for tying down a load is still there. I secure the boards, push the cart into the corral and head to the driver's side of the truck. That's when I notice a blur of royal blue plowing toward me. It's the same WHNT reporter from yesterday racing in my direction, blond hair flying behind her like a silky cape. Her hulk of a cameraman is right on her heels.

I execute an about face and head back toward the store entrance. The faster I walk, the faster they walk. I feel them closing in. How she moves that quickly in high heels and a tight skirt is beyond me.

"Emma! Emma, I have a few new questions for you."

If I reach the store, I'm certain she won't dare follow me inside. Maybe I should have climbed into the truck and driven away but there were so many cars and pedestrians milling about that backing out of the slot and driving away would have taken forever. And then she would only have followed me home. I need an alternate egress. Maybe Howard will come pick up the truck for me. I'm certain he will be more than happy to do me a favor since he's courting my mother and no doubt desires my approval.

"Emma, what are you afraid of?" the tenacious woman asks as she follows me through the store entrance.

More posters of the missing girls mock us.

I keep walking. Take a right and cut through the gathered crowd in front of the paint department. I rip off my cap, shove it into my back pocket as I emerge from the other side of the throng of bodies awaiting their shaken cans. Then I dart down a side aisle and rush back toward the lumber department. A quick look behind me ensures I've lost her for the moment. A left and then a few more aisles over and I hide behind the rolls of chain link fencing stacked in the farthest corner of the huge store.

My pulse is pounding and a sheen of sweat coats my skin. "Shit." I don't know Howard's number. Calling Mother would only worry her. Then it hits me and I realize exactly who I need to call. I slip my cell from my back pocket and tap the name listed as Dangerous, which is code for my sponsor.

"Hello."

His deep voice is instantly soothing. *Idiot.* This was a very bad idea. "Mr. Beckett, this is Em—Beth Taylor."

"Beth." Pause. "Are you all right? You sound upset."

Deep breath. "Actually, I'm in a bit of a bind. My car won't start and I need a ride. You're the only person in the area I know. Would you be able to give me a lift?"

More lies. Jesus, I'm becoming so good at this that maybe I should go into politics.

"Of course. Where are you?"

The announcement that a customer needs assistance in plumbing echoes over the loudspeaker system, forcing me to wait before answering his question.

"Hold on, are you at Home Depot?"

A frown nags at my forehead and I stare at the screen for a sec. "Yes, why?" Then it hits me that he just heard the same announcement as I did. I roll my eyes. *Get it together, Emma.*

"So am I. Where are you?"

I glance around. See the sign for the restrooms. "Meet me at the restrooms."

Carefully checking in both directions first, I slip from my hiding place and hurry along the aisle until I reach the sign. A quick sidestep into a short corridor and I'm standing at the drinking fountain between the men's and the ladies' room doors.

Joey Beckett appears, his expression confused, but he smiles and I feel the frustration about the reporter seeping away. Mercy, this man is gorgeous.

"So, you work for Home Depot?"

I blink, suddenly as confused as he looked five seconds ago. "No, I…" Then I smile. "Actually, I'm a quality control inspector. I do spot visits all over the country." I shrug. "I look for store cleanliness, interact with personnel as if I'm a customer, and report back to headquarters."

"Wow. You're like a spy." His smile widens to a grin. "I guess I should watch my P's and Q's around you."

Emma Graves, this is your life—a tower of lies. One slip and the whole thing could fall apart like a game of Jenga.

"That's right." I force a smile. "So, thanks for giving me a ride. I'm really in a bind. As you can imagine, I can't ask anyone who works here."

"This way," a female voice shouts. "I'll check the ladies' room."

I spin around and catch a glimpse of long blond hair bouncing around royal blue clad shoulders. For the love of God, that reporter is still looking for me.

"Shit." I turn to head for the men's room but abruptly realize I cannot leave the man I called to rescue me standing here without an explanation. So I grab him by the arm and haul him into the men's room with me. The reporter won't expect me to make this move.

I hope.

The door closes behind us and I brace myself before turning to face him. This is where things will get tricky.

Surprise and then amusement flickers across his too handsome face. "Beth, are you," he glances at the urinals nearby, "having an identity crisis?"

At least he didn't ask if I've been drinking. For the record, I would give anything for a double shot of tequila right now.

"Okay." I draw in a big breath. "The truth is my car is fine, but I'm being followed." It is the honest to God truth, as ridiculous as it sounds. Sadly, I can't rally a follow up or explanation to the statement.

Those assessing blue eyes peer straight into mine. "Who's following you?"

Exactly the question anyone would ask. I should have thought of that.

"A disgruntled employee." I immediately latch onto a way out that allows the two of us to part ways before I have to dig myself anymore deeply into this hole. "May I borrow your hoodie?"

The fact that he's wearing jeans that mold flawlessly to his muscular thighs just as he did the first time I laid eyes on him and that the Life is Good tee that contours to his equally well defined chest has not escaped my attention. My shoulders sag with a kind of defeat that's all too familiar. *Do not go there.* All I need is the gray hoodie that rounds out the trendy and somehow intensely sexy wardrobe.

I blink away the idea of how good he looks. "I'll get it back to you, I promise. I just have to ditch this...*creep.*"

He's shouldering out of the garment before I finish the statement. "Sure." He hands me the hoodie. "No rush. I have others."

"Thanks." I drag on the hoodie. It falls warm and smelling like clean soap against me. "I'll...I'll explain another time."

He smiles again. "No rush."

"Really, I appreciate this more than you can imagine."

Before I can reach for the door behind him, he puts his hand on my arm. "Remember, if you need *anything* I am always just one phone call away."

That is definitely my cue to go. "I won't forget."

I do the right thing. I grab the door, but I can't for the life of me follow through with the necessary action. All I have to do is pull and yet I cannot. I tell myself it's because I'm concerned the reporter whose name I don't even know could be waiting just on the other side of the door. That maybe I need to give it another few seconds.

It won't be the first time I've lied to myself.

I pivot, reach up and grab this gorgeous man—my AA sponsor—by the face before going up on tiptoe and locking my lips with his. I melt against him and escape my current dilemma for a few mind-blowing seconds before I regain my senses.

As quickly as I latched on, I let go and retreat, bumping into the door I should have fled through half a minute ago. "Sorry. I shouldn't have done that. I have a habit of doing the wrong thing." Big breath. Square the shoulders. "But now that it's out of my system, you have my word it won't happen again."

Before I can run away there comes that smile again. God, help me. This was a bad, bad idea.

He crosses his arms as if he, too, must ensure he doesn't go for a repeat performance and studies me for a moment, his expression bemused. "Don't beat yourself up about it. Sometimes you have to do the wrong thing to make the right thing happen."

"Good point." I think. At any rate, I lift the hood over my hair. "Thank you...again. I'll call..."

I hurry away, uncertain which represents the greater threat —spending one more second alone with him or going out there and potentially facing the reporter. Since she and her cameraman now likely wait at my dad's truck, I decide for the moment that she is the least of my worries. So I hurry to the outdoor garden department and take a position where I have a good view of the truck.

Half an hour later the reporter and her cameraman give up and climb into the station's van and drive away. Probably to Helen's house.

I guess I'm not going home for a while.

10

THE SCHOOL I ATTENDED IN JACKSON FALLS LOOKS
exactly the same as it did when I graduated fifteen years ago.
Two-story Greek Revival with bride white siding punctuated
with fluted columns flanking the entrance and a copper
topped dome perched like a crown above it all. The first
settlers in Jackson Falls were quite wealthy. They had no inten-
tion of sending their children to school in anything less than
an architectural wonder. Despite the boom of business and
newcomers to the surrounding area, Jackson Falls remains a
small town, leaving no reason to expand or to divide the k-12
school then or now.

One of the oldest schools in the state and inarguably of
historical and architectural significance to the community, the
building has been maintained in pristine condition. Any and
all additions have been in keeping with the architectural
integrity of the original structure—primarily due to the trusts
left behind by wealthy benefactors. The school was and is
populated by people, teachers, staff and students alike, who all
know each other's history from birth. Good, bad or indifferent, labels and destinies are set by the time a child reaches
kindergarten age.

The curse of small town life.

Case in point, I will forever be frozen in the image shaped by tragedy.

Slowing to hardly more than a roll, I pass the front of the school. It faces Bank Street, the main business thoroughfare in Jackson Falls. The small front parking area is for school visitors only but today it's packed to overflowing with people carrying signs. People stand on the steps to the grand front entrance, on the sidewalk, on the grass and on the narrow strip of asphalt that serves as a drop off lane. The gathering extends all the way to the street. An older man looks out over the crowd from the top of the steps. Those assembled appear to hang on his every word.

Easing over to the curb, I roll the window down and listen. I can hear his voice but can't make out all the words. I hear the terms *failure* and *police* repeatedly. Each statement is followed by chanting from the crowd. Jackson Falls PD uniforms linger around the periphery of the throng.

A protest of some sort, I decide.

Then I spot the feisty news reporter that has been following me around. Her van is parked in a visitors slot in front of the building, surrounded by the crowd. She and her cameraman are a few steps down and off to the right of the man speaking. So this is why she abandoned her pursuit of me.

I pull out my cell and give Letty a call. Her rich voice makes me smile. "Hey, Sheriff," I tease.

She laughs. I know she is overwhelmed so I should be quick. "What's going on at the school? Looks like a rally or a protest of some sort."

"Delbert Yarbrough. Poor guy. He's been raising hell since before the Shepherd and Baldwin girls went missing. It's like that twenty-fifth anniversary documentary WHNT did set him on a mission. He's pressuring all of us to finally solve... you know, the old case. With this new case, he's taken his frustration to the next level. The Shepherds and Baldwins are probably there, too."

I know from personal experience that the twenty-five-year anniversary business reopened old wounds. It certainly played havoc with my mental well-being. "Can't fault the man for trying to find justice for his daughter."

God knew my dad and mother hounded the police and the FBI for years. Mother was relentless in doing all she could. Stacy's mother had died the year before. I can't remember if or what Mr. Yarbrough did back then, but I'm certain he was as vigilant as my folks. Frankly, I blocked as many of those details as possible. It was too painful.

"I know," Letty admits. "But we're doing all we can."

"Deep down, I'm sure he's aware of all you're doing," I say. "Emotions, you know. They make us do things sometimes and sometimes it's not the right thing."

"Yeah, I know." She was quiet for a moment. "So, do folks look pretty calm over there?"

I scan the crowd. "I don't see any issues." I want to ask her what she's doing but I remind myself again that she doesn't have time to keep me up to speed. "Hey, did they find those missing cavers?"

Finding those two seems far more doable than the other. Hopefully I'm not bringing up another subject that will make her even more stressed than she already is.

"Not yet. If we don't find them soon, we may be looking at a recovery rather than a rescue."

Damn. "Well, I won't keep you." I pull the gearshift back into Drive. "Let me know if there's anything I can do."

Letty insists we must have a real girls' night as soon as she has another break and I agree. We end the call.

I watch Mr. Yarbrough a while longer. Our families drifted apart after *that day*. It was like we couldn't bear the mutual agony. Passing each other on the street was nearly too much. If Stacy hadn't been with Natalie or the other way around, would that day have turned out differently? If Helen had been home instead of in Birmingham she would have realized the bus was late and started looking for us. But she had a doctor's appointment in Birmingham that day. Mr. Yarbrough's office was in Huntsville and Dad was working on a house in town. So no one noticed we were unaccounted for until hours after the crash.

It wasn't anyone's fault, it simply was.

As I drive away from the school I spot one of the big yellow buses in the rear parking lot. My heart skips a couple of beats. The seemingly innocuous details of that final ride rolls through my brain. Before I realize what I'm doing, I am driving toward Long Hollow Road...toward the place where my life was once normal and happy. At least as normal and happy as a four-eyed, chubby eight-year-old's life could be.

I'm surprised to find two new residential subdivisions along the road that was once nothing but fields and the occasional pasture. The cookie cutter homes are a startling contrast to what my mind recalls. Bradford Pear trees and wooden fences border the brick and rock houses with their small square yards and sleek concrete driveways. They look uncomfortable and out of place against the backdrop of the mountains. A turning lane for the new subdivisions has been added to the two-lane road.

Another three miles and I see the place where the bus toppled onto its side. I pull over and get out, my heart racing, thudding painfully against my sternum. Weeds and thatch crunch under my feet as I descend the bank and cross the ditch to the memorial my parents erected a year or so after that day. The two white crosses remain as white as the day they were driven into the ground. Helen or one of her friends, maybe Mr. Yarbrough, probably keeps them painted. A photo of Natalie and one of Stacy hang on their respective crosses. Mother ordered special cases for the photos to protect them from the elements. In her photo Natalie's long blond hair hangs in lush waves and her big blue eyes are filled with laugher. The smile on her face makes my chest tight. There were never—not even now—adequate words for how very much I miss her. She was my sworn enemy at times, so frustrating I told myself repeatedly that I hated her and yet she was my hero, the person I admired above all others.

She was my sister and I loved her—still love her—with every fiber of my being.

I touch the fresh green blades of the daylilies that Mother planted more than two decades ago. The mature clumps will produce a ring of yellow blooms all summer long. Anyone passing on the road will appreciate the beauty. Some might say memorials like this one are a distraction or foolish, but this was the only memorial we could give Natalie and Stacy. Mom and Dad refused to bury an empty coffin and call it done.

Plopping onto the grass, I sit for a long while and listen to the silence around me. There is no silence in Boston. Maybe the noise helped to push me over the edge. I'm accustomed to dig sites in the oddest and often the remotest of places, not typically in a metropolitan area.

I like my solitude; I need the quiet.

I stare at the photos. For years we played the what-if game. What if they came back? What if they escaped their captor and found help? What if they finally climbed out of the sinkhole that swallowed them—like the Jonah and the whale story in the Bible? Every time the phone rang, for the space of three or four rings the whole family would experience the excitement of what if it's *the* call. What if it's the good news we've been waiting for?

But news never came.

Of course it's possible that Natalie and Stacy were sold off into slavery of some sort. Human trafficking is as old as time. But it's more likely that they are dead. No matter how many times I tell myself this I still don't completely believe it. I mean, there's no evidence to prove that theory any more than there is to prove any other. They're gone. Vanished. Missing.

Dad said a thousand times that the hardest part was the not knowing.

The parents of the girls who went missing this very week are no doubt already suffering the agony that goes with the little voice that just won't shut up—the one that keeps telling you this is bad…so bad. No matter how desperately you want to cling to hope that relentless, heartless little voice warns you to give up…to admit defeat.

I stand, dust off my butt and slog back to the truck. A twist of the key in the ignition and the engine fires. I close my fingers around the steering wheel and instantly hear Dad's voice telling me to put my foot on the brake and then pull the gearshift into Drive.

"God, I miss you, Daddy."

I putter along the road until I arrive at the farmhouse where my life began. The place where we were happy…the place where our family was complete. Mother and Dad kept the farm. In part because it had been in his family for several generations and in part so that if Natalie ever found her way back she would not find a new family living in her home. Though the house is closed up, has been for twenty-four years, the necessary maintenance has been kept up-to-date. Other than the missing rockers on the front porch, it looks exactly the same.

I shut off the engine and climb out. My heart doesn't do that fierce pounding now. It hangs low in my chest, overwhelmed with sadness for what was and can never again be. I climb the steps and peer through the front windows. Even the furniture is still there. Not everything. Mother brought the sentimental pieces to the new old house. But the sofa we gathered on to watch movies and the rug where Sam stretched out like a small horse are still there. Beyond the living room I can see into the kitchen to the window over the sink where Mother placed a bouquet of fresh flowers every week for as long as I can remember. Even after we moved away, once a week she added fresh flowers to the glass vase there. She never said but I knew she left them there just in case Natalie came home.

My sister had been gone for years before Mother finally stopped.

Back down the front steps I wander to the big Dogwood tree. White blooms make it look like a cloud and draw me to its gentle shade. I drop to my knees at another memorial that is near and dear to my aching heart, Sam's grave. As Labradors go, he lived a long life. I missed him so much after we moved into town but he absolutely would not stay there. I sweep my fingers over the white pebbles that line his grave. He held on for years after Natalie died before he gave up and went to sleep for the last time.

I think Sam is the real reason I could never have another dog. What animal could possibly live up to my memory of him? He was loving and brave and completely loyal. I remain convinced that his body heat saved my life that cold night twenty-five years ago. He was my hero.

Not being able to find Natalie broke his heart, too.

I get up and take one last look around. How I wish things had been different.

Feeling defeated, I wander back to the truck. My stomach rumbles and I realize that it's well past noon and I'm starving. The idea that the last thing my lips touched was my sponsor's mouth makes me groan. What an idiot I am. What the hell was I thinking? Calling him again would be a mistake. I know myself far too well to take that self-destructive detour.

You have enough trouble right now, Emma.

I climb back into the truck and head toward town. The air that flows through the windows is cooler today than yesterday. But the long sleeves of the hoodie keep me warm. I glance down at the gray fabric and shake my head. *Idiot.*

Before making the final turn into town, I decide to press

on and turn instead onto Stackhouse Road. Already flowers and stuffed animals are piling up at the site where the Baldwin and Shepherd girls' bicycles were found. Flashbacks from that same scene on Long Hollow Road makes me tremble, desolation fills me. The fear, the hope, the total exhaustion…it was all so overwhelming. I don't have to imagine what these families are going through.

I know it well.

At the next road I turn around and head home. The sooner I get there, the sooner I can start replacing the fascia. Helen will stand right under me watching. Maybe Howard will drop by and take her out to dinner or to a movie. Anything to get her out of the house and off my back.

Thankfully the street and driveway are clear of reporters. I pull the truck all the way around behind the house near the shed. I would like to think the reporter wouldn't knock on the front door or walk into the yard, but she might. She damn sure followed me around the Home Depot.

Mother meets me at the backdoor, glass of iced tea in hand. "I thought you'd gotten lost."

I set the two gallons of paint on the porch. "I rode out to the farm." Dodged a crazy reporter. Kissed my AA sponsor. I feel my face heat just thinking about the latter. I really do need to get back into therapy. I am broken in so many ways. Like Humpty Dumpty, a whole slew of king's horses and king's men would never be able to put me back together again.

Mother's eyebrows rear up. "Really? You should have stopped by and picked me up. I would have gone with you."

"There's a rally at the school," I say to change the subject as I untie the boards and lay them flat on the porch.

"Delbert Yarbrough," she says. "Ginny told me he was planning to hold one. He's been pushing Letty and the rest for weeks now. I don't know what else he expects them to do."

She follows me into the house. I hang Dad's cap on the hall tree. "He expects them to do the undoable. You know."

"I do." She moves through the mudroom into the kitchen. "I made your favorite chicken salad."

My stomach rumbles again. "Great. I am starving." I collapse into a chair, perfectly content to allow my post heart attack convalescing mother to wait on me. I'm really not a good daughter. "You didn't tell me that Ginny is the post-mistress now."

Virginia Cotton, like her daughter Letty, is one of the hardest working people I know. No one deserves a great opportunity more than her. She and Helen have been friends forever, just like Letty and me.

"I'm sure I did. You probably weren't listening."

Though I would never admit it out loud, my mother is likely correct.

Helen measures her famous chicken salad onto a plate with an ice cream scoop. Grapes, pickles, pecans and mayo, combined with freshly cooked chicken and then chilled. My taste buds have my mouth watering. The piece de resistance is the sweet, buttery croissant. To. Die. For.

"Tea?"

"Sure." The only time I drink iced tea is when I'm at home. How can I be in Alabama and not drink iced tea? *Sweet* iced tea.

Tea poured and plates prepared, Mother joins me at the table. "I was thinking."

Oh, God. The potential for trouble in that statement is utterly limitless. "Really?"

I sink my teeth into the salad and moan. I haven't had anything that tastes this good in ages.

Beaming, she goes on. "Yes. I was thinking about your wardrobe."

I freeze, not daring to breathe. This means one thing: she has rifled through my duffel. Jeans, tees, socks, underwear and not much else. Thank God I didn't have a stash of vodka or tequila in there.

"What about my wardrobe?"

She takes a bite of soft, fluffy croissant stuffed with delicious salad and chews for a moment. A sip of tea follows. "Tomorrow's Sunday. What are you going to wear to Mass?"

I knew that little white lie would come back to haunt me. Foolishly I had hoped she would forget.

Her lips stretch into a broad smile at my startled silence. "Not to worry, I dropped by Monique's this morning. You remember that shop? Monique carries only the trendiest fashions. It's so chic. You should stop by while you're here. It's my favorite shopping spot."

I grunt, too worried to form a reasonable reply.

"Anyway, I found the perfect dress for you. I even bought the shoes to match."

I swallow the lump of croissant that has turned as hard as gravel. "You shouldn't have gone to so much trouble."

She waves me off. "I have the perfect handbag, too. You're going to be so gorgeous!"

God help me.

11

SUNDAY, MAY 13

I'M STUMBLING. MY FEET FEEL HEAVY AS IF I'VE WALKED A hundred miles. I am so, so tired. It's too dark, I cannot see. I'm so afraid. My heart squeezes. I want my mommy and daddy. Please, please, I just want to go home.

My eyes fly open and my breath catches in my lungs.

"Dream...just a dream." I dampen my dry lips, swallow against the parched feeling in my throat.

The whirring of the old fan reminds me of where I am. *Home.* I sit up, shove the sweat-dampened hair out of my face and take a deep breath.

I glance at the Backstreet Boys wall clock. As much as I want to, I can't lie in this bed and feel sorry for myself. There's just time for a shower—drying my hair takes forever—before *Mass.* It's Sunday and my mother tricked me into promising her I would go. I stare at the pink A-line silk dress. Sleeveless, jewel neckline with a hem that hits a couple of inches above the knee. The matching shoes are classic high heel pumps in that same soft pink.

"Oh God," I grumble.

An hour later, hair whipped into shape and the dress clinging to me like a second skin, I clop down the stairs in the three-inch heels. If I don't break an ankle or my neck it will be a miracle. I don't do heels and rarely do dresses. This is the feminine style my mother wishes I possessed.

Wrong daughter, Mom.

Natalie was the one who loved to dress up and to wear makeup. At fifteen she looked as glamorous and sophisticated as any senior in school. Maybe I was supposed to be a boy. Natalie pointed out that fact early on.

All you do is play in the dirt and trail after Daddy. You should've been a boy, Emma.

Maybe so. But I like being a woman. I'm just happier without make-up, in jeans and flip-flops. So shoot me.

Mother stands at the hall mirror painting on lipstick as I descend the stairs. My breath catches a little. No matter that she's heading toward the back half of her sixties, my mother is a beautiful woman. Beautiful and strong. I can only hope to ever be as strong as she is. She would never lie to herself and to the people she cares about the way I have—except she didn't tell me about her heart attack. She would justify this decision with the idea that she's protecting me and since I'm keeping secrets from her I'm not about to call her on it. She has always bravely faced whatever obstacle fate tossed in front of her and driven on. People assume I'm strong like that, but I'm not.

Somehow I muddle through.

"There's still time for you to have toast and coffee, dear," Helen assures me before rubbing her lips together and checking the result in the mirror.

She wears a burgundy dress that fits well to her toned body. The hem settles at the knee. The colorful scarf nestled at her throat displays splashes of the pink that is her trademark color. She wears low-heeled pumps in the same burgundy color as the dress. Her hair is tucked into a flattering French twist with soft wisps curling around her face.

"Thanks." Leaving the house without coffee would be

putting every member of St. Mary's at risk of encountering my worst.

I head for the kitchen hoping coffee will infuse my veins with enough caffeine to carry me through the next two hours. The Mass won't last so long but it's the social encumbrances before and after that I dread.

Oh well, it won't kill me to be the good daughter for one morning.

LIKE THE JACKSON FALLS SCHOOL, St. Mary's is as old as the town, one of the oldest Catholic churches in north Alabama. Built of limestone in the Romanesque Revival style, it stands tall and proud on the west side of town, just off the square. Where else were all those original wealthy settlers going to attend Mass? Only the best would do. Two towers flank the façade, one houses the bell and the other has windows all around. During the civil war, soldiers used that tower for a lookout.

Before we go inside I vividly recall how the double door entrance leads into the vestibule. Rich Carrera marble floors flow from the front entrance all the way to the altar. Just inside the door, the coatroom and the church offices are to the right, the restrooms to the left. In the nave, mahogany pews are split by the red carpet that runs the length of the main aisle. The stained glass windows draw the eye up to the soaring ceiling and its hand hewn wooden beams. It is a lovely old church full of history and dignity for the most part. Over the nearly two centuries of its service to the community there has been the occasional scandal. Like when I was nine and the choir director announced that the child she carried was the priest's. That was the last time St. Mary's had a new priest —until now.

I sigh. All I have to do is survive the next hour or so. The horde of people milling about on the steps and swarming through that entrance remind me why I've only been to Mass once since I left for college. *The gathering.* Everyone wants to say hello and ask how you are and how long you're staying and a dozen other questions I don't want to answer. Or maybe I can't answer those questions because I'm far too busy pretending I don't notice how I am. It's easier that way. Denial is such a comfortable friend of mine.

As we climb the steps I'm grateful that most folks appear to be focused on the subject of Delbert Yarbrough and the rally he's holding over at the Methodist church this morning. Maybe I'll get through this without too much discomfort.

"Come this way." Helen encircles her arm around mine and ushers me to the right where a small crowd is assembled. "I want to introduce you to Jake."

"Your priest," I remind her. "Father Barnes." I don't know why it bothers me that my mother calls him Jake. She called Father Estes by his given name, John, for as long as I can remember. But he was a good ten years older than Helen. Her calling this younger man who seems to make her so giddy by his first name feels weird.

"You're going to love him."

As if the folks gathered around the priest recognize a force of nature is descending, the crowd parts like the Red Sea clearing a path for my mother. I toddle along a mere step behind her, mainly because she has a death grip on my arm.

"Helen, good morning."

That deep voice seeps into my brain sending up warning flags and launching a powerful shot of denial before my brain interprets what my eyes see.

Joey Beckett.

My AA sponsor.

Nooo that is just not possible.

The black garb and the white collar confirm that he is indeed a priest but the dazzling blue eyes and killer smile remind me like a slap to the face that he is the man I kissed in the Home Depot men's room about twenty-four hours ago.

Sweet Jesus. I kissed a priest on the mouth with salacious thoughts roaring through my head…with heat exploding in the rest of my body. I am the latest scandal at St. Mary's without having even set foot inside.

This cannot be.

"Jake, this is my daughter, Emma."

Panic flashes in those dazzling eyes for one split second and then he extends his hand, his face relaxing into a welcoming expression. "Emma, I've heard so much about you."

Somehow despite my horror my hand finds his and he squeezes it warmly. The spark of electricity rushes up my elbow. Even more shocking, I find my voice in spite of the adolescent reaction. "Ditto, *Father* Barnes. Mother talks nonstop about you—her new *priest*." I tell him with my eyes what a lying sack of sheep shit he is.

Our hands fall apart.

Helen is going on and on about something but my stunned brain cannot process the words. We are staring at each other, this sneaky priest and I.

He lied to me.

And I lied to him.

I suppose one could say that we're even.

No, no. Not even close. You see, I am a mere human and he is…a *priest*.

Anger ignites in my veins. The first opportunity I have I am going to give this guy a piece of my mind—Boston style.

IRONICALLY THE HOMILY is about forgiveness. Father Barnes hesitates more, I presume, than is normal for him, which convinces me that he is improvising. These are not the words he had prepared for this morning. Rather, he is openly, publicly pleading for my forgiveness.

Not in this life, buster.

I stare at him unblinking as I accept communion from his hand. Finally he announces 'Go in peace,' and I am the first person out the door. I need to get far away from him right now. Confused and struggling to keep up, Mother and Howard follow close behind me. I forgot that Howard the hardware man attends St. Mary's.

Lucky for me, as it turns out.

"Are you all right, sweetie?" Mother senses my distress no matter that I haven't lived in the house with her in fifteen years. I suppose it's a mother's instinct. The bloodhound thing.

I wonder if that instinct failed to warn her that her new priest is a liar and perhaps far worse. After all, I admit to having started the kiss but he participated.

I hesitate. I am a liar as well. No better than him on that score, but I'm not a man of the cloth.

"I'm fine." I pat the hand she places on my arm and tell another lie. "I totally forgot I promised Letty I'd come by and help her with...the case."

Helen blinks. "Oh. All right. Do you need my car?"

Definitely a stroke of luck that Howard is here. "That would be great."

She nods. "I can ride with Howard." She flashes him a smile. "We always go to lunch on Sundays."

"Okay." I snag the fob she produces from her purse. "Have fun, you two."

I don't look back as I rush down the steps.

I know what I need and there is no putting it off any longer.

~

JOHNNY'S

There is only one bar in the area that serves alcohol before noon on Sundays and it also features strippers. What the hell? If you need a drink badly enough you can deal with anything, right?

I need a drink. Not a glass of wine. A real drink. And I need a smoke. If I'm smart I can steer clear of the third part in my habitual unholy trinity—Alcohol, Smoke and Sex—since it usually makes an *ass* of me.

Not a slip I want to make within a thousand miles of home.

The alcohol and the tobacco are both readily available at Johnny's. The guy sitting two stools away slid his pack of smokes and his lighter down the counter to me before I even asked. I guess he saw the envious way I watched him take a drag and exhale.

"I think I know you," he says.

Not exactly original and not at all inspiring. "Well, thanks for the smoke but I'm certain I don't know you."

"Emma Graves," he says with a nod. "I do know you."

I cringe.

Thankfully he makes no move to slide to the empty stool between us. "You don't remember me, I'm Mark. Heather's older brother."

Mark Beaumont. I look at him now. Then I remember, the blond-haired jock who was two-plus years older than my sister and who won all the best awards every year, including his senior year, before disappearing from the limelight. He vanished around the same time and almost as completely as Natalie. Natalie would be forty now, so that would make him about forty-two or three. His once trademark blond hair is peppered with gray and his face is a road map lined with bad choice routes and the subsequent unpleasant detours. The most startling part is the way his skin seemingly lies against nothing but bone and judging by the fifth of Vodka standing next to his glass, we battle at least one of the same demons.

Maybe all the Beaumonts aren't perfect.

I rest my elbow on the counter, plunk my face in my hand and meet his bleary gaze. "Yes, I remember you." Letterman jacket, full of himself, it all comes back in a rush.

"Yeah." He pours another double shot of Vodka. "I was an asshole. Now I'm just a drunk." With that he knocks back the shot, then he looks at me again. "Strange you being back at the same time those girls are missing." He jerks his head toward the mirror behind the bar where amid the liquor bottles are more of the missing posters.

I stare at those two faces for a moment then quickly look away. "Strange, yes."

He slides off the stool and gives me a nod. "Good to see you. Keep the smokes."

"You, too," I say automatically without really meaning it. Mark Beaumont, like everything else around here, reminds me of the parts of the past I've tried so hard to forget. "Thanks."

He staggers away and I wonder if he's planning to drive in that condition. Lorraine probably has a car waiting outside for him. No member of Lorraine Jackson Beaumont's brood would ever risk a DUI. I vaguely recall a third Beaumont, a younger brother. Maybe five or so years younger than me. I wonder whether he inherited the perfect genes like his sister or the shitty ones like Mark. I can definitely sympathize. Natalie was the one to get all the good genes in my family.

The bartender plunks a shot of tequila and two lime wedges in front of me and I forget all about Mark, bad genes and the posters on the mirrored wall not ten feet away. I stare at the vices before me and swallow hard.

This is the moment that has been more than a year in coming. I haven't had a drink—other than the occasional glass of wine, maybe more if I count what I had at Letty's—since before I went to Iraq. I did have a smoke while I was in the hospital recovering from surgery. The PT guy wheeled me to the smoking area with him.

Right now, I need this more than I need to breathe. Another lie, of course, but it feels entirely true. The need tingles and twists inside me and I resist with the last, unraveling thread of fight remaining in my damaged soul. I lick my lips in anticipation of the burn I know will provide such wondrous relief—if only temporarily. Frustration and guilt and anger and all those other emotions I don't want to feel will just slip away. I take a deep breath, remind myself just how good it feels to not give a damn about anything.

The battle goes on this way until I'm unsure how long I've been sitting here staring at the relief I so desperately desire.

Unable to bear the tension any longer I reach for the pack of cigarettes. I can do this one thing without having to worry that I'll end up embarrassing myself. Only my lungs will know. I flick the lighter and draw the nicotine and the dozens of other chemicals into the farthest recesses of my chest. The urge to cough tugs at my throat but I ignore it, hold the smoke deep inside for a few seconds and then close my eyes. When I can hold my breath no longer, I exhale. The room spins a little. It's been a long time. The tension leaches out of me like static electricity discharging into the ground with a harmless crackle.

As I savor the cigarette I continue to stare at the shot. Enough of these and I wouldn't care about handsome liars or missing little girls and I certainly wouldn't allow thoughts of my vanished sister or my aging mother to invade. I would go off into that pretend world where nothing matters except the buzz…the feel of freedom completely uninhibited by rules and expectations.

"If you have to talk yourself into it, maybe you shouldn't do it."

I jerk my face to the right. The liar—the priest—slides onto the stool beside me. He still wears his uniform.

"Really?" I glare at him. "You are aware what this place is."

He smiles, not the megawatt power show that first hypnotized me, something a little more subdued. "I am."

Jesus H. Christ.

Before I can launch the fury that's been building inside me since Helen introduced us, the bartender strolls up. "What you having today, Father Barnes?"

My jaw drops and I am unable to close it.

"The usual," the liar tells him.

I sit, mouth open, in stunned disbelief as the bartender pours a glass of *cranberry* juice and sits the virgin drink in front of him.

"Thank you, Riley." The liar smiles. "We missed you this morning."

The bartender—Riley, apparently—shrugs. "Cadence called in sick. I had to fill in."

When the bartender moves on, the liar leans toward me. "You should probably close your mouth."

I snap it shut, furious all over again. "You lied to me, Joey Beckett."

He gave a slow nod. "I did, Beth Taylor." He lifts his glass and takes a drink. "And I'm sorry about that, but there are some things I prefer to keep between me and the Man upstairs."

I reach for an ashtray and stamp out the cigarette. "What about your congregation?" I glare at him some more. "What about my mother who thinks you hung the moon?"

For a long moment he stares back at me, his eyes showing a weariness I hadn't noticed before. "We all have weakness, Emma."

Hearing him say my name makes me feel exposed, naked and angry all over again.

"The fact that I'm an alcoholic," he goes on, "does not lessen my faith or make me a bad priest. It makes me human.

I haven't had a drink in ten years and I will never have another."

I want to ask how he can be a priest and avoid at least wine but I'm still too pissed to pretend to care. I suppose he's like me and takes his chances with wine. It's the hard stuff that always does me in. Just another way we lie to ourselves.

"While you're here visiting your mother," he goes on, "I will do all in my power to help you in any way you need me. I only ask that you keep my secret."

To pretend what he is doing is any worse than what I do every day of my life is hypocritical. Something my dad hated, something I despise. I may be many things but I am not a hypocrite. "I can do that."

The showstopper smile that blew me away the first time we met appears. "Thank you."

He pushes the shot of tequila away and motions for the bartender. "Riley, my friend needs a..." He turns to me in question.

"Coke or Pepsi. Whichever you have."

Jake nods. "Good decision."

The weight of anger and frustration lifts and I smile in spite of myself. "Thank *you*."

My cell rings and I almost don't reach for it. It's probably Helen wanting to know where I am and what I'm doing. Or maybe she and Howard drove past Johnny's and saw her Cadillac in the parking lot. No, not likely. If she saw her SUV anywhere near this establishment she would have demanded that Howard come inside and see what I'm doing.

"Is that your phone?"

I nod as I drag it out of the small pink clutch Helen insisted I carry.

Letty Cotton.

A line of worry splits my forehead, making me aware of the headache that has begun there. I accept the call. "Hey, Letty. What's up?"

There's a hesitation before she responds. I hear muffled voices in the background and realize that she is either listening to what someone is telling her before she can answer me or that she has butt dialed my number and is unaware I'm on the line.

"Hey, sorry, Emma. Listen, we've got a problem."

Immediately the image of a brutal car accident looms in my mind. Has Mother been in an accident? A band tightens around my chest. "What's going on?"

"Remember those two lost cavers?"

I nod, realize she can't see me and say, "Yes. Of course."

"Well, the rescue unit found them and they're a little dehydrated and a lot delirious but I've got to check out their claim anyway."

I'm confused. I can't imagine what this has to do with me. "Okay."

"Our coroner—Glenn Wallace—has cancer and he's in the hospital in the middle of a chemo cycle so I can't call him. If I call the state lab it could be days before they get someone down here. I can't wait that long, Emma. I need to do this now. I need to know if these guys are full of shit or if there's really something down there."

I'm thinking if she needs a coroner there must be a body. Images of the two missing girls zoom through my head. I stare at the missing poster and a knot ties in my gut. I'm an anthropologist. My training could be of assistance and I'm certainly not afraid to go down into a cave. "What can I do to help?"

"I need you to go down in this cave with me." There's a lingering moment of silence. "It may be nothing, but these guys both swear they found bones down there. *Human* bones. Bones and graves."

For a moment I can't speak. Images of Natalie smiling and Stacy whispering in her ear flood my mind. Then I remind myself that these could be animal bones or the bones of a civil war soldier who hid in the cave or a centuries old native

inhabitant who died there. It happens. Bones and other arti-
facts are frequently discovered in the area. Could be the
remains of a long lost caver who wasn't so lucky as the two
recently rescued.

"Text me the directions. I'll run home and change and be
right there."

"I'll pick you up at your house." She hesitates a moment.
"Thanks, Emma. I will owe you big time."

Excitement rushes through me. Now this is something I
can do and keep my mind off all this other stuff while simultaneously staying clear of both Helen, the handsome priest and
that persistent reporter.

I am very, very good at digging up bones.

12

HELEN

EMMA DIDN'T TELL me what is going on, only that Letty needed her assistance. Though I try not to, I can't help but worry that this has something to do with the missing girls. If anything, I hope they've been found alive and unharmed. No mother should have to go through the agony of discovering her child has been murdered. Sometimes I am torn about which is worse, learning the horrible truth or never knowing exactly what happened.

Either way is an unbearable place.

I stare out the kitchen window as the sun starts its drop westward. I smile at the mason jar on the windowsill full of pink tulips. They remind me of how pretty Emma looked at church this morning. We haven't had a minute to ourselves for me to ask what all the tension between her and Jake was about. If I didn't know better, I would say they have met before though I don't see how.

The clatter on the table has me turning toward my phone. It vibrates against the wooden surface. My pulse jumps at the possibility that it's Emma. She's a grown woman and I know it's foolish but I can't help but worry. I rush to grab it, read the name and my hopes fall.

I muster up a lighthearted tone. "Hi, Ginny. Are you home from church already?" Ginny's congregation usually has lunch potluck style and continues on with an afternoon service. I'm surprised to hear from her this early in the afternoon.

The mewling sound that whispers out of my dear friend reaches deep inside me and twists my heart into knots. "What's happened, Ginny?"

"They found bones, Helen. In a cave…just like *he* said."

Misery lances through my chest. The words I want to say feel frozen on my tongue. I struggle to expel the words from my mouth. "Has Letty made any identifications?" The idea that Emma is with her presses against my sternum.

"She didn't say." More of those painful sobs echo across the line. "She and Emma are going down in that cave to bring the bones out."

Tears roll down my cheeks. My heart is racing and it's difficult to breathe. *Oh God. Oh God. Oh God.* Somehow I manage to steady my voice. "We'll know soon I guess."

Ginny clears her throat, struggles to speak without breaking down again. "Letty will tell us."

The idea of Emma in some damned hole in the ground uncovering her sister's bones makes my head swim. I pray she can handle it. No matter that she does this all the time, this time is different. This time it could be her sister.

Agony swells inside me. For so long I poured every part of myself into the search for my precious Natalie. Even when the police and the reporters stopped, I kept going. I could not stop. Could not give up. I didn't notice how dangerously close I was to a very dark place until I fell, felt the change in velocity as I tumbled into that abyss. Every ounce of willpower and strength I possessed was required to climb out of that hole— for my sweet Emma. She still needed me. Andrew needed me.

"Call if you hear anything else," I urge, trying with all my might to sound strong.

"Helen…"

I know what she's going to say. "We made a pact, Ginny. I will never tell anyone what happened. We've left letters for our girls when we're gone. There is no need to ever speak of what happened again until that time comes. Not to anyone. Not even to each other."

The silence that fills the line is heavy with the misery that has been ours alone for two decades.

"All right. I am truly sorry you've had to carry this burden with me all these years. You are a dear friend, Helen." Her voice breaks on the last.

"This burden belongs to both of us. We did what we had to do. I have no regrets."

We end the call without saying more. There's no need. It is what it is.

I scrub at my cheeks, cursing the tears there as I climb the stairs. Memories swirl in my head—memories I never wanted to think of again but today I have no choice.

In my room there is a box hidden on the top shelf of my closet. I scoot a chair there and retrieve it. I haven't touched this box for twenty years. It's too hard or perhaps I am just a coward. Either way, as soon as I sit down on the bed and open the lid I inhale the scents of the past…the scent of my sweet, sweet Natalie.

The many fissures in my damaged heart widen. A smile touches my lips as I rifle through our—mine and Andrew's—favorite pictures of Natalie. So beautiful. Smart and talented. Just like Emma. We were so blessed to have two such beautiful, intelligent daughters.

I finger the ballet slippers she wore in her final recital. She so loved dance. Inside one of the slippers is the necklace we bought her for her fifteenth birthday. Lovely silver chain with a single charm—pink ballet slippers. Anger stabs into my heart. I close my eyes and will it away. Anger won't change anything now. Inside the box is a letter Natalie wrote the day Emma was born. I laugh whenever I read it. She warns her new sister that she will never be the favorite. So funny. Her kindergarten report card and the retainer she hated wearing. I move through the memories, packing them all back into the box one by one. On top, I'm careful to leave the letter I wrote to Emma twenty years ago. When I die, she'll find it.

That was the agreement Ginny and I made.

Whichever of us survives the other will answer any questions our daughters have and hope for forgiveness.

I remember the day I wrote this letter and first placed it in the box. It was the day before old Sam died. I had gone alone to him that day—before Emma got out of school. There were things I needed to say that I couldn't yet share with Emma or her father. I sat on the porch next to the loyal animal. He was so old, but Andrew and I refused to put him down as long as he wasn't in pain and he ate well. We made that decision years before. We allowed him to live out his life doing what he wanted to do—watching for our sweet Natalie to come home. Every single day for five long years he lay on that porch and watched for that damned bus to stop but it never did.

On this day, nearly five years after Natalie disappeared, I went to him, to tell him the news I had hoped I would never learn. Natalie wasn't coming back. I have no idea if dogs understand our words but I believe my tears were explanation enough. Sam stared at me with those big brown eyes, so weary, so sad. I am convinced he understood that our girl was gone forever. If I'd had any doubts, when he laid his head in my lap I knew. I scratched behind his ears, stroked his head and his face, felt the dampness of his own tears. We sat together for a long time before I left that day.

It would be the last time.

The next day when Emma and I arrived after school Sam was not on the porch. We found him in the house in his bed.

We both cried and went to where Andrew was working to tell him. As quickly as we could gather what we needed, we returned to give our sweet Sam a proper burial.

I had selected Natalie's favorite teddy bear from when she was just a little girl. Emma placed it in the blanket with Sam before her daddy wrapped him and then covered him with the warm earth.

As Andrew and Emma loaded up in the truck to go home, I told Sam how very much we would all miss him. Before walking away, I asked a favor of him.

"Please take that teddy bear to Natalie in heaven."

In my heart I knew without doubt that he was with my precious Natalie delivering that teddy bear even as I walked toward the truck where Emma and Andrew waited.

13

EMMA

IF TRAVELING BY ROAD, the cave is about ten miles from the farm where I lived from birth until I was almost nine. Even farther from where I was found half frozen the morning after the bus crash. Yet somehow my muscles remember the terrain…the place. These mountains have stood here for thousands of years. Most of the trees were here before I was born and will be here long after I'm gone.

My nerves are taut, like the high wire in a trapeze act. Once we left the road, ATVs took us the better part of the distance up the mountainside, but eventually the woods became too dense so we walk. Thick moss cushions our path like a velvet ribbon curling through the forest. The air is heavy with humidity and I am winded by the time we reach our destination. I haven't been on a jaunt like this one since the injury. I feel the climb in my thighs.

Letty stops and takes a moment to catch her breath. "They entered the cave on the other side of that ridge and came out here."

She gestures to a slit in the ground at the base of a rise that's no more than five feet wide and maybe two feet at its tallest point. It looks like an all-seeing eye in the mountainside. Saplings and underbrush camouflage it, encircling the odd rupture in the earth like thick rows of lashes. I move closer and peer into the darkness.

"It's pretty much straight down for about fifty, fifty-five feet," Letty warns.

"If my calculations are correct," Colton Tanner, a cave expert from the National Speleological Society, says, "this portion of the cave once had a fairly large opening that we could have walked through, located about ten yards that way." He points downhill in the direction from which we came. "I'm guessing the collapse took place less than twenty years ago." He waves a hand between the possible location of the original opening and the hole we're looking at now.

I see what he means. The vegetation along that area is dense, but the trees are not nearly as large as the ones nearby. The underbrush is jungle thick, the ground noticeably springier. My instincts are buzzing. I remind myself that I don't know what's down in that hole and allowing myself to become overly agitated will not help me get the job done. Letty is counting on me.

"What we're left with is a gap where the ground split after the collapse. This opening wasn't listed in any of the society's records. Until these guys were found, I'm guessing it's been decades since anyone even came near it."

It's easy to see why no one noticed the opening the cavers crawled out of before today. Unless you stepped on just the right spot and fell in or poked your head through just the right clump of bushes, you would miss it altogether. Some of the undergrowth was trampled down by Letty's deputies and a couple of the rescue squad members. Made getting through easier for us.

"Going in from the entrance where our guys started,"

Letty says, "we might end up as lost as they did and never find the bones they claim are down there. They walked and crawled for miles. So we're going in from here. Once we have our feet on the ground down there, the graves are supposed to be about half mile or so in."

"Nothing I haven't done before," I assure my old friend though my hands shake the tiniest bit.

Letty jerks her head toward the expert. "Mr. Tanner was kind enough to bring us all the equipment we'll need for getting down there. He'll go in with us but he'll stay clear of the gravesites."

The Cave and Rescue Unit is not particularly happy that Letty backed them off this part of the adventure. But if there are bones from a homicide down there, the recovery has to be done by the book with every effort made to preserve the crime scene and to protect the chain of evidence. I am qualified for crime scene evidence removal. Letty deputized me to make it official.

"Let's do this then," Tanner says.

I'm impressed with his gear. Top of the line fiberglass helmets, state of the art LED lighting mounted right on the helmets. At home, I pulled on socks and jeans and my hiking boots and the only long sleeved shirt I brought with me. Since I didn't have a jacket I grabbed the lying priest's hoodie. I pull it on now, his scent lingering on the fabric. Sometime between leaving him at the bar and Letty picking me up I decided not to hate him for now. Maybe his message on forgiveness got through. I tug on the knee and elbow pads as well as gloves, completing the ensemble.

"He brought the equipment you requested," Letty says. "If there's anything else you decide you need, we'll have one of my deputies bring it up the mountain."

"Thanks." I haven't been around Letty on the job. I'm already impressed with how capable and competent she is. Nothing I hadn't expected.

Tanner wears a pack carrying water, a few snacks in case we're down there a while, and first aid supplies. A five-gallon bucket containing a portable spade, a trowel, dental picks, two medium size collapsible soil screens and a couple of paint-brushes will be lowered first. Both Letty and I have packs as well. In hers she carries a camera with flash and other items she will need for documenting the scene and the remains in situ. My pack contains a number of plastic evidence bags in varying sizes as well as a few paper sacks.

The Sheriff's Department's two forensic techs will remain above ground to bring up and properly store for transport all evidence we collect.

A slightly pared down version of the team and tools I generally have at my disposal on a dig but I can make it work.

With the ropes and rigging for descent in place, we gear up with the harnesses and prepare to rappel down into the cave. The drop is fairly quick but too tricky for a rope ladder since parts of the cave wall jut sharply outward. Our first priority is to get this done alive and unharmed. Another reason to be thankful I didn't throw back that shot at Johnny's. I guess the handsome, lying, I-have-weaknesses-too priest did me a favor.

I may have forgiven him but that doesn't mean I'm not still pissed. A little.

One at a time, we go down into the dark abyss. Tanner first, then Letty and finally me. This part of the cave is larger than I expected. The uninviting crack in the ground led me to believe it was a long narrow space. Not true. By the time my feet touch the ground again any light that filters in from the opening above has vanished into the darkness. Our helmet lights reveal a large room surrounded by perpetually weeping limestone walls. Water seeps through, trickling down like tears. Time and water have left designs in the rock, almost like faces watching as we arrive to investigate the claim of bones in its depths.

The layers of rock stack up like shelves on one side of the space, which is the only reason the two lost cavers were able to climb out. I look from the top shelf to the opening and shudder inwardly. They still took a tremendous risk making that final leap. I guess it was better than dying down here without ever trying.

Moving forward is slow. The rocks are slippery and some jut upward like spikes. Overhead the stalactites remind me that we are traipsing into territory that could very well date back to the beginning of time. The temperature is cool, maybe fifty degrees. The air smells dank, like damp dirt and decomposing plant life. One of the delirious guys who'd gotten lost down here insisted he left a small orange stake flag, the kind surveyors use, to mark the spot. The site is a ways in so we keep moving.

Four maybe five minutes later Tanner announces, "The flag is dead ahead."

I spot the small orange flag and the alien terrain seems to shift around me. The lightheadedness comes out of nowhere. Steadying myself, I shift the bucket I carry to my other hand. The unexpected and abrupt urge to tell Letty I can't do this hurls into my throat. I want to turn around and run. But I can't.

Letty needs me...*I* need to do this.

"We'll make this the outer perimeter of the scene for now," Letty says to Tanner.

This is as far as he goes. He doesn't argue though I can see the curiosity as well as the disappointment on his face. "Standing by."

My pulse flutters as I move toward the marked location. I think of Helen and how she asked me repeatedly what I would be doing to help Letty. I trust my mother, of course, but some part of me resisted telling her about the find. After twenty-five years you would think we had stopped anticipating the discovery of the truth about Natalie and Stacy's disappearance, but that is not at all the way it is. I cannot help but wonder about the bones. Helen probably thinks the two girls who went missing just this week have been found. Since the find is only bones that isn't possible.

I crouch near the mounds that do indeed give the appearance of graves. The soil has been disturbed on one of them, a human skull and a tibia lie atop the loosened dirt.

"Holy shit." Letty breathes the words as she squats next to me. "I guess they weren't as crazy as I thought."

I draw in a long, steady breath, let it out. "The graves appear fairly shallow." Which is why the two men spotted the bones. Time and the elements have shifted a layer of the soil. My spotlight reveals other glimpses of white against the dark earth. I steady my nerves. "I'll proceed using the trowel. I don't want to use the spade unless I have to."

Letty nods. "I'll take photographs and make some measurements before you begin," she reminds me.

"Right." I move back. "I can help with the measurements." This is something we do at all digs. The routine is second nature to me.

Letty snaps pics of the general area. Then, as I hold the tape measure at different vantage points, she takes more and then makes notes. As much as I want to dig in, particularly to see if I can find any sort of ready identification, documenting the scene is extremely important to the investigation moving forward. If the bones are those of victims of a crime, those victims deserve our utmost care.

Once Letty has completed her work, it's finally time for me to begin.

"Tell me what I need to do." Letty steps back, giving me plenty of elbow room.

"Be ready to bag."

"Gotcha."

My hands slip into a rhythm that is as familiar to me as breathing. The emotional baggage lifts and my mind focuses solely on the work. I note fractures in the frontal, parietal and temporal lobes of the skull. Three distinct blows to the head, at least one is noticeably depressed.

I hesitate. It's possible some sort of fall caused the injuries but most likely it was murder. Although it is not my job to make any conclusions about cause of death, I mention this to Letty as we bag the skull and the single tibia the cavers discovered.

She nods and that solitary action causes a buzzing to start in my ears.

I close my eyes a moment and silence the sound, remind myself to breathe deep and slow, then I say, "It appears the skull and the tibia came from this mound." I gesture to the first of the two graves. "Let's operate under that assumption and keep what we find in this section together."

Letty nods her understanding. She packages the skull and the tibia, and labels each with a Sharpie, then waits for my next move.

Slowly, I float the trowel through the reasonably soft soil. I hit a rock now and then. Flinch and then continue. One by one, the skeletal remains emerge. As I reveal more of each bone, I choose the larger of the paintbrushes to sweep away the soil without risk of causing further damage. Both arms are intact. A leg. The second leg has separated at the knee. Not unusual. Once all the tissue that holds together the pieces has completely decomposed, joints can and will fall apart.

My fingers gently ply the next piece from the earth. Pelvis. *Female*. My heart thumps hard against my sternum. There isn't sufficient light for me to hazard a guess at the age. I would need my measuring instruments and plenty of light for that part. Again, not my job. Renewed purpose has my hands moving a bit more swiftly.

Could this be Natalie or Stacy? The question ricochets in my brain. I could be touching my sister's bone...or Stacy's. My hands tremble and my throat goes so dry I can hardly swallow. I should take a break and have some water but I cannot stop. I need to know. Whatever I find, I cannot be certain of anything until the remains are properly identified using dental and medical records.

I remind myself of this over and over as I continue.

I find a metal snap and what appears to be a zipper, both consistent with those found in jeans or some other type of pants made of cotton or linen that have long since decayed. Cotton and organic fabrics decompose quickly, most of the time within a few months. A small square of synthetic material appears to be the tag from a t-shirt or blouse of some sort.

Ribcage. I hold it in my hands for a moment, an ache throbbing deep inside my own.

Keep going.

Feet. Right one, left one. Partially decomposed sneakers. Blue. Natalie wore sneakers that day but they were pink.

Deep breath. The first set of remains is complete as best I can determine.

I move to the second mound and repeat the process, my movements steady and methodical. Thankfully the bags are large enough so far. There are a considerable number of bags piling up so we may have to rethink how we transport them back up through the entrance and down the mountainside.

"Tanner," I shout to the man still standing several yards away.

"Yeah?"

"Check with the Rescue Unit to see if they have some small tarps for making bundles to bring up the remains. If not, we're going to need something like that or maybe a small stretcher."

"Got four of those six by eight blue tarps they sell at Walmart in my truck. Will those work?"

I am immensely grateful for his state of readiness. "Perfect. We'll need rope or duct tape to bundle them in small enough parcels to get through the opening."

"Got that, too."

"I do love a prepared man," I say, all the more grateful since this is an aspect of the work I should have thought of before descending into this dark hole.

Again I discover a zipper, but this time there's a metal button instead of a snap. Jeans, for sure. I can just make out the logo pressed into the metal. *Levi's.* My breath catches. Natalie loved Levi's, but so did most of the other kids her age. Another tag from a blouse or tee. Patches of satiny type fabric and u-shaped metal strips consistent with the remains of a bra with underwire support. Again my hands slow, tremble. Natalie was well endowed for a fifteen-year-old. She may have worn underwire support bras. I can't be sure.

Mother would know.

I steady myself and plunge my gloved fingers into the dirt once more. Voices and images from my childhood reverberate inside me, causing that damned trembling in my hands to spread…along my arms, down my torso and into my legs. My head begins to spin as if some dark place in my gray matter already knows what is coming.

Steady. Calm. Focus on the work.

I find the nylon string before I feel the shoe. I exhume the sneaker.

One by one the hairs on the back of my neck stand on end. Goosebumps spill across my skin.

Pink.

My pulse quickens. I turn the shoe, to look at the outer side. The letters and shapes made in black permanent marker are faded, partially disintegrated but enough is there for me to recognize hearts and stars and two letters: NG.

Natalie Graves.

14

"YOU'RE SURE YOU'RE OKAY TO KEEP GOING?"

Letty stares at me, looks deep inside me, waiting for an answer. The worry in her eyes tells me she is as sick as I am. All these years we have waited for this moment. The police, my parents and numerous other people have searched, always hoping and praying they would not find what we have at last unearthed.

We now have the answer to the question that has haunted our families and this town for twenty-five years.

What happened to Natalie and Stacy?

The remote and ever fading possibility that they might be alive somewhere is gone. The theory that the girls tried taking a shortcut, as I did, got lost and died in their sleep in the cold somewhere in those hills around the farm is gone.

Both skulls were fractured in the same manner. Most likely blunt force trauma—multiple blows.

Natalie and Stacy were murdered.

The words pound in my brain, echoing over and over.

I feel numb. Numb and empty. I cannot adequately articulate what I expected to feel in the event my sister or her remains were ever found, but I don't believe this is it. I anticipated some level of relief, certainly a final jolt of grief and perhaps closure, physically and emotionally.

I feel none of those things.

My hands won't stop trembling. My skin burns from touching her bones—my sister's bones…beautiful, perfect Natalie's bones. Once I exhumed that sneaker with her initials, I tore off the gloves. I needed to bury my fingers in the dirt that had blanketed my only sister for twenty-five long years. I needed to touch her bones…to touch her. To feel the last thing she felt as she died.

Emotion burns my eyes and I swallow back the urge to gag.

My stomach has pitched upward, against the useless, shuddering organ that is my heart, which hangs and quivers in my throat. I alternately need to vomit and to scream. I feel like I'm eight years old again and I am oddly lost. I do not want this to be. I want to go home and throw myself into my mother's arms. I want to talk to my dad.

But I can do neither of those things. I am a grown woman and many people—my mother, Mr. Yarbrough and the woman staring at me right now—are counting on me to follow through with this somber, miserable task. I've done it hundreds of times. I am highly trained and amply experienced.

I square my shoulders and do what I do best. I lie. "I'm fine. Don't worry about me. Let's get this done."

An hour later I watch as each bundle is carefully lifted up and removed from the cave. As the last of Natalie's remains rise out of this damned place I tremble and I cannot stop the tears.

She is finally found. Free of this dank, dark prison that has held her for so very long.

Drawing in a steadying breath, I mentally walk through

the steps that happen now. The techs will transport the remains to the Forensic Lab in Huntsville where they will be thoroughly examined and officially identified. A pair of sneakers is not an official identification by any means. But I know—deep in my soul I know. I didn't say as much to Letty but the age range is right. Even without my tools or better lighting I've looked at enough human remains to judge the age with a fair degree of accuracy. Both sets of remains belong to females between thirteen and eighteen years of age.

Though a forensic team is scheduled to come behind us and complete another search for evidence, first we will sift through the soil for any missed skeletal remains no matter how small. I don't expect to find any since the remains looked and felt intact, but it's important to be thorough. Letty has cordoned off a sizeable area where the graves are with yellow crime scene tape. This is the part we will screen before anyone else sets foot down here.

I pull on new gloves and we begin at the outer perimeter, then as we move into the cordoned off area we're kneeling on soil that has already been sifted for remains and evidence. The process is slow and painstaking. If it takes all night, we won't stop until we're done.

"I've asked the lab to process the remains ASAP." Letty pauses a moment. "We've waited a long time."

I nod. "A long time."

Her hands delve into the soil once more. "Besides, we have all these protests going on and the missing kids. We need any and all evidence that might be even remotely related processed immediately."

"You're right." I say the words though I am lost in my own thoughts. The last school bus ride my sister and I took keeps playing again and again in my head. I try to push it away but it refuses to go. It streams over and over like a video on a loop.

I will not melt down like I did in that classroom. Letty

needs me. I focus on my hand movements, on the richness of the soil. Scoop, shake. Scoop, shake.

"We won't be able to share anything about what we've found." Letty hesitates but she doesn't look at me. When wearing helmets with spotlights you learn fairly quickly not to stare at each other.

"I won't tell Helen." I understand she's gently warning me not to discuss the case with my mother. I can't help wondering how this news will affect my mother. She just had a heart attack. Has she secretly continued to hope Natalie will come home one day? God, I hope not.

Can I say without doubt that I haven't harbored that same hope, ever so slightly?

"I'm sorry I have to ask you to do that." Letty's voice draws me from the troubling thoughts. "I'm used to withholding information but I realize it feels wrong to a civilian."

I stop, my fingers deep in the dirt. "It doesn't feel wrong. I understand. We operate at digs with similar constraints."

A weary chuckle escapes my friend. "Do you know I've never taken a real vacation? I want to go on a dig with you someday."

I laugh, tension making the sound brittle. "This is a dig, sort of, though it's about as far from a vacation as I can imagine."

Letty chokes out a laugh and then suddenly we're both laughing so hard we can't catch our breath. It's like when we were kids and we watched The Christmas Story for the first time. Mother bought me a Polaroid camera that Christmas. Letty and I snapped dozens of photos of each other with a bar of soap in our mouths.

Suddenly we aren't laughing anymore and we sob. Our helmets bang against each other as we hug so hard we can't breathe. When I was a child I cried almost every night, wishing Natalie would come home and that my parents wouldn't be so sad. As I grew into a teenager I just felt depressed. I was angry a lot with Mother for allowing this terrible thing to happen. Deep down I knew it wasn't her fault, still I had to blame someone. I imagine she did the same thing.

Then the indifference settled in. I just wanted to get out of this town—get away from this place that had damaged me so. Never, not once in my life have I ever spoken to anyone save that damned therapist in Boston after the meltdown about what happened to me—to my family—when I was a child. No one outside Jackson Falls with whom I've worked or met has a clue about *that day*.

I wanted to outrun it. To escape the deep, festering hurt. I didn't want to be that four-eyed, chubby kid whose sister was lost. I didn't want to be the only one who came back. I didn't want to be regarded with pity. I just wanted to be me.

Emma Graves, the woman who digs up bones. The woman who wasn't afraid in that hole while her assistant and friend lay dying. The woman who made it out of that goddamned hole alive.

The strong woman who comes back home and takes care of her ailing mother and finds her missing sister after a quarter of a century.

Except I am not strong. I cry harder.

When we run out of tears and our faces are smeared with tears and mucus and dirt, we sit back on our heels, our knees furrowed in the loose dirt, and attempt to pull ourselves together. Our lights shine forward as if we're mesmerized by the craggy rock wall.

"Well." Letty clears her throat. "Now that we've gotten our little breakdowns out of the way…"

I laugh, can't help it. I feel strangely giddy now. "Nat would say we're acting like babies."

"Oh my God, you're right. She must've told us that a thousand times."

We lapse into silence for a long moment.

"Someone murdered her, Letty." The words are a whisper in the musty darkness that surrounds us. Where we sit, the area marked off with yellow tape, is lit up like a spotlight focused center stage on the actors in a macabre play.

"Looks that way." Letty's fingers ball into fists against her thighs. "I have a killer to find."

The fractures on the two skulls were far too similar to have happened coincidentally as if they fell into this godforsaken hole. And they sure as hell didn't bury themselves. Besides, based on what Tanner said, twenty-five years ago the entrance wasn't a hole with a fifty-foot drop. Whatever happened in here, at least one other person was involved.

"He beat them and then he buried them," I say out loud. The grim words echo off the damp walls. I am grateful no one else is down here. Tanner went up with the final bundle of remains.

"He felt remorse."

I frown at the idea. "Maybe he just wanted to hide what he'd done."

"Maybe, but in my experience a killer who regrets what he's done tries to do something right—something kind for the victim. They were buried carefully. The graves were mounded the way you expect a grave to look. He wasn't just covering them up."

I scrub my dusty forearm across my face to swipe away the tears and snot. I almost laugh as I think that the lying priest might not appreciate me using his hoodie as a handkerchief.

"Now all we have to do is find the son of a bitch," I mutter as I fill my screen once more.

"If we're lucky," Letty scoops dirt into her screen, "he got emotional and careless down here. That's when they screw up, when they get emotional or in a hurry."

We dig and sift in silence for a time, the soil shaking across the screens, sifting through the hundreds of small holes and sprinkling down like cake flour. Piece by piece we carefully inspect anything that doesn't filter through the screens. Lots of small rocks. Another rivet from the jeans.

The jingle of metal on metal rattles in my screen. I still, then lower my screen and inspect the contents. Rocks. More rocks.

Metal. The air halts in my lungs. Partially caked with dirt and visibly rusty, the dog tags dangle from a beaded metal chain.

The beam of Letty's headlamp joins mine. Her screen lowers to the ground. She doesn't speak, only stares.

The silence in the cave echoes inside me. Even my heart seems to have failed.

I rub the dirt away and read the letters stamped into the metal.

Cotton. James D.

I recognize the string of numbers as a social security number. B positive. Baptist.

James Cotton. Letty's father. Why would his dog tags be *here?*

Letty turns to me. I squint against the bright light. She does the same since mine shines in her face as well. Simultaneously we adjust our headlamps. That's when I see the paralyzing terror in her eyes, on her beautiful face. Everything inside me weeps.

I shake my head. "This is a mistake."

Letty extends her hand toward me. I drop the dog tags into her gloved palm.

She inspects the tags for a long while. The muscles of her throat work with the effort to swallow, to breathe. I want to say something comforting, something reassuring.

There are no words.

Slowly, as if her muscles are so cold they cannot move quickly or smoothly, she reaches for an evidence bag. I help her open it and she deposits the dog tags into the plastic and seals it.

"We should stop now."

Her soft words reverberate through the dank space.

I am aware we probably should have stopped as soon as I pulled that pink sneaker out of the dirt. "We should."

"If we stay, we compromise the evidence."

I nod my understanding and begin packing up the tools. I fold the screens and tuck them into the bucket. The shovel, the rake, it all goes back into the bucket. We stand and dust off our knees.

"I'll let them know we're coming up."

My entire being aches for Letty. If her father did this awful, heinous thing, why would he be so foolish as to leave his dog tags? The chain wasn't broken so it's not likely that he accidentally left the necklace he wore all the time. I don't recall ever seeing him without them.

It doesn't make sense. The experts will say it's because he was mentally ill. He wasn't thinking. He lost control. Murdered the girls and then became frantic, desperate. Or maybe he actually wanted someone to find the truth.

Except I do not believe James Cotton was a murderer. I do not believe he would have harmed Natalie for any reason.

My mother has spoken many times about how he searched for us that night. He could not have done this.

"Letty."

She turns to me as she fastens her harness into place.

"Your father never laid a hand on you or your mother. He broke things. He yelled. He walked away. But he never hurt a person."

My friend—the one true friend I have in this life—shakes her head. "I can't talk about this."

I, of all people, understand her feelings to the very core of my being.

I nod and harness up.

Only a few minutes are required to make our way out. Night has fallen and the thick canopy of trees blocks the moonlight and stars. I check my cell, it's 8:45. Floodlights operated by a generator were set up to chase away the coming darkness in the immediate vicinity of the cave opening. Tanner and three deputies have been standing by for further orders.

"Sheriff Cotton," the deputy named Lamont steps forward, "I called in back-up. The media got wind of what's going on up here and there's half a dozen reporters parked down by the road. Hill and Shaw are keeping them out of the woods. I guess one of those rescued cavers spilled the beans."

Letty and I exchange a look. She walks over to the box of bags and other potentially needed materials. After a bit of poking around she pulls out a paper sack. She drops the plastic evidence bag containing the dog tags into the sack and takes it to Lamont.

"I want you to hand carry this to the lab. Tuck it under your shirt, whatever you have to do to get past those reporters without them seeing that you have something. Okay?"

"Yes, ma'am." He pulls his khaki shirt free of his trousers, puts the bag under his shirt and then re-tucks the tail. Flashlight in hand he heads down the mountainside.

"Anderson, you and Syler," she glances at the other deputy, "stay put until the next shift gets here. I'm setting up around the clock guard duty. I don't want anyone going into that cave."

"Yes, ma'am," the two call out together.

Without saying more Letty begins helping Tanner pack up his gear. I do the same. Letty tells the caving expert that they will likely need him again tomorrow and maybe for a couple of days after that. He assures Letty he's happy to help for as long as it takes. We start down the mountain together, the three of us. Letty asks Tanner more questions about how and when the opening of this cave collapsed. Is it possible a person caused the collapse? An explosion or something along those lines?

Her reasoning makes sense. She wants to rule out the possibility that whoever buried the bodies there tried to cover up the evidence.

"To be absolutely certain," Tanner admits, "you might need someone above my pay grade, but I'm pretty confident this was a natural phenomenon."

"Tell me why you're pretty confident," Letty tosses back at him.

"The lack of unnatural interior damage," he explains. "It's like when a tree falls. If you're a logger or an arborist you know enough about trees to recognize when one falls on its own and when it was pushed over by some outside element like the wind or a bulldozer maybe."

Makes sense to me.

"As a cave expert," Letty asks, "what precisely convinces you that this was a natural occurrence?"

"The stalactites for one thing. There are broken and shattered ones in the area where rock and dirt hit rock and dirt, but the ones nearby are solid. An explosion would have sent energy outward around wherever the charge was placed. Everything around it would have been affected to some degree. On top of that, we have the opening that's left behind. I doubt we would have had an opening at all if explosives had been utilized. We know heavy equipment hasn't been up here. The formation of that opening is natural from the slow shift and slide of the earth. And based on the vegetation and trees in the area, I estimate that collapse occurred fifteen to twenty years ago."

"I appreciate you explaining it to me." Letty stops. We've reached the ATVs we'll use for the trip down to the road. She thrusts out her hand. "No one can know what we've found just yet. Not until we're ready to issue statements."

Tanner clasps her hand in his and gives it a shake. "I won't speak to anyone about this without your permission."

Letty thanks him again and suggests that he go on ahead. At the road, the deputies will escort him to his vehicle.

When Tanner is gone, she turns to me. "I'll call Chief Claiborne, the ABI and the FBI, let them know what we found. The feds or the state will likely take lead on the case from here."

I'm surprised. Somehow I expected she would be lead and that I would help her. "Okay."

When Letty turns to move on, I touch her arm. She hesitates but doesn't look at me. This is eating her up and I can't bear it.

"I could spend the night at your place. We can talk or get shitfaced. Whatever you need."

She shakes her head. "I appreciate the offer, I really do, but I need to be alone. To think." A shrug lifts her shoulder. "And I have this other case—two little girls I'm hoping won't be found this way."

"I understand."

In silence we climb onto the ATVs and make the final leg of the journey back to the road. Dusk has settled but the eight —no nine—vehicles lining the opposite side of the road light up the night with their spotlights. Four police cruisers as well as Letty's SUV are on this side of the road.

The reporters rush toward the faded centerline of the pavement and the deputies meet them with arms extended and firm warnings being issued.

Questions are shouted at Letty and at me. We ignore them and climb into her vehicle. As we drive away, the weight of knowing presses down on me. The mystery of what-if is gone. No more wondering.

Natalie is dead. The only question now is who killed her.

I glance at Letty. I refuse to believe it was her father.

The headlights cut through the darkness, lighting the black road and sending shadows over the woods on either side of us. Finally my sister is found…but along with her precious remains we discovered a whole new nightmare. But we also confirmed another element of this never-ending saga.

There really has been a monster in our midst all this time.

15

I STARE AT THE FAUCET, WATCH THE DROP OF WATER SWELL and swell until it falls free of the spout and plops into the steaming water. I have pulled the stopper chain loose twice already, let the tub drain part way and then tucked the stopper back in and turned on the hot water again—all with my toes because I'm too exhausted to move any other part of my body.

I need the hot water and the steam to soak the dirt from that damned cave out of my pores and off my skin...to expel the dank odor from my lungs. But there is nothing I can do to scour the images out of my brain. Those precious bones...the fractures and depressions in the skulls. The pink sneakers.

I blink, the movement strangely sluggish. I feel as if the world around me has abruptly slowed to an odd crawl in the wrong direction. Like the secondhand on a clock moving backward. Sound—even the droplets of water—are abnormally loud. Another bead swells, breaks free and then slaps the water like the belly flop of an awkward, inexperienced swimmer.

I flinch.

When I came home tonight Mother stood in the middle of

the kitchen. For a moment she only watched as I tugged off my hiking boots and rolled off the socks. Finally, she asked if I was hungry. After another half minute elapsed and she wanted to know if I was okay. If I was injured in any way. I suppose I looked as if I might be hurt. My clothes were filthy, dirt stuck to my skin. I felt as if I had been on the losing end of a wrestling match. I think I said no. Not sure I answered at all.

She didn't ask what Letty and I found. I chugged a bottle of water. She watched without saying more. To break the thickening quiet that appeared to have enveloped her, I told her I needed a bath and I walked out of the room.

Denial. I am well acquainted with the strategy. If you pretend it's not happening, maybe it will go away...won't be real. I have practiced this method of coping a million times. It works only temporarily.

The trouble always comes back.

My sister is dead. Her friend is dead.

This revelation is no surprise. They've been missing for most of my life and still it has stunned me. Wounded me. There was always a strong possibility that Natalie and Stacy had been murdered. Always. I know this. I have known this all along. Still, I am shattered anew. My brain does not want to accept this conclusion. I do not want to know this thing that I cannot tell my mother.

She knows. I am certain. This is why she didn't ask. In her heart, she knows. But, like me, she doesn't want to know. She doesn't want to think it or to say it out loud or to hear me say it. She wants Natalie's disappearance to remain a mystery. To continue clinging to that tiny fragile thread of hope that she is alive. That she will one day come back. That she is out there somewhere...

Natalie is dead.

I suck in a breath, abruptly aware that I'd gone too long without one. Clearly, I was ill prepared for today. I admit this now because I have no choice. My muscles ache. I am sadly out of shape. I haven't run in months. Haven't worked out at all in nearly as long. Mentally, I'm a wreck. Today isn't likely to help.

I drop my head back against the rim of the claw foot tub and close my eyes. Vaguely I'm aware that the water has grown cool once more. I've scrubbed my skin and hair, soaked my aching muscles. There is little else I can do to avoid what comes next. I should dress, go downstairs and eat something no matter that I have no appetite. Letty will need me tomorrow. We agreed to meet at her house to develop a plan. She has a task force briefing at seven so as soon as she's free we rendezvous.

There's something I need to do first so I should get moving by seven.

I sit up, water sloshes around me. I want to curl up into a ball and cry some more. I want to moan and curse God. I want to go to sleep and wake up tomorrow with no memory of this day.

Enough wallowing in self-pity. I drain the tub and step out onto the fuzzy rug with its yellow daisies. I dry my hair as best I can with the towel. I refuse to bother with a hair dryer. When I've dried my skin, I toss the towel over the shower curtain bar and go in search of clothes. I didn't bring a lot but I do have one pair of sweat pants. A tee and a clip for my damp hair and I'm good.

Downstairs Mother sits at the kitchen table cradling a cup of tea in her hands. I inhale the aroma of fresh brewed coffee and my mouth waters. But coffee isn't what I need. The caffeine will only rob me of badly needed sleep—assuming I can sleep at all. I walk past the coffeemaker and the table and into the pantry. Though my mother has never been much of a wine drinker, she maintains a nice variety for visitors. I select a Chateauneuf-du-Pape red and locate the opener. Once the cork is free I pour a nice big glass. I tuck the bottle under my arm and grab a second glass just in case Helen decides to indulge.

I place the bottle and extra glass on the table, curl up in a chair and down a hefty swallow. A fruity, licorice taste with a hint of smoke and cracked pepper rouses my lethargic taste buds. At the moment I really don't care how it tastes, I only want it to work. That the flavor is pleasant is a bonus. I need to relax and the hot water just didn't do the trick to the degree desired.

How could a tub of hot water ever warm the cold that is deep within my bones, in my very soul?

"You should eat something with that."

At first I don't answer. But then I think of her heart and how this news could cause another heart attack. Stress, grief, anger are all triggers of the chemical reaction that can create the perfect environment for cardiac events. So, rather than argue with her assessment I nod and somehow dredge up a ghost of a smile. Obviously grateful for something to do, she scurries around and gathers cheese and crackers, then places them on a plate. When she settles it before me I eat no matter that it tastes like cardboard.

Helen reclaims her seat and continues watching me.

I nibble at the cheese, the crackers, down more wine. She alternately stares into her cup and at me.

She says nothing.

I say nothing.

"The two missing cavers were found," I announce as if this is the only news I have to share. As if this is the announcement for which she waits. I couldn't bear the silence any longer.

Playing along, Helen nods. "I saw it on the news. That reporter, Lila Lawson of WHNT, interviewed them."

Lila Lawson. I now know the name of the wart on my ass currently bugging the shit out of me.

More wine slides down my throat. I am grateful for the

warm, relaxed feeling that begins to settle in my brain, forcing my mind to clear and my muscles to loosen. "They were delirious. Probably drank cave water."

"They're alive, that's what matters."

"For sure."

Her gaze locks with mine and I know the question I cannot answer is coming.

"They said there were bones in the cave. Is that why Letty needed your help?"

This question I can answer but I am aware the unhurried, seemingly offhanded interrogation will not stop there. "Yes."

The soft hum of the heating system fills the hush. Forced air rises from the floor vent near the bank of windows that overlook the backyard, shifting the lacy curtains. I suddenly want to share with her all that I learned today. It burgeons in my throat, crushes against my heart.

She deserves to know.

Pounding reverberates through the house. I jump. What the hell?

Frowning, Mother turns toward the sound and rises from her chair. It's not until that moment that I realize she's still wearing her church clothes. The burgundy dress is wrinkled. Her feet are bare, the shoes abandoned by the back door. I remember seeing them as I came in tonight. More tendrils of hair have fallen around her neck. Her lipstick has long since worn off.

Maybe she called Howard to come over and help with an intervention or to provide moral support while she questions me with a bit more force. This quiet, tentative Helen is unfamiliar to me.

I doubt it's Letty. She would call and let me know what's happening before showing up at the door. Could be the reporter. I open my mouth to warn Mother but I'm too late. I hear raised voices in the entry hall. One sounds deep, male I think. Maybe the cameraman who follows Lila Lawson around.

With a fast gulp I down the last of the wine in my glass and hurry to Mother's aid. This reporter will not get away with harassing my family. She's gone too far this time.

My brain fails to identify the brusque voice before I reach the entry hall. My eyes work a little more quickly. I stall as if the hardwood has turned to quicksand. The air grows too thick to draw in and out of my lungs.

Delbert Yarbrough.

His gray hair stands up in tufts, his face is beet red. He, too, still wears church clothes. Though I didn't see him today, I recognize the lightweight wool trousers and button down shirt as well as the leather oxfords that personifies the typical Sunday best in the small town south.

"You need to go home, Delbert," Helen tells him. "It's late and you're upset."

Yarbrough spots me and pushes past her, bullying his way into our home. "Letty won't tell me what the two of you found in that cave."

His voice is raw, the words wrapped in decades of misery. My soul aches for him. Nothing I can say will provide the relief he seeks. We have all spent twenty-five years believing that if we only knew what really happened, we could move on. We could let go and put *that day* behind us.

Not true.

Knowing has not given me one iota of closure. I still have no idea why Natalie and Stacy were taken or who took them. I ignore the flash of metal in my brain that reminds me of the dog tags we found.

Not possible.

"Mr. Yarbrough," I fold my arms over my chest, acutely aware of the thin tee shirt and worn out sweat pants I wear, "if there was information I could share with you, Letty would have told you already."

Mother stares at me, dark circles under her eyes, fear and uncertainty lining her face. I must tread carefully here. Both of the people standing right in front of me are just as wounded as I am. No, I amend, they are far more hurt and injured than I can possibly fathom. They want to know the truth and yet they don't.

Part of me wishes I still didn't know.

"Please." He moves in toe-to-toe with me. "Please just tell me what you found in that cave. They're saying on the news that bones were found. I need to know if it's my Stacy."

He's not as tall as I remember. His back is hunched with age or despair or both. Craggy lines mar his face. But it's the agony in his eyes that tears me apart. The not knowing, the hope has eaten at him for a quarter of a century. Stacy was his only child. He had no one else to distract him from the agony. No wife, no one.

Mother and Dad had each other…they had me.

"Yes." I say this knowing I should keep my mouth shut but I cannot. I am not as strong as Letty, apparently. "The cavers found bones. But" I raise my hand when he opens his mouth to no doubt launch into more questions "there has to be an official identification, Mr. Yarbrough. The bones could be anyone's." Another lie. "They've already been sent to the lab in Huntsville. Letty put a priority on the analysis. We will know soon."

His shoulders slump. "Did you find anything else that might tell us who was down there? I can tell you what my Stacy was wearing that day, in case you don't remember."

The hope in his voice tugs at me but I've already said too much. "The clothes were gone, completely decomposed. I'm sorry I can't be of more help, Mr. Yarbrough. You have my word that Letty is doing everything possible. We will know soon."

I hold my breath, hope against hope that he doesn't bring up my training and start asking other questions like were the remains those of females? What age? Any visible injuries? Any other evidence?

The dog tags plaster themselves across my vision once more. I blink them away.

At last Yarbrough nods. "Thank you." He exhales a heavy breath. "Thank you for talking to me."

I nod. I don't trust myself to do more.

He apologizes to Helen and leaves. As she closes the door I see the WHNT van on the street. They're watching us. Probably snapped photos of Yarbrough at our door.

"I'm sorry, Emma. I shouldn't have opened the door, but I couldn't pretend he wasn't there. I know just how he feels."

"You did the right thing."

She crosses the room and sits down on the third step of the staircase. She looks so tired. So uncharacteristically old. I consider going back to the kitchen and finishing off the bottle of wine. Instead, I do the daughterly thing and sit down beside her. I can always drink the wine later.

"Twenty-five years," she says, her voice thin and fragile, so un-Helen like.

"You shouldn't allow this to upset you the way it has Mr. Yarbrough," I warn. "The stress could cause another heart attack. We can't be sure of anything yet."

The big old grandfather clock my mother's great-grandmother brought all the way from England chimes the hour. Ten o'clock. The news is on. Mother muted both the televisions before I came downstairs. I suppose she couldn't bear to hear any more. The lead story tonight will be about the bones found in the cave. Right behind that breaking story will be an update on the two missing girls. There is nothing new to report on the latter. The find in the cave is diverting resources from that search. Every step taken by the Sheriff's Department and Jackson Falls PD will be scrutinized and dissected over and over.

I close my eyes and wish the whole thing was over. Mostly

I need to sleep and recharge my drained emotions. I suppose I should have brought the sleeping pills I stopped taking days ago. Enough of the wine should have basically the same effect.

"Did you find Natalie?"

My eyes open but I do not look at my mother. Honestly, I'm surprised she waited this long to ask. "The lab will do an official identification. Dental records. That's the way it works. Then we'll know."

My words sound hollow even to me. Robotic and emotionless.

"I don't care about the lab analysis and the official ID." Her frail voice rises, the hurt evolving into anger. "Did you find Natalie?"

She looks at me now. I feel the weight of her gaze, the misery radiating from her anguished being.

"Yes." My breath catches on the word.

Her gaze drifts away from me, she stares forward as I do. "Thank you."

Half a minute, maybe more lapses before she speaks again.

"Is there anything else you can tell me?"

I'll have to text Letty and let her know that I told Mother. How could I not? If I hadn't been so damned tired and emotionally drained I would have pointed out that detail when Letty first mentioned not telling our mothers.

"We can't talk about the rest yet."

Helen nods her understanding.

We sit in silence for a long time. A piece of our lives—the not knowing—has suddenly been extracted from our existence, leaving yet another gaping hole. Though the previous hole is now filled with this new knowledge, there is undeniably another void. Like screening the dirt at a dig. The scoops of displaced soil that go into the screen sift down and refill the space left behind. The items removed—a rock or piece of bone or another item from the past—leave an empty place.

Finding Natalie's remains has left an empty place where wonder and hope once dwelled.

My sister is dead.

"Are you going back to Boston?"

The question surprises me. Does she want me to leave? Does she need to be alone to digest this new reality? I assume she will want to have a funeral Mass and of course there's the burial. I want to be a part of those things. I want to help her.

More than anything else, I want the truth. I need to help Letty find the truth otherwise her father's name won't be cleared and we will never understand what really happened.

Doubt attempts to intrude but I refuse to believe that James Cotton did this. Even in a fit of rage he would never have hurt Natalie or Stacy. The idea is ludicrous.

I take a breath and turn to my mother. "Do you want me to go back to Boston?"

"What a foolish question!" She looks away. "Of course I don't want you to go back."

I take a moment to remind myself that this hurts her far more than me. Natalie was my sister but she was her daughter. Despite my childless state, I fully grasp the magnitude of the difference.

"I plan to stay and help you with the next steps." I shrug. "Nat's final arrangements. I promised Letty I would help her with the case. We still don't know who took Natalie and Stacy. We need answers. They deserve justice."

"What difference does justice make now?" Helen drops her face into her hands.

On some level I feel the same way but I traced those fissures in Natalie's skull, felt the depression indicative of blunt force trauma. Fury detonates inside me. I want whoever did those things to my beautiful, perfect sister to pay. I want it more than anything just now.

"He could do it again," I remind my mother. "He may have already, there are still two girls missing."

She shakes her head. "It's not the same. Whoever took those little girls is not the same devil who took Natalie and Stacy."

I agree for the most part, but Helen doesn't simply agree she feels adamant about it. The conviction echoes in her voice, in the way her muscles clench with anger. I remember a time when she ran from town to town tacking up posters with pictures of Natalie and Stacy. I remember the calls, the letters. She worked like a crazy woman trying to draw attention to and gain support for the search. She wanted Natalie and Stacy found. We all did.

Now they have been found. But not the person who caused them to disappear.

Why has the fire for justice grown cold?

I say, "I'm staying until this is finished."

With that announcement I push to my feet and head upstairs. I call a good night to her over my shoulder but she doesn't answer. I choose not to take it personally. She needs to grieve.

The years of wondering and hoping and searching are over.

There's nothing left for her except to bury the dead.

I, on the other hand, am going to find a killer.

16

MONDAY, MAY 14

JACKSON FALLS DOESN'T HAVE A STARBUCKS SO I BOUGHT the largest coffee sold at the Mini Market and loaded it down with cheap powdered cream and lots of real sugar. The taste isn't the same but the results should prove similar.

Maybe I should have bought two. I'm uncertain whether large doses of caffeine combined with sugar will be sufficient to clear my head of last night's lingering nightmares. During the hours of fitful sleep I floated along that damned final bus ride about twenty times. Not one thing changed as the images rolled through my sleep. I watched Natalie and Stacy walk away from the bus each time. The big difference with these dreams was the ending. Each time my sister and her friend were struck repeatedly by someone I couldn't see, they fell to the ground and their screaming woke me every damned time.

I banish the images and force my full attention on the road. My throat aches and my chest feels tight. I try and dampen my throat with the wholly awful coffee but it doesn't help the parched sensation. All it does is make me want to hurl.

Letty is still in her meeting, leaving me with time to kill. Before I left the house I made up my mind to drive to the cemetery. School buses are out, it's that time. I stop for the bus to pick up a couple of kids. I survey the faces in the bus windows. Some look the same way I feel—as if they still aren't ready to face the world, others are animated, talking and laughing. At this stop the two girls who climb onto the bus wear jeans, tees, and sneakers. I guess the uniform around here hasn't changed very much. The taller of the two girls looks to be thirteen or fourteen. I think of my sister. When we were kids she seemed so much older to me, so mature, but she was just a child. A child who was bludgeoned to death after God only knows what other manner of travesties.

The organ in my chest squeezes and flops uselessly. In the deep recesses of my soul I know that I cannot leave until I find the person who did this. For the first time since I was eight years old having the knowledge of where Natalie is and if she is dead or alive is not enough. Growing up all I wanted was for her to come home, to be my sister again…for things to return to the way they were before *that day*. In time, as I matured, I realized those things would never happen so I wished to know what happened to my sister. Had she been sold into slavery? Was she living in someone's basement? Had she been murdered or had she gotten lost in the mountains and starved to death?

Now I know and those answers are not enough.

I must know the rest.

Traffic is as heavy as it gets around this town. The folks who don't put their kids on the buses and the kids who drive themselves are rushing to school. Others are headed for the interstate to get to Huntsville or to Decatur for work. My destination is only a few more blocks. The cemetery is on the same street as St. Mary's, which reminds me that there's a chance I could run into the lying priest.

I'm not so worried. He likely has some sort of breakfast with members of his congregation or authority figures in the community. Puttering around in the cemetery is probably not a Monday morning ritual.

In an effort to throw the reporter off my trail, I drive the Prius this morning. To that end I removed the plates and used the one from my father's truck so the car looks like a local's. Totally illegal but obeying the state codes governing motor vehicles and traffic is not a high priority of mine at this time. I just have to remember to put it back. I wouldn't want Howard getting pulled over by Jackson Falls PD next time he takes the truck for a drive.

I park inside the cemetery near a copse of trees. Narrow paved lanes wind through the largest and oldest cemetery in town. The founders are buried here. Generations of Jacksons and Turners and Beaumonts, though the Beaumonts aren't actually founders. But one—Matthew—married a Jackson, which put their name on the map, so to speak. My ancestors helped found Jackson Falls as well. As did Letty's, but you won't find her father buried in this cemetery. He's in the one on the other side of town where Letty's ancestors are interned. There was a time when blacks and whites weren't buried in the same cemeteries. That part of life in Jackson Falls had all but disappeared by the time I was born, but my mother's mother told me the stories. She ended each one with the warning that if I remembered her words I would always know better than to make the same mistakes. I think she was right. We need to remember the wrongs our ancestors committed so we don't repeat their stupidity.

I find the section of the cemetery where generations of my mother's and father's ancestors are buried. I walk past the towering headstones. By the time I reach my dad's there has been considerable downsizing. After his terminal diagnosis, he and Helen selected a headstone that suited them both. My parents have never been showy people. The only reason they bought that big old house on Tulip Lane was because there wasn't another one available in town at the time. People who move to Jackson Falls rarely leave. It's the perfect, genteel small town—two murdered girls and an additional two missing notwithstanding—and its position on the map is right between two thriving metropolitan areas. The school gets a Blue Ribbon from the state just about every year. What's not to like?

I crouch down next to Dad's grave. My chest tightens as I read Helen's name on the other side of the headstone. Reaching down I tug a weed or two from the small white pebbles that blanket the double plot. There's a plot between this double headstone and the one that marks my dad's parents' graves. Mother wanted to leave space for Natalie to be ensconced between them. We've never discussed Natalie's final arrangements beyond that point. I guess because it was easier not to talk about it. To pretend she would be back one day.

"Hey, Dad." I draw in a big breath and let it go. "I'm sorry I haven't been back since the funeral, but I've been calling Mother often. I haven't forgotten what you asked me to do." For the most part anyway.

I hear some people drop by the cemetery and talk to their dead relatives on a regular basis but this is my first time. I glance around the cemetery, don't see anyone. Feel grateful I'm alone.

"I found Natalie yesterday." My voice shakes and I clear my throat. "Stacy, too. As soon as the police release the remains we can give Nat a proper burial." I close my eyes for a time and consider how to say the rest. "We always knew they were probably dead, but I guess somehow I pushed away the idea that they'd been murdered. It was too terrible to think about. But they were, murdered I mean."

For a minute I stare at the shiny black granite, reading his name, allowing the memories to drift through my mind. "Letty and I will figure out who did this. I want you to know I'm not leaving until we find the truth, so don't worry. And, I guess you know Mother had a heart attack. I'll make sure she's doing okay before I…go."

I shake my head, place my hand on the cool granite and push to my feet. I don't know what I was thinking coming to Dad's grave and saying all this out loud as if he can hear me. I pretty much lost all my religion in that hole in Iraq—not that I'd retained that much anyway. I deal in facts and tangibles. The one thing I can guarantee you that comes after death is the wasting away to bone. The bones are what remains of the greatest among us as well as the least. If there is some spirit world I can't see it or touch it or sense it so I'm not exactly a believer. The fact that I even came to the cemetery and spoke to my dad as if we were seated around the dinner table could be a bad thing considering my breakdown a couple of weeks ago.

"Maybe I am losing it completely."

"Whether you have faith or not, it never hurts to voice your feelings."

The priest. Oh hell. "You shouldn't sneak up on people like that," I accuse as I turn to face him.

He smiles and I find it impossible to hang onto a thread of irritation. "I'm sorry. I don't usually encounter visitors this early. I walk the cemetery each morning. It's my hope that it gives those who reside here comfort."

I almost suggest it might be more fitting if he wore his religious garb rather than jeans and a pullover sweater, but I decide not to be unkind. He did help me out at Home Depot and at Johnny's. It's just that the jeans and the sweater make him look like any other guy and I'm having trouble dealing with that aspect of this man.

"I'm sure the families appreciate your efforts." A nice, noncommittal way to give him a compliment. Mental pat on the back for me. "If I had known I would run into you this morning, I would have brought your hoodie."

The truth is the hoodie is in the washing machine. This

morning's cool temp sent me into Helen's closet for a sweater. I finally found a plain tan one about as old as I am. Despite the chill in the air, the jacket I'd left Boston wearing was too heavy for weather in Alabama.

"Use it as long as you as you like." Another smile tugs at his lips. "I saw you on the news last night."

"I swear all the dirt will wash out." I'm sure he cringed when he saw the condition of his hoodie.

"I'm glad you wore it yesterday." He shrugged. "It makes me feel a part of the important work you and Letty did."

The pain and concern on his face tells me Helen called him.

"She wasn't supposed to tell anyone." I don't want to be angry with my mother but I told her about Natalie and Stacy because I couldn't *not* tell her, but she shouldn't have told anyone else.

"Emma, your mother sharing her feelings with me is the same as you coming here this morning to share them with your father."

"I don't think so." I need to go. "He can't blab to anyone else."

"You can trust me, Emma. Completely."

I laugh. Can't help it. Thankfully my cell vibrates in my back pocket. I check the screen. A text from Letty. I'm to meet her at her house ASAP.

"I have to go."

"I'll walk you to your car."

Since it's a free country, I don't argue.

"Helen is concerned about you being involved in the investigation of what happened to Natalie. She's worried it won't be good for you."

"Helen shouldn't worry about me." I keep my attention on my car. Another fifty yards and I can escape.

"You're right."

This time I stall and stare at him.

"You're a strong woman, Emma. You've done incredible things in your life. If you choose to do this, you will do it to the best of your ability and you won't stop until you're done or it stops you."

How can he see inside me so completely? I hug my arms around myself to block his too perceptive eyes. "You don't know me."

"I know you very well. You and I are a great deal alike."

"Now that I agree with. We're both compulsive liars and we both want things we shouldn't want."

His flinch tells me I hit a nerve.

I continue on to my car and, surprisingly, he follows. Before I can, he opens the door like a true southern gentleman.

"I'm sorry I lied to you, Emma, and I'm even sorrier to be yet another cause for your loss of faith."

This time I'm the one who flinches. "Your little harmless lie didn't do this to me, Jake. Life did this to me and the worst part is that I allowed it." From somewhere deep inside me more words gush out before I can stop them. Every fiber of my being feels too full with hurt and the need to release the pent up misery abruptly overwhelms me. "I ran away because I couldn't be here anymore. I couldn't be the daughter who survived anymore. I couldn't take the curious stares and the questions anymore. But I found out there are some things you can't run away from—like yourself. So, yes, I'll stay until I find who did this. I think it's the only way I'll ever find the part of me I lost that day."

My heart is pounding so hard I can hardly breathe and the crappy coffee threatens to reappear. I cannot imagine why I felt the need to spew all that to him, but there it is, lying on the ground, the stench of it floating in the air between us.

"I hope you'll allow me to be a part of your journey."

I scrub a hand across my mouth terrified that more unexpected words will fly out of me. I nod and drop behind the steering wheel. He closes my door and I drive away. I point the Prius toward Letty's, acutely aware that he watches.

The short drive to her place allows me to clear my head and get my racing heart under control. For the first time in a very long time I feel the urge to run a couple of miles. I feel like a bird trapped in a cage far too small. Seeing Letty's face grounds me.

"We'll take my Jeep," she says.

I grab my cold crap coffee and lock my car. "Is there anything new on the search for the girls?"

My coffee goes into the console alongside hers. I climb into the Jeep Grand Cherokee. I like that it's black and seriously cool. The quintessential cop vehicle. That's the ticket, Emma. Think normal thoughts. Focus on the here and now.

"Nothing yet." She puts the gearshift into reverse and backs out of her drive. "The FBI and the ABI have pretty much taken over the Shepherd-Baldwin case. Between their resources, the city's and the county's they're doing all they can. We still have a lot of tips coming in to the call center but nothing useful so far."

"What's *our* plan?"

Letty glances at the console and makes a face. "There's a coffee shop over by the Pig called Beans. You shouldn't drink that shit they sell at the Mini Market."

I laugh. "No kidding."

Letty ignores my question for a full minute. I let her. I have an idea, particularly since she's wearing jeans, a tee and a jacket this morning. Not her official sheriff's uniform of khaki shirt and trousers.

"I took some personal time," she finally says. "After I turned over the dog tags, I was off the case anyway. Conflict of interest. There's not a lot I can do that my department, PD, the feds and the guys from the ABI aren't already doing to find our missing girls. I thought you and I would start our own unofficial investigation into what really happened to Natalie and Stacy."

"You sure that's the right thing to do?" God, I sound like Helen now.

Letty nods. "I have to figure this out, Emma. Someone set up my dad. I'm not going to be the reason this new, forming as we speak, mini task force proves those allegations were right all along."

"I couldn't stop thinking about you and your dad last night." I reach for the crappy coffee. "I know he didn't do it. He wouldn't have hurt Natalie for anything. Plus, he was out there searching that night just like everyone else."

"I appreciate your support," Letty says, her voice low, weary. "But that isn't going to be the popular thinking. You'll be painting a target on your back, the same as me."

I stare at her, my heart swelling into my throat. "I will always be on your side, Letty. No matter what."

She glances at me, a faint smile clearing the clouds of worry on her face. "Thanks. I doubt there will be anyone else on my side after those dog tags become public knowledge."

"You and your mom will always have me and Helen." I face forward. "So, what's our plan?"

"I say start at the beginning. Retrace every step. Find out who was where and doing what. First thing, we make a list." She gestures to the glove box. "There's a pad and pen in there if you want to get started."

I open the glove box and retrieve the needed items. "Natalie's and Stacy's names are at the top, I presume."

"Right. Then the two of us and our parents. Add Mr. Russell. It's a long shot but let's find out if he'd been sick just before the crash and if anyone knew about his health issues."

Definitely a long shot but then I'm not a cop.

"What about the neighbors who lived on Long Hollow Road at the time?" I suggest.

"Yep. Friends and teachers of Natalie's and Stacy's. Everyone. We won't leave anyone out."

I scrawl names as fast as I can. "Hold on, I need to catch up." I shake my head. "I'll never remember all Natalie's friends." My sister was one of the most popular girls in school and it was a long time ago.

"Look in the backseat. I put the yearbook from that year back there."

"You are a very smart lady." I unbuckle and fetch the yearbook. Seatbelt back in place, I ask, "Where are we headed first?"

"To your old house."

"Good starting place, I guess."

"That's not our starting place." Letty flashes me a grin. "It's going to be our command center."

I point a finger at her. "I was wrong. You're not smart. You're a genius."

"I have the case files in the back. The ones from twenty-five years ago as well as the Shepherd and Baldwin file."

My mouth gapes. "How did you get away with those?" I felt reasonably confident the investigators reopening the old case would need them. Certainly the new case files were needed in the Shepherd-Baldwin investigation.

"I spent most of the night at the station making copies."

"Geez, should you be driving?"

"I'm good for now. I may crash and burn later."

We park around back of the house to avoid nosy passersby. I locate the hidden key and unlock the backdoor. Once the boxes of case files are unloaded, I open a couple of windows to air out the place.

"We need a coffeemaker," I mutter, wondering why Letty did all the preparing and I did nothing but show up. I should have asked her what I could do.

"Your mother is bringing a coffeemaker, coffee and breakfast."

My lower jaw sags again.

"Don't worry," Letty assures me, "she's not staying. I asked her if we could use the place and she said of course but she insisted on bringing a few comfort items."

A few comfort items turned out to be a vast understatement. Mother showed up half an hour later with the promised coffeemaker, a couple of pounds of freshly ground coffee beans, pancakes and sausage, bottled water, a six pack of each of our favorite sodas, chips, apples, cheese and crackers. She added a fresh bouquet of flowers to the mason jar in the window over the kitchen sink and stocked the two bathrooms with toilet paper and hand towels. Helen Graves can never be accused of being anything less than thorough.

With the supplies unloaded, she gave each of us a hug and went on her way.

"Did you tell your mom?" I sent Letty a text last night and told her about my inability to keep part of the news from Helen.

"I went by her house and told her," Letty said. "I realized I couldn't keep it from her since those dog tags will probably end up in the news today or tomorrow. She needs to be prepared for being questioned all over again." Letty exhales a heavy breath. "And the reporters. It wouldn't be right to let her be blindsided like that."

"I'm glad you did."

"She swears she took them off Dad's neck right in front of the coroner." Letty clears her throat. "She wanted to keep them for me. But she lost them at some point later on."

I frown. "The coroner should be able to confirm what he saw when he certified cause of death."

"I'm planning to talk to him as soon as his doctor gives the okay."

We line three of the dining room chairs under the double windows and place the file boxes in the seats for easy access. Our notepads, pens, the school yearbook, and other useful items go on the table. Letty even managed to dig up an old phone book.

"Let's get started." She pulls out one of the three remaining chairs and gets comfortable.

I do the same. I've spent my life digging in the dirt so this is a different kind of dig for me but I look forward to the challenge.

If Natalie and Stacy's killer is still alive, I hope he's afraid.

No, I hope he's terrified.

We're coming, you bastard.

17

I HAVE EXHUMED THE REMAINS OF PEOPLE BRUTALLY murdered by the leaders of their own countries and then buried in mass graves as if they were nothing more than cattle grouped together in the wrong place when lightning struck.

Just when I believe I have seen it all, I witness something more depraved—the very worst man can do to man. Days and weeks, even months of my life have been spent examining remains and the environment in which they were found in an effort to determine the events leading up to the day their existence ended. I've evaluated cause and manner of death.

But I have never worked a case from this aspect—determining the identity of the killer.

Letty created a timeline on my mother's china cabinet. Photos and pages listing events are taped to the front of the cabinet, top to bottom. The timeline begins on Tuesday, April third, one week before the bus accident twenty-five years ago. Photos of Natalie, Stacy, me, Letty, all the parents as well as the bus driver are taped along the top of the cabinet. She left space below those photos to affix pages with the names and hand drawn heads (like the placeholder images used for social media profiles) of other persons of interest; POIs, she calls them. So far we have several additional friends who were close to Natalie and Stacy, dance instructors, teachers—like the cheerleading coach and the yearbook sponsor—with whom both worked closely beyond the usual school curriculum.

The few neighbors who lived on Long Hollow Road at the time are listed though several are now deceased. Still, it was necessary to include them. No one who had opportunity can be excluded. Once the names of every person with opportunity are assembled, that list will be narrowed down by motive. I have a feeling the china cabinet will never be large enough.

"If we go strictly with the interviews conducted by the investigators who handled the case in real time, most of these POIs can be ruled out." Letty braces her hands on her hips and paces the length of the dining room, her gaze fixed on the timeline. "But we're not ruling anyone out based on what they told the police twenty-five years ago."

"Do you have reason to believe one or more didn't tell the whole truth in their interviews?" Letty has read all the reports and would certainly recognize any aspect that appeared suspicious. She is trained to look for the holes in a story, I am not. I am, however, reasonably competent at spotting lies—a secondary result produced by years of honing my own skill at telling lies.

"This girl." Letty taps one of the photos.

"I remember her," I say as I study the photo. "Mallory Carlisle. She was one of Natalie's close friends. Her folks were divorced or something."

"Mallory Jacobs now," Letty pointed out. "Her dad left when she was about ten. Her mother spent all her time trying to find a new husband. According to my mom, Mallory ended up home alone a lot. I guess that's why she found herself pregnant at eighteen and married right after high school graduation."

"Jacobs?" I try to remember someone Natalie's age or older named Jacobs.

"He was from Huntsville," Letty explains. "They divorced a couple of years later but not before having another child. Two girls, both married really young just like their mom. The younger one—" her forehead pinches in concentration "—I can't remember her name, she's a senior at one of the local universities. She married Heather's little brother, Marshall. They had a baby six months later."

I really can't recall any details about the youngest Beaumont. "How old is he?"

"Marshall is twenty-eight. He's with some big time law firm in Huntsville."

Nothing like his older brother, apparently. The image of Mark flickers through my mind. "I saw Mark the other day." I opt not to mention the circumstances of our chance encounter.

"He's spent most of his life in and out of rehab." Letty shakes her head. "Mom says Mark changed after his father's accident. Threw his future away."

"I'd forgotten about that, too." I've obviously blocked far more of the past than I realized. "Didn't Mallory and Mark have a thing for a while?"

Letty nods. "It ended badly."

"Yeah." I frown. "That's right." More ancient data long ago exiled to some unused area of gray matter.

Letty rolls her eyes. "Mallory is so thrilled that one of her offspring landed the most eligible bachelor in all of Madden County."

I roll my eyes, too, as much at Letty's sardonic tone as at the news. "How exciting for her."

The older two Beaumont children ruled our small world back in the day. You would have thought they were royalty when the truth was they were mere humans just like the rest of us. I wonder if Heather has figured out that part yet. Evidently not based on the fit she pitched in the Pig about her preferred yogurt.

"Anyway," Letty says, turning back to the timeline. "Of all the friends interviewed, Mallory is the only one who stated that Natalie was seeing someone—someone older."

"I guess it's possible." I shrug, struggle to look at the possibility with some measure of objectivity. I can't help Letty find the truth if I can't keep the proper perspective about all this. "She was very popular. Mature for her age. I don't think Mother knew about a boyfriend. I certainly didn't."

Snippets of memories I haven't thought of in years file through my mind. Natalie fussing over what she would wear to school. Spending more time than usual on the phone. "I suppose if she was hiding a relationship there must have been a reason—maybe the boy was considerably older, a senior maybe. Freshmen cheerleaders are usually considered fresh meat to the seniors."

Letty nods and joins me at the table. "That's my thinking. I've asked your mom to come back over. She was closer to Natalie than anyone. She can help us with some of this." She gestures to the china cabinet.

Letty's right. Helen will remember accurately far more than the two of us. We were so young. It's possible much of what we remember was shaped more by emotions we were too immature to comprehend and sort than by actual events.

"We were all in shock back then." I survey the photos. "Terrified of what had potentially happened and hoping against hope it would turn out okay...that we would find them. The way they found me."

"I remember being so scared that night," Letty says. "When Mom came to Granny's house and told me they'd found you I was so happy." She gifted me with a sad smile. "I couldn't imagine ever going back to school without you." Her smile faded. "But Granny just started crying and crying as if the world had ended. Mom hugged her so hard. She cried, too. I didn't understand then, but I do now. They were afraid Natalie and Stacy were gone for good."

A shiver rushes up my spine. "People always said your granny could see things."

"I wish she was still here so she could tell me how to figure this out." Her gaze settles on the collage of people and information.

"Me, too."

I've watched my fair share of television and movies. Read more books than I can call to mind. But the story that stuck with me as a kid was The Wizard of Oz. When Natalie and Stacy didn't come home that first day after the bus crash, I kept thinking that all they had to do was click their heels three times and repeat the words: *There's no place like home. There's no place like home.* Then God or His angels or some good witch would help them find their way home again.

Except they never did.

I don't think we ever watched The Wizard of Oz again after that year.

I banish the thoughts and sit up a little straighter. "I hope Helen brings lunch." For the first time in a long time I am not just hungry but starving. This is unusual, mark-the-calendar unusual. I want to satisfy this raging hunger and then I want to get out there and find the answers no one else has been able to find.

Maybe deep down I want to be the hero, the good witch or the angel that never came when my sister and her friend first went missing.

"Hey, girls!"

Mother's voice rings through the house. My heart seizes at the memory of all the times she came home and called out to Natalie and me exactly that way. She closes the front door and walks into the dining room, arms loaded with a picnic basket. I push to my feet and grab the basket. I heft it onto the kitchen counter since the table is covered with interview reports.

"Did you bring everything in your fridge?" I ask. The basket weighs more than one of my dig packs. I'm certain she shouldn't be lifting anything this heavy. Obviously the two of us are going to have to sit down with her doctor and discuss her limitations.

She smiles. "I figured you two had built up an appetite."

"God, it smells good," Letty says with a groan of appreciation.

As we watch, mouths watering, Mother unloads fried chicken, mashed potatoes, sweet peas and rolls from the basket. And, of course, homemade cherry cobbler and mason jars filled with iced lemonade. Melamine plates along with packaged plastic dinnerware she's saved from take home orders.

"Let's eat and then you can tell me what you're doing." Helen surveys her china cabinet. "Maybe I really can help."

The hope in her eyes, in her voice tugs at the most tender place inside me. I recognize the tactic. She wants to help, but more than anything else she wants something meaningful to do. I've spent most of my adult life ignoring my own feelings and needs using that very maneuver.

"For the purposes of full disclosure, did my mother ask you to spy on us?" Letty tosses out the question as she covers the pink roses on her plate with potatoes and peas. A golden brown chicken breast follows.

Curious how Mother will answer this direct question, I keep quiet and follow Letty's example, loading up my plate. Maybe I don't generally eat like this because no one cooks like my mother—which might explain why I was a chubby kid.

"No, she absolutely did not." Mother pushes a mason jar toward each of us and reaches into the fridge for a bottle of water for herself.

Apparently the fridge was stocked and plugged in sometime before we arrived. I never noticed the motor humming until now. I can already see that I'll make a less than sharp detective.

Letty grunts, her opinion on the matter as plain as the nose on her face, as Helen would say.

"Well now, if you'd let me finish before you started snorting like a pig, you'd have heard the rest of the story."

Just like old times. Letty always liked to cut to the chase and Mother always reminded her that one should never jump to conclusions. However, on this one I stand firmly with Letty. Mother will report to Ginny whatever she learns and Ginny would do the same.

"Your mother is worried about the two of you, just as I am," Helen scolds. "We've had a terrible shock and I doubt a one of us is thinking as clearly as we should."

The glimmer of emotion in her eyes is difficult to look at. I wish I could spare her what is to come. She has no idea just how terrible it is. I scoop a wad of potatoes into my mouth. Pain impales me when I think of those damaged skulls—my sister's skull and her best friend's.

Add to that the dog tags and this nightmare has barely begun.

"Ginny would be right beside me," Mother presses on, "offering to do whatever possible to help, but she has to work. The post office won't run itself. As for your question, she did not ask me to spy on you, only to keep her informed as to your welfare." She hesitates long enough to draw in a big, emphatic breath. "Now that we've gotten that out of the way, let's get down to business. What exactly is it the two of you are doing out here? Liam O'Neal told me you'd taken some personal time." This she says to Letty.

I sip my lemonade—hand squeezed—and savor the taste of summer. Mother made this same lemonade all season every summer of my childhood. I stare at the thin slices of lemon floating in the mason jar. If I close my eyes for just a moment I can hear Natalie giggling in her room. Right down the hall. A thin wall separates our old rooms and she was always on the phone. Letty was the only person who ever called me. Until my junior year of high school anyway.

"I can't officially be a part of the investigation." Letty shrugs. "It's a conflict of interest. O'Neal is my chief deputy; he'll be in charge for a while."

Helen considers this information. "On the news they said there's still nothing on the Shepherd and Baldwin girls."

Letty lowers her head, as if she's ashamed she hasn't singlehandedly solved the case. "They have nothing. In that respect, it's like twenty-five years ago all over again."

I remember that first night at Letty's. She was determined not to let this new case be like Natalie and Stacy's. Now everything is turned upside down. The past is suddenly the present and finding the bones and those dog tags has knocked all of us off balance.

"The remote possibility," Letty goes on, frustration heavy in her words, "that the two cases are connected prevents me from being a part of the Shepherd-Baldwin investigation as well."

Another frown furrows its way across my forehead. Letty and I have spent very little time together as adults. What I know about the grown-up Letty comes mostly from the things Helen has told me rather than anything I have personally observed. No matter, I recognize several things about my friend. She is not a quitter and she is one of the strongest people I know. She would never have allowed alcohol to become an issue and she absolutely would never have lost it in a classroom full of kids.

"Refresh our memories about Natalie's friends," I suggest, moving on to something we can do. "Starting with Mallory."

Mother sets her plate aside and walks to the timeline. "Mallory Carlisle—Jacobs now—was a year older and a sophomore but she was one of Natalie's closest friends, next to Stacy. That year was different though, Mallory was so busy with her first real boyfriend that she dropped out of dance and cheerleading. Natalie and Stacy were really disappointed. They didn't spend as much time together anymore, but they were still friends, I believe. Things change when boys come into the picture," she adds in case Letty and I don't remember the less pleasant side of puberty.

"What about teachers?" Letty asks. "Any difficulties with teachers or school staff? Or any other adult around town?"

I wonder if this is Letty's way of getting around to the "older" guy theory?

Helen settles wearily into one of the three chairs not loaded with file boxes. "All Natalie's teachers loved her and she adored them. She was an honor student. On the student council. Beta Club. Interact Club. She didn't have any enemies."

Mother presses her hands to her face for a moment before she can go on. "I know it sounds like I'm bragging, but it's true. Everyone loved Natalie. Stacy, too, as far as I know."

I reach across the stacks and pages and squeeze her hand. "We know you're not bragging. It is true. Everyone loved Natalie and Stacy."

Except at least one person.

"During her interview," Letty walked over to the table and picked up one of the reports, "Mallory said she thought Natalie might be involved with someone older."

Mother throws up her hands and shakes them from side to side. "That's not true. Natalie was far too busy for a boyfriend and if she'd had one, I would have known. We shared everything. I told the sheriff and the chief that all those years ago. Mallory was wrong."

I look at Letty and raise my eyebrows in an I-told-you-so.

Letty drops into the chair nearest Helen. "Think about that answer for a minute, Helen. If Natalie had her first serious crush—particularly on someone you and her father might not have approved of—are you sure she would have told you?"

173

Mother hesitates but only for a second. "I believe so."

Letty looks to me again.

"You and Dad have lived here your whole lives," I say, taking another approach. "Surely there was someone during the investigation that you thought should have been a suspect —at least in your minds."

Mother surveys the pages and pages of reports covering the dining table. "No. There wasn't a single person in this community that we felt would hurt our daughter. No one."

"Someone new in town at the time," Letty offers. "There was a Benton Culver. He'd recently been released from prison on an attempted rape charge. His alibi checked out and he moved away, but you didn't once consider he might have been involved? Or someone like him?"

Mother moves her head from side to side. "No. We spoke to him twice. It wasn't him. There just isn't anyone I know who would have done such a thing."

The emotions she displayed a few minutes ago are gone. She seems oblivious, almost indifferent. Chipper even. I can't decide if she's still suffering from a bit of shock or if she's hiding something.

"Mother."

She looks at me, startled as if I snapped her from a faraway place. "Hmm?"

Maybe her doctor prescribed something for anxiety. I should have thought of that. Of course he would under the circumstances. "Are you sure you're okay? Did your doctor give you something to help you stay calm?"

"What?" She frowns. "No. I'm fine. I'm just having a little trouble with the tears. Please, ask whatever you like. Really, I'm fine."

Letty looks uncertain, but I do as Mother says and plunge onward. "What do you truly—deep in your heart—believe happened to Natalie and Stacy?"

For half a minute or more she contemplates the question.

"I think perhaps they got lost. Like you did," she says. "I spoke to Colton about the cave where they were found—"

"Please tell me," Letty interrupted, "that he didn't pass along anything about that crime scene."

Mother shakes her head adamantly. "No. Of course not. He only told me how the cave had sunk in all those years ago. You know, like a sinkhole. I think maybe they were lost and fell into the hole. He said it was a big drop." She shakes her head, draws in a shuddering breath. "That has to be what happened."

Letty and I exchange a look. It's a reasonable theory, except Natalie and Stacy didn't bury themselves. I keep that part to myself.

"I doubt we'll ever know what actually happened," Mother says, almost to herself.

"We will know," Letty assures her. "Twenty-five years ago, the police only had a starting place. They had no evidence and no direction. They had nothing."

My attention is riveted to my mother's face as Letty speaks. She almost looks afraid of what Letty will say next. Why would she fear finding the truth? Is she afraid for us? It's the only explanation that feels even remotely logical.

"Now we have an ending place," Letty goes on. "Somewhere between the beginning place and the ending place we'll find the intersection where Natalie and Stacy encountered the person who took their lives. You have my word on that."

More of that suffocating silence lapses. I can't take it. "Our plan is to retrace their steps, Mother. We're starting the week before they disappeared. From that day forward we're going to know everyone they spoke to, everywhere they went, every little thing they did. Someone somewhere knows something that matters; they just might not realize it matters. It's like Letty said, it's a whole different ballgame now that we know the ending place."

I am suddenly on fire. Maybe a little full of shit but a whole lot psyched.

We are going to do this. For Natalie and Stacy.

And for our mothers.

Even though, for some odd reason, mine doesn't look so thrilled at my revelation.

18

DESPITE OUR SHAKY START, HELEN PROVIDED CONSIDERABLE insights into most of the faces hanging on the china cabinet and she suggested a few names Letty and I hadn't thought to add. We now have quite the list. We decided the best way to move forward was to do so separately. The names on my list are the easier ones to approach, the ones who gladly cooperated with the original investigation.

Letty is taking the folks who might prove less cooperative. She's the sheriff. As long as she doesn't mention that she's taken some personal time, those people will see her questions as official police business. Even the toughest nut to crack will often yield to a badge.

The first name on my list is Mallory. Though I remember her, she never really paid attention to me. No doubt she will recall the name. Emma Graves, Natalie's younger sister. Emma Graves, the girl who came back when no one else did.

Mallory owns a European style boutique in town. This shop was established after her divorce, about ten years ago. Rumor has it that the tidy settlement she received helped to launch her longtime dream. According to Helen, Mallory likes to travel so she chose a career that allows her to write off all that travel as a tax deduction. Maybe Mallory is smarter than I recall. Of course all the girls Natalie's age seemed dumb to me because their worlds only appeared to encompass clothes, popularity and celebrities.

I glance in both directions before I get out of my car. I've spotted numerous reporters since I left the farm, all no doubt looking for a story to tell. Someone who knows the missing girls. Someone who knows bones have been found. The police have been fairly tightlipped with comments. I imagine that will change soon enough.

The Royal Boutique is on the square in downtown Jackson Falls facing the Classical Revival style courthouse built in 1884. As the legend goes the original courthouse burned to the ground at the hands of Frank James' supporters while he was on trial in nearby Madison County. My grandmother was an avid storyteller when I was a child and she insisted that the burning of the courthouse story was completely inaccurate. Her tale was that a number of Jackson Falls' most prominent families, including the mayor, the sheriff and a couple of judges, arranged to have dinner in the jail with the notorious outlaw on numerous occasions while he was incarcerated. Certain Jackson Falls church-going extremists burned down the courthouse in retaliation for their wicked behavior.

Whatever the case, the courthouse was rebuilt exactly where it once stood for close to a hundred years. As the center point of the town, the courthouse is bounded by four streets. The rest of the town expands from there in a grid of square city blocks. Mallory's shop is brick with large windows like the others along the block. I decide it must be French week or month since mannequins dressed in very French Couture fill her storefront windows.

At the door the faces of those two young girls who are missing stare at me. The giant red letters that spell out the word MISSING demand action. *I can't help you. I couldn't help my sister.*

How the hell do I think I can do this and make a difference?

I close my eyes and banish the negative thoughts. I have to do this.

I will do this.

The bell over the door jingles as I push through.

"Welcome! I'll be right with you!" floats from somewhere beyond the counter. There's an open doorway that leads into a back room, maybe a storeroom.

I'm impressed by the glamorous vibe. The shop would be right at home around Fiftieth and Fifth in Manhattan. I check a tag on one of the dresses. "Ouch." The prices are reminiscent of those as well.

"Oh that would be perfect with your winter coloring."

I turn toward the voice. Mallory looks surprisingly like the teenager she once was. The only surrender to aging I note are the typical lines that have etched themselves into her face but even those are minimal. At forty or forty-one she's still slender and dresses young with no sign of gray in her long red hair.

She recognizes me and her mouth forms a circle of surprise. "Why, Emma Graves, how are you?"

"I'm good. And you?"

"I'm just wonderful, thank you."

I spin slowly, admiring the extensive collection of chic apparel. "Your shop is very nice."

She beams. "Thank you. I take great pride in my work." Her expression slips a bit. "I heard your mother had a heart attack. I hope she's doing all right now. I feel just terrible that I haven't dropped by and checked on her. I guess you've had to come home to see after her."

I smile at the suggestion that a mere heart attack could slow Helen down or require anything beyond minimal assistance. Yet, in the back of my mind I know that the next cardiac event could be far more serious. I could lose her. My heart squeezes.

"She's doing well, thanks."

Mallory's hand flies to her throat. "Oh, my, I just realized you're probably back because of the bones. I can't believe it took all these years to find Natalie and Stacy."

My brain stumbles for a moment. *How can she know this?*

"Oops." Mallory covers her mouth for a moment, her eyes round with something like surprise. "I'm sorry. I wasn't supposed to say that, but, of course you must know."

"How did you hear this?" I ask, careful not to confirm her statement.

She busies herself with refolding a scarf. "I might have overheard something about it at the mayor's office this morning. I pop in for coffee sometimes before I open the shop."

I'll just bet she does. She probably has a spy on the staff who keeps her up to speed on all the juicy news and rumors. Nothing ever changes in a small town.

A big sigh bursts across Mallory's freshly painted lips. "Lord, I have prayed so many times they'd be found, *alive*—of course."

"I appreciate your prayers." It's the expected thing to say when a person makes that announcement. No matter how many years I have spent away from the south that reaction was drilled into my head along with please and thank you. "I stopped by to see if maybe you had a few minutes to talk about Natalie and Stacy."

Curiosity claims her face now. "Well, Lord yes. Would you like a water or coffee?"

I shake my head. "You and Natalie were close," I say. This is not a question. I remember Mallory spending the night on several occasions.

"We were." She smiles sadly. "I regret now that I let having my first real boyfriend get in the way of our friendship. I think I hurt Natalie by always being busy. Plus I really couldn't stand Stacy. I pretended to like her for as long as I could. Truth is, I had just turned sixteen." She shrugs. "Let's face it, sixteen is a stupid age. Lucky for me I eventually found a good man—at least for a little while—and had two beautiful daughters."

At that point the offspring photos came off the shelf behind the counter. Both daughters look exactly like Mallory, red hair and blue eyes. She goes on and on about the youngest being married to Marshall Beaumont. By the time I see half a dozen photos of the grandchild my eyes are glazing over.

"I'm sorry, I have a tendency to go on and on about my girls and my little angel. I'm sure that's not what you wanted to talk about."

I smile patiently. "I understand. Actually I wanted to follow up on something you said twenty-five years ago. I'm wondering if Natalie had any other close friends who knew about the older guy she was involved with at the time of her disappearance?"

Mallory's face shows surprise at the question, but the reaction doesn't reach her eyes. "Older guy?"

"You said in your statement to the police that Natalie had a new secret boyfriend and that he was older."

"Oh, well." Rather than answer right away, Mallory made a production of putting the framed photos away.

I recognize the ploy. She's about to lie to me.

"The truth is I was the one flirting with an older guy. One of the cops spotted me in a car with him and I lied and said it was Natalie. My hair was pulled back and he didn't get a good look so he believed me. Like I said, sixteen and stupid. It's a miracle any of us live through it."

She blinks as if she abruptly realized that some didn't live through it.

Anger stirs deep in my veins. I force a smile onto my lips. "We've all done stupid things, that's for sure. Still, I wonder if there wasn't someone. Natalie seemed more secretive than usual those last few months. Even Mother noticed."

This particular lie is not for my benefit. It is only for the sake of the investigation. Even the lying priest felt comfortable protecting the greater good with a little white lie.

Again, the other woman looks away. "I'm sorry. I really don't remember anything about her and an older guy. Maybe the cops confused me with another of Natalie's friends. They interviewed so many of us and emotions were running high."

Ha. Not likely. "I thumbed through the yearbook and you were the only one of her friends with red hair. I can't see the detectives who interviewed you confusing you with Natalie or any of her other friends."

Her smile is brittle this time. If her face tightens anymore her skin will crack. "Maybe so, but I think I would remember if I mentioned Natalie having a secret boyfriend. There was obviously a mistake or a miscommunication."

A razor thin edge of irritation vibrates in her voice. Maybe she is telling the truth. It wasn't impossible that one of the cops involved with the investigation made a mistake or maybe covered for someone else. Letty knows—at least by reputation—all the cops involved in the investigation. Tonight she and I will discuss the possibility that one of them fell down on the job…or purposely covered for someone.

Anything was possible. Except it feels like Mallory is the one doing the lying.

"Just one more thing," I say before deciding to put her out of her misery and head for the door.

She waits for me to continue, her eyes wide with what looks like uncertainty.

"You love your children and grandchild. My mother loved Natalie that same way. Wouldn't you want the whole truth if something happened to one of your daughters?"

The catch in her breath and the horror that claims her

face should have made me feel bad for having suggested such a thing, but I don't.

I walk out, leaving her to ponder the question. As I drive away Letty calls to let me know an official statement has been issued. The bones discovered were those of Natalie Graves and Stacy Yarbrough.

No matter that I knew this before anyone else, tears slip down my cheeks. Now the world knows, too.

TWENTY-FIVE YEARS ago Ms. Stella Larson, only twenty-four at the time was a new teacher at Jackson Falls and being the low woman on the totem pole she was tasked with taking over as cheerleader sponsor. Old Mrs. Stedman had retired the year before. Someone had to do it. As it turned out, Larson had been a cheerleader in high school and in college. Unmarried and childless, she was happy to fill her after school hours with extracurricular activities.

Funny how people always assumed if you didn't have a husband and/or kids you had nothing better to do than their bidding.

The current school year was nearing an end but next term's squad would already be working on routines and organizing summer camp. I find Ms. Larson and her squad behind the new gym—the one that was built the year after I graduated. The girls are jumping around and doing flips on the field. The ones with the experience are critiquing the new girls. In my opinion high school is painful enough without adding some extra activity that involves pointing out your faults and belittling your form.

I haven't set foot on school property in fifteen years. Reunions always seemed to come on the wrong date. I was either out of the country or in the middle of a dig, sometimes both. Not that I would have come anyway. It wasn't like there was anyone from my school days—besides Letty—that would draw me back for such an event.

I should ask Letty if she'd ever attended one. As the sheriff she might feel compelled to make community appearances in hopes of maintaining support.

Something else to which I have no desire to serve—the mercy of the public. Too many politicians are either fools or egomaniacs. In some cases, maybe both. I wonder if Letty's job will change her over time. Will she be forced to pander to the wealthy and the powerful to stay in office?

I can't see that happening.

Shifting my attention back to the here and now I watch Larson for a moment. Like Mallory, Stella Larson is physically fit and youthful looking. She wears khaki shorts and a white polo along with the same blue sneakers her cheerleaders wear. As I approach her on the lower run of the bleachers she glances up, shielding her face from the sun setting behind me.

"We have another half-hour of practice," she says, evidently believing I've arrived to pick up a member of her squad.

Do I look old enough to have a teenager? I certainly feel like it most days.

"You probably won't remember me," I begin as I take a seat a few feet from her.

"Emma." She smiles and her hand immediately reaches for mine. "Sure I remember you. Not to mention you've been in the news a couple of times lately. It's wonderful to see you." Sadness touches her face. "I'm so sorry to hear about Natalie and Stacy." She inhales a deep breath. "Of course, there was little reason to believe they were still alive, but it's nevertheless painful to lose that slight hope even after all these years."

"It's a difficult time," I agree.

I feel guilty that I woke up more focused on finding the truth about what happened than aching at the loss. I'm not sure that's how I should be feeling but I am certain this is what

I need to be doing for now. Maybe that's how Mother feels. Perhaps my need to dissect her reactions to mine and Letty's questions caused me to misinterpret what I saw and heard. Mother has struggled to be strong, and to have faith all these years. Now that task is behind her, maybe she just needs something else to do but isn't quite sure of her footing in this new territory.

"You know," Larson says, "Natalie was so helpful to me that first year. She was a mere freshman but she didn't let any of the girls run roughshod over me. I can't tell you how wonderful it was to work with her if only for that one year."

I notice she isn't wearing a wedding band and wonder if she's still single. Not that I can fathom a reason it matters but I do wonder. "My sister was a leader and a very compassionate person."

"She was."

Before I can venture into the subject of my sister's potential boyfriends, Larson shouts an order to repeat the routine to the girls whispering and laughing behind their hands. God, teenagers are all alike no matter the decade.

Larson turns back to me. "The news said the investigation is being reopened. I hope that means they found evidence that will help bring the girls' killer to justice." She presses a hand to her mouth. "I'm sorry, I'm assuming things that may be untrue. I've heard some say they may have wandered off in the woods, got lost and died. It was very cold that night." Her cheeks flush a deeper red. "Well, of course you of all people remember exactly how cold it was."

I can't be sure whether Larson is genuinely remorseful about her statement or if she's fishing for information. "I don't believe the police have reached any sort of definitive conclusion at this point."

A line forms between her brows. "I'm sorry, I don't know where my mind is. If you're not here for one of the girls, was there a reason you stopped by? I really am glad to see you but

I feel as if there might be more to your visit than to say hello to your old gym teacher."

Definitely fishing, but also genuinely concerned.

"Actually." I hesitate, memories of Natalie prancing around this very field suddenly pouring through me like water slipping over the falls. Her long blond ponytail and brilliant smile making her standout from the rest of the team. I blink the images away. "You probably knew Natalie as well as most of her friends."

Larson laughs softly. "I don't know about that, but she confided in me from time to time. I was very open about our relationship with the detectives who questioned me after she and Stacy disappeared."

"Did you have reason to believe Natalie might be involved with an older man? One of her friends seems to believe she was, but my mother and I weren't aware of a boyfriend in the weeks before…"

Since I now know she's dead it would be more appropriate to say before her death but I don't want to say it. I don't want to think it. All these years Natalie has been with us, haunted our dreams, whispered in the dark places we find ourselves when we're all alone. There was always the possibility—the tiniest seed—of hope that lived deep inside us that she would come back one day.

Now that hope is gone.

"There was someone." Larson purses her lips and seems to pick through her memory banks before saying more. "She never told me his name but I sensed that he was pressuring her."

"Pressuring her?" My heart stalls and then starts to gallop toward some unseen finish line. I hold back the urge to launch a barrage of follow up questions. I need to give her time to think, to pick through the memories tucked away for so very long. So I hold my breath and I wait for her to go on.

"He wanted her to agree to something she didn't want to do and she was uncertain how to proceed."

"Do you have any idea what he wanted her to do? Have sex? Run away with him?"

She shakes her head, her face crestfallen. "I wish I knew. She would only share so much."

"Did you advise her in any way?"

"I did. I told her she should never feel pressured to do anything she didn't want to do and that if he persisted she should speak to her parents. We had a lengthy discussion about relationships and how that while there is often compromise there should never be tyranny."

"Good advice." I'm grateful Natalie had a friend in this woman.

"Did she speak to her parents? She never mentioned anything to me after that day." Larson's expression is heavy with the worry I suspect has haunted her for twenty-five long years.

"She didn't." The worry morphs into pain but I press on before she finds the words she wants to say next. "Can you remember the timeframe when this conversation took place? Days or weeks before she disappeared?"

"About a week before. She really seemed happy and relaxed after that. I was certain she'd ended the relationship."

Knowing Natalie the way I did, she probably had. And that may have cost her life. My throat tightens at the idea but I press on. Finding the truth trumps my need to grieve.

"She never made any reference to what grade he was in or what he looked like?" I ask. "Maybe he was from one of the colleges in Huntsville or Decatur?"

Larson shakes her head again. "I really wish I knew. Whether the information proved relevant or not, I would love to be able to help, but she never mentioned who he was or where he lived. She was very careful about that part."

Another thought occurs to me. "Is there a chance Natalie

worried that you might know him? That could explain her reluctance to mention him by name."

Larson considers the suggestion a moment. "It's possible but I was so new to the area I doubt I would have known him anyway."

True. "Thank you, Ms. Larson. You've been very helpful and I appreciate your time."

She takes my hand again. "I've asked myself a million times if I could have helped more when the girls first went missing. But I told all of this to the police and they assured me the possibility would be thoroughly investigated."

"Ms. Larson, I'm sure you did everything you could to help Natalie and to help the police."

A sad smile lifts her lips. "Please feel free to ask me anything. If I can answer it, I will."

I stand and prepare to go. "I appreciate your help."

Before I can turn away, she asks, "Are you hoping to do what the police haven't been able to do in all these years?"

I consider the best way to answer that question. Though Ms. Larson has been very helpful and kind, the prospect that anything I say might end up in a reporter's ear is not lost on me. "I want to help. That's all."

I leave her my number and head back to my car. Climbing out of the van parked next to my Prius is the reporter from WHNT and her cameraman. What was her name? Mother mentioned it. Lila something.

Well, hell.

Beyond sprinting across the ball field and disappearing into the woods behind the school, I'm not avoiding this confrontation.

Maybe it's time I give the woman something to get her off my back.

"Emma," she says brightly, "I'm glad I caught up with you at your old school."

The camera is rolling. I decide not to lie and tell her the feeling is mutual.

"Emma, how did it feel to find your sister's remains? Was this the ending you expected?"

The lady knew how to cut straight to the heart of the matter.

"It's not the ending we'd hoped for obviously, but it's the one we were prepared for." How's that for quick and evasive?

"Going down into that cave didn't cause you to start suffering flashbacks again, did it?"

Anger and frustration stir again. The lady has done her homework. Of course she has. This one is clearly intent on making a name for herself. "No. No flashbacks."

"When this is over are you planning to return to Boston to your position at Boston University?"

"I'm undecided."

"I understand you may not be invited back after the mental breakdown you had in the lecture hall."

For a single instant I am frozen with fear, dread, maybe both. Then I just get angry. Her goal is to make me angry. I realize this. She wants a breaking newsworthy reaction. "Some uncertainty as to whether you'll be invited back the next semester is always the case with an untenured position. I'm fine with either option. Frankly, my heart is in the field. The classroom isn't really where I feel at home."

A clear and logical response.

"You're a survivor, Emma. You've walked away twice now when others didn't."

Her digging into Iraq shouldn't come as a surprise. I have no idea what she expects me to say to the remark so I don't say anything. Mostly the idea that now everyone in Jackson Falls will know about my meltdown keeps ringing in my ears.

"How do you feel about your friend Letty's decision to step away from the investigation after her father's dog tags were found with your sister's remains?"

The question sucker punches me and I am not ready.

I walk away.

She follows with more questions.

I ignore her.

No matter that I knew this was coming, I am devastated for my friend.

19

TUESDAY, MAY 15

ALL FOUR LOCAL TELEVISION CHANNELS LED WITH THE SAME story on last night's ten o'clock news: the dog tags belonging to James Cotton. I refused to watch. Helen sat transfixed as reporters who were still in diapers at the time Natalie and Stacy disappeared retold the events from twenty-five years ago with a passion and an urgency meant only to boost ratings. The segments were immediately followed by a previously recorded plea from the mothers of the girls who had been missing for six days now.

I hate this part. I hated it twenty-five years ago even when I was insulated by my parents and I hate it now.

I called Letty. She was staying the night with her mom. My friend's voice was steeped in the misery of having her father's name dragged through the mud all over again. I wish there was something I could do to stop where this is going. If the task force released or leaked the information about the dog tags that means just one thing: they are poised to go with that theory. Letty fears the team will focus solely on that scenario and forego the trouble of looking for others exactly the way those involved with the investigation did twenty-five years ago. I share that same concern.

Which is why we will not stop until we prove them wrong.

I arrived at the farm at eight this morning. Letty would have been here already but she was diverted by the mayor. Unlike the Jackson Falls chief of police who is appointed, the sheriff of Madden County is an elected position—elected by the people of the county. No matter, Letty cannot ignore a summons from the mayor, not and hope to get along in crucial political circles. Powerful people like the Jacksons, the Beaumonts (by virtue of Matthew's marriage to Lorraine) and the Turners carry a great deal of influence. Letty had a feeling the meeting was about any impropriety our unofficial investigation might represent.

My only question is who ratted us out?

My money is on Mallory. Her daughter is married to the mayor's brother. I can see her calling Heather the moment I walked out of her fancy little shop right downtown in the middle of nowhere.

I don't want anything I do or any misstep I make to be part of the reason Letty's career is jeopardized but I cannot and will not back off until we find the truth. Not unless Letty asks me to stop and I don't think that's going to happen.

We have the same goal.

My own career is in trouble, which ensures that I have a strong grasp on how it feels to watch one circling the drain. I will not be a part of that happening to Letty. Maybe I should do this alone.

Like Letty would ever go for that.

Still, the concept rolls around in my head as I chug my coffee. The bitter taste reminds me I should pour out the remainder in the carafe I made nearly two hours ago and put on a fresh pot. As I go through the motions I stare at the clock. Doing so won't make Letty show up any sooner than she can so I set the coffeemaker to brew and wander over to the stack of reports on the dining room table.

It feels good to be at the farm. Feels like home.

Retracing the steps of the previous investigators is something I feel confident I can do on my own. I could consult Letty if I find myself stuck or at a loss somehow on moving forward. It isn't necessary for her to be involved and risk her career and her standing in the community. Not to mention her mother's. Ginny Cotton worked far too hard for way too long to make a decent life for herself to have the past come back like this to damage that accomplishment. I can't bear the idea of people looking at her as if she is as guilty as her dead husband was presumed to be.

Whether Letty is responsive to the concept or not I feel obligated to put it on the table.

Pounding at the front door pulls me from the troubling thoughts. I hustle in that direction. Why the hell did I lock it? The knob turns freely. I frown. I didn't. So why the hell doesn't Letty come on in?

Standing on the porch as I draw the door open is Delbert Yarbrough. He glares at me as if I'm the one who pissed in his coffee this morning. I resist my initial instinct to step back and slam the door shut, then lock it.

"Mr. Yarbrough, hello." I glance beyond him to the truck parked in the drive behind my Prius. He came alone. Of course he would. His wife is dead. I can't ever remember seeing him with a friend. He was a grumpy old man twenty-five years ago, I doubt his disposition has changed much.

"I want to know how you and your mother can pretend the Cottons are your friends?" He shakes his head. "That bastard husband of hers lost his goddamned dog tags while he was burying my baby—while he was burying your sister! How can you still pretend he was innocent?"

The last part he yells. I jerk at the sound. "Mr. Yarbrough, I understand you're upset by this news but finding those dog tags is not definitive evidence that Mr. Cotton had anything to do with their murders. I knew him. You knew him. He was a good person who suffered immensely. He wouldn't have hurt Natalie or Stacy."

The fury burning on his face has him fisting his hands at his sides. Oddly I am not afraid of this man. Though I haven't lived in Jackson Falls for a very long time, I know he is not a bad person, only a broken person like me.

"You're a fool and so is that mother of yours."

His words give me the impression that he has confronted Helen in this same manner. Now I'm angry, too. "Mr. Yarbrough, you're aware my mother recently had a heart attack. I hope you haven't confronted her like this. I'm certain you wouldn't want to be responsible for damaging her health in any way."

The fury clears briefly and I see the deep hurt in his eyes but all too quickly the rage is back. "I know what the two of you are doing." He glances at the table beyond me. "You're trying to prove James Cotton didn't do this. That's why the sheriff has taken off some so-called personal time with two little girls out there somewhere needing to be found. What kind of sheriff does that?"

His voice grows louder with each word.

"Mr. Yarbrough, an entire task force is working on finding the girls. Search parties are going out every day. You know this. Letty's personal decision is not in any way hindering the search."

"It was God, you know."

I blink, confused. "I don't understand."

"It was God who caused those men to get lost in that cave. He wanted the truth to come out. After speaking to them I am convinced God led them to those graves. If I had trusted His purpose the other wouldn't have been necessary." He puts his face in his hands and begins to sob.

Braced for another outburst, I move close enough to put a

hand on his arm. I see blood on his right hand and start to say as much then I realize it's not blood, it's paint or some sort of stain. "Mr. Yarbrough, I know how difficult this has been for you. My family has suffered right along with yours. What's happening right now is like slicing open all those old wounds and pouring salt into them. It's hard, it hurts. But we need the truth. Letty and I only want to find that truth, no matter what it turns out to be."

His head snaps up and despite the tears on his face the fiery glare is back. "Mark my word, her daddy did this. I only wish he was still alive so I could drag him down into that goddamned hole and bury him the way he did my baby."

Delbert Yarbrough executes an about face and storms off to his truck.

I lean against the doorframe and watch him roar away. I watch until I can no longer see his old white truck and the sound of the engine fades into nothingness. He is hurting. I understand his pain. In his shoes I might feel the same way. If I had not known James Cotton the way I did, if our families had not been close, I would likely feel as Yarbrough does.

For the first time in all these years I ask myself if it's possible...could Letty's father have harmed Natalie and Stacy? He was a soldier who watched his fellow soldiers die, who fought his enemy as necessary. An enemy he didn't truly understand. An enemy who could be a child as easily as a grown man. Was it possible that he suddenly, inexplicably saw Natalie and Stacy as enemies?

Yes, of course. There is no logical way to deny the possibility and yet every cell in my body resists the idea.

Letty's Jeep rolls into the driveway and my heart aches at the sight of her. As much as this hurts me, quite possibly it hurts her more. No one is saying terrible things about my dead sister. She, on the other hand, not only has to deal with reliving her father's suicide, she also has to face the viciousness of the resurrected accusations regarding his involvement with Natalie's and Stacy's deaths.

I straighten from the doorway. "So what did our esteemed mayor have to say?"

No need to mention the strange visit from Delbert Yarbrough. Judging by the agitation in her step the meeting with the mayor was trouble enough.

Letty waits until she's inside to respond. She closes the door and sags against it. "We just received our first official warning."

"Well damn. And I missed it." I gesture toward the dining room. "Shall we have coffee while you fill me in?"

"I'm on caffeine overload."

We migrate toward our mini conference room. I make a stop at the fridge and grab a bottle of water, then set it on the table. "Sit."

She watches as I place an apple next to the bottle before giving me one of those pure Letty looks that states loudly and clearly "Really?"

With a fresh cup of coffee, my fourth, I join her at the table. "So what did Heather have to say?"

She bites into the apple and chews for a moment. It's obvious she is attempting to get her frustration under control.

"First, she demanded to know what it is that we think we're doing."

"I take it you told her." I occupy my hands by cradling the warm mug. The urge to march down to the mayor's office and shake the hell out of the woman who wouldn't even hold the position if not for her mother throttles through me.

"You're a private citizen and I'm on personal leave. It's a free country. We have the right to review and theorize in any way we choose about the case as long as we don't infringe on anyone else's rights or in any way obstruct the official investigation."

She tears off another chunk of the apple.

"She didn't care for your response," I offer.

Letty fakes a smile. "She didn't like my attitude. Said I was disrespectful of her position."

Funny but not a good thing.

"I'm sure you weren't disrespectful." I say this in hopes that I'm right. Letty's nerves are raw right now, as are mine. This is not a good place to be when attempting to carry on a reasonable conversation. Or perhaps reasonable is the wrong word. Heather wants her universe to operate a certain way and those within that universe to act just so.

"She doesn't want the truth." Letty finishes off the apple and plops the core onto the table.

"Because it will make the previous investigation look bad?" I propose since I can see no other reason she would be so concerned.

She nods. "Chief of Police Barker Claiborne—one of her mother's cronies—was lead on the investigation. If he looks bad, she looks bad and Mommy can't look bad because she just got engaged to Senator Ned Baxter who's in the middle of a reelection campaign."

"I saw the billboards the night I arrived—I thought the woman standing beside the senator was Lorraine Jackson Beaumont—but I was too focused on my own problems to care. So this is a really bad time for Mommy dearest to have any past issues arise."

A logical conclusion given the current mayor's mother was the mayor at the time and is now moving into Alabama state politics—even if only by marriage. Jacksons have held the position of mayor in Jackson Falls for four generations, nearly a century. Of course Lorraine married a Beaumont but she was still a Jackson just as her daughter is no matter that her father was a Beaumont and her husband is a Turner. Scandals related to the family name have been as scarce as hen's teeth. I have my doubts as to whether it's because the Jacksons were and are above reproach. I suspect it has more to do with not getting caught. But then I am biased. I despise Heather Beaumont Turner more than a case of bedbugs —something I've unfortunately dealt with twice in my life after staying in ratty motels in third world countries.

"She warned me that she would be watching," Letty admits. "Which means she'll have someone watching us. Maybe a friend, but more likely a member of her personal security team."

"She has a personal security team?" I don't know why this surprises me. She is the mayor. More and more public figures are targets. I suppose being from one of the wealthiest families in the state and marrying into another of those wealthy families adds to the worry of kidnapping and the like.

"Oh yeah," Letty goes on. "She has the one the city pays for and then she has the one her momma pays for."

"Speaking of the Beaumonts." My conversation with Mallory bobs to the surface of the river of thoughts rushing through my brain. "So Mallory's younger daughter married Heather's baby brother because she was pregnant." This still amazes me on some level. "It's different these days than it was when we were kids. I'm surprised there was a forced marriage. Why not just pay her off?"

Letty smiles. No doubt her first of the day. "Apparently little Marshall was in love with the girl and refused to break it off. And the girl was spilling the beans about the baby all over town. I've never seen a high profile wedding thrown together so fast."

"I'll bet Lorraine was fit to be tied." I laugh at my use of one of my mother's favorite adages. Lorraine Jackson Beaumont was her rich daddy's only child and she has proven every inch the conceited bitch he raised her to be—another of my mother's favorite sayings. Helen and Lorraine have disliked each other for as long as I can remember. I'm not entirely sure why. Maybe I'll ask Helen one day.

"Don't you know it." Clearly this gives Letty great pleasure. "Of course she never let on. You would've thought the two had been promised since before they were born." Her brow folds with thought. "Come to think of it, Mallory's older daughter is a city councilwoman. She was elected not long after the wedding." Letty shakes her head. "The woman is nice and she really seems to care about the community, but she has zero personality. In fact, she was the long shot in the race, behind in all the polls, then our lovely mayor and her mother began to support her and she was suddenly a shoo-in."

Some things never change. "Just goes to show how far some people will go to take care of their kids. Lorraine couldn't very well have her youngest offspring married into a family of what she considers nobodies."

Letty opens the bottle of water and downs a long swallow. As she absently replaces the top back onto the bottle she mutters, "Sometimes I hate this place."

Of all the people in this town, I can understand this senti-ment better than anyone. But it pains me deeply to hear Letty say those words. She has built a life and a career here. Some-thing else has happened...something bigger than the mayor's reprimand.

"What else happened this morning?"

Her attention intent on the bottle, she turns it around and around with her fingers. "Someone spray-painted awful things on my father's headstone."

"Oh God." I go around the table and crouch at her side. "I'm so sorry. When did this happen?"

"Late last night or early this morning I guess." She plucks at the label on the bottle. "I ask myself how the hell could someone do that, but I know. I know. People believe he's a killer, a monster. Doesn't matter that he was dead and could no longer defend himself before they officially labeled him a suspect. Doesn't matter that he served his country and his life was devastated because of it. It doesn't even matter that he was innocent."

I take her hand in mine. "I'll go to the hardware store and get something to clean it up. Don't—"

"Our mothers have already cleaned it up the best they can. It wasn't easy to get the spray paint off, especially the red, but somehow they managed."

I think of the red stain on Yarbrough's hand. But I can't be sure it was actually paint or that it had anything to do with defacing James Cotton's headstone. The last thing I want to do is make accusations without proof and cause even more pain for another innocent man. Though he has a different way of showing it, Yarbrough is hurting just like the rest of us.

"Tell me what we should do now." We have those long lists of names. "Should we start interviewing the next people on our lists?"

Letty surveys the table, then nods. "Yeah. To hell with the mayor. We're going to do this whether she likes it or not."

"I agree." I stand as Letty pushes her chair back. "But we need to proceed with a bit more caution. This is your home, Letty. Your career. We can't jeopardize what you and your mother have built here."

"This is your home, too," she reminds me, "and your mother's. We all deserve the truth. Natalie and Stacy deserve justice. My dad deserves peace. I intend to find that peace and that justice no matter the cost."

What more can I say? Letty is right. We all need the truth no matter how many people we have to rub the wrong way to find it.

After a few minutes more of planning, we proceed with the same strategy as yesterday: I go one way with my list, she goes the other with her own.

Except I have a stop to make first.

If Delbert Yarbrough can show up at my house unannounced, I can do the same. Maybe I'll get lucky and he won't be home. Maybe he's busy organizing another of his pointless protests and I can have a look around.

We all have secrets.

We all tell lies.

It won't hurt to learn what secrets Mr. Yarbrough keeps.

20

HELEN

My fingers tighten around the steering wheel as Ginny and I sit in silence. We cleaned the ugly graffiti from James's headstone as best we could but there is more work to be done. At least the worst of the vile painted words are no longer visible.

Monster. Killer. Evil.

I called a professional cleaning service but they won't be able to get to the job until later in the week. What we accomplished will have to do until then. Ginny's cell phone rings and I jump. We both do. She answers and I sit quietly listening to her end of the conversation. The voice on the other end sounds like Letty. I can barely hear so I can't be certain. I hope nothing else has happened.

I think of Emma and her out at the farm and I worry. I worry that this new nightmare will scar them both more than they already are. God Almighty, I want this to be over. My sweet Natalie is gone. She is never coming back. Why can't we just leave it and have some peace? I should be glad her remains were found. I should be thankful for the opportunity to lay her to rest...

I am not. The timing could not be worse.

I know my Emma. I know Letty. They will not stop until they know the whole truth and I am terrified.

"Please be careful," Ginny says. "Love you."

She puts her phone away and exhales a heavy breath, outrage making her face twitch. "Mayor Heather called Letty on the carpet about this unofficial investigation she and Emma are conducting. She warned Letty to watch her step. You know her Momma put her up to that shit."

I grit my teeth a moment to prevent screaming. That bitch Lorraine Jackson Beaumont has been running this town for most of her worthless life, through her daddy before she was mayor herself and now through her daughter. I wish I could tell her just how pathetic she really is, but I cannot. I can only keep my mouth shut and hope her fiancé wins this damned election and takes her off to Montgomery. It will be such a blessing to know she is gone. She dragged out the grieving widow image for nearly two decades after the lowdown piece of shit she'd married right out of college died. I almost smile at the thought that he is rotting in hell while his precious wife chases after her happily ever after with another man. I force away thoughts of her dead husband and think of how when the image of widow no longer suited Lorraine's purposes, she found wealthy, handsome international businessman turned politician Kurt Carlton.

Though Lorraine may soon be gone, her daughter is proving equally ruthless and utterly self-centered but I doubt she will ever be as good at either as her momma.

"I'm worried about them." I say this because it needs to be said. Emma is all in the world I have left, just as Letty is all Ginny has. We cannot allow them to make the same mistakes we made. "We have to do something."

"Those dog tags were in my car," Ginny says, her voice

seething and so very quiet as if the rage is sinking deeper inside her, curling its way through her and meshing with the pain and agony she has had to carry all these years.

We spent hours on our knees scrubbing her husband's headstone. James Cotton was a good man. A broken man, but a good one. He was a veteran who came back damaged in ways that twenty-five years ago there was no good way to fix. He was guilty of nothing more than being misunderstood.

"Think, Ginny." I turn to her. "Think very hard. Are you sure they were in your car after James died?"

Renewed fury flashes hot and swift in her eyes. "I took them off his cold, dead body myself. That old bastard Glenn Wallace saw me do it. He knows I did. I cleaned them off with the hem of the dress I was wearing and the next day when I found them in the bottom of my purse I hung them on the rearview mirror in my car."

"Why would Glenn lie and say he doesn't remember seeing them?"

Glenn Wallace, the coroner for the past thirty years, apparently signed a statement in the past twenty-four hours asserting that the only jewelry worn by the deceased James Cotton was a wedding band. When the chief and that new ABI fella questioned Ginny this morning they told her what he said and she told them the coroner was wrong. If Ginny says those dog tags were hanging around her husband's neck when he died, then by God they were. I guess it's possible the cancer and the treatments have scrambled Glenn's memory.

I tell myself it was an honest mistake except I cannot see how.

It pains me to know that Glenn would do such a thing. I would never have believed he was that kind of man. But then, I know Lorraine. She probably blackmailed him with some knowledge she has kept all this time for just this moment. That's the danger in lies and secrets. Once they happen they take on a life all their own. They invade our existence, burrow in deep, winding around the truth and then it becomes impossible to separate them, to pick them apart. Slowly but surely it becomes a part of your memory, your past and your future… until someone or something unearths that place where it all started. And then you can't take it back. Can't make it go away or pretend it never happened.

It seethes and grows and you cannot stop the momentum.

"I want to know what purpose it serves for him to lie!" Ginny glares at me.

I take a breath, banish the disturbing thoughts and shake my head though I know her words were not a question.

"I asked him right there in the shed where James shot himself if I could keep his dog tags. I knew how much they meant to him and I wanted Letty to have them when she was older. He said, 'why course you can, Gin' and that's what I did."

My soul aches at the idea that someone would want to hurt Ginny and Letty like this. I feel outraged at Glenn's betrayal. I keep that to myself for another time.

"There's only one answer then," I say and our gazes lock. "Someone took them out of your car. The someone who helped cover up the truth about my Natalie's murder."

The hurt swells and undulates. My eyes burn and my chest aches with the effort to hold it inside. It's been twenty-five years but the pain of losing a child will go with me to my grave. It cannot be assuaged.

Ginny nods. "That's the only explanation and we both know it. Glenn, the chief, all of them are part of the cover-up."

I don't have to ask if she locked her car, no one in Jackson Falls did back then, most of us don't now. Back then folks didn't even bother locking their houses if all they were doing was running errands in town or picking up kids from school.

Who would have imagined a killer was lurking in our midst?

The worst kind of murderer—one who preys on children.

The agony presses against my breastbone and I lose my breath. I fight the hurt and struggle to pull myself together. Now is not the time to fall apart. Whatever else I do, I must protect Emma.

"What if...?" I struggle to draw in a breath, the air squeezes past the misery and goes grudgingly into my lungs. "What if James didn't kill himself? What if he was chosen as the scapegoat?"

He was the perfect option. Mentally ill. Prone to outbursts. Every day he walked the very road where the girls disappeared. Twenty-five years ago we believed that the strain of being a potential suspect in the investigation pushed him over the edge, but more than once since then I have dared to wonder if someone had set him up. Ginny would never talk about it. But the time for ignoring possibilities is over.

Ginny shakes her head. "He killed himself, Helen. He'd been telling me for days he couldn't take no more. I did all I could to help him, but there was no way to stop his mind from dragging him to that awful place. When Letty first became sheriff she looked at the case file. She said there was nothing to suggest anything other than what it was."

I nod my understanding. "If Letty was satisfied, then we should be as well."

Still, I am convinced we must look at each piece of the past, no matter how agonizing. Someone took those dog tags after James was already dead and buried. They took them to use as evidence to seal his fate if Natalie and Stacy were ever found. I say as much to my friend.

"But he died a whole week after the girls disappeared," Ginny reminds me. "I don't see how that's possible knowing what we know."

She's right. I chew on that detail for a moment and then I measure my words carefully before suggesting another terrifying scenario, "Is it possible someone else knows what really happened? That person may have taken the dog tags from your car for that same purpose, which would mean…" Again I swallow back the misery. "You get what I'm saying."

"It would mean that piece of shit wasn't the only person involved."

Disbelief and shock thickens between us.

"If that's what happened," Ginny dares to venture, "we both know there's only one, maybe two people it could be."

A strange anticipation starts to build inside me, quashing the disbelief and the shock, fueling my wavering strength and courage. I look my old friend straight in the eye. "If that's what happened, how in the world will we ever prove it?

I cannot imagine any possible way.

"I don't know." Ginny swipes the tears from her cheeks. "I just don't know."

I grab her hand with both of mine. "But we have to try."

21

EMMA

THERE ARE lines that officers of the law, like Letty, cannot cross. In my work there are also strict rules and procedures that must be followed when excavating remains. I am fully aware that what I am about to do is completely illegal.

But I'm doing it anyway.

Delbert Yarbrough lives on Little Indian Creek Road. It didn't occur to me until I decided to drive to his house that his home is located along a narrow side road right off the larger road that runs alongside the woods at the base of the same mountain where my sister's remains have lain all these years.

Indian Creek Road. I realize as I turn onto the side road that will take me to the Yarbrough's home why I remembered the terrain in the area of the cave. I had never been to that cave until I went down with Letty. But, long ago as a child, I went fishing in Indian Creek with my dad, Letty and her dad. We walked a good distance through the woods, maybe just a few hundred yards from the opening to that very cave. Of course, my memory dates back to before Natalie disappeared.

Died. She died, I remind myself.

A new sort of pain trickles through me. It feels different from the pain of the past twenty-five years although we all understood on some level that Natalie was never coming back. Still, this is a new ache that burrows in a different place in my chest—the very center of my heart where hope once resided.

Indian Creek begins at the Tennessee River and twists through the woods for miles, growing smaller until it ends on the north side of neighboring Madison County. Along this part of the greenway that follows the creek there is nothing but trees and the mountains on either side of the long, winding road that cuts through it. The occasional house pops up, mostly older residences that were once a part of vast farms. Little Indian Creek Road where Yarbrough lives was, obviously, named for the smaller tributary that trails off from the main creek. More modern homes have popped up on Little Indian Creek Road over the years.

The Yarbrough home sits a few hundred yards from the road, overlooking the creek. I pull into the driveway before Yarbrough's and park at a gate maybe fifty yards from the main road. A large wooden sign marks the property as belonging to a hunting club. Since it's the middle of the day on a Tuesday I don't worry about my car being in the way. Hunting clubs have bought up wooded property all over Alabama for seasonal use. Even in season, the members rarely show up except on weekends. At least that was the way of things when I was a kid.

I guess I'll find out if that routine has changed.

The chill in the air has me lifting my shoulders up around my ears and hugging my arms around myself. Ironically the priest's hoodie continues to come in handy. I traded Helen's old sweater in for the freshly washed hoodie this morning. I tell myself this was not because I wanted to be reminded of *him* but because I'm not really a sweater girl. Considering all the other problems I have at the moment, I decide not to ponder the notion.

I walk back to the road and continue on the short distance to the next driveway. I check my cell, make sure it's on silent and tuck it into my hip pocket as I start down the gravel drive to the Yarbrough property. I used to ride over with my mother or dad to pick up Natalie when she had spent a Saturday night with Stacy. Natalie usually went to church with Stacy when she was at her house and vice versa.

Glancing up at the tree canopy over the road I wonder if Stacy and Natalie ever explored the woods near the cave. Cold trickles through me and I shiver. This is too far from where the bus crashed to believe they walked here and just left Mr. Russell and me to fend for ourselves. Someone had to have driven them those nine or ten miles. The Yarbrough place is only five or six miles from town but there is no cross-road from Indian Creek to Long Hollow Road. However my sister and her friend got to the cave, they had to travel back past the bus into town and to the other side, closer to the western town limits, and then down Indian Creek Road.

Would Natalie have ridden right past the bus knowing I was still there with the dead bus driver?

Not willingly. I am certain of this.

I reach the end of the drive where the trees have been cleared and a two-story log house stands. It's so quiet I can hear the water beyond the house. Mr. Yarbrough's truck is not in the drive. I glance at the garage but decide to go to the front door and knock. I can always tell him that my car started acting up and I pulled onto that other drive to avoid blocking traffic. Not that there is a lot of traffic but I doubt he will question my reasoning, after all I've lived in large cities for the past fifteen years.

My excuse will be that I felt compelled to come and apologize for not keeping him informed of mine and Letty's efforts to figure out what really happened to Natalie and Stacy. Of course that's another of my lies but he won't know. I'm a very good liar. Only recently have I realized that perhaps the reason I am so good is because I've been lying to myself for twenty-five years.

I have pretended that I could live with never knowing the whole truth.

I cannot.

After several knocks with no answer I check out the garage. The side door is unlocked. Two skylights prevent the interior from being dark or the need for turning on lights. Yarbrough's truck isn't in the garage. There's a four-wheel ATV and a riding lawn mower. On the far side of the garage is a large gun safe. Not surprising. Most males and a considerable number of females below the Mason-Dixon Line own at least a hunting rifle or a handgun. There's a large chest style freezer. Shelves line the walls. Paint cans, tools and plastic storage containers fill the shelves. Because I watched far too many horror movies when I was a kid I check the freezer. Meat and vegetables fill the large frozen space.

I set my hands on my hips and survey the garage once more. No cans of spray paint. Nothing else that looks out of place. I head back outside. Behind the garage two large garbage cans stand at the end nearest the house. I open the lid on the first. White kitchen trash bags fill the can to capacity. No loose trash, no spray paint cans. I shake my head in resignation and heave a sigh. No matter that I can't see any cans of spray paint, I smell them.

One by one I remove the four heavy kitchen trash bags. The can is empty otherwise and spotless. Who scrubs their garbage cans? Probably Helen does exactly the same thing. Shaking my head, I start with the bag that was on top. Sure enough, under a wad of damp paper towels and soiled paper plates I find three cans of spray paint, two red, one black. I stuff the trash back into the bag and heft all four back into the trashcan.

I should call Letty but I'm torn between giving her the pleasure of seeing that the person who defaced her father's headstone is arrested and causing Mr. Yarbrough more pain.

I move to the back of the house. Might as well have a good look around while I'm here. If he shows up before I leave I'll stick with my story of my car acting up. I climb the steps up to the rear deck. From there I can see the water of the creek. The drop from the backyard to the water isn't more than thirty or forty feet. A wall of glass that peaks at the vaulted ceiling looks out over the backyard and the water. I cup my face and lean close to the glass. Inside the house looks exactly as I remember. Same leather sofa, worn and wrinkled with age. Two wood and leather chairs that I now recognize as classic Mission style flank the fireplace.

Before I can stop myself my hand lights on the doorknob and turns. The door is unlocked.

I freeze.

There is no way I'm going into this house. To do so is vastly different from walking onto the deck or even going into the garage. A home is intensely personal. This is Mr. Yarbrough's private space.

This is breaking and entering, locked door or no.

I leave the door closed and head down the steps. It's not until I'm on the ground again that I realize my heart is flailing. I can just imagine what Helen would say if she saw me now. She really would think I'd gone around the bend.

Maybe I have.

Before I head back around front I walk to the other side of the deck. Another set of steps, these concrete, lead down to a door that is apparently an exterior access to the basement. I scan the foundation of the house and see none of those small, narrow windows that suggest a basement, but that only means this one is completely underground.

"I've come this far." Without giving myself time to change my mind, I descend the twelve steps to the door. It's metal. No glass. I resist turning the knob and do an about face to go back up the steps. I stall. Near the toe of my hiking boot, lying against the riser of the first step up is a narrow, shiny object about four or five inches long.

I reach down and pick it up. Lip gloss. Pink lip gloss. It's fairly new. Not damaged or worn as it would be if it had lain in the elements for more than two decades. I imagine that Yarbrough has had his share of girlfriends. Maybe a friend who has a teenage daughter.

Even as I tell myself these things adrenaline is pumping through my veins.

Every instinct warns me to go. Now.

This time I don't walk. I run. My boots seem to mire in the gravel as I push as hard as I can toward the road. If I can just make it to the road, I can walk through the edge of the woods to the other drive. If push comes to shove I can veer into the woods before that but I have no desire to get lost in these unknown woods or to go plowing through the thick underbrush and end up falling into a sink hole. A shudder quakes through me.

I make it to the road and relief weakens my knees. Still, I keep running until I'm out of sight from the road and well down the hunt club driveway. I stall at the driver's side door of my Prius and realize I left my fob and my bag in the car and that it's unlocked.

"Jesus Christ."

Not until that moment do I realize that I am still grasping the lip gloss. I thrust it into my back pocket and reach for the car door. I check to make sure all is as it should be before climbing behind the wheel. Enough three-point turns later to equal about fifteen and I speed toward the paved road then screech to a halt just in time to ensure no one is coming before I blast out onto the Little Indian Creek Road.

The oncoming vehicle to my right doesn't register as any

sort of threat at first. As it grows nearer the white color clicks in my brain. Closer still and I recognize the driver.

Delbert Yarbrough.

He recognizes me at the same time and slams on his brakes, sliding to a stop right in front of me and simultaneously blocking my path.

The smell of hot rubber fills my nostrils and I almost gun it hoping to cut between the ditch and his rear bumper. Not even this damn Prius is that small.

Before he can get out I do. I march right up to him as he climbs from his vehicle. "I was headed to your house."

I hope to God that my face looks more relaxed than it feels. My lips are posed in a smile but they are fighting me. They want to tremble. My entire body is suddenly shaky. "It's been so long I took the wrong turn."

His eyes nothing but slits, I feel him assessing my face, my body language. His casual button-down shirt and jeans tell me he has either retired or has taken some time off himself.

I work hard to appear innocent. I'm usually quite good at this part but it's that damn lip gloss and what it might mean that's messing with my ability to remain calm.

"What are you doing out here?"

"I wanted to apologize." I tuck my thumbs into my pockets to prevent crossing my arms. "Letty and I should have told you what we were doing."

He stares at me, his eyes wider now, searching mine. "So tell me."

I push onward as if we're on the same page. "You were right about Letty. She has taken some personal time. We believe we can find the whole truth about Stacy and Natalie. Our concern is that the task force will be so focused on proving James Cotton killed them that they won't look at anything or anyone else."

He steps in toe-to-toe with me. I stand my ground.

"Are you stupid or just crazy? That bastard did kill them."

I flinch but I refuse to be bullied. "Maybe I am and maybe Mr. Cotton did do it. But we need to be sure, Mr. Yarbrough. Let's just consider for a moment that Mr. Cotton didn't do it. That means whoever did has gotten away with murder for twenty-five years. Can you really spend the rest of your life convinced that justice has been served when all we have is a piece of evidence that anyone could have put in that cave?"

For a moment he stares at me as if he remains convinced that I have in fact lost my mind. His expression is hard, unyielding. Then his face softens the slightest bit. "And if you find that he's the one, can the two of you live with that?"

Though his question gives me pause, I say what I feel. "The truth is what we want, whatever that is."

He looks away, his arms hanging at his sides. "You know, I used to dream about her all the time. I had no idea she was so close."

I reach out, put my hand on his arm. "I still dream about them sometimes. I've taken that bus ride a million times, I think."

His gaze collides with mine, the misery I see in my mother's eyes and in my own stares back at me. "And you don't remember anything besides them walking away?" he demands.

"I wish I did. I've even had regression therapy and there's nothing."

I hesitate for a few seconds on the rest of what I've been thinking but I figure I need to go the distance to ensure his suspicions about me being this close to his house don't stir again.

"Obviously to get from Long Hollow Road to Indian Creek Road they had to be riding with someone." That part was the only logical conclusion, now for the supposition part. "I know my sister. She would never have ridden past the bus again without stopping to get me and to check on Mr. Russell. We both know she didn't get to Indian Creek Road in a car or truck or whatever without passing the bus. There are no side roads that connect that road and this one." I point toward Indian Creek Road.

"Maybe they did stop and you'd already set out on foot."

I shrug. "Maybe so, but the point is Natalie and Stacy were with someone and it wasn't James Cotton because he and his wife only had one car and my mother and Letty's were in Birmingham in the only car the Cottons owned. When they returned, James was already out in the woods with my father looking for Natalie and Stacy."

His eyes narrow again. "He could have kept them at his house until he had access to his car. They had that old storage shed out back. The girls could have been in there."

"That's possible, too. But the police searched their house, the shed, the car. Do you really think Mr. Cotton was capable of covering his tracks that perfectly? Not a single hair was found in his vehicle. Not a single trace of evidence anywhere in the house or the shed or in the yard. Nothing. Even if Natalie and Stacy got into the car with someone they knew versus some stranger, there came a point when there was a struggle. Struggles leave all manner of trace evidence behind. Hairs, blood, other body fluids. Where is the evidence?"

Delbert Yarbrough has no answer for that question.

The problem is, neither do I.

22

MY CELL IS BLOWING UP BY THE TIME I REACH INDIAN Creek Road.

I drag it from my back pocket. Letty.

"Hey." I make the turn onto Indian Creek.

"Where are you?"

"Where are *you?*" I echo.

"I was just about to head back to the farm but Chief Claiborne wants to see us in his office ASAP."

Oh hell. "I swear to you that I did not break the law...*much*." If Yarbrough has already called the chief of police, then he was more pissed off than I realized when we parted ways. Usually I read people better than that.

"I'm afraid to ask what you're talking about."

Oh hell. "Why does Claiborne want to see us?"

"Really? You're going to do this to me?"

I blow out a breath and admit defeat. "I was still mad at Delbert Yarbrough when we parted ways this morning so I decided to have a look around his place."

"Oh my God. Please tell me you did not go into the man's house."

I switch the phone to the other hand. "I did not go into the man's house."

"Just tell me what you did, Emma."

"I walked around the yard. Peeked into a few windows and I might have gone into the garage." Did the man have cameras? I should have thought to look for a security system. Damn it!

"You do understand that you've just admitted to having committed a crime?"

I shrug. "Yeah, well, I wasn't thinking."

"Clearly. And what if he'd arrived home and found you on his property—in his garage?" Her voice grew louder with every word.

"He didn't. I was already in my car and down the road before we ran into each other."

"There are a couple more houses on that road, but he had to know you were at his house."

"I told him I was." I stop again, check for oncoming traffic and make the right turn that will take me back into town. "I told him I wanted to apologize for not sharing with him what you and I are doing."

Letty kept interrupting me with demands but I finally got the story told. I left out the parts about the spray paint cans in his trash and the lip gloss. I will get to those troubling details when she calms down.

"You're lucky he isn't at City Hall right now pressing charges."

"So I should meet you at City Hall?" In my self-serving opinion it's time to move on.

"I'm in the parking lot."

"Almost there," I say.

"See you in a minute then."

She ends the call without a goodbye and without telling me why we've been invited to the chief's office. The 'Welcome to Jackson Falls' sign comes into view. I guess I'll know what the summons is about soon enough. Maybe the chief wants to reiterate the mayor's position on our unofficial investigation.

I stop for a traffic light and my cell vibrates.

Letty

I read the text.

Reporters have arrived.

"Great."

I tug the lip gloss from my pocket and tuck it into the glove box. The short drive to City Hall is uneventful. I spot Letty's Jeep and park in the slot next to it. I count six news vans. Reporters and their cameramen spill toward our vehicles before we can emerge.

I meet Letty at the hood of the Prius. We huddle close and head for the entrance.

"Sheriff Cotton, do you still stand by your father's innocence?"

"Emma! Emma!"

The familiar voice of Lila Lawson cries out above the others. Letty and I keep going.

"Emma, how do you feel about the reality that your best friend's father murdered your sister?"

I stall.

Letty grabs me by the arm and ushers me forward.

Two uniformed officers spill out of the entrance and usher the reporters back. I refrain from asking what took them so long. Inside, another officer ushers us past security and into a conference room filled mostly with faces I don't recognize. On the wall are two televisions, one displays the crowd outside while another shows a discussion between what appears to be two reporters about the Shepherd and the Baldwin girls, their photos line the bottom of the screen. The sound is muted on both screens.

"Sheriff Cotton, why don't you and Ms. Graves have a seat and you can make the introductions?"

This comes from an older man I recognize from the news as Chief Barker Claiborne.

We pull out the only empty chairs around the long conference table and sit. Seated at the head of the table is Jackson Falls' esteemed mayor, Heather, who requires no introduction so Letty skips her and gestures to my left as she starts calling off names. Special Agent Nile Jansen is with the Huntsville FBI office. Special Agents Jimmy Watwood and Paul Anderson from the Alabama Bureau of Investigation in Montgomery. Finally, Chief Deputy Liam O'Neal who's sitting in for Letty while she's on leave.

I brace in preparation for the chief to lower the boom. There's not a lot he can do to me unless he has learned I trespassed on Yarbrough's property, but he can cause serious repercussions for Letty.

"We wanted to include the two of you in this briefing," Claiborne says, "before we make a statement to the press. We'll rely on you to pass along the news to your mothers."

Letty and I exchange a look.

"Has the medical examiner's report come in?" Letty asks.

The chief nods and passes what I presume is a copy down the table to Letty.

My heart begins to pound, faster and faster. I can't breathe, can't swallow.

"The ME has determined cause of death to be blunt force trauma to the head. This determination applies to both victims," the chief explains.

I stare blankly at the report. This is not news to me but with the ME's report released I can no longer avoid telling Mother the rest of what I learned in that damned cave. I feel sick and relieved at the same time. I need to get this off my chest but I hate the idea of shifting it to hers.

"Additionally." The chief passes another report down the table. "We found traces of blood on the dog tags and we sent that for DNA analysis. The lab was generous and put our request at the front of the line."

Letty glances over the report, then places it on the table.

Her face tells me the report is damning.

"The blood on the dog tags found in that cave," the chief goes on, "is a match to your father's, Letty. I don't see any way to avoid naming him as the killer. I just don't see any way."

I look at my friend, keep my mouth clamped tight. This is her world. I don't want to say or do the wrong thing but staying quiet is killing me.

"How did the dog tags get into the cave?" Letty demands. "My mother took my father's tags off his body *after* he was found dead. Eventually she hung them on the rearview mirror of her car. We all know," she surveys those seated at the table, "that anyone could have taken those dog tags from her car and placed them in the cave."

A beat of silence expands in the room, pushing the oxygen out and making it hard to catch a breath. Not one person in the room endorses Letty's assessment.

"Except the coroner has no memory of those dog tags being on your father's body," the chief argues. "I have discussed this point with him this morning at your mother's insistence and he says that if they weren't in his report then they were not there."

"My mother is not lying." Letty holds her ground. "She has no reason to lie. In twenty-five years most everyone in this town has believed that my father abducted Stacy and Natalie and killed them. What purpose would it serve for her to suddenly start refuting that claim now that there's actual physical evidence?"

Letty makes an excellent point. Though both Ginny and Letty have always believed as Helen and I do that James Cotton was innocent, once the case went cold, Ginny let it go. We all did. It was the only way to move on with our lives.

I marvel at the idea. Have any of us really moved on or

have we simply been muddling through? Stalled at a place where the past overlaps the present and moving forward is impossible.

Those at the table look at each other and then at the files lying on the table in front of them. None have an answer for Letty's question. None want to look at her or at me.

"Excuse me." I push back my chair and stand. "I just have to say something. My mother and I have waited twenty-five years to know what happened to my sister. The same goes for Delbert Yarbrough. What's a few more weeks? Have you sifted through more of that cave floor? Where are the backpacks? Those were fabricated from mostly nylon, chances are they would still be in reasonably good condition. Where is my sister's necklace? She wore that necklace every day of her life. She was wearing it that day. If you look in your case files you'll find a photo of it." I touch my throat. "The chain is silver and there are pink ballerina slippers."

None of those listening open their folders but that didn't stop me. I'm on a roll and I intend to get this said.

"You found none of those things in the Cotton home, on the property or in the car. And speaking of the car," I'm flat out angry now, "Virginia Cotton drove my mother to a doctor's appointment in Birmingham that day. This was an all day trip in the Cotton's only vehicle. How would you propose that James Cotton got the girls from Long Hollow Road to Indian Creek Road or to wherever he took them first?"

"Ms. Graves, that was covered in the original investigation," Claiborne reminds me. "Cotton could easily have kept the kids in the shed behind his home until he had the car in his possession. The next day even, when everyone else in this town was out there looking for those girls."

Letty stands next to me. She places her hand on my arm to assure me she understands I've done what I can but I am far from finished.

"That's right," I allow. "He could have, except Natalie and

Stacy were walking toward my house when they left the bus. The Cotton home was in the other direction. Why would they have turned around? The crash happened closer to my house than to Letty's. It's an illogical theory. But let's say Mr. Cotton was taking one of his long walks that day while his daughter was at home alone and sick with the flu. He'd never left her home alone before, but let's say that day he did. He may have been walking back toward his house when he ran into Natalie and Stacy. What did he do? Wrestle the two of them into submission and drag them back to his house? Two or more miles? If so, where are the injuries related to the struggle and the necessary restraints? The only fractures I noted on any of the bones were the ones from the trauma the medical examiner found. Why were no signs of a struggle found on Mr. Cotton? God knows the detectives interrogated and inspected him to their hearts' content."

More of that goddamned silence is the only response.

Letty's hand tightens on my arm. "Let's go."

"If he kept them in the shed for a time, where was the physical evidence? Why didn't his wife or his daughter hear any sounds? Even a gagged hostage can make sounds." I shrug. "Not a single hair was found. Both girls had long hair. That's virtually impossible."

The chief holds up both hands. "I hear you and you make a number of valid points."

I look from one stony face to the next. "And here's the kicker. The real game changer that you won't find anywhere in those files" I point to the stacks on the table. "To be honest I only thought of it just this moment. I'm wondering why no one in twenty-five years has thought of it. A room full of trained investigators—much like the room full who investigated this same case all those years ago." I shake my head. "James Cotton was out there in those woods with my mother and my father searching for us. All night and all day for days after that. Where were Natalie and Stacy then? Oh wait, in the shed right? Probably struggling to get loose from their restraints. And yet you found no evidence and Letty and her mother never heard a sound."

"Unless they were already dead," the FBI agent says.

I stare at him, want to slap his face. "True. But again I ask, where was the trace evidence? He bludgeons them to death and they stay overnight at least in that shed and then he carries their lifeless bodies in the trunk of his only vehicle to the drop location. He drags their limp bodies through miles of woods and still nothing was discovered. Wow, he was really good. Or your forensic folks were really bad."

I don't wait for Letty to usher me to go, I walk away.

That sickening silence follows us out of the room.

Once out of the secure area and in the lobby she turns to face me. I brace for a rebuke. I'm sure my outburst did little to help her standing with those people.

"Thank you."

Tears well in my eyes and I hate myself for not being strong enough to hold them back. "I'm just sorry I was too young to think of all those things twenty-five years ago. Apparently no one else did."

We hug and then we walk out into the throng of reporters. There are nearly a dozen now. This time Letty walks up to the woman who has been hounding me, probably her as well.

"I'd like to make a statement."

She glances at me and I give her a nod of approval, not that she needs my approval. Letty squares her shoulders and holds her head high while she lays out all the holes in the theory that James Cotton abducted and murdered Natalie and Stacy. Amid the crowd of reporters I see Delbert Yarbrough. Worry nudges me. Will he start a protest against Letty now?

Rather than attempt to shout her down, he meets my gaze and nods. The move is so slight I almost miss it but with that almost imperceptible acknowledgement I know he is in agreement.

As much as I want to be relieved by his about face regarding Letty's father and our unofficial investigation, the pink lip gloss in the glove box of my car won't allow me to trust him. It's foolish and likely nothing and still I can't let it go.

"That's all I have to say."

Letty's announcement is our cue to go.

Uniforms hold back the crowd while we make our way to our respective vehicles.

"I have to check on Mom," Letty says. "I'll meet you at the farm in an hour."

"See you there."

We drive away. Letty heads toward the post office and I drive toward the house on Tulip Lane. I definitely don't want any of the reporters following me to the farm. I make the turn onto Tulip and I notice Yarbrough's truck is tailing me. I pull to the curb and put the gearshift into Park. Maybe his change of heart wasn't the full one-eighty I hoped for.

As he approaches my car I lower the window. I peer up at him, don't see any anger in his expression. Definitely a good thing.

"The police will be releasing a statement," I say in hopes of heading off any questions he might have. I'm not about to be the one to tell him how his daughter was bludgeoned to death. I flinch at the thought.

"There's something I should tell you, since you and Letty are trying to find the truth."

I'm suddenly holding my breath, hoping for the one clue that will make the difference.

"A week or so before they disappeared, Stacy mentioned something about a teacher giving Natalie trouble."

A frown mars my face before I can stop it.

"I know," he says, reading my expression. "Everybody loved Natalie. I questioned Stacy about it but she wouldn't say more. She did slip up and say *he* so I know it was a man. The

227

day after the girls went missing I told this to Claiborne and he said he'd look into it. A week or so later," he rubbed his head, "I can't recall for sure the exact date, I asked him about it again. He said he'd checked it out and none of the teachers, male or female, had any idea what I was talking about. Natalie had perfect grades. She and Stacy were both model students."

I almost tell him that I've already heard from Ms. Larson there was an older guy in Natalie's life. And Mallory Jacobs had mentioned one in her interview twenty-five years ago though she denied it when I asked her about it.

Rather than say any of that, I hold back.

"There's nothing in any of the reports about you talking to the chief." I decide it's safe to tell him that much. "I read all the interviews with Natalie's teachers and no one was asked about any sort of involvement beyond the classroom."

Yarbrough braces his hands on my window and leans closer. "I'm telling you, there was a teacher giving Natalie trouble. My Stacy would never have made up something like that. She loved Natalie like a sister. She was worried which tells me it was real."

I thank him and he walks back to his truck.

My instincts start to hum. My dad always said the third time is the charm. I have three different references to an older man close to Natalie.

Bottom line: we're looking for a man who was close to Natalie and he's probably a teacher.

I rush to the farm.

I need that school yearbook.

23

I PACE THE FLOORS WHILE I WAIT FOR LETTY. I CALLED Mother twice. Drove by the house. She wasn't home and she didn't answer her cell. Finally, out of desperation, I called Letty's mom. She sounded strange. Of course she does. Letty has just shared the news about the dog tags. I asked Ginny if she had seen or spoken to Helen. She had not. Rather than leave her with something else to worry about, I pretend I'm looking for information on Yarbrough, which I am, really. I asked her if he had a history of violence? No. Heavy drinking? Not that she had ever witnessed. Odd behavior before this recent plunge into strangeness? Not at all. Social life? Church. There were numerous others. Her answers did nothing to assuage my certainty that something is off with him.

The thud of a car door draws me to the front window.

Letty.

I unlock the door and open it. She climbs the stairs, weariness visible in her every move.

"How's your mom?" Dumb question. She is broken to pieces just as Helen is, just as Letty and I are.

"She's okay."

I nod. "I spoke to her for a minute. I couldn't get in touch with Helen. I thought maybe she'd talked to her."

"She didn't mention it."

"She said she hasn't heard from her." I close the door behind my friend and twist the lock. "There's something I need to tell you." Two somethings, actually.

Letty drops into one of the dining chairs and pulls her knees to her chest. "Shoot."

I walk to the table, withdraw the lip gloss from my back pocket and place it on the table in front of her. "I found this on the steps going down to the basement at Delbert Yarbrough's house."

Letty picks it up and turns it over and over between her fingers. "Okay."

"It isn't old enough to be Stacy's," I state the obvious. "I asked your mom about Yarbrough. She said that he never had much of a social life beyond church before Stacy went missing and that he hasn't had one at all since then as far as she knows. No rumors about him dating. No drinking, no trouble. Nothing until a few weeks ago when he started pushing the reopening of Natalie and Stacy's case. So, if he has no social life, doesn't date," I point to the lip gloss, "where did this come from? It's new. Dropped on those steps recently."

Letty inspects the tube again. "This only proves he had company and that company dropped her lip gloss." She tosses the pink tube onto the table. "We're going to need more than supposition and a random tube of lip gloss to make this relevant."

I'm not ready to throw in the towel just yet.

"When he showed up here this morning ranting about the cavers he said something like if he had trusted His—meaning God's—purpose the other wouldn't have been necessary. That statement started to gnaw at me so I pulled the files on the girls who are missing." I open the Baldwin file. "These are photos taken of her bedroom. Look." I say this knowing Letty is fully aware. I point to the white dresser in the girl's lavender room. A square glass cube holds what appears to be several tubes of lip gloss not unlike the one I found. "The Baldwin girl loves her lip gloss."

Letty looks from the photo to me. "You think Yarbrough took those girls to get back at the police for failing to find his daughter's killer?"

"I think the twenty-fifth anniversary did the same thing to him it did to me, pushed him over some edge. I had a meltdown in the classroom and he started this chain of increasingly radical protests. I think maybe his protests weren't prompting the hoped for reaction so he took things up a notch. He abducted those girls in a similar manner to Stacy and Natalie's disappearance to draw media attention. Not to hurt them, but to prompt the desired effect."

Letty studies the photo for a second longer. "So the case is reopened for comparison purposes and Yarbrough gets what he wants—a fresh look at the old case."

I point a finger at her. "He's desperate. Figures he has nothing left to lose. His family is gone. He was forced into retirement—according to Helen."

"You could be onto something with this."

"What do we do about it? Go to Claiborne?"

She snorts. "No way. Not enough evidence. He would laugh us out of his office. We'll have to start keeping tabs on Yarbrough. Get a look in that basement."

"Won't we need a search warrant for that?"

"There are ways around warrants." She picks up the lip gloss and considers it again. "I'll look into this, see what I can figure out."

For the first time in days I feel excited, in a good way. "Let's talk about Natalie's teachers, specifically the male ones. I have a new theory."

We go over what Mallory, Larson and Yarbrough stated about this mysterious older guy in Natalie's life. The strangest part is that nothing any one of them said exactly confirms or supports the other. And it's all hearsay, according to Letty. The strange part is that the only mention of Natalie and an older man in any of the police reports and interview statements from twenty-five years ago was Mallory's comment. Why would Yarbrough or Larson lie? Or was Mallory's comment appearing in her official statement a mistake?

If someone was covering up the truth, it was likely someone working on the case. Either that or it was shoddy police work.

"Your mom doesn't remember anything about trouble with a teacher or Natalie acting secretive?"

I shake my head. "I don't either. The really weird thing is how Mallory changed her story to her being the one involved with the older guy—who she chose not to name—and that she only said it was Natalie to avoid getting into trouble. Why change her story after all this time?"

Letty picks up the yearbook. "How many male teachers did Natalie have?"

"Five. One, Mr. Couch, economics teacher, who died before Natalie and Stacy disappeared and one who was confined to a wheelchair—remember Mr. Jeffries? He retired before we reached high school. The wheelchair pretty much rules him out."

Letty nodded. "Jeffries was the Spanish teacher. He died a couple years ago."

"So that leaves Frank DeSoto, the boys' basketball coach and gym teacher," I point out. "Matthew Beaumont, biology teacher, and Trenton Caldwell, Algebra and Geometry."

Letty looks at their photos in the yearbook. "I don't remember any of them being this handsome but Caldwell and DeSoto are pretty hot."

"Beaumont is older," I note, "but still attractive in a proper gentleman sort of way."

"He was also Heather's father."

"Yeah." I tap the photo. "I can't see Mr. Beaumont cheating on his wife. She would have castrated him."

"Maybe her selfish, overbearing personality is the reason he would."

Letty has a point. "I was thinking I would talk to Ms. Larson again, see what she will tell me about the three."

"I need to pay Mr. Wallace a visit tomorrow morning and press him about the dog tags." Letty leans her head in her hand and rubs at her forehead with her fingertips. "He's lying and it's time he admitted it before it's too late. I don't want him taking the truth to his grave with him."

As unpleasant as the task sounds, I second that one.

"What about Yarbrough?" I can't stop thinking that those girls could be at his house right now.

"We'll watch him in shifts. We need something to take to Claiborne. A random tube of lip gloss won't cut it, especially coming from one of us. I'll pay a surprise visit to his place with the excuse that we need more information about this mystery man he mentioned."

"Sounds good." This is the right direction. I can feel it. "I'll find a reason to do the same in the morning. If he leaves his house, I'll follow him. Later, after school, I'll follow up with Ms. Larson."

I hesitate. If I tell Letty the other part her emotions may get the better of her. But I can't not tell her and have her going to the man's house blind. "I found one other thing when I was at Yarbrough's house."

She looks at me expectantly.

"Remember when I was in the garage nosing around?" She nods. "The trashcans sit next to the garage so I had a look. Everything inside the can was stowed in kitchen trash bags so I couldn't see anything but I smelled it. When I dug through the top bag I found two red spray paint cans and one black one tucked into a bag. I noticed a red stain on his hand earlier. I think he might be the one who defaced your dad's headstone."

Anger and frustration cloud her face. "You couldn't tell me this earlier?"

"We were a little busy."

She heaves a heavy breath. "Okay, I'll find a way to question him about it. I can say someone saw him or his truck near the cemetery."

"I think he's just hurting, like the rest of us. He wants the world's attention on this case in hopes of finding the same truth we want to find. I know what he did was wrong and hurtful, but someone said to me recently that sometimes you have to do the wrong thing to make the right thing happen."

I guess the priest made an impression after all.

Letty doesn't agree with my conclusion but she doesn't disagree either. "Let's just hope if he took those two girls that he hasn't done something that can't be undone."

I can only imagine how terrified those children are and I know full well the nightmare their parents are suffering.

If this whole thing was some attempt for attention and the girls are safe, then it's a far better outcome than what happened to my sister and her friend.

I wonder if we will ever know exactly what happened.

LATER I DRIVE to the school and sit in the visitor's parking area for a time before going home. Helen finally called me back but she was in a hurry. She said we would talk when I got home. The conversation was strange. She sounded strange, just as Ginny had when I spoke to her earlier. I'm certain Helen had seen the press conference by the time she called me but she clearly didn't want to talk about it.

Maybe that's why I came here. Maybe I'm not ready to go home and face her. I stare up at the school that is as familiar as my own reflection. It's dark but I want to be here, to remember the classrooms, the corridors...the teachers.

No matter that I never truly fit in, my life was innocent and happy in this place...until Natalie went away.

I can't help wondering how all our lives would have been different if the unthinkable had not occurred. Natalie would no doubt be a dance teacher with a couple of beautiful children of her own. Her husband would be someone important and, of course, incredibly handsome. She wouldn't have it any other way. Helen would be happy playing the part of grandma. Maybe if my dad hadn't spent so many years being worried and sad he wouldn't have developed cancer. Studies have linked depression and anxiety to higher risks.

As for me, I'm sure I would still be the peculiar daughter. The one who digs in dirt and unearths bones. I even wonder if I would have stayed had Brad not decided Heather was more his type. Probably not. I was born to be the quiet one but my mind was never still, it was always wandering far away. I suppose on some level I was destined to travel the world. Maybe all those genes I inherited from the Graves side of the family determined my future for me right from the beginning. Graves and what they hold are my specialty, after all.

I'm fairly confident my life would have turned out exactly as it did except maybe for the whole ASS thing. I might not have overindulged in alcohol, smokes and sex quite so much and avoided making an ass of myself if *that day* hadn't happened.

"Isn't this what coming home is about?" I stare up at the prestigious school. "Asking yourself what if? Thinking about what might have been?"

A rap on my window next to my head makes me jump. The squeal that escapes my lips sends the man hovering outside my car staggering back.

I blink. The older man's face looks vaguely familiar.

"You're not supposed to be in this parking lot after dark

unless there's a school function going on," he says, his gruff voice muffled by the glass.

I start the engine and power down the window. "I'm sorry." I produce a smile, feel completely humiliated that I squealed like a little girl. "I haven't lived in Jackson Falls in a long time. I'm only visiting for a few days. This is where I went to school."

"Why Emma Graves, is that you?"

He comes closer, leaning down to get a better look at me with only the streetlamp and the dim glow from the dash to see me in the near darkness.

"Yes, I'm Emma." It's possible this man has seen me on the news but he does look vaguely familiar. My mind automatically browses through my memories until I find the right one. "Mr. Brewer, are you still working for the school?"

Surely he's just out for a walk. He was an old man when I was a child. He must be nearing eighty. Although, he appears fit and as sharp minded as ever.

"Sure do. Mostly I tell others what to do these days. I'm the chief of the janitorial department. I take a nice long walk every evening, gives me a chance to see that all is as it should be around the school."

"Congratulations on your promotion. I apologize for breaking the rules. I was about to head home anyway."

We chat for a few minutes more. He asks about my mother and offers his sympathy about Natalie.

"Well, I'll get on home," he says. "The missus will have supper on the table by now."

"Mr. Brewer?" It suddenly occurs to me that he might remember something useful. "In the weeks before Natalie disappeared, do you recall her having any trouble at school?" I broach my intended subject carefully. "Perhaps with one of the teachers?"

He removes his cap and scratches his head. His thick dark hair now gray. "First off, I'm pretty sure you recall that everybody loved Natalie. She never got into trouble. Never failed to be kind and thoughtful. Always on the honor roll. Popular too. I'm sure she would have broken a few hearts if things had turned out differently."

I nod patiently. "My sister was a wonderful young woman." It's not until that moment that I consider Natalie more than a child. She was always my big sister but also just another kid. Yet, hearing all that I have these past few days, I realize she was far more than that. She was fifteen, quite mature for her age and sporting the body of a woman. Maybe she was already breaking hearts without knowing or understanding the power she possessed.

Teenagers are so full of fire and passion…sometimes it erupts, sometimes it can become dangerous. I doubt many realize the power they possess over those toward whom all that fire and passion are aimed.

"But you don't recall any trouble." I smile again, hoping he will indulge me. "I know it's been a long time but Mother and I were talking about how we thought there might have been something going on at school that we didn't know about."

He tugs his cap back onto his head and appears to consider my comment for a bit. "I sure can't remember any sort of trouble. All the teachers adored her." He nods. "But I'll think on it. If something comes to mind, I'll call your momma and let you know."

"Thank you, Mr. Brewer. Give my best to Mrs. Brewer."

I watch him walk away before driving the few blocks home. It's possible the teacher issue is a dead end. I don't trust Mallory and it's possible Mr. Yarbrough is lying to me. Though I can't see why he would unless he's hoping to throw me off the scent of what he's really up to. I think of that tube of pink lip gloss and worry storms me all over again.

Whatever he's doing, we have to find out if it involves those two little girls.

I park behind the house, grateful there are no reporters waiting out front. I'm not very happy that Letty refused to allow me to go with her to visit Yarbrough. I get her reasoning —we can't go at him from different angles if we go at him together on this one angle. Better to divide and conquer. She pushes him about his efforts to draw attention to the case and I stay after him about the teacher scenario. That way he doesn't feel like we're ganging up on him.

Letty ordered me to go home and get some rest. She promised to call after she spoke to Yarbrough.

I am tired. No doubts there. Chief Claiborne's press conference likely dumped a lot of information, not the least of which was an in-depth discussion on cause of death. I should have been with Helen when she learned that news—if I could have found her.

Was she avoiding me or did I not try hard enough? Some would say this is further proof that I am not a very good daughter. I was so caught up in the trouble with the teacher scenario that I ignored my own mother when Letty went straight to see hers first thing.

Except I couldn't find mine.

Inside my mother is watching a movie, *Pink Cadillac* with Clint Eastwood. She dabs at her eyes with a tissue, seemingly completely focused on the screen. I stand at the door to the living room.

"Don't mind me," she says with a glance in my direction. "I always cry when I watch this movie."

I don't believe her but I let it go.

"Your dinner is in the microwave. It should still be warm."

I walk across the room and sit down next to her. "*Pink Cadillac* is a comedy. Why would you cry when you should be laughing?"

"Is it true?"

I pick up the remote control and mute the television. It isn't necessary for me to ask her what she means.

"Where were you when I tried to call you? I was worried."

She lifts her chin, stares me straight in the eye. "I'm here now. I want to know if what Claiborne said is true?"

"Yes."

"So, so, he hit her in the head with something and that's what killed her?"

Her voice wobbles and quavers and my heart threatens to fail me.

"It's the only conclusion the medical examiner can make since there is no tissue to test for other causes."

I wish for the proper words—any words—to say that might give her comfort as I answer the deluge of questions, but there are none. Is it possible Natalie felt no pain after the initial blow? Sure. Is it probable? No. Was she terrified? Depends upon whether she was drugged or not. And the ultimate question: Did she suffer for long? Seconds? Minutes? Hours? There is no way to know the answer with any measure of accuracy.

We sit, staring at the screen for a while before she speaks again, "We don't know if other bad things were done to her?"

My faltering heart twists. I have tried very hard since finding the bones not to consider the other possibilities.

"There's no way to be certain. There were no other fractures. If a violent struggle had taken place more likely than not there would have been indications. Wrist or forearm fractures from where she tried to get away or attempted to defend herself. There was no indication of that kind of struggle."

"I guess that's good." Her attention settles on the muted antics on the television screen.

"I believe so," I agree. I hesitate for a moment before saying the rest. "I examined each one very carefully." There is no need to explain that I mean the bones. "They were all perfect and," for lack of a better way to phrase it, "just as they should be."

She asks no more questions. We sit. Watch the muted

movie for several minutes. I need a shower. My body warns that I should eat and sleep but I cannot leave her sitting here like this. No matter that she says nothing I can feel her misery expanding inside her, around us and I want to comfort her but I fear if either of us moves or speaks that we will both shatter into a million aching pieces.

The wail that issues from her throat rips the very heart from my chest. I wrap my arms around her and hold her close. Her entire body shakes with the tide of agony washing over her.

I sink into the ocean of desolation with her and hold on tight to ride out the tsunami that has been years in the making.

24

WEDNESDAY, MAY 16

THE NEXT MORNING I SIT OUTSIDE BEANS, THE COFFEE
shop located next to the Piggly Wiggly. Delbert Yarbrough is
inside having breakfast. He sits at a window table, unmindful
of my surveillance. It isn't necessary to follow him around.
Letty told me last night that she'd slipped a tracking device
under the rear bumper of his truck when she stopped by his
house. She talked to him about the Shepherd and Baldwin
case. Pushed him pretty hard, she said. Then she broached the
subject of the graffiti on her father's head stone. Before she
could mention the made up eyewitness, Yarbrough confessed.
He begged her forgiveness and promised to pay for any and all
necessary repairs.

How could a man who couldn't bear the burden of
defacing a headstone abduct two little girls?

I think of the lip gloss and I know what I have to do. After
starting the engine, I roll away from the coffee shop. I woke up
thinking about those girls. Their mothers were on the news
again this morning pleading for their safe return. Breaking
into the Yarbrough basement won't be difficult. To that end
I'm driving dad's truck. The tools I need for the job sit in the
seat next to me. Letty is dropping by the coroner's house this

morning. He was released from the hospital yesterday. She intends to question him about her father's dog tags and her mother's insistence he was wearing them when he died.

I'm halfway to the Yarbrough home when Letty calls.

"Hey, did you learn anything new?" I hope for hers and her mother's sakes that Mr. Wallace's memory has improved.

"He's standing by his report."

The frustration that has become too constant a companion fills me now. "The man is dying, isn't he? Why the hell doesn't he just tell the truth?"

Both questions are rhetorical. There is always the chance that he *is* telling the truth.

But that is not the answer we need to hear.

"I'm headed to the farm," Letty says. "Meet me there. There's someone who might be able to help us."

I take the next left and turn around. For now I let the other go but I will get into that basement in the next twenty-four hours come hell or high water.

When I arrive at the farm a green Taurus sits in the drive next to Letty's Jeep. The Taurus sports a Montgomery County tag. A disabled-person placard hangs on the rearview mirror. Has one of the ABI guys come over to the dark side or is he a spy?

My money is on the latter.

Letty and the stranger from Montgomery are seated at the table. This isn't one of the men from yesterday's task force meeting.

"Emma, this is Marvin Timmons. He's one of the two ABI special agents who worked Natalie and Stacy's case."

Timmons stands and thrusts out his hand. "My partner, Freddy Boone, passed away three years back."

I give his hand a shake. "Did your friends send you to find out what we're doing?"

Letty laughs. "Told you she'd ask that question."

I pull out a chair and drop into it. Timmons resumes his seat.

"Actually, Agent Watwood did mention that you and Letty appear to be working your own investigation."

I lift my eyebrows at Letty.

She gestures to our guest. He says, "Watwood and Anderson don't know I'm here. I came because I've always felt like something went wrong with our investigation but Claiborne and the FBI were running things so we followed their lead."

"They still are," Letty grumbles.

"How can I help?" the retired agent asks.

Letty and I exchange a look. The question at the top of both our lists is the same.

"We've only been able to find one reference to an older man—possibly a teacher—who may or may not have been involved with Natalie and that was in the girl Mallory Carlisle's statement. Yet the scenario has been mentioned by two other people we've interviewed in the past few days."

It isn't necessary to mention that Mallory Carlisle is now Mallory Jacobs or that her younger daughter married into the mayor's family. None of that is relevant to anyone but us.

Timmons leans back in his chair. He still wears the off-the-rack suit of his former profession, but the cane propped against the table is an accessory he didn't have twenty-five years ago. Though his hair is more salt now than pepper, I do remember his gray eyes. Now that I've listened to him for a bit, his voice echoes in my memory.

Are you certain you didn't see anyone else with your sister and her friend? How long did you stay on the bus after Natalie and Stacy left?

He pushed me hard during his questioning. I decide not to hold that against him. He was doing his job.

"The Carlisle girl was the only person to bring up the subject." He shook his head. "Her recounting of what she'd seen was told half a dozen different ways. In my opinion she was lying. I believe that was the general consensus."

"Stella Larson mentioned this same theory," I say. "A man, possibly pressuring Natalie. She said she told this to the police but there's nothing in the case files. The same with Delbert Yarbrough. He told the police his daughter was worried about a male teacher that Natalie was having trouble with, yet there's nothing in any of the reports."

Mr. Timmons surveys the piles of reports. "The first thing I will tell you is that every teacher and staff member of the school, the dance studio and the employees of any other place either of the girls went were interviewed and alibis were checked. It's always possible that one of the investigators or agents listed a POI as having an alibi without confirming. But the question I would be asking of your three witnesses," he suggests, "is to which investigator were these incidents reported?"

That is a very good question.

I LEAVE Letty and Mr. Timmons going over the files. According to Letty's tracking app, Mr. Yarbrough has spent most of the morning in Huntsville but now he's back home so checking out his basement is a no go. Another research idea occurs to me but I decide not to mention it to Letty. It's a long shot but one I plan to check out. Nothing ventured, nothing gained. I glance at the clock on the dash and realize I have half an hour to make it.

The drive to St. Mary's takes less than twenty minutes. I park in the lot and head for the entrance. I'm about to do something I haven't done since I was a kid. I shake my head, realize I haven't thought of that day in ages.

At the ripe old age of twelve guilt had driven me to walk down to St. Mary's on a Saturday afternoon and slip into the confessional. I confessed my sins to Father Estes, the priest who came to St. Mary's when I was nine and remained until Barnes showed up. Father Estes assured me that my transgression wasn't the worst thing a kid my age could do. I did my penance and never thought of it again…until just now.

As I enter the sanctuary I dip my hand into the Holy Water and bless myself, however grudgingly. If there's anyone else here for confession he or she is already in the confessional. I make my way there and see that the light is off so I go on inside, close the door behind me.

Within moments a curtain slides back and I stare at the priest's profile behind the tinted mesh screen. My big plan suddenly feels like an idiotic idea and I almost cut my losses and make a hasty exit.

At my hesitation he says, "When was your last confession?"

"I dunno. Like twenty years ago."

He's the one hesitating now. Obviously, he recognizes my voice.

"I'm here to listen to whatever you would like to tell me."

I notice that he carefully words this statement so that it doesn't sound religious. In fact, it's completely unreligious. I suppose he realizes this is not a typical confession.

"Well, I guess my last confession was when I was twelve and I wanted to get back at this girl who was always making fun of me."

"Making fun of you in what way?"

I frown. "You aren't supposed to interrupt like that, are you?"

"I'm sorry, please go on."

"If you must know," I say, my voice snappish, "she called me names and made fun of my glasses." I think about it a minute. "My clothes, my lack of a manicure. My hair and my nose."

This time he keeps quiet and still he makes me uncomfortable. Mostly I think it's the scent of his soap that's invading my side of the screen.

I sigh. "Anyway, we were at a school assembly and I was sitting on the bleacher below her. She was so preoccupied whispering with her friends that she didn't notice me tying her shoes laces together." The memory of blood gushing from her nose after she fell makes me flinch. "I felt really bad about it afterward. Especially since she wore braces." I touch my mouth. "She had to have two stitches in her upper lip."

"Did you do your penance?"

"Of course. I was twelve. Father Estes was God to me. I trusted him completely."

Father John Estes was the first and last man besides my dad I ever really trusted.

"I regret that I broke your trust, Emma."

I make a face. "What happened to the veil of anonymity?"

"It's the soap," he said, his voice lower as if he fears someone will hear, "I knew it was you the moment I moved the curtain aside."

The fact that I noticed the same thing about him rattles me. I shake it off. I'm on a mission here. "I need your help but it's not about what I did when I was twelve."

"Confess your sins and they will be forgiven."

This was the tricky part. "Actually, it's not my sin, it's someone else's."

"You don't have to do that with me. You really can tell me anything."

"No, seriously, this is about what someone else did."

After a brief hesitation he says, "Let's proceed with caution then and I'll do my best to help."

"Twenty-five years ago my sister and her best friend were abducted and murdered." I take a breath and drive on. "Letty and I have learned there may have been a man— maybe a teacher—pressuring Natalie. I believe the person who killed the two of them attended this church. A true

Catholic would have confessed his sins. Father Estes may know the identity of the killer—he may not realize this person killed anyone but he may be aware of an older man's obsession with a young girl."

"Confession is a sacrament," Barnes reminds me. "The sacred seal of confession cannot be broken."

I roll my eyes. "I know this. I'm not asking him to reveal what was said and by whom, but if he could confirm that there was an older man involved with her, we would know if we're moving in the right direction. We don't want to waste time on a dead end."

The fact that he doesn't immediately say no gives me hope.

"To gain Father Estes's confidence on the matter, I would be forced to lie to him."

"You've lied before," I remind him. "For the greater good," I tack on.

The hesitation that follows has me thinking I've gone too far. When he steps out of the confessional my conclusion is confirmed. Reluctantly, I reach for the door handle and do the same.

Those searing blue eyes stare directly at me. "I'll make a deal with you."

My first instinct is to run, but I need this piece of information. "What kind of deal?"

"I'll ask him—though I can't promise you I can share his response—if you'll volunteer at the women's shelter with me once a week for the remainder of your stay in Jackson Falls."

I almost laugh. Since I'll be gone as soon as Letty and I learn the truth, why not?

"Sure. I will gladly volunteer with you every week during the remainder of my visit if you confirm or rule out this rumor."

He offers his hand. "Deal."

Reluctantly I place my hand in his and we shake. The zing

of electricity that zaps me each time we touch sparks. "The sooner the better."

"I have lunch with Father Estes in Huntsville every Thursday."

"That'll work."

~

THE SWEET TEA & Biscuits is right next door to Mallory's fancy boutique. Helen wanted to meet for lunch so I chose the place. After lunch I can drop in on Mallory again. So far she's the one who has changed her story repeatedly to suit the moment, which should make her an easy target.

Helen waves from the other side of the window as I pass. She's already grabbed a booth. I reach for the door but someone else beats me to the draw.

"Why, Emma Graves, I can't believe it's really you."

Lorraine Jackson Beaumont drops her hand from the door and beams a smile at me that is as fake as the sleek thin nose and the unlined skin on her artfully and surgically perfected face. Her salon enhanced blond hair hangs free on her shoulders as if she is half her age. The red power suit tells me she is likely going door to door in support of her new fiancé.

How nice.

"Mrs. Beaumont." I muster up a smile. "In the flesh. I'm sure you've seen me on the news," I suggest, unable to resist tossing in a dig.

"I have." All signs of politeness and kindness vanish instantly. "I saw you *and* Letty. What a shame to see a promising young black woman making such tremendous and career shattering mistakes."

Outrage quakes through me. "I'm not sure I know what you mean."

The smile is back but the menace in her eyes is undeniable. "Why, I'm sure you're aware that for every action, there is always a reaction. Everything we do in this life has consequences, Emma. Unlike you, Letty lives in a small town where certain powerful influences make the important decisions. Perhaps you might serve your friendship with Letty best by reminding her of all she and her mother have to lose."

With that the former mayor turns and struts away, sleek red high heels clicking on the cobblestone. I guess she decided she didn't want to have lunch in the same place as me.

Anger and dread clash in my chest. I yank the door open and walk inside. Helen watches me storm toward her, her own face a study in worry.

"What in the world was that about?"

"A warning," I confess. "She doesn't like the investigation Letty and I are conducting."

"She said as much?"

Helen appears stunned that Lorraine would come right out and say how she feels about our investigation. I, on the other hand, wonder why it took her so long.

"Oh, she took a roundabout way of getting to her point but the message was loud and clear. She wants us to stop or there will be consequences."

The former mayor is right about the power of the few in a small town. Letty and her mother are unquestionably the ones with the most to lose and I need to be sure they are both looking at this with their eyes wide open.

A killer has gotten away with murder for twenty-five years. If he is still alive he's not going to sit idly by while we prove he did it.

Determination stiffens my spine. *Give it your best shot, pal.*

We are doing this.

25

HELEN

"She's not in there," Ginny insists.

"How can you be so sure?" I stare at the big house across the road from where we parked.

I have known Ginny Cotton for fifty-five years, since we were little girls at Jackson Falls school. I recall as vividly as if it were yesterday when she showed up at senior prom with a white man—James Cotton, a recent transplant from Chicago. She is and always has been a good woman, a caring woman. The hardest working, most loyal woman I know.

But right now I fear she is on the brink of an awfully steep cliff and I am terrified she will slip over that edge.

"I cleaned that big ass mansion all by myself for fifteen long years. I know when she's there."

The bitterness that taints her voice dwells deep inside me, too. Somehow over the past twenty years I've learned to hide it well. Most of the time Ginny does too but things have changed of late.

Those damned dog tags.

I shake my head. "I can't believe she would go that far."

Ginny's head whips around, her gaze colliding with mine. "How can you say that? You know the kind of bitch she is."

My chest tightens. God almighty I did not mean to belittle her feelings on the matter. "But we're talking about murder— the murder of children. She has three of her own."

I try my best to keep my voice steady but it's impossible. I have been strong for so long...so very long. But I feel myself weakening now. I don't know if it's age or just the idea that everyone knows what happened now. There is no more pretending.

Natalie is dead. My girl is gone.

"I wouldn't put anything past her." Ginny stares toward the house once more. "I know it was her."

I think of Lorraine's warning to Emma and my fingers tighten on the steering wheel. But words are not deeds. "What if it was *him*? He may have lied."

She stares at me, the self-righteous outrage still tightening the features of her face. "Couldn't have been him. He had that accident, remember? He was laid up for a couple of weeks, couldn't hardly walk by himself. I cleaned up enough of his shit and piss."

Lord have mercy she is right. James wore those dog tags until the day he died—*a week after the girls went missing.* "So we know the dog tags were taken seven or more days after Natalie and Stacy disappeared."

The reality of what my words mean sinks into my weary brain at the same time they do Ginny's.

"The girls must have been..." She looks away from me, toward the house. "Right here on this property until then."

I close my eyes and block the idea that my sweet girl could have been alive for days before she was murdered. If only we had found her in time. And Ginny is right. Natalie and Stacy could very well have been right here for however long they lived after being taken by that monster. I don't say as much but I drove over here yesterday. Watched the house for I don't know how long before going to the cemetery to talk to Andrew. It broke my heart to tell him what I'd heard in that press conference. That was the reason I couldn't answer Emma's call. I couldn't bear to talk to her. Couldn't risk telling her the whole truth. The words had swelled in my throat, twisted there like barbed wire. It took hours to pull myself together.

"Helen."

Ginny's hand covers mine and I take a deep breath. I don't trust myself to speak. It takes every ounce of fortitude I possess to keep from squalling like a baby.

"We don't know how long they were alive after he took them," she says softly. "But we do know it wasn't long or Natalie would have found a way to escape."

I nod. "She would've."

Ginny clears her throat. "I listened to everything Letty said in that statement to those reporters. They didn't find any other evidence against James twenty-five years ago because he was already dead when those precious girls were buried. He had to be. We both know the only way that bitch got her hands on those dog tags is if she took them off my rearview mirror. And there was only one reason for her to do such a thing—to incriminate my husband if the bodies were ever found."

"You're right." I watched Letty's eloquent delivery of the facts as well. "Emma believes since the backpacks were made mostly of nylon they would still be intact, and they didn't find them in that cave."

"One or both could be on that property somewhere," Ginny offers with a glance across the road. "He kept her necklace, why not her backpack?"

Fury brands every inch of me. I stare at the Jackson home place. Lorraine Jackson Beaumont's great-great-grandfather built the massive house more than a hundred and fifty years ago. Over the decades the house was remodeled and expanded until it became one of those mega mansions like the celebrities live in. It still looks like the proud plantation house it once was but it is far bigger and fancier. Horses graze in the fields around it. Beautiful barns stand on the rolling hills at the back of the cleared portion of the property that abuts the woods and mountains.

However pleasing to the eye, the only thing good that ever happened in that damned house was when Matthew Beaumont died there.

"The bottom line is," Ginny says, her voice cold and hard, "whether Lorraine had anything to do with the taking or the killing, she helped him bury those girls and she damned sure took James's dog tags. That makes her just as guilty in my eyes. A devil willing to do anything to protect her own. Just like her no account daddy. He whored around and did whatever he pleased and everyone worshipped him like a god. I hope he's roasting in hell right alongside his piece of shit son-in-law."

I close my eyes. "He lied to you about the way they died."

Neither Ginny nor I had summoned the courage to discuss the medical examiner's announcement that cause of death was blunt force trauma to the head. Agony roars through me.

"I'm not surprised. He was so doped up and scared he would have said anything to keep me from killing him."

The silence that lingers is one I know well.

"Don't even go there, Ginny," I warn.

"What I did," she goes on, completely ignoring my warning, "forced you to have to carry this burden with me. We've kept this secret. Lied to the people we love most for more than two decades. Maybe it's time I told the truth. There's no need for you to have any part in this."

I turn to her. "I will not lose anyone else I love to this nightmare! I know how it will go. They'll charge you with murder. Lorraine and her ilk will swear you were trying to

254

clear your dead husband's name and ended up killing an innocent man."

Ginny shakes her head. "I don't care. This is destroying my daughter."

"Letty is strong. She'll get through this. These trials are only temporary. You tell anyone what we did—"

"What *I* did," she corrects, fire in her eyes.

"That's something Letty will have to live with every day for the rest of her life. How would it look to have a sheriff who didn't even know her own mother was involved in something like that?" I shake my head again. "We can never tell anyone. The girls will know when we're dead and gone when no one can use us to hurt them."

Ginny heaves a heavy breath. "I know you're right. I do. I just hate that it has to hurt you, too."

I reach across the console and hug my friend. "We'll get through this." I shore up my slumping courage and say the rest of what's on my mind. "But there is one thing we can do to help the girls."

Ginny looks expectantly at me.

"We can find the evidence we need to prove Lorraine was involved and that James is innocent."

"I don't want her to get away with this." Ginny's voice quivers. "She's gotten away with too much already."

My friend is right. "This time, she's going to get what's coming to her."

One way or another.

26

EMMA

STELLA LARSON BLEW her whistle and the sophomore girls set off around the track. I guess gym class hasn't changed that much.

I press down the corners of my visitor's pass to prevent it from peeling off my tee. The bleachers aren't any more comfortable now than they were the last time I sat with a twisted ankle and watched the rest of the girls in my class trot around this track. Thankfully I don't have to wait long. Satisfied her class is following instructions to move faster than a walk, she joins me on the bleachers.

"I saw you and Letty on the news." She moves her head from side to side. "There are so many questions about what really happened. For the record," she turns to me, "I agree with you and Letty. I feel like they decided James Cotton was guilty and didn't really look at anyone else. Now they have the evidence they need to stick with that theory. It's just not right."

"I've been thinking about what you told me," I say. "We've

found more witnesses who say Natalie was having trouble with an older man. Most believe it was a teacher."

Larson watches the girls jog past. "I wish I could say that isn't possible but we both know it happens all too frequently."

Teachers having relationships or encounters with their students show up in the news far too often. I think of the man who abandoned his wife and children to drag a teenager across the country in hopes of starting a new life. Deep inside I shudder at the idea that Natalie may have fallen victim to exactly that sort of depravity.

"These girls," Larson says, "don't understand the power they are only just beginning to come into possession of. Their bodies have suddenly gone from girls to women. Their skin is young and smooth, their breasts firm and high, their mouths oh so tempting. Hormones are causing them to think of things and to feel things they've never wanted to think and feel before. They are daring and terrified at the same time."

"But they're still children." I say the words, remembering well how the girls who matured more quickly flaunted their new womanly assets.

"They are, even as they tease and tempt any male who crosses their path." She shrugs. "It's human nature. The urge to procreate. They have no idea this is what their bodies are doing, they only know it feels good. It feels empowering. But it's dangerous."

I don't want to think about Natalie or Stacy that way but I also don't want to pretend that my perfect sister wasn't human. "Was Natalie doing that?"

Larson nods. "A little. Not as much as some of the others. But she teased and flirted, far more subtlety than most."

"Letty and I have three names we want to ask you about."

Larson looks at me then. "You realize that if I had seen or heard anything I would have reported it?"

I nod. "I do."

"I never witnessed any improprieties from any of my

colleagues not with Natalie or anyone else. But I did see *things*. Like the way the girls crushed on certain teachers. Fortunately I have never known one of my colleagues to fall into that tender trap."

"Twenty-five years ago the big crushes were Frank DeSoto, Trenton Caldwell, and Matthew Beaumont," I guess.

Larson nods. "Frank and Trent were only in their twenties back then, like me. The girls really gave them a hard time—no pun intended. Matt, being older, handled the attention better. On the other hand, since he was a father, the girls felt more comfortable with him."

"Was there one of the three that Natalie gravitated toward?" Even as I ask the question I dread the idea of having this conversation with Helen. She still sees Natalie as a little girl. The last thing I want to do is cause her more pain but I fear before the truth is fully uncovered, there will be more hurtful revelations.

My mutinous brain forces me to consider Heather and her brothers. One of the teachers is their father. Somehow I cannot work up any potential sympathy for her or for Mark. The Beaumont offspring, discounting the younger brother, were always bullies. Their superior attitudes evidently were coded into their genes. Those unpleasant traits came from somewhere. It's easy to point a finger at Lorraine, their mother. As for their father, I don't really remember him either. He was a high school teacher and by the time I was in middle school he had died.

"If she did, I never saw it. Matt was popular with all the kids, boys and girls alike. I don't know if you remember but he was in an accident around the same time Natalie and Stacy went missing. Wait." Her face creases in concentration. "I believe it was that same day. He was never the same after that. Looking back, I'm confident his brain injury caused the dramatic changes in his personality."

"He suffered a traumatic brain injury?" Letty and I talked

about Beaumont having had an accident. I vaguely remember him returning to school with a cane.

"Oh I think so. He was in a coma for a while. They wouldn't have known as much about the brain injuries back then. It was a terrible accident. His right leg was broken to pieces, there was internal bleeding. It was a real mess. Oh yes, and there were a couple of fractures to his spine."

I'm well acquainted with injuries to the spine. "So no one ever mentioned any trouble with Natalie?"

"Never." She smiles at me. "Your sister really was an extraordinary young woman."

Unfortunately we need more than that. "I realize I'm putting you in a tight spot, but let's theorize for a moment. If this person who was pressuring her was a teacher, who would you look at first?"

Sympathy fills the other woman's eyes and I want to scream. I need her help not her pity.

"Keep in mind that I saw nothing untoward from any of my colleagues."

"I understand. I'm not trying to prod you into pointing a finger at anyone, I just don't want to waste time. I'm only looking for the right direction moving forward."

"But, if forced to point out the most likely candidate or candidates, I would say DeSoto or Caldwell—simply because they were younger at the time and not as experienced in handling the issues that come with teaching teenagers."

"Do you have any suggestions on how I might approach DeSoto? I had Caldwell for Algebra and Geometry, but I didn't have any classes with DeSoto."

Larson checked her watch. "Caldwell has his planning period next hour. You can probably catch him then or after school. He still has the same classroom."

"First floor overlooking the quad, right?"

"That's the one." Larson calls one of the girls over and

tells her she's in charge. "Come on, DeSoto's over on the base-ball field."

"Thanks. Your help means a lot."

As we walk toward the field, she says, "Just so you know, DeSoto came out about ten years ago. He's gay."

"Was he ever married? Maybe he had a girlfriend?" Just because he finally announced to the world that he was gay, didn't mean he wasn't involved with numerous females first.

"Never married but there was a girlfriend a few years before he came out of the closet. Another teacher. Over in Huntsville. They've remained friends and she's married with a van full of kids now."

As we reach the baseball field I spot DeSoto. He is still a handsome man and extraordinarily fit. He wears the khaki shorts and white polo shirt that appears to be the Phys Ed staff uniform. A sprinkling of gray highlights his dark hair at his temples. His face is pleasant as he turns toward us. I hope he can offer some insight into Natalie's life but I have my doubts. Since he worked with the boys—still does apparently —Natalie wouldn't have interacted with him often. Then again, there were the ball games and she was a cheerleader.

"Coach DeSoto," Larson says as we approach. "Do you remember Emma Graves? Natalie's little sister."

The coach looks me up and down. "Why of course I do." He thrusts out his hand. "Emma, I've been watching you on the news."

Nothing like being a celebrity. I shake his hand. "Then you know I'm trying to learn more about what happened to Natalie."

A frown furrows his brow. "I've heard talk about you and Letty reexamining the case. I hope you find what you're looking for."

The sincerity in his brown eyes is refreshing. I'm certain he means what he says.

"I'm looking for someone who was around Natalie frequently who might remember any issue she was having."

His eyebrows rear up. "Issue? Natalie was the model student. I don't think she had issues." He looks to Larson. "Did I miss something?"

"She was having trouble with someone," Larson says. "She told me this older man was pressuring her. Did you hear any rumors to that effect or about any trouble she might have been experiencing?"

DeSoto's face reflects his regret at the news. "I don't recall ever hearing anything even remotely negative about Natalie." A sad smile lifts his expression. "She was always a ray of sunshine. Genuine and caring." He exhales a heavy breath. "I wish I could be of some help but I don't recall anything like that."

As if he only then realizes the real reason I might be talking to him, his face falls again. "In case you're wondering, I was at a spring training camp in Tuscaloosa with our football team. School records will confirm those dates."

"I'm talking with anyone who spent time with Natalie on a regular basis, Mr. DeSoto," I offer. "Please don't take my questions the wrong way."

He nods. "I understand. I would do the same thing."

I thank the both of them and head for the main building and Mr. Caldwell's room. The central corridor divides the first floor in half. Caldwell's classroom is on the left in the east wing. Most of the math classes were held there. The west wing is, ironically, where the history and government classes were held.

I scan the numbers on the lockers until I spot the one I had senior year. I pause and touch the cool navy metal. Brad and I stole kisses behind this door. Photos of us and of me and Letty filled the interior. I still keep that one photo of me and Nat. No matter where my work has taken me, I have always kept it with me. It sits in a frame on my mantel back in my

Boston apartment. I turn around and stare out the windows onto the quad. The building forms a massive square around the inner quad where picnic tables and benches as well as fountains and mounds of beautiful flowers fill an outdoor space meant for studying and creating a sense of contentment.

I remember crossing the quad on the way to the cafeteria and almost always I would spot Natalie sitting at one of the fountains surrounded by friends.

My heart feels heavy as I continue down the hall to Caldwell's classroom. I look through the glass in the door and spot him at his desk, head bent over a stack of papers. I knock on the door and he looks up. I wave, doubtful that he will recognize me.

He motions for me to come in and I do.

I close the door behind me and produce a smile. "Mr. Caldwell, I'm sorry to bother you."

"Emma Graves." He rises and walks toward me. "I've been watching you on the news."

"I keep hearing that." I don't know why everyone makes it sound like a good thing.

Rather than offer his hand he pulls me into a hug. Like DeSoto, he has kept in shape and is still quite good looking.

He releases me and gestures to the nearest desk. "Have a seat. What brings you back to school?"

I settle into a desk located directly in front of his. As he sits his expression tells me he has just realized why I'm at the school.

"You're looking for information about what happened to Natalie. I thought this new evidence proved James Cotton is the one who took her and Stacy."

"Letty and I still have questions."

"Well, ask away." He turns his hands up in an open gesture. "Any way I can help, I'm happy to do so."

I decide on a different approach for Caldwell. "You and Coach DeSoto were quite popular with the girls back then."

He laughs. "They liked yanking our chains, that's for sure."

I smile. "A lot of girls had crushes on the two of you."

He purses his lips and nods. "True."

"Was Natalie one of those girls?"

"Natalie was a brilliant young woman and beautiful," he says. "We had many great discussions on logic, but she never looked at me as anything other than her teacher. I believe the same can be said for Coach DeSoto. Natalie was not your typical teenage girl. She was far too mature for childish crushes."

His enthusiasm and kindness make me feel guilty for coming into his classroom and asking these questions. But this is something I have to do. "I have a couple of witnesses who believe she was having trouble with an older man. That man may have been pressuring her in some way. Did you get any feeling from her that she might be under duress?"

He considers my question for a time. "I will say that Natalie and I had a talk the week she disappeared about her grades."

"Her grades? My sister was a straight A student." I didn't mean for the words to come out so defensive but they did.

He smiles, the expression sad. "She was. I was one of the teachers who recommended she and Stacy be awarded an honorary diploma. They were both very smart. But Nat's grades slipped just a little her last month of school. She was still making A's but there was a measurable drop. I asked her about it and she just shook her head and said life got in the way sometimes."

"Did any of her other teachers mention this issue?" It was the first I had heard about it. I'm certain Helen would have mentioned something this relevant.

"It was the same across all her course work. Nothing significant but the drop was there. We all figured Nat had her first boyfriend or something. It happens to everyone, boy or girl, eventually. No one was concerned, but I felt compelled to nudge her a little."

"She didn't mention any particular life issue getting in her way?"

He shakes his head. "She did not."

I bite my lip and then take the plunge. "Mr. Caldwell, do you mind if I ask where you were the day Natalie disappeared?"

Another of those sad smiles tugs at his lips. "I was right here until seven that evening conducting SAT prep classes. I was supposed to have those classes every evening that week, but I rescheduled so I could help with the search. I'm sure the school has a record of it somewhere."

"Thank you, Mr. Caldwell." I stand, my vision glazing with tears. "I really appreciate your time."

I head for the door.

"The truth is, Emma, Stacy is the one I was most concerned about."

His voice stops me cold in my tracks. I turn back to him. "How do you mean?"

"I probably shouldn't be talking about this to anyone besides the police or her father." He shakes his head, stares at the floor a moment. "But if it'll help you and Letty find what you're looking for, I'll take the risk."

"Letty is the only person who will know whatever you tell me." I make this promise understanding that I may not be able to keep it completely, but I will try my best.

"Stacy went through something in the middle of the first semester that school year. Her grades fell dramatically. She seemed depressed, but she came around by Christmas. I wanted to talk to her father but she begged me not to. She said he'd been going through some issues of his own since her mother died the year before. Frankly, I assumed at the time that was her problem as well and maybe it was. I urged her to speak to the school counselor but she never did." He stands and moves toward me.

This is exactly why Letty and I decided to question everyone—even those like this man who had confirmed, airtight alibis. Time changes perspective, allows emotional distance and sometimes, *sometimes* it causes us to rethink what we felt was important in the past.

"Then that spring," he goes on, standing close enough for me to see the hope as well as the regret in his eyes, "she began behaving the same way all over again. Depressed, agitated. Once more I tried to talk to her about the issue but she wouldn't open up to me. After they disappeared I mentioned my concerns to Sheriff Claiborne—that was before he became the chief—but he chalked it up to her mother's death as well. Didn't seem to think it was relevant. Still," he shakes his head again, "looking back, it feels like it was more. I'll always wonder if I missed something. Of course she had Natalie. I imagine Natalie knew whatever was going on."

I would bet my life Natalie knew.

The question is: was that knowledge what got my sister and her best friend killed?

27

MIDAFTERNOON LETTY AND I RENDEZVOUS AT THE FARM TO compare notes. Mr. Timmons left for his hotel in Huntsville. Letty is dubious about his participation. I'm undecided but I trust her instincts on the matter. She would certainly have a better sense for this sort of thing than me.

"You're worried Timmons is pretending to help so he can keep Claiborne or whoever informed about what we're doing."

"Yeah." Letty sips her coffee. "Too many missing pieces lead back to Claiborne. Like information from witnesses that was never documented in any of the detectives' reports—that was Claiborne, I checked. I don't know. It feels like a good portion of the original investigation was glossed over because they thought they had their man. Going through the motions was just for appearances."

My dad had trusted Claiborne. Mother still does as far as I know. She has never mentioned any scandals related to him or his position as chief of police now or sheriff then. But I have been gone a very long time and Letty has been right here. As certain as I am that she is biased to some degree since Claiborne is the one who first pointed a finger at her father, she is the sheriff. She is also a woman, and she didn't reach that position without being very, very good at her job.

"Would Claiborne be that careless or are you suggesting he purposely ignored details that pointed to someone besides your father?" Even the top cop was only human. He wanted his citizens to feel safe, he wanted to close the case—maybe even if there was a chance he had the wrong man.

Letty sets her coffee aside and walks to the window over the kitchen sink. "I honestly don't know, but what I do know is a shoddy investigation. The statements made by at least three people are missing. Either they were never added to the case file or they were later lost or removed. None of the interviews were recorded. Alibis were checked off a list and at times not fully documented."

She lapses into silence. I imagine she is struggling to conquer her emotions. I wait. The scent of fresh brewed coffee tugs at my senses so I grab a mug. Might as well have a shot of caffeine to add to my jumpiness. I savor the dark, rich flavor and consider how to frame my next query.

"Tell me about the current political hierarchy in Jackson Falls." This is a good starting place.

"Heather, as you know, is the mayor, but I'm pretty sure her mother still has a hand in running that office." She turns to me, leans against the counter. "The city council is filled with the usual suspects, more friends of Lorraine. Basically, the same people who've always run Jackson Falls still do. The town's hierarchy hasn't changed that much since we were kids. Hell, since my grandparents were kids."

Like my grandparents, Letty's are all long dead but I get what she's saying. "Maybe that explains what Lorraine meant with that veiled threat she tossed at me when I met Helen for lunch today."

I've already filled Letty in on what I learned from the teachers I interviewed. Lorraine's hateful words were the

furthest things from my mind after hearing what Caldwell had
to say about Stacy Yarbrough.

Suddenly Lorraine's words feel far more relevant than they
did a few hours ago.

*For every action, there is always a reaction. Everything we do in this
life has consequences, Emma. Unlike you, Letty lives in a small town
where certain powerful influences make the important decisions. Perhaps
you might serve your friendship with Letty best by reminding her of all she
and her mother have to lose.*

"You ran into Lorraine at Sweet Tea & Biscuits?"

"Sort of. I was going inside and she said hello." I tell Letty
the rest. As I speak, I watch the anger flare in my friend's eyes.

She opens her mouth to say something then snaps it shut
and holds up a hand for me to give her a moment. I hate that
I had to repeat those obnoxious words but this is not the time
for paraphrasing the truth. We have to operate on the facts,
good or bad.

"Screw her," Letty growls.

I nod. "I couldn't have said it better myself." I take a
breath. "But she does have a point."

"Screw her point." Letty paces the floor now.

"Moving on," I suggest, "my biggest question coming
away from those interviews is why hasn't Yarbrough
mentioned the trouble his daughter had the first semester of
the school year?"

"He doesn't know."

Letty states this with complete conviction and, considering
what I've seen in recent days, I have to agree. Delbert
Yarbrough would have torn the school apart if he had
believed for one minute that his daughter had been in any way
harmed or harassed by another student or a teacher. Our
mothers would remember the fracas. Caldwell did say that
Stacy begged him not to tell her father and there was nothing
in the documented interviews of the case file about the trouble. I shake my head. Yarbrough had no way of knowing.

Apparently there were a lot of things the families of the victims didn't know.

Letty stops her pacing, her expression a study in concentration. "If our killer was a teacher, based on what you learned we can rule out DeSoto and Caldwell for sure. We've already ruled out two of the others." Letty searches my face one long moment before she continues, "That leaves Matthew Beaumont and we know that he was in an accident that same day."

I nod. "Larson mentioned his accident. He died a few years later."

"Five years later," she confirms. "My mom was their housekeeper back then, remember? She cleaned that house the very same day he died. He was at home sick—she said that happened a lot those last couple of years. She thinks he was addicted to painkillers. He was a mess. Lorraine is probably the only reason the school didn't fire him. Anyway, the kids came home after school and found him dead."

"Damn." Why didn't I remember those details? "I guess her being mayor at the time, she could keep all those unsavory details quiet."

"Oh yeah. And Mom said she played the grieving widow to the hilt. She never remarried, you know, just focused on her kids and being mayor—not necessarily in that order." Letty frowns as if she's trying to recall some other relevant detail. "I overheard her talking recently about her engagement. She said that her kids were settled and it was time for her to indulge herself for a change. With Heather in the mayor's seat and Marshall, her youngest, sitting pretty in the area's top law firm, she was just happier than a dead pig in the sunshine. Course that was before Mark had to be whisked off to rehab again last month."

"I told you I ran into Mark the other day." I make a face. "At *Johnny's* on Sunday."

Letty gives me a look. "Do I want to know why you were at Johnny's?"

"Probably not, but Mark was there and he looked like hell."

"Yeah, he has problems. Except, on paper," Letty explains, "he's the model citizen. He works for the city, runs the Environmental Department, which is a fancy way of saying he oversees garbage and recycling. He's been married three times, been in rehab about a dozen times and he lives in a house in the historic section of Decatur that his momma bought. She doesn't like him too close to the rest of the family since he's prone to wild parties and drinking binges."

"How does he run the Environmental Department?" I ask, using air quotes for emphasis.

"His sister makes sure things run smoothly."

"With all those problems of her own," I venture, "why does Lorraine care what we're doing? Beyond not wanting the investigation conducted under her watch to look bad, what's her issue?"

Letty laughs but her face turns immediately somber. "Maybe Lorraine's afraid we'll bring up some unsavory suggestion about her dead husband since he was one of Natalie and Stacy's teachers—he is the only one we haven't ruled out. Now definitely isn't a good time for her to be seen in even the most remote bad light. The wedding date hasn't been set and her man has to get himself reelected."

"So," I take a mental step back and evaluate what we have, "if the trouble Natalie and/or Stacy were having originated in school with an older man—possibly a teacher—we're left with Matthew Beaumont. If the accident was his alibi, then we shouldn't waste our time and Lorraine shouldn't care. Either way, my only question to you is: when and where was this accident? We might as well rule him out by confirming his alibi the same way we have the others."

"Only a mile or two from his house on…" Letty's gaze connects with mine. "On Indian Creek Road."

We both know the fact that he lived on *that* road doesn't make him the one. We also both recognize that we're grasping at straws with every step we make in this unofficial investigation. But we have to follow every lead. We agreed in the beginning that our investigation would include everyone, that we wouldn't leave anyone out.

That includes Lorraine Jackson Beaumont's dead husband.

I DRIVE to Indian Creek Road while Letty goes to her office to get a copy of the accident report. She'll catch up with me. Since I have some time, I make a detour past the Yarbrough home. I even pull into the driveway. All is quiet. No sign of his truck. My fingers tighten around the steering wheel, but rather than get out, I turn around and head back to Indian Creek. Letty is expecting me and I don't need to go off halfcocked and break into the man's house.

No matter how much I want to.

As I reach the Jackson home—the house will always be referred to as the Jackson home since Lorraine's forefathers built it—I slow. Beaumont was leaving home when he had the accident, that much we know. I turn around in the driveway and head back in the direction of town.

As I round the curve I spot Letty's Jeep a quarter of a mile away, on this side of the bridge. I pull onto the shoulder and she does the same. We climb out and meet at the yellow line. Tension crackles between us. As certain as I am that this is likely just another dead end, it feels like more. Or perhaps it's simply because we're on this road…so close to that damned cave. She turns the pages of the accident report until she finds the map the deputy created.

"Deputy Tubbs said Beaumont took the curve too fast." Letty gestures back in the direction I'd come. "He went off the road into that ravine."

We walk the few hundred feet to the location listed in the report, then to the edge of the road and peer into the deep ditch. I can see why he was so badly injured.

"Shit." I turn to Letty.

She looks from the report to me and shakes her head. "Couldn't have been Beaumont. His accident occurred about the same time as the bus crash. Both accident times are only estimates, but the timing is too close to believe Beaumont left school, picked up Natalie and Stacy, took them somewhere and then came back to this location and had his accident."

"Damn. It feels like every direction we take leads nowhere." Frustration expands inside me.

Letty crams the map and the report into her back pocket. "We have to be missing something."

"We've been focusing on the idea that the person who took Natalie and Stacy was a man—the same man who may have been giving one or both trouble at school."

Letty's lips slowly form a smile. "You're thinking maybe it was a woman, a woman who wanted to protect her man."

"Lorraine would do anything to protect her family." I'm off and running. The possibilities rush into my brain. "Even if it wasn't her husband, what if it was Mark? He was seventeen or eighteen at the time and full of himself. Maybe he picked up Natalie and Stacy and did something horrible, then called his dad for help. Dad has an accident rushing to his aid so Mommy has to finish the job."

I hate throwing Mark under the bus but he does have issues. Big issues based on what Letty has told me and they started around that same time. Whatever he did or didn't do, we have to rule him out. It's the only way to be sure.

"Oh my God," Letty pops her forehead with the heel of her hand, "I should have thought of that. Maybe Mr. Beau-

mont was pressuring Natalie and Stacy to drop whatever issue
one or both had with his son. They wouldn't drop it and the
son decides to clean up his own mess only he goes overboard
and..." She lets out an unsteady breath. "And he kills them or
someone helps him kill them and then they have to hide the
bodies."

"Oh damn." My heart is racing. "Do you think Lorraine
could commit cold blooded murder?"

Letty nods. "Yeah, I do."

She frowns, drags her cell from her pocket. "Yarbrough is
sitting on the road outside the Shepherd's home."

"The Baldwin girl lives two houses down, right?"

She nods in answer. "If he has something to do with their
disappearance, maybe he's feeling remorse. I think it's time he
and I had another talk. You want to come with me?"

"I believe I'll visit our old friend Heather."

"Don't tip our hand about Mark," Letty warns. "We're
running out of potential leads. The last thing we need is
Lorraine covering up any more tracks."

My friend needn't worry. If there's one thing I am very,
very good at, it's hiding the truth.

THE MAYOR'S office was moved to an elegant corner shop on
the square about a hundred years ago. Walton Mercantile
went out of business after the owner died and the historic
property came on the market. The Jackson family bought the
corner shop with its massive windows that look out over two
sides of the square and donated it to the city for the purpose
of making sure their accommodations were suitable.

The lobby is elegantly decorated and the receptionist is
young and attractive. She smiles and welcomes me to the
mayor's office. Within moments of my arrival I'm sitting in
Heather Beaumont Turner's office. Rich wood paneled walls

and mahogany furnishings are softened by luxurious curtains and elegantly upholstered chairs. Awards and prized photo ops with distinguished businessmen and other politicians line the walls.

"I saw you and Letty on the news yesterday." Heather smiles but it's fake. "You seem to be showing up there more and more." She looks me up and down, from my braided hair to my well-worn jeans.

"I promise it's not because I want to be there," I assure her. "It's the bones."

Another of those plastic smiles nudges at her lips. "You always were *different*."

"I can't deny that one. But this time it's not really about me. Everyone is poised and ready to finally know the truth about what happened to my sister and her friend Stacy." I push out of my chair and walk to the shelves where framed photographs of her family sit. "Your children are beautiful."

Of course they would be, both she and Brad are attractive.

"Thank you. We're very proud of them."

I notice a photo of Mallory's daughter and Heather's brother Marshall. "I guess you and Mallory mended your longtime rift."

Heather and Mallory were never really friends—Mallory was far older than her. But there was a time when Mallory and Mark were inseparable. Then suddenly Mallory started calling him brace face and began using lunch period to point out every pimple that appeared on his face. It wasn't until the drive over here that I remembered Natalie telling Mother about Lorraine showing up at school to put an end to the bullying. I wonder now what Mark did to Mallory to make her so angry.

I don't see any relevance to the truth Letty and I are looking for but I can't help thinking that dear old Mallory likely contributed to Mark's journey toward alcoholism and whatever other addictions he suffers. Kids can be so cruel, especially bitches like the one watching me so intently at the moment.

"We're family now," she says in response to my comment about Mallory but her tone is brittle.

I pick up a photo of her mother and father from before his accident, study it a moment and then settle it back into its spot. "Do you still miss him? I'm not sure I'll ever stop missing my dad."

I wander back to the chair in front of her desk.

"I still miss him, yes. He influenced so many lives."

I smile, hoping mine doesn't look as fake as hers did a few seconds ago. "He did. I'm sure your brothers had a particularly hard time after his accident, especially Mark. Wasn't that his first trip to rehab?"

Anger flashes in her eyes. "We all did. As *you* well know, we all have our own coping mechanisms."

"Maybe I'm remembering it wrong. I was thinking your father was rushing to help Mark—his car had broken down or something like that—when he had the accident." A little theory I made up but it sounded plausible enough.

"No," she said pointedly. "He was hurrying back to the school. There was an emergency with one of his students. If not for the accident, he would have been with the search teams forming to look for you and the others."

"That's right. It was that same day." I shrug. "You know my memory of that day is a little foggy sometimes."

"Understandable." She glances at her Rolex. "Is there something I can do for you, Emma. I do have another meeting."

"No, not really. It's just that Brad and I spent some time catching up the other day and he mentioned getting together while I'm here. I thought I'd better check your calendar." The pinched look on Heather's face is priceless. "You know, I think it was Mallory who said the two of you have an anniversary coming up. Anyway, maybe we can have dinner while I'm in town. Share a toast to your anniversary."

"Sounds fabulous." Her lips thin as she picks up her cell and taps the screen. "I'll check mine and Brad's calendars and get back to you."

"I look forward to it."

I walk out of her office and exit the building with a new sense of purpose. It has been a really long time since I felt this good. Who knew making Heather Beaumont Turner second guess her husband as well as whatever alliance she and Mallory have formed would feel so good.

I'll bet she's chewing out Brad's ass right this second.

As soon as I settle behind the wheel of Dad's truck, my cell rings.

Helen.

"Hey, what's up?"

"Mr. Brewer called me. He wanted to get a message to you. He said he needs to speak with you as soon as you have time."

Anticipation fires through me. "Does he still live in that house down the block from the school?"

"He does."

"I'm heading there now."

Helen asks if I'll be home for dinner and I promise I will. I wonder if Natalie ever mentioned Stacy having trouble. I ask Helen before letting her go.

"Not that I recall. Have you learned something that suggests otherwise?"

"I'm not sure yet, maybe. We'll talk more when I get home."

I check with Letty on the drive over to the Brewer house. She brings me up to speed on Yarbrough. He explained that he'd decided to sit for a while on the street where the missing girls live in hopes of gaining inspiration for the theme of his next protest but Letty isn't buying it. She intends to follow him until he's back home. We agree to check in with each other as soon as I talk to Mr. Brewer.

The Brewer home is a modest ranch style house that was built after a nineteenth century house burned to the ground. In the downtown area any modern homes were built where the older, historic homes burned or were torn down. Mr. Brewer's truck is in the drive.

He meets me at the door and welcomes me inside. As soon as we're seated, his wife insists on bringing me a glass of iced tea.

When she leaves the room, Brewer rests his gaze on mine. "I could hardly sleep last night for thinking about your question."

"I'm sorry if I caused you any discomfort. That wasn't my intent." I say this even as my pulse hammers in hopes of learning an important detail—one that might help Letty and me find the truth.

He puts his hand up and shakes his head. "No worries. Anyway, it was about two this morning when I remembered an incident. But there was only one and it wasn't exactly a big production. It was over in an instant."

Anticipation is killing me but I strive for patience while Mrs. Brewer serves the tea.

When she returns to the kitchen, he says, "This was in March of that year. Maybe three weeks before Natalie and Stacy went missing. I remember stepping out of the janitor's closet and seeing Beaumont and Natalie standing outside his classroom. That in itself wasn't so unusual. The teachers often counsel their students in the hallways. It gives some sense of privacy from the rest of the class without the formality of going to the principal's office."

"Was there something about what you saw that made you feel uncomfortable?" I can scarcely hear myself think with the blood roaring in my ears as it does. *Please let this be something useful and not another dead end.*

"The discussion looked intense—as if they were arguing."
He shrugs. "Beaumont reached for her arm like he meant to
calm her down or console her somehow but Natalie jerked
away from him as if she feared he might hurt her. She said
something that looked angry then she stormed back into the
classroom."

Goosebumps pebble on my skin, my heart thumps harder.
I clear my throat and ask, "You believe they were quarreling?"

"At the time, I didn't think too much of it. But, looking
back maybe I was wrong to ignore it. This wasn't the typical
teacher-student dressing down. This was almost intimate. Like
a boyfriend and girlfriend arguing. Or maybe a husband and
wife."

His words disturb me deeply. Anger joins the wild mixture
of anticipation and uncertainty. I take a moment to find my
voice again. "Thank you, Mr. Brewer. Please call me if you
think of anything else."

He walks me to the door and I cannot get away fast
enough. I climb into the truck and start the engine. I head
toward home, my mind reeling, my stomach lurching. I drive
barely a block when I am forced to slam on the brakes and
veer to the curb.

I plaster my hand over my mouth and grapple for something. My hand clenches on the plastic bag from my stop at
the mini market yesterday or the day before.

I get the bag open just in time to vomit.

I squeeze my eyes shut as my stomach roils again at the
idea of my beautiful, perfect sister being touched by a man
she should have been able to trust.

Her teacher.

28

"I'M HEADING TO MOM'S. MEET ME THERE."

I listen to the voicemail twice. Letty sounds heartsick. I slow and do a U-turn. The taste of bile is bitter in my mouth. I reach for the water bottle in the seat but it's empty.

Lowering the window a bit, I lean toward it and let the cool air hit my face. My stomach still roils. I waffle between wanting to cry and to scream. I always felt safe at school. Sure some of the other kids tortured me but I never felt *unsafe*.

I refuse to believe my sister would have done anything to purposely tempt any teacher with her body. I can't be sure about Stacy. Ms. Larson is right about that age being a difficult one. That place between childhood and womanhood. Hormones and developing bodies. Passions and dreams.

But Natalie wouldn't have done such a thing.

Would she?

I try to remember how I felt between fourteen and sixteen but it was different for me. I was stick thin and gangly. I was not poised and full of confidence as Natalie had been. I spent most of that time wanting to crawl into a hole and stay there. Natalie was performing on a dance competition team and giving speeches as part of the student council. It's impossible to find a commonality between us for that period. Except no one has memories of Natalie suggesting that sort of behavior. Even Ms. Larson said she wasn't like the other girls her age.

That has to mean something.

Considering Mr. Beaumont's accident, it's far more logical that it was Mark who went after Natalie and Stacy. The cover up—framing James Cotton—was about protecting the son.

It all makes sense. Mark Beaumont's inability to be the kind of good son expected to sprout from the loins of Lorraine Jackson Beaumont is precisely the reason Heather was groomed for bigger things while Mark was ensconced in a controlled space and sent off to rehab as necessary.

The blue lights in front of Ginny Cotton's home have me slowing down. Letty's Jeep is there and so is Mother's Cadillac. I pull to the side of the road and park. The sun has set but there's sufficient light for me to see the hateful words painted across the front of the clapboard siding.

A MONSTER LIVED HERE.

Hurt crushes against me. I want to demand who would do such a thing but I know—those who are convinced that an innocent man abducted and murdered two young girls.

I will no more believe James Cotton was a monster than I will that my perfect sister was a temptress who lured her teacher or his son into a forbidden relationship.

As I approach the house the two uniformed officers are leaving, the cruiser backing out of the drive. Helen has her arms around Ginny. Letty stands in the driveway staring at the words.

"Was it Yarbrough again?" I ask as I reach her.

Letty shakes her head. "He hasn't been anywhere near here. I went to his house after he left Stackhouse Road. I was pretty frank with him. He let me in the house to have a look around."

At my look of surprise, she adds, "The basement, too. No missing girls. Nothing at all suspicious."

I can't say that I'm disappointed she didn't find the girls. I hoped Yarbrough hadn't gone that far. But that means the girls are still missing and no one has a damned clue who took them.

I stare at the viciousness strewn across Ginny's house "Maybe one of his protest followers did this."

I'm grasping at straws. Anyone in the area who thought James Cotton was guilty and who had the balls could have done this. Especially with the news reporting over and over that James Cotton was the killer. As for Yarbrough, I'm pretty much convinced he's leaning toward our side where James is concerned.

Letty shrugs. "Doesn't matter. The whole town believes it was him."

"Hey." I step in front of her, blocking her view of the malice. "Not everyone."

I quickly bring her up to speed on what Brewer said. It's becoming more and more obvious that the only trouble Natalie had in her life was with one particular teacher—Matthew Beaumont. And possibly his son, Mark.

"We might be on the right track," Letty agrees. "I talked to the guy, Kellie Pike, from the junkyard who picked up Beaumont's car after the accident." Letty steps closer to me and lowers her voice. "He says he got the call to recover the car about eight o'clock that night. He had to wait until the next morning to do it because of how dark it was and how deep that ditch is."

"Is that typical?" I've never been involved in a car accident. I have no idea how long after it occurs that a wrecker service is called. "Or are you thinking the accident happened later than the time specified in the report?"

Letty glances beyond me. The mothers are coming. "I don't know but I'm damned well going to find out."

"The two of you have to stop."

We both turn at Helen's stern words. With nothing left to

illuminate the macabre scene except the porch light I can't see her eyes but the anger and something like fear weigh heavy in her voice. Ginny leans against her as if she can no longer bear the burden pressing down on her. I want to beat the hell out of whoever did this but first I intend to know what bug crawled up my mother's butt.

"What does that mean, Helen?" I demand.

Letty touches my elbow. "I'm going out to the shed to find some paint."

"Get two brushes," I tell her. If she doesn't have any I'm pretty sure there's at least one in the toolbox in the back of Dad's truck.

"You're treading into things you don't understand," Ginny says before Helen can figure out how she wants to answer my demand.

I walk toward the two women who suddenly look far older than their years. Part of me wants to hug them tight and protect them from this horror but the other part wants to shake the secrets out of them. I am sick of the secrets and the lies—including my own—lurking like ghosts among the four of us.

"What things?" I look at Ginny rather than Helen. She's the one who made the ominous statement. We're standing no more than three feet apart, and I watch her face, her eyes for tells. The very ones I work hard to keep off my face when I'm lying.

"Things you don't need to know about," she says, fury snapping in her dark eyes.

"Lorraine showed up at my door," Helen says, drawing my attention to her. "A few minutes after I called you with that message from Niles Brewer. She says you went to see Heather and upset her with questions about her father and her brother."

I scrutinize the two women—these lifelong friends. "What if I did? Is there some reason you don't want me to hurt

Heather's or Lorraine's feelings? Something perhaps I should know about the past? Say twenty-five years ago?"

"You don't know what that woman is capable of," Ginny presses. She glances around me. "She can ruin Letty's career. I don't care what she does to me, but I won't have her tearing my girl's life apart."

Now I'm just flat out angry. "Like she did my sister's? Like she did Letty's father's?"

Ginny flinches.

"Emma," Helen warns.

I look from one to the other. Somehow, beyond my anger, I remind myself that Mother isn't well. Ginny might not be either. They're both getting older. I take a second to calm myself and then I ask, "What are you two hiding?"

Both stare at me like deer caught in the headlights of an oncoming truck.

"Found the paint and the brushes."

Letty's announcement shatters the tension and Helen ushers Ginny toward the front door.

"I'm taking Ginny inside for some tea," Helen says. "You girls can handle this."

I watch until the door closes behind them, fury still pumping through my veins.

"What was that all about?"

Lies, I want to say, but I don't.

"I'm not sure but I think those two are keeping something from us. Something important."

Letty hands me a brush. "I'm staying here tonight. I'll see what I can find out."

We begin the frustrating work of covering the black spray paint. It will take several coats of the white paint and I doubt that will cover it completely. We'll need a good stain block formula to do the job right. For now we can live with making the words more difficult to read.

I think of the grand home Brad and Heather built on the

lake and the prestigious home place where Lorraine lives. How would they feel if they woke up tomorrow and horrible words like these were painted across the fronts of their homes? I dip my brush into the can of white paint and stroke it across the foul words. No point in wondering because they will never know. They are protected by privilege, surrounded by the insulation of generations of wealth and powerful influence.

Well, I'm not afraid of Heather or her damned mother. I will keep digging until I unearth every buried secret and every hidden skeleton I can find with the Jackson or the Beaumont name on it.

Before I'm finished they will beg me to stop.

For the first time they will know how it feels to be at someone else's mercy.

I SIT IN THE BATHTUB, arms hugged around my knees. I have gone over all that Letty and I have learned and we still have nothing earth shattering. Nothing that proves there is another person of interest in the case. I have played *that day* over and over in my mind. I have relived the days and weeks after Natalie and Stacy's disappearance.

Nothing new bobs to the surface.

When the water grows cold, I climb out and dry off. I find my sweat pants and tee and drag them on. I have been so preoccupied I haven't even thanked Mother for keeping my laundry done. Since I brought a very few things it's only because she washes them every night that I have clean clothes. I don't know why I didn't bring more. My intent was to stay two weeks. But the goal was to stay holed up in the house. I didn't expect to be interviewing people and rushing around all over town like some PI. And I certainly didn't expect to be a feature in every damned news cycle since the day after I arrived.

I go to the top of the spiral stairs and listen. The house is silent. Helen has gone to bed. For several days now Letty and I have been going over those statements and reports from the original case file. We've studied the school yearbook from front to back. We've relived that time until we are both sick of thinking about it.

But there is one place I have not dared venture for fear Mother would be too upset. No matter how strong she appears as she did tonight standing in alliance with her friend, she just had a heart attack and I cannot forget that reality. I have to protect her to the degree possible.

So I creep down to the second floor. When we moved from the farm Natalie's room was left just as it was even though they decorated a room in this house for her. Used the same color paint, similar furniture and bedding. Then, a few years later Mother transported everything from Natalie's room at the farm to this house. She carefully placed each item just as if it had always been right here—just as Natalie left it. At the time I remember thinking it was weird but whatever made her happy was fine by me.

I reach the end of the hall on the second floor. My parents' room is at the other end so hopefully I won't wake her. Once in Natalie's room I close the door and flip on the light. I am immediately transported back twenty-five years. From the Bon Jovi posters to the cheerleading and dance trophies, the room looks exactly as I remember my sister's room. Mother went to great lengths to recreate the room unerringly.

The white bed with its pink canopy and spread is loaded with colorful pillows and stuffed animals. The two teen magazines that had come in the mail that month lay on the end of the bed, one opened to the exact page Natalie had been looking at before she left for school that day.

Across the room the shelves are filled with her favorite novels. Natalie loved historical novels. *Pride and Prejudice. Little*

Women. On her dresser there are tubes of lip gloss just like in the Baldwin girl's room. Make-up, nail polish and perfume. Her hairbrush. I finger the bristles.

I move to the closet. Her clothes are all there; except for the ones she wore the day she disappeared. The jeans along with her underthings and the pullover sweater she wore the day before she went away are in the laundry basket in the corner of her closet.

My fingers trail along the hanging blouses and tee shirts. Shoes and boots and sandals line the floor. I sit down and survey the many pairs. My sister was a clotheshorse.

I scoot over to the laundry basket and pick up the sweater. I hold it to my face and inhale deeply hoping to catch just the tiniest whiff of my sister. The lingering scent makes me smile. Maybe it's my imagination but I believe I can smell her. I reach for the jeans next. Levi's, of course. I smooth my hand over the soft denim. My eyes fill with tears when I think of all the wonderful things Natalie would have done with her life. She would have been such a good daughter.

"Way better than me."

I swipe away the tears and stare up at the shelves around the top of her closet. Colorful boxes hold many of her papers and keepsakes. I consider sorting through all those. Natalie didn't keep a journal. She insisted they were too cliché.

Deciding to prowl in those boxes I reach to toss the jeans back into the basket but I hesitate. A small lump has me digging through the pockets, one by one. In the right front pocket my fingers encounter folded paper. My heart starts that foolish pounding as I withdraw the find.

The paper has been folded into a small square. I open it very carefully and then I smile. It's a drawing of a rather unattractive bird. The bird is colored blue and in the upper right hand corner of the note is the sunshine. At the bottom of the page are three hand printed words, the letters poorly formed and hardly straight.

I love you.

My hands begin to tremble and I try very hard not to cry. I don't remember when I made this note for my sister but it makes me immensely happy that she carried it with her at least on that one day.

"She loved you."

I look up at my mother. She stands at the door in her pink flannel gown with those vintage pink foam rollers in her hair.

"I know." I refold the note and tuck it back into the pocket, then place the jeans in the basket.

I push to my feet and face my mother. "I won't stop until I finish this."

Rather than argue, Helen throws her arms around me and hugs me tight. Her body shakes and I realize she is crying.

As hard as I try to hold back my own tears, they fall like rain.

29

THURSDAY, MAY 17

"Will you and Letty be at the farm today?"

Mother's question stops me at the back door. She wants to know what our plan is for the day. I want to assure her we'll be fine. I don't want her to worry, but there is little I can say to give her what she wants.

She wants me to let it go.

I can't reconcile what she wants me to do with what needs to be done.

"Yes." I glance over my shoulder, give her a smile. "We'll be reviewing the case files again. I'll probably pick up a gallon of Kilz to go over the graffiti at Letty's mom's house."

"I know she'll appreciate your help."

I reach for the door.

She doesn't stop me this time.

I cross the porch, descend the steps and climb into Dad's truck. There is something comforting about being in his vehicle.

My cell vibrates in my pocket and I withdraw it, expecting to see Letty's name on the screen. The number is local but not one I recognize.

"Hello."

"This is Delbert Yarbrough."

The sound of his voice makes me shiver or maybe it's just the cool morning air. "Good morning, Mr. Yarbrough."

"I'd like to talk to you if you could come by my house this morning."

Anticipation rushes through me. "Sure. I can come now, if you'd like."

"We'll be waiting."

The call drops and I stare at the screen. *We'll be waiting.*

I start the truck and call Letty.

"I'm on my way," she says before I can speak.

She means the farm but our morning agenda has just changed. "Yarbrough called. He asked me to meet him at his house. He said 'we'll be waiting'."

"I'll meet you there."

I check the street and ease out of the driveway. I end up behind a school bus and have no choice but to make every stop for six blocks.

The kids in the backseat wave at me. I wave back. One sticks out her tongue, I do the same. A memory broadsides me. Natalie and Stacy in that backseat, huddled together. Laughing...no, crying. Stacy is crying. Natalie is consoling her. I push my glasses up my nose and turn back to my own window. We're almost home and leaves swirl across the road. It's almost Thanksgiving.

A horn blares and I blink, stare at the taillights of the bus disappearing down the street while I remain sitting still. I move my foot from the brake to the accelerator.

Something did happen to Stacy the fall before they went missing. Whatever it was, it flared up again in the spring.

I intend to ask Yarbrough. He wants to talk and so do I.

The ten minutes required to reach Indian Creek Road are the longest of the week. As I turn into his drive Letty pulls in behind me. His house comes into view and I slam on my brakes. Behind me, Letty does the same.

The WHNT news van sits not ten yards from the house.

"Son of a bitch."

If Letty wasn't right behind me I might just back out of the drive and leave. Instead, I roll forward and park several yards away from the WHNT van. Letty pulls up beside me. We meet in front of the vehicles.

Letty stares at the other vehicle. "What is he up to?"

I shake my head. "No idea."

As we round the van and head for the front porch, Lila Lawson and her cameraman climb out of the van's side door.

"Well," the reporter says, "this just gets more interesting by the minute."

"What're you doing here, Lawson?" Letty crosses her arms over her chest and blocks the steps.

"Mr. Yarbrough called and asked me to meet him here."

Letty and I exchange a look. I have a very bad feeling that we've been had.

I lead the climb up the front steps.

The door opens before I reach it.

Yarbrough stands in the doorway. If possible I think he looks far older than he did just two days ago.

"Come in."

I follow him inside. Once we're all in the living room, he says, "Have a seat. I have an announcement to make."

"Is it okay if we set up the camera for a live broadcast?" Lawson asks.

Christ, the woman cares about nothing but getting the story. Then again, that is her job, I suppose. But it doesn't make me like her.

Yarbrough shakes his head. "We're not doing this live. I'm giving you the exclusive but no camera." He jerks his head toward the front door. "He can wait outside."

Lawson is too smart to argue. She sends her cameraman out to the porch. The blinds are closed tight so he's not going to be able to sneak a shot.

Letty, Lawson and I settle on the sofa. I'm grateful Letty took the middle spot.

"May I use an audio recorder?" Lawson asks.

"I'll need to see it first." Yarbrough holds out a hand for the small recorder.

Damn! Can we not get on with this?

Satisfied there's no hidden camera, he passes the recorder back to Lawson.

"I called you here this morning to confess my part in a hurtful scheme that should never have happened."

My breath stalls in my chest. I feel myself leaning forward in anticipation.

Before Yarbrough can continue a door on the other end of the room opens and two teenage girls walk in.

Shepherd and Baldwin.

Letty launches to her feet. "Mr. Yarbrough, I need to warn you that you have the right to an attorney and that anything you say from this point may be held against you."

He holds up his hands. "I'm well aware of my rights, Sheriff Cotton."

Letty withdraws her cell and prepares to call for backup.

"Wait," Sharla Shepherd says.

Letty's fingers still.

"We have a statement we'd like to make." Deana Baldwin moves up beside her friend.

"One month ago," Shepherd begins, "Mr. Yarbrough started an uprising against the Jackson Falls PD in protest of the way the investigation of his daughter and Natalie Graves' disappearance was handled. Deana and I watched the news reports. All his efforts, all the support he rallied, brought about no reaction from the police department. It was as if they didn't care about the truth anymore—that Stacy and Natalie didn't matter."

Deana spoke then. "Two weeks ago our government teacher asked our class to do a project on something we think requires change within our government. We chose to focus on local government and how powerless the people of Jackson Falls really are. We decided to see exactly what it would take to force the police department to do what they should have done twenty-five years ago."

"We decided," Sharla continues, "to create a kind of reenactment of Stacy and Natalie's disappearance to see if that would prompt the proper reaction. We knew we couldn't do this alone since we would need a place to hide and food and water. So we came to Mr. Yarbrough for help."

I honestly don't know for whom to feel the sorriest—these girls whose harebrained plan was reinforced by a grown man who knew better or the grown man who was manipulated by two teenage girls.

"Mr. Yarbrough refused," Deana says as if she read my mind.

Yarbrough drops his head.

"That's when we told him we were proceeding with or without his help. Rather than see us trying to hide in the woods where we would not be safe and protected, he reluctantly offered his basement."

I knew it! The lip gloss belonged to one of them.

"Mr. Yarbrough," Sharla says, "in no way influenced our decision and he tried his best to get us to call our parents on several occasions. Now that we feel we have accomplished our mission, we're ready to go home."

I expect Yarbrough gave them an ultimatum after Letty's visit. Which is likely why he visited the road where they live yesterday. He knew from personal experience how the parents were feeling.

The parents are called as is the chief of police. Before the crowd can arrive I corner Yarbrough.

"Do you remember Stacy having some sort of trouble at school in the fall and then again in the spring before...?" It wasn't necessary to say the rest.

"What do you mean trouble?"

"A drop in grades. Maybe she was withdrawn, depressed?"

He shakes his head, then stops. "Wait, there was something going on right before Thanksgiving. She'd spent the night with Mallory and I thought maybe they had a fight. They didn't seem to hang around each other anymore after that. I asked her about it but she assured me it was nothing. You know how teenage girls can be." He glances at the Shepherd and Baldwin girls. "Unpredictable."

"Mr. Yarbrough," I glance at Letty who is questioning the girls, "you really should call your attorney."

He shakes his head. "I'm prepared to face the consequences of my actions."

I think of the warning Lorraine issued to me. What consequences has she faced for her actions? She is hiding something related to the day Natalie and Stacy went missing. I know it. Why else would she care how much digging Letty and I did?

My cell vibrates and I pull it from my hip pocket. Dangerous. I really need to change that to Jake Barnes or to the Priest.

I step away from the crowd and take the call. "What's up?"

"We need to talk. Can you meet me at Johnny's in about fifteen minutes?"

I frown. "Johnny's is open at this hour?"

He chuckles. "As a matter of fact he serves a very good breakfast and a mean mimosa."

I glance across the room, still a little stunned at what transpired this morning. "I'll be right there."

I make my way to Letty and whisper the news in her ear. She nods and urges me to go. I'm only too happy to do so. By the time the chief or sheriff or both get here, reporters will be crawling all over the place. I shudder at the thought.

JOHNNY'S HAS a few regulars but no real crowd. Jake is sitting at the bar. I'm surprised to see him in a sweatshirt and jeans. I slide onto the stool next to him.

"You hungry?"

I give him a look. "I'm staying with my mother. It's impossible to get out of the house without eating something in the mornings."

"Coffee then?"

"Sure."

He waves to the bartender and points to his cup and then to me.

"So you have something for me?" I sound like a cop speaking to one of my informants.

"I do."

I feel guilty holding back so before he shares his news I tell him about the girls. By the time I get to the point where he called me tears shine in his eyes. The reaction is so tender I can hardly stand it.

He grabs me and hugs me, almost pulling me off the stool. We draw awkwardly apart.

"This is great news."

I nod.

He clears his throat. "I spoke to Father Estes."

I don't ask but I wonder how much wine was involved— for the older man anyway.

"There was a man, of course you're aware I can't say who. In fact, the only reason I can speak to you at all on the matter is that this man chose not to confess his sins or to seek absolution from Father Estes. He only wanted to talk so what I am about to share with you is nothing more than the gist of a casual conversation between two men sitting on the porch having a few beers."

It hits me at that moment just how far I have pushed this man of God. It's selfish of me to have gone down this road. "I shouldn't have asked you to do this." I say the words before my brain can overrule my heart. "If you feel we shouldn't discuss your talk with Father Estes, I'll understand."

I hold my breath and wait for his decision. He opens his mouth to speak, but the bartender appears to leave a steaming mug of coffee in front of me. My heart thuds painfully.

Jake looks around then goes on. "I can do this since the conversation was not privileged by the seal of confession and Father Estes knows that I'm sharing this with you. His only request was that I not *directly* reveal the name of the other person."

I nod eagerly, grateful for whatever he can give me.

"This man agonized over this terrible thing he had done. Father Estes was surprised by his sudden fall into the depths of despair when he'd never known this particular man to show such desolation. But during this dark period, whatever he had done, it weighed heavily on him."

Could he possibly be any slower getting to the point that might actually give me something useful? "And?"

Jake looks away. I catch his gaze in the mirror behind the bar. "This plunge into despair happened after Natalie and Stacy disappeared."

I shrug. "Could be coincidence." Surely that is not all he has to share.

He huffs a breath of frustration. "Father Estes believes his depression was related to the terrible *accident* he survived."

I turn my face to his, holding my breath all over again.

"But, I'm thinking it was more than that." He shifts to look at me and I see the worry in his eyes.

I jump off the stool. This time I do the hugging. "Thank you."

"Emma, listen to me."

I draw back but he keeps his hands on my arms, holding me close.

Then I remember our deal. "I know, I know. I promised to volunteer with you at the women's shelter."

A faint smile touches his lips. "Don't worry, I haven't forgotten." The smile vanishes. "Emma, there are people in this town who do not want you digging into the past. I worry about you."

I have no idea why my eyes are suddenly burning and my knees feel weak. What kind of priest would he be if he didn't worry about me?

"Perhaps," he offers, "you should reevaluate just how deep you are prepared to dig."

I smile, the real McCoy for the first time in a very long time. "Thank you for your concern, but I've spent my life digging up things, I'm not about to stop now."

He nods. "I thought you might say that." He reaches beneath the neck of his sweatshirt and fiddles with something. When his hands come away he drags a silver chain and medallion from his neck and reaches around mine.

The feel of cool metal settles against my chest.

"This is Saint Benedict. The patron saint against evil." He smiles. "I've got your back, Emma. And so does the Man upstairs."

30

HELEN

I CAN'T ASK Ginny to stay out of work again today. She has already taken too much time off and today there's just no one to take her place. I was at the post office with her when the news aired that Naomi's and Patricia's daughters turned themselves in. As thankful as I am, I can't help wishing there had been a happy ending for Natalie and Stacy.

No amount of wishing will change what happened.

Now I have to do the thing part of me has wanted to do for twenty-five years. Yet, to do so was to admit that Natalie was never coming back. Once I discovered she wasn't, I couldn't do this part for other reasons—one being the fact that I had no idea where her body was. I only knew that she was in a cave somewhere.

This morning shortly after Emma left, Chief Claiborne called and told me that Natalie's remains would be released to me tomorrow.

I can now make her final arrangements.

First thing after leaving the post office I drove to the cemetery and shared the news with Andrew. Our girl will finally be laid to rest next to him. When we chose our headstone, we selected one for Natalie as well. I wasn't sure if her remains would ever be found but if they were, I wanted her final resting place to be ready when the time came. The headstone will be delivered this afternoon.

I park in front of the funeral home and take a deep breath. This part is one I haven't done. A sense of excitement stirs inside me. Although there is no body to dress, I bring Natalie's favorite dress and the shoes that match. I even bring the little pink purse that she adored. And I have her necklace, the one she was wearing when she died. The bastard stole it from her and I intend for her to have it back.

Mr. Harlowe is waiting for me inside. I called and made sure he was available this morning. He had an appointment in Huntsville but he canceled it to meet with me. I appreciate his flexibility. I also trust him to help me make the best choices. I have waited a very long time to bring my daughter home.

I want everything to be perfect.

The brisk spring air cools my too warm face as I emerge from the car. I've tried awfully hard not to cry, but it's impossible. I retrieve the bag that contains Natalie's things from the backseat and square my shoulders.

As I walk toward the entrance another vehicle pulls into the lot. The familiar idle of the engine has me turning back to look. Andrew's truck sits beside my car. Emma bounds out of the driver's side door and rushes toward me.

"Why didn't you tell me? If Letty's mom hadn't called her, I…" She shakes her head.

No more crying. My eyes refuse to obey the command. "I didn't want to bother you. I saw you and Letty on the news. I'm so glad those girls are safe."

I realize tears are slipping down my cheeks but I cannot stop them. I dab futilely at them with my mother's handkerchief. It's the same one I used at Andrew's funeral Mass.

Emma hugs me tight. "I want to do this with you," she whispers in my ear.

We cry together for a few moments before drawing apart.

"Come along," I say. "Mr. Harlowe is waiting."

Together Emma and I select a beautiful pearl white coffin with a pale pink lining for Natalie. Mr. Harlowe was kind enough to arrange for Lisa from the Jackson Falls Floral Shop to be at our meeting. We select flowers and decide to have the funeral Mass on Monday at ten. I've already checked the date with Jake and he promised to see that the community knows about the arrangements. Lisa kindly offers to call a local caterer who will take care of the refreshments at the house after the burial.

As we leave the funeral home, Emma and I hug again.

"Thank you so much for doing this with me," I say. "It means more than you know."

"Why wouldn't I? She was my sister. Of course I wanted to help."

My sweet Emma. I look at her and her beauty takes my breath. I want so desperately for her to be happy. I don't want her to suffer any more nightmares. I want her to put this behind her and to move on, but she refuses until this is done.

I want so to end this here and now but I cannot risk Ginny's future, not to mention what it would do to Letty. If Ginny and I could only find a way to prove what we know the risk might be worth it.

"I have to meet Letty," Emma says.

"I hope the two of you are being careful," I remind her.

She nods but I know she's not listening.

Before turning away, she hesitates and asks, "At any time during the school year before *that day*," she begins, "did Natalie mention anything about Stacy having trouble?"

I think back, trying to recall but nothing comes to mind. "I don't remember anything being said. Why do you ask?"

"I just remembered Stacy crying on the bus. Natalie was

comforting her. Mr. Caldwell mentioned that Stacy had some difficulty that year. Maybe what he said triggered the memory. It might have been around Thanksgiving."

"I can't remember anything but girls that age often keep secrets from their mothers. Do you think this has something to do with what happened?"

"I don't know." Emma shakes her head. "Mr. Caldwell mentioned Stacy's trouble that year—depression and falling grades. Mallory had that falling out with Natalie and Stacy. Three different people have suggested that Natalie was somehow involved with an older man, perhaps a teacher, and Mr. Brewer witnessed an incident between Natalie and Mr. Beaumont."

The more Emma says the more terrified I grow. "Why haven't you mentioned any of this before?" My voice sounds hollow. My knees feel weak.

She shrugs. "It just all came together this morning. There's something there, I can feel it. I think their disappearance leads back to what was happening at school."

"I am certain Natalie was not involved with any older man." I bite my tongue at how bitter the words sound. "As for any trouble the girls had that year, Natalie never said a word except maybe once she mentioned being disappointed in Mallory." I shrug. "Thinking back, I think maybe Stacy was at our house around Thanksgiving that year, but I assumed she and her father were having a little trouble. It happens with teenagers. Especially considering she'd lost her mother around that same time the year before. But how in the world is any of that possibly relevant anyway?"

Emma searches my face and eyes and I know she's wondering why I would be angry or maybe she recognizes my lies. I've decided she is very good at spotting untruths.

"I don't know how it's relevant yet, but think about it. Mallory states in her interview with the police that Natalie is involved with an older man. A statement she later recanted.

Now Mallory's daughter is married to one of the Beaumont sons and her other daughter is on the city council, her win sealed by Lorraine's support. A tense exchange was witnessed between Matthew Beaumont and Natalie at school. Natalie disappeared and Matthew had a terrible accident followed almost immediately by his son Mark being rushed off to rehab. Oh and let's not forget that Lorraine warned me that actions have consequences. Seems to me the one common denominator in all of those things is the Beaumont name."

My heart rises into my throat.

"Gotta go, but if you think of anything call me."

I wave to my daughter as she drives away, then I sag against my car, my legs like rubber. Somehow my hand finds my cell deep in my purse. I call Ginny. When she answers it is all I can do to say the words.

"We can't wait any longer."

31

EMMA

I FIND Letty back at the farm.

"Sorry," I say as I close the door. My heart is still heavy from making the selections at the funeral home.

Letty looks at me as if I've lost my mind. "What're you apologizing for? You needed to be with Helen."

I grab a bottle of water from the fridge. "What happened with Yarbrough?"

"Claiborne arrested him for obstructing an official police investigation and harboring minors. I don't think he'll do any time. Probation for sure. The parents can always file civil suits. He made a mistake but it was a doozy."

"I'm just glad the girls are okay."

Letty waves her arms over the table and the pages and photos stacked there. "All of this comes down to just a few loose ends. First, we have Mallory *and* Mr. Caldwell saying that Stacy was having trouble that school year."

"Helen says she didn't know anything about that. She did remember that Stacy was at our house more often than usual

around that time. She thought there was trouble at home."
She also sounded odd to me. I am more convinced than ever
that Helen knows something she isn't sharing.

Letty nods. "Then we have Mr. Brewer saying he
witnessed a tense exchange between Natalie and Mr. Beaumont. Add to that the couple of folks who suggested Natalie
was involved with an older man and Lorraine's threats about
consequences."

"Like I told Helen," I speak up, "The common denominator is the Beaumont family."

"You would make a good cop." Letty grins. I laugh.

"Seriously, my money would be on Matthew Beaumont," I
confess. "Except for that accident. The runner up, in my opinion, is Mark."

"The accident is the one hitch," Letty agrees. "In fact,"
she picks up a report lying in front of her, "I couldn't sleep last
night for thinking about that hitch."

I feel sure part of what kept her awake was the damned
vandalism at her mother's home. I wonder if Lorraine Beaumont would stoop to vandalism. She'd probably just pay one
of her minions to do it.

"So," Letty says, "I reviewed the accident report again,"
she looks at me, "and again. I thought about what old man
Pike said about when he got the call to pick up the car and
what I found was a disconnect. When an officer or a deputy is
called to the scene of an accident, one of the things he does is
call the wrecker service. Why would Pike have gotten the call
so late if Deputy Leo Tubbs was on the scene by four?"

A new anticipation ignites inside me. "You think the police
report was doctored?"

Letty stares at the paper in her hand. "I hate to think such
a thing. Tubbs was a good cop. Retired about five years ago,
died last year. He was the first one on the scene when my
dad..." She hesitates, lost in the memories. "He held me so
tight. Kept whispering to me that everything would be okay

while my mom screamed in the background." Her eyes, dark and heavy with emotion, meet mine. "Your mom and dad cleaned up the mess so that when we got back home the next day it was like it never happened. We spent the night at your house, remember?"

I squeeze her hand. "I do. Mother let us watch TV until we fell asleep."

"Anyway." Letty clears her throat, scrubs at her eyes with her sleeve. "I did a little digging while you and Helen were taking care of business."

My stomach rumbles. I realize it's after two o'clock and breakfast was a very long time ago. I'm betting Letty hasn't stopped for lunch either. "Keep talking. I'll make peanut butter sandwiches."

"Good idea."

She watches a moment as I smear the crunchy blend on the bread. I imagine she's having trouble suggesting Deputy Tubbs falsified the accident report. Understandable. Cops don't want to believe other cops would do such a thing.

"Six months before the Beaumont accident, Mrs. Tubbs fell off a ladder at her home and injured her spine. She spent a good long while in the hospital. In the end she was para-lyzed from the waist down. They were drowning in medical bills. Suddenly, about two months after Beaumont's accident, all the medical bills were taken care of and the Tubbs's mort-gage was paid in full."

"Shit." I bring the sandwiches wrapped in paper towel to the table. "So the Beaumonts paid him off."

"Looks that way to me."

"How did you find out about the mortgage and the bills?"

"When Mom started delivering mail, she used to hand carry their mail to the door. Mrs. Tubbs didn't get a lot of company so she would inevitably talk a mile a minute to Mom. She went on and on about how they would have lost everything if it hadn't been for the department raising all that money for them."

I frown. "I thought you said the Beaumonts paid the bills."

Letty's lips spread into a sly smile. "I called the one deputy who was friends with my father and asked him about that fundraiser. He confirmed what she said, except they raised less than a thousand dollars. Not nearly enough to pay off medical bills and a mortgage."

"Deputy Tubbs is dead. How do we prove any of this?" I take a bite of my sandwich.

Letty takes a couple of bites of hers before she answers. "Maybe his wife will talk."

"Won't hurt to ask," I say.

"Won't hurt," Letty agrees.

I glance around the room. "What happened with Agent what's his name? The ABI guy who worked the case twenty-five years ago?"

"He called me this morning." Letty goes to the fridge and grabs a can of Pepsi. "His brother-in-law passed away and he had to leave for Chicago. He said he'd check in with us when he's back home."

I guess he wasn't a spy after all. "So it's just you and me again."

Letty pops the top on the can. "It was always just you and me, but don't worry, we've got this."

CLARE TUBBS LIVES in the same house she and her husband purchased forty years ago when they first married. They raised their daughter and son here and this is the same house she was attempting to paint when she had her fall.

This reminds me that I'm supposed to be painting Mother's house. I guess she wasn't trying to scare me when she mentioned the woman who fell off the ladder. Tubbs appears to be about the same age as Helen. She handles the wheel-chair well and her home, a neat rancher, is handicap equipped. Framed photos of her children and grandchildren fill the mantel and any available flat surface.

We've declined tea and listened through her life story. We've talked about how good it is that Natalie and Stacy can finally be laid to rest and what good news it is that the Baldwin and Shepherd girls were found. I hope she remains as talkative when she finds out why we're really here.

"Mrs. Tubbs," Letty says, "do you remember when Mr. Matthew Beaumont had his accident? You know, it was that same day of the bus accident?"

The older woman stares at Letty for a long moment before she answers. "I do."

"I found an inconsistency in the accident report and I was hoping you might remember something your husband said about that day? Maybe with the bus crash and all that happened, things got mixed up."

I'm impressed with Letty's approach. When my attention rests on Tubbs once more I see that she is not so impressed.

"I wondered how long it would be before someone came along asking about that day."

Letty and I exchange a look

"What do you mean, Mrs. Tubbs?" Letty asks.

Since Clare Tubbs is a cop's wife, it's better for Letty to handle all the questions. I keep my mouth shut and sit here as a reminder of my lost sister.

"First off," Tubbs says, "this is completely off the record. I ain't saying another word until we're all clear on that."

"We're clear," Letty says.

"Clear," I agree.

"I saw the news this morning." Tubbs looks at Letty for a while before she continues. Somehow a news crew managed to snap a few photos of her mother's home before we were able to cover up those hateful words. "You've been a cop long enough to know that sometimes things just have to be done a certain way or they get confused and the right thing is done for the wrong reasons or vice versa."

Letty nods.

I stare, wondering if what she is about to tell us will be the thing we need to find the truth. I guess it depends upon whether she sees the truth as the right thing.

"That day was one of those times. My husband was a good man, a good cop. He did what he was told and respected the chain of command even when he didn't agree with it. Except once."

My heart thuds. All we need is one piece of corroborating evidence.

"What happened that once?" Letty's voice is gentle.

"He refused to obey a direct order."

The realization that Claiborne was the sheriff back then is not lost on me.

"Life was difficult for us at the time. I'd fallen off that damned ladder and the medical bills were eating us alive. We were on the verge of losing our home." She shook her head. "We were desperate. I'm the reason he changed his mind and did what he didn't want to do."

"Is that why all your medical bills went away and your mortgage was paid?"

"Well," she adjusts her hands in her lap, "I don't know where those things came from. We received all sorts of donations from *anonymous* sources and there was that department fundraiser. Money just kept showing up at the door so I can't rightly say why or how."

"What time did Deputy Tubbs receive the call about Mr. Beaumont's accident?"

"Six-thirty. He had just come home to get a heavier coat. He was going out to help with the search."

The ability to breathe deserts me.

"You're certain of the time?" Letty asks.

"Positive. I had an appointment with the physical therapist at four twice a week. I had to make the appointments late in the day so my daughter could drive me after school. That day I was feeling particularly bad so we got barbecue on the way home. By the time we got to the house it was quarter after six. The kids had me in the house by the time Leo stopped for his coat. That was the first we heard about the bus accident. I remember looking at the clock and thinking how it would be pitch dark soon and those girls would be out there all alone. Leo said he didn't have time to eat, he had to get out there and help find those lost girls."

She looks at me as she says this.

"But dispatch called Deputy Tubbs before he could join the search?"

Tubbs shakes her head. "Sheriff Claiborne called him."

"You're sure it was Claiborne?" The tension along Letty's jaw tells me this news makes her furious.

"I am. I answered the phone." Tubbs nods resolutely. "After he hung up, I asked Leo if was he going to help with the search and he growled that the sheriff was sending him to an accident on Indian Creek. The ambulance was already en route and he needed Leo over there ASAP." She looks from Letty to me and back. "You might not remember but it was the very next year that Sheriff Claiborne got appointed as the Jackson Falls chief of police. I hear tell he lusted after that job for a long time before luck shined on him."

Everyone in the room knew luck had nothing to do with it.

"Did your husband ever talk about what he was asked to do regarding the accident Sheriff Claiborne sent him to work?"

Tubbs shook her head. "He would never talk about it but I knew whatever happened, it didn't sit right with him." She looks at the two of us then. "It stuck with him until the day he died. He always said that eventually even the devil himself had to pay his due."

"Mrs. Tubbs," Letty says, "I know this conversation is off the record, but my dad deserves justice. Natalie and Stacy deserve justice. To make that happen, we need your help. Would you be willing to make an official statement?"

Tubbs eyes us each in turn, then she says, "You sure you can take them all down? I don't want Claiborne or old Lorraine giving my family no trouble."

"You have my word," Letty promises.

Air rushes into my lungs. This is big.

We are back in Letty's Jeep before either of us speak.

"That son of a bitch knows my dad is being set up."

I understand that Letty means Claiborne.

She turns to me. "There's no question the Beaumonts are involved in what happened to Natalie and Stacy. We might not have enough to prove it, but we will find what we need."

I think of how far these people have gone to cover up the truth and I suddenly understand why Mother is so worried about Letty and me digging into this.

"We have to be careful," I say.

Letty nods. "Yeah."

My cell vibrates and I dig it from my pocket. I don't recognize the number but it's local and I think of the visit to the funeral home this morning so I answer. "Hello."

"Emma, it's Mallory. I need to talk to you privately. It's urgent. Can we meet now?"

I look at Letty. "Sure, Mallory. Where would you like to meet?"

LETTY DROPPED me by the farm for my dad's truck. She headed to Pike's Wrecker Service with a statement for him to sign regarding the call about Beaumont's car. Between his statement and the one from Tubbs, we're moving forward.

I park on the square in front of Mallory's shop. Though I

doubt the woman intends to give me anything usable against the Beaumonts since her family is part of their family now, I might as well hear her out. She might just let something slip.

The bell over the door jingles as I enter the shop. Mallory hands the receipt and the bag to the customer at the counter. She thanks her and the woman leaves, flashing me a smile as she passes.

"Give me a minute." Mallory hurries to lock the door and turn the sign to closed.

She wears enough jewelry on her arms and around her neck that she clinks when she walks. Her emerald midi length dress is layered with a multi-colored sweater in deep jewel tones. Chic ankle boots with low heels complete the look. She's a walking advertisement for her classy store.

I wait at the counter until she hustles back over.

"What's up?" I try not to sound too hopeful. Mallory is the sort of person who likes to play games. I was too young to notice when Natalie was alive, but I've realized this since coming home last week.

She grabs both my hands. "Let's sit."

She pulls me to a bench in front of the lingerie table. We sit, knees to knees, her bejeweled fingers still clamped around my hands.

"I lied to you, Emma."

I feign surprise. "You did?" Of course, I know this already. She isn't a very good liar.

She nods, tears brimming on her lashes. "I feel just terrible about it but I thought I was protecting you and Natalie. I've prayed on it and I've come to realize that you need to know the truth. You deserve the truth."

"I appreciate that, Mallory."

"You remember Matthew Beaumont? Science teacher? He was dead already by the time you reached high school."

"I remember him."

"Natalie had a big crush on him." Her hands release mine

so she can put hers to her chest with the dramatic flair that is all Mallory. "I mean really big. Scary big."

I blink.

"He kept trying to reason with her but she wouldn't stop. She was like…I don't know—stalking him. That's why we had our big falling out. I always tell everyone it was about my first boyfriend and that big mess with Mark but it was really about Natalie's obsession with Mr. Beaumont. I tried to persuade Stacy to help me convince her to stop but she was completely on Natalie's side."

As difficult as I find this to swallow, I sit quietly and let her talk. To keep my cool, I focus on seeing myself reaching out and punching her dazzling white teeth down her throat. No one has teeth that white. Crowns or veneers. Has to be.

"She tried every way in the world to seduce him. It was really embarrassing." She makes a sad face. "I'm so sorry to tell you these awful things but they need to be said. I felt telling you directly, privately, was best."

I nod, imagining myself strangling her now, her eyes bulging, tongue hanging out.

"Poor Mr. Beaumont was so patient with her, trying to reason with the unreasonable. It all blew up *that day*."

"How do you mean?" I clasp my hands together to prevent acting out my fantasies.

"Mr. Beaumont told her that he was taking the issue to the principal. You can imagine Natalie's reaction. That would ruin her perfect record, her reputation. She couldn't have that but she just couldn't bring herself to let him go. She wanted him all to herself. He gave her every chance, you know. He told her to go home and think about what was more important to her, this foolish adolescent crush or her family and her future."

Images of Natalie and Stacy huddled together in the backseat of the bus flash through my mind. Frantic whispers echo through me.

"I didn't tell Mr. Beaumont, but I knew Natalie would never go for his offer. She wanted what she wanted."

I pick up on a pinch of anger and maybe jealousy in her voice. But then, most of Natalie's peers had been envious of her.

"When Mr. Beaumont got home from school that day—the day Mr. Russell had his heart attack and the bus crashed—he found a note from Natalie in his jacket pocket. The note said she was going to kill herself if she couldn't be with him."

This floors me. My body jerks with the shock. *Impossible.* In spite of the shock, I manage to ask, "What did he do?"

"Mr. Beaumont, bless his heart, was rushing back to school to show the note to the principal when he had his accident. It was horrible, just horrible." Her hands go to her throat. "At first I honestly thought Natalie and Stacy had run away. Maybe she thought Mr. Beaumont would regret what he said if he thought she was lost. But then when they didn't come back I realized some bad person had probably picked them up and hurt them." She exhales an exaggerated sigh. "It's hard to believe it was Letty's father. Do you think he might have been obsessed with Natalie the way she was with Mr. Beaumont?"

I stare at her, unable to speak now.

She grabs my hands again. My entire body shudders in revulsion.

"I know it's hard to believe. Everyone thought Natalie was so perfect. She was so beautiful and she had those big boobs and those lush lips. She was hard to resist."

Her hands squeeze tighter around mine as she speaks.

"But she wasn't so perfect or beautiful inside. She was mean and selfish." Her gaze locks on mine. "I'm so glad you never had to see how evil she really was."

The medallion on the chain that Jake hung around my neck burns against my skin.

DEBRA WEBB

"What about the note?" My voice is small. I can hardly squeeze the words past the lump in my throat.

She shakes her head. "That's the saddest part. I guess it was lost when they cut Mr. Beaumont's clothes off him in the ER. He never had the evidence to prove what really happened. I suppose the family felt it was better not to get involved, you know? What purpose would it serve if they dragged all that ugliness up? By the time Matt—Mr. Beaumont—was able to explain what happened, everyone knew James Cotton did something bad to Natalie and Stacy."

Incredibly, beyond the red of rage floating before my eyes, I find the ability to ask, "How did you know about the note and all of this?"

"Oh my Lord." Mallory launches to her feet. "Look at the time. I have to pick up my granddaughter. Her mother has class tonight." She rushes to the door, unlocks it and opens it for me to go.

I push to my feet and walk to where she stands but I don't go.

"I'm not leaving until you tell me how you could possibly know this." The words are cold with fury.

Her face pales. Clearly she didn't expect this reaction.

"Lorraine," she says in a rush, her gaze straying to the street. "After Mr. Beaumont died I mentioned to her about Natalie's infatuation with him and how I worried about his accident being somehow related to...to his ultimatum to Natalie."

She shrugs, glances at me, but then sets her attention on a passing car. "She—Lorraine—sat me down and told me the whole story. She didn't see any reason to embarrass your family with those awful details." She looks at me once more. "What purpose would it have served?"

"None," I say, pretending to agree with her.

She hugs me and whispers, "I'm so sorry, Emma. None of that matters now." She draws back. "We should all strive to

318

remember Natalie the way she used to be before she turned into that..." She shakes her head. "I'm so sorry."

I nod and walk out the door, but I can't go without giving her and Lorraine something to think about. I'm confident that Mallory has just regurgitated what Lorraine instructed her to say to me.

Mallory stares at me, her face frozen as if she fears what I might say next.

She should be afraid...very afraid.

"Back then school let out about three in the afternoon. I'm just wondering about the timing. Mr. Beaumont claimed he drove straight home after school and then was returning almost immediately," I smile, "for the urgent reason you've just shared with me. What was he doing between three thirtyish and when his accident actually occurred around six or half past?"

Mallory's head gives a jerky shake. "I think his accident was way earlier. Either way I don't understand the relevance of the time. He may have lain in the ravine for hours before he was found."

"That's what time the deputy who responded to the accident received the call. We found confirmation of the time a few hours ago. Mr. Beaumont's accident didn't happen right after school. If it had and hours passed, as you suggest, before he was found, he would have died from the internal hemorrhaging related to his injuries."

The last part was a stretch since I haven't reviewed his medical records. I am going based on hearsay, but it seems to have worked. Mallory is speechless.

I walk away.

My movements are strangely disjointed.

My mind is spinning.

It's not until I'm in the truck and driving away that I scream.

32

HELEN

MY HANDS SHAKE SO I fist my fingers together. My table is set and dinner is ready. Emma and Letty will be here any moment.

Ginny stares at a framed photo of Emma and Letty that stands on the mantel. Several of my favorite photos of my daughters and their friends and my dear husband are on that mantel. I sometimes sit at night just staring at those captured memories, wishing that things were the way they once were.

Sadly they will never again be as they were. But I still have Emma. No matter the price, I must protect her. She and Letty have veered too near the truth and I know with complete certainty that Lorraine will not risk the danger to herself and the life she has built for her family. She will stop them as she has anyone who ever dared to challenge her.

I cannot allow this to go any further. Emma and Letty must know the truth. They must understand what we did and why.

As if I said the words aloud Ginny turns to me. Her fearful

gaze tears at my heart. "Are you all right?" I ask the foolish question knowing the answer.

Ginny draws in a deep breath. "I might be closer to all right if I had a shot of Andrew's bourbon."

"Why didn't I think of that?" Frankly, I could use a drink as well.

We go to the liquor cabinet in the dining room and pick through the bottles.

"That one will do," Ginny says when my hand closes around the bottle of Jim Beam.

I set the bottle aside, pull a couple of glasses from the small shelf in the cabinet that was once a Victrola. Andrew painstakingly restored and repurposed the junked phonograph as a liquor cabinet. He made it beautiful once more as he did all things he touched.

I pour a hefty serving in each glass and pass one to Ginny, then lift my own. "To letting go of all the secrets and lies."

Ginny taps her glass to mine. "Amen."

We savor our drinks, and our memories...a lifetime of memories.

Emma and Letty arrive and I insist that we eat first. I've prepared Emma's favorite vegetable lasagna and a fresh green salad. I even made garlic bread and picked up a fresh baked cherry pie from the shop on the square.

Ginny offers to help with coordinating the gathering after the burial service on Monday. I thank her. She also says that Lisa dropped by the post office to check her box. Lisa said Delbert Yarbrough had scheduled Stacy's memorial for Sunday afternoon. We all intend on going to the Yarbrough memorial. Natalie's funeral Mass is not until Monday so there's no conflict.

By the time the pie and coffee are served silence has invaded our nice, comfortable evening. It's time, I realize. The girls sense the evening was a precursor for something, that is obvious. I imagine they expect Ginny and I will do more pleading for them to back off this unofficial investigation.

Strange, their unofficial investigation has gleaned far more in just a few days than the official one has gathered in decades.

"We have something to tell you," I say.

Ginny nods, glances at her cup as if she wishes the coffee were bourbon.

"First," Emma says, "the two of you need to know where we are with the investigation."

Ginny pipes up. "You two don't need to go any further with your investigation."

Letty sets her coffee aside. "Mother, just listen to what we have to say and then we'll hear the two of you out."

I look to Ginny and she shrugs. "We're listening," I say, relenting.

Letty lays out what they have found so far which covers the things Emma told me in the funeral home parking lot today and more. They are so very close to the truth.

"Today," Letty goes on, "we discovered another stunning cover up by the original investigation. The widow of Deputy Leo Tubbs, the deputy who responded to Matthew Beaumont's accident, stated that the accident didn't occur until much later than originally reported. This is a significant find. Matthew Beaumont no longer has an alibi."

My throat grows so tight I can't speak.

"Out of the blue Mallory asked me to meet with her," Emma says. "I think Lorraine instructed her to give me a story that might explain the discrepancies we've been uncovering, like Brewer's account of the incident between Natalie and Beaumont."

"Of course," Letty points out, "unless Mallory goes on record, what she said is just hearsay."

"She claims Natalie had been stalking Mr. Beaumont," Emma says.

My stomach turns over and the few bites of dinner I managed to swallow threaten to reappear.

"According to Mallory, Beaumont had been struggling to get her under control for weeks. She claims his accident was related to a note Natalie wrote to him the day of the bus crash. He supposedly drove home after school, found this note from Natalie saying she was going to kill herself so he was rushing back to the school to show the principal when he had his accident."

I cannot hear any more of this. I launch to my feet. "Lies," I roar. "All lies."

Ginny holds up a hand. "Stop, all of you. I want to tell you what really happened." She looks up at me. "Sit down, Helen. It's going to be all right."

My hands fly to my face and I collapse back into my chair, my legs no longer able to support me. The very idea that bitch Lorraine would make up such things about my Natalie makes me want to tear her apart.

"After your father died," Ginny says, looking to her daughter, "I had to work even harder to make ends meet. I didn't have the luxury of wallowing in grief or in the loss of our sweet Natalie."

Ginny and I share a look, and I know her heart is breaking just as mine is. All these years we wanted to protect them from this.

"Nearly five years after that day," Ginny goes on, "I was still at the Beaumont house cleaning like the slave they considered me to be. I worked two to three days a week for Lorraine. Sometimes her husband would be home having one of his *spells*. That's what Lorraine called them but Helen and I both knew what it was. He got addicted to those pain killers they gave him after the accident and every so often he tried to quit 'em cold turkey. He always went off the deep end whenever that happened."

"Why are you just now telling us whatever this is?" Letty

demands, already irritated that her mother has apparently kept something from her.

"Hear her out, Letty," I implore.

She doesn't like it but she doesn't disrespect me either.

"This particular day he was having a bad spell," Ginny goes on. "I could hear him taking on and turning stuff over in their room. Lorraine always told me just to leave him be and not bother cleaning their room. I don't think they really shared that room anymore anyway. I think Lorraine had already moved to the big guest room on the other end of the upstairs hall."

I stare at my Emma. I feel some amount of relief that we are finally telling the truth but I am terrified that she will never forgive me for keeping these awful secrets from her. God only knows how Letty will react when she learns what poor Ginny had to do.

It hurts my soul to think about it.

"It was just about lunchtime that day when he started taking on so bad I was sure he had hurt himself so I went into the room." She swiped at the tears sliding down her cheeks. "He was sitting on the floor in his underdrawers staring at something in his hand and rocking back and forth like a baby."

I stand and walk across the room for the tissues. I remove several for myself and then pass the box to Ginny.

She swipes her eyes and her nose. "I got down on my knees next to him and asked him if he was okay. He went to wailing that he didn't mean to hurt them. I kept asking him what he meant. I didn't understand." She exhaled a big breath. "Until he said, 'my Natalie'. That's when I saw that he was holding Natalie's necklace—the one with the ballerina slippers. It took every ounce of strength I had to sit back on my heels and let him spill his guts. I was terrified that if I said a word he would stop talking."

She hugs her arms around herself. "He cried and said he

was in love with her. He planned to run away with her and start a whole new life, but Stacy got in the way. He was certain Stacy was filling Natalie's head with lies." Ginny looked from Letty to Emma. "That day, Natalie sent him a note all right. She told him unless he turned himself in for what he'd done, she was going to turn him in herself."

"Turn him in for what?" Emma asks, her voice thin.

Ginny shakes her head. "I can't say for sure. He kept repeating the same thing, how he loved her and wanted to run away with her and that Stacy turned her against him. He was headed to the farm after he found the note. He knew me and Helen were gone to Birmingham. He figured he would persuade Natalie to go away with him and they would leave then and there. He didn't expect to find Stacy with her. He drove right past that wrecked bus." Ginny shakes her head again, her lips compressed in anger. "He forced Natalie and Stacy into the trunk of the car at gunpoint. He took them to his place, tied them up, put tape over their mouths and locked them in the storm cellar under that stand of oaks beyond the driveway."

"He told you all this?" Letty asks as if she is having trouble absorbing the full implications of what her mother is saying. Perhaps she is in shock.

Ginny nods. "He had bought a car that he intended to use for their getaway. He had clothes for both of them, money, fake IDs—everything he would need for running away. He stored everything at one of their rental properties that was vacant, but when he set out to go get the other car he had the accident."

"Who found them?" Emma asks.

My precious daughter's face looks so pale. I wish I could go to her and hold her but I need both her and Letty to listen, to believe and to do the right thing.

"Natalie and Stacy weren't found until he came out of the coma, more than a week later. By then it was too late."

"Oh my God." Emma stands and starts to pace the floor. She stalls at the double windows that overlook the backyard.

Letty stares at her mother. "Why in the hell would you keep this a secret all these years?"

"Ginny tried to make him tell her what he did with...the girls," I speak when Ginny's voice fails her. "The bastard scrambled up and stumbled out of the bedroom. Your mother followed him. They argued. Ginny kept screaming at him to tell her the rest. Then he fell down the stairs. The fall killed him and Ginny didn't know what to do, so she called me."

"Did you call 911?" Letty demanded, her expression and tone filled with disbelief. "Jesus Christ!"

Our silence is answer enough. "Oh my God." Letty shakes her head. "What were you thinking?"

We have no answer.

"You knew about all this?"

Emma's question and the look in her eyes are like a spear to my heart. "Yes."

Letty holds up her hands for quiet. "What the hell else did he tell you about Natalie and Stacy?"

Ginny dabs at her eyes. "He said that when he told Lorraine she rushed home but it was too late, the girls were dead. With no food or water..." She shook her head, unable to continue.

"He lied." Emma turns toward us, fury tightening her beautiful face. "Cause of death was blunt force trauma. Did Lorraine do that?"

Ginny and I look at each other. "He swore," she says, "that they were dead when Lorraine found them. He said they took the bodies into a cave and buried them."

"Who is they?" Emma demands.

Ginny shakes her head adamantly. "I don't know. I was in a rage. I wasn't thinking clearly. Of course, he had to have help. I can't remember exactly how many days he was in the hospital. I assume Lorraine helped him. But I don't know for

327

sure. Maybe Mark and Lorraine did it while he was still in the hospital. Whoever helped him, they also took your daddy's dog tags off the rearview mirror in my car. I thought I lost them, but they stole them. They planted them with the bodies so if they were ever found everyone would believe James was guilty after all."

"Just tell me why Claiborne didn't believe you?" Letty's voice is hollow now, her eyes bleak.

"We didn't tell him," I say for Ginny.

Before either daughter can demand to know why, I finish the story. "When I got to the Jackson place after Ginny's frantic call, he was lying at the bottom of the stairs. His body was twisted at an odd angle. His neck..." I shudder at the memory. "Blood had poured from a massive gash to his head. Ginny had his blood on her blouse where she'd tried to help him. She told me everything and we cried together. When I pulled myself together again, I pried my Natalie's necklace out of his cold, dead fingers." Fury tightens my face. "I wanted to tell the world what he'd done but I knew that Claiborne would find a way to make it look as if Ginny killed him in an effort to clear James's name. Or maybe Matthew caught her stealing and she pushed him down the stairs to shut him up. Just another black woman who tried to take advantage of her wealthy white employer."

I look directly at Letty. "You had lost your father, I could not risk you losing your mother, too. Ginny had no witnesses. It was the word of a killer's wife against the word of an influential pillar of the community."

When neither says a word, I go on, "I helped Ginny finish cleaning so she could leave and let the family believe he fell after she left. Whenever he stayed home like that, he was generally out of his mind on drugs but no one except Lorraine would ever know that part because of course the coroner would and did rule his death accidental. I'm certain there was no mention of the drugs."

"You," Ginny said to her daughter, "know what Lorraine Beaumont is capable of. She will never allow the truth to become public knowledge. She will say I made up the story or that I killed her husband. This will never be about anything bad she and that bastard husband of hers did."

There were questions. Many we couldn't answer, some we could.

"Beaumont lied," Emma says. "I'm not saying he didn't kill Natalie and Emma, obviously he was involved. But if he left them as he said—"

"Maybe the trauma," I swallow the lump that bobs into my throat, "was caused somehow when they buried them. They could have thrown them into the cave and then climbed down to bury them."

"The damage was almost identical on both skulls," Emma argues. "If the bodies were arbitrarily thrown down into a hole, there's little chance they would have sustained exactly the same injuries in the same location on the skull and there would have been other injuries. Other broken bones and there were none. Besides, there was no reason for them to throw the bodies down into the cave. At the time they would have been able to walk to the area where the burial was done. The collapse probably hadn't occurred yet."

"What you've told us," Letty says, "only confirms what we already knew. There's a very good possibility that the person who killed Natalie and Stacy is still out there."

"Lorraine," Emma says, outrage simmering in her tone. "It had to be her."

"Or Mark," Letty suggests. "He wouldn't have wanted his father to go to jail." She looks from her mother to me. "Your story narrows the suspect pool, and for that I'm grateful."

If I had hoped this revelation would stop Letty and Emma from pressing on with their dangerous investigation, I was wrong.

There is only one other thing I can do.

33

FRIDAY, MAY 18

EMMA

I STARE at the stack of neatly folded clothes on my dresser. Helen and I said little after Letty and her mom left last night. I haven't seen those two argue since Letty and I were little kids, but they locked horns last night.

Ginny announced she would go to the FBI agent on the task force and confess. Letty did not handle this well. Ultimately, the decision was that the mothers would keep quiet while Letty and I moved forward with our unofficial investigation. I have no idea how far we can go with this or what our next step might be. I'm leaving that in Letty's experienced and capable hands.

I drag on the usual tee and jeans, socks and hiking shoes and I'm good to go. I'm at the door when I notice the silver chain lying on my bedside table. I took it off when I showered last night. I've never really been a superstitious person or even a particularly religious person, still I snag the necklace and drop it over my head, then tuck it under my tee. The cool metal rests between my breasts.

Descending the stairs I wonder where Helen went last night. She said she and Howard had planned to watch a late movie but she lied. Ten minutes after she left I drove past Howard's house and her car wasn't there. I even drove past the Beaumont place just to make sure she hadn't decided to do something really crazy.

No Helen.

She arrived back home a few minutes after I did, which turned out to be a good thing since I was circling the liquor cabinet like a crippled plane coming in for a crash landing. The urge for a good stiff drink had been hounding me since the mothers called last night's meeting. Instinctively I had known whatever the news it would be surprising, maybe even shocking.

I did not expect earth shattering.

Part of me is concerned that I haven't run screaming through the town. I feel too calm. Perhaps it's shock. I want to be angry at the Beaumonts, at God and anyone else who had anything to do with what happened twenty-five years ago.

But all I feel at the moment is numb.

Downstairs the smell of coffee draws me to the kitchen.

"Good morning." Helen smiles. "I've made a basket for you to take to the farm. I believe Letty mentioned the two of you would meet there this morning."

I try to read her but she's purposely avoiding eye contact. "So Howard was feeling poorly last night?" I ask, using her words.

"Hmm-mm." She nods and tucks the foil wrapped biscuits into the basket. She pushes the basket across the counter toward me. "Coffee's ready. Y'all be careful today."

With that she leaves the room. I stare after her. What the hell?

Okay, enough. I follow her path, find her in the living room on the sofa holding a book. "Are you feeling all right?"

I think of the heart attack she had ten, eleven days ago and worry churns in my belly. Yesterday—this entire week has been extremely stressful.

"I'm fine, thank you."

Oh hell. "If you need me," I say, "just call. I don't know what the plan is for today but I won't be far away."

She lowers the book and looks directly at me for the first time. "Please stay away from that den of snakes."

"How we proceed is Letty's call." I pass the buck.

"You don't understand what Lorraine is capable of." Her voice is too soft, almost weak.

I can't leave her like this even though my brain is demanding coffee so I sit down beside her. "Mom, we are not going to put ourselves in danger. Letty is really careful. There are rules about how we proceed even in an unofficial investigation."

Helen searches my eyes, hers watery and for the first time in my life I realize how truly fragile she looks. The realization terrifies me.

"Lorraine and her husband killed your sister. I don't know if we can ever make her pay for her part in this and clear James, but I do not want to risk losing you. This nightmare has stolen enough from me."

I hug her tight against me. "You're not going to lose me." I give her a final squeeze and draw back to find her crying. "We'll be careful." I smooth the tears from her cheeks with my thumbs. "I love you, Mom."

"I love you."

We hug some more and then I load up and head to the farm. Letty is waiting.

"Helen sent breakfast." I place the basket on the counter next to the sink.

"Is she okay?" Letty digs in to the heavenly smells emanating from the neatly packed goods.

"I think so. How about your mom?"

"We fought some more when we got home, but we ended up making up and going to bed. I stayed at her house. I was afraid if I didn't she'd do something crazy like go confess to watching Matthew Beaumont fall down those stairs and not calling 911."

"They lied to us all these years." I say this with just a touch of reverence. I always knew my mother was strong but I had no idea the burden she'd been carrying. Who knew she could lie as well as me? I'm kind of impressed. Terrified, stunned, but strangely impressed.

Letty slathers a biscuit with strawberry jam. "Yeah." Her gaze meets mine. "We probably would have done the same thing."

I nod. "Definitely. Only you would've pushed the guy down the stairs."

The laughter bubbles up from deep inside me and I can't stop. Letty almost chokes on a mouthful of biscuit because she can't stop laughing either. The laughter turns to tears and we end up hugging in the middle of the kitchen where Helen served us homemade chocolate chip cookies and milk after school...where cold winter nights were spent sipping my dad's special blend of hot chocolate. And Natalie entertained us with her imitation of some movie star or pop singer.

By the time we pull ourselves together we are sitting on the floor, arms hugged around each other, faces red, cheeks damp with tears.

"I think we'll start calling this the Cry Center instead of the Command Center." I laugh a little more. "We've had a few of these sessions."

"Good therapy, I guess." Letty swipes at her nose.

"What now?" I have no clue where to go from here. My heart wants to go to that damned reporter—Lila Lawson—and tell her everything, but my brain reminds me that what we have is merely hearsay.

"Brewer's statement combined with Tubbs's and Pike's casts suspicion on Matthew Beaumont but it doesn't prove anything," Letty explains. "The story our moms told is hearsay—the words of two lifelong friends who want to clear my father's name."

"We need evidence, right?"

Letty swipes at her eyes with her sleeve and nods.

"What about Natalie's necklace?"

"Helen could have had it all along," Letty argues, playing devil's advocate. "My mom could have found it among Dad's things."

"Damn." I close my eyes. "It feels like the closer we get, the further away we find ourselves." Another thought occurs to me. "Wait." I turn my head to look at Letty. "What about Mallory?"

A burst of dry laughter pops from her throat. "Like that crazy bitch is going to shit in her nest. Whatever her reason for telling you what she did, she will swear you're lying if you take it to the press or the task force."

"We need tangible evidence," I say, amending my previous comment.

Letty nods. "If we had a warrant to search the Beaumont property we might find something. God knows there was nothing else in that damned cave."

"What if we watch for Lorraine to leave and do it without a warrant?"

Letty sighs. "The search would be considered unreasonable and therefore any evidence found would be inadmissible."

"What about probable cause or, what's the term? Exigent circumstances?"

"Neither applies in this case. The only way we could search without a warrant is if we had consent."

I laugh, the sound dry and humorless. "Like that's going to happen."

"I'm not saying Beaumont was a serial killer," Letty says, "but he did keep that necklace because he was so in love with Natalie. What if she wasn't the first?"

We stare at each other a moment.

"Stacy was all depressed and having trouble keeping her grades up the latter part of the first semester of that school year." I take the ball she tossed and run with it. "What if Beaumont was fixated on her first?"

The idea that Natalie would let the man touch her still doesn't sit right with me.

Letty gets to her feet and offers her hand. "Exactly. If he kept Natalie's necklace he most likely kept a souvenir from the other girls he lured into relationships—assuming there were others."

I take her hand and pull up. "And what about the backpacks? They have to be somewhere. They weren't in the cave. What if they're hidden somewhere on the property? Beaumont may have had a special place where he kept things so he could touch them and relive the memories."

I almost gag at the idea.

Letty rubs at her temples with the tips of her fingers. "I can go to the FBI—someone not associated with the investigation—and plead my case. I could emphasize the idea that I believe the entire original investigation and all the folks involved were tainted by Claiborne's machinations."

"Is there a chance they would believe us?"

"Hold on." Letty reaches into her pocket and retrieves her cell. "Cotton."

While she talks I finish off a biscuit with jelly and down my coffee. I try to imagine how it felt to live with this burden for twenty years. What Helen did for Letty's mom is the very definition of true friendship. I look at Letty; I can't read her expression as she listens to her caller. I know without doubt she would do the same for me. I would do it for her, no question.

In that moment, standing in the kitchen of my early child-hood, and watching my oldest and dearest friend, I suddenly realize that I've stopped having those nightmares about Iraq and the bus crash the past couple of nights. I haven't had an anxiety attack or anything other than a passing desire for a drink in days. With all that's happened I have more reason than ever to have suffered a double whammy of both.

"That was Mr. Wallace's wife."

The coroner. "Did he…?"

As soon as I ask the question I feel guilty about hoping he hasn't died because as long as he's alive there's hope he'll tell the truth about the dog tags. How sad is that?

"No," Letty says. "He wants to see us."

No matter that I'm fully aware this may not be informa-tion that will help our investigation, my hopes rise anyway.

GLENN WALLACE'S wife greets us at the front door. Before inviting us into the house, she steps onto the porch and pulls the door closed behind her.

"He's very weak. Don't stay too long and don't say anything to upset him."

"Yes, ma'am," Letty says.

I nod. "Of course."

The older woman stares at each of us in turn. "I don't know why he wants to see you. I can only assume it's about the old case since your momma," she glares at me, "paid him a visit last night. He never got over that case, refused to talk about it even to me. All of a sudden after Helen left last night he's wanting to talk to the two of you." She shakes her head. "I guess he's got something to get off his chest."

We follow her inside though she doesn't officially invite us. As we trail behind her through the house, my mind is turning over the idea that Helen visited Mr. Wallace after last night's dinner and entertainment. At least now I know where she went when she claimed to be going to Howard's.

The bedroom smells of death. A hospital bed stands to the right of the full size bed that matches the other furniture in the room. The night table between the two is loaded with bottles of medication. A small lamp stands amid the sea of bottles, its dim bulb the only source of light in the room. Blinds are closed tightly over the windows.

"May Ellen, close the door behind you," Wallace says.

His wife looks less than happy but she does as he asks.

"Come on over here," he says, his voice frail and thin. "I can't talk very loud and I need to be sure you hear what I have to say."

We move closer to the bed; Letty goes right, I go left. We stand on either side of him. His skin is so pale and translucent, whether from the disease or the treatment, it's difficult to assess. Faint blue veins trace paths under the paper thin skin that lies against bone, making his face and every other visible part of him gaunt and skeletal looking. The rise of his chest is shallow, the fall a jerky tremble.

He looks to Letty first. "I have no idea what your daddy did or didn't do but if those dog tags are the only evidence they have of his presence in that cave, then they have no evidence because he was wearing those dog tags when he shot himself."

My knees go weak and my breath stalls in my lungs. I hear the sharp catch in Letty's respiration.

"But you—"

"I did what I was told to do," he cuts her off.

"Tell us what happened, Mr. Wallace." I speak quietly, not wanting to upset him no matter that my entire being is vibrating with emotions. The numbness I first felt this morning is long gone.

He swallows, the movement jerky along the frail column of his throat.

"Do you need a drink of water?" Letty asks, her voice oddly calm as well.

"I'd love a drink," he says with a rusty laugh, "but not water."

I smile, my face feeling like glass about to shatter.

"Claiborne was desperate." He clears his throat, the sound like rotting tissue ripping. "The girls had been missing for over a week and they had nothing. Everybody on the investigation wanted it to be James Cotton. He was an easy mark. He had opportunity." He pauses to catch his breath. "He fit the profile the FBI provided."

My heart is pounding. I want to scream but I keep my feelings inside. This part is harder on Letty than me. I need to stay calm for her.

"With his history of violent outbursts, Claiborne was determined to nail him and make the community happy. My part was cut and dry. I examined the body and certified the cause of death as a single gunshot to the head and the manner of death as suicide. I found no reason whatsoever to believe otherwise and that was that on my end." Another shaky breath escapes his mouth. "Then you two found his dog tags in that cave. The very next morning the chief and Lorraine showed up at the hospital with a statement for me to sign saying Cotton wasn't wearing the dog tags when I examined his body." He clears his throat. "Like I said, I did what I was told."

Letty and I look at each other over his failing body.

"Why would you lie for them?" Letty asks.

I want to move to her side and put an arm around her shoulder. She has lived with the lies about her father for nearly her whole life.

"Everyone lies for Lorraine," he says and coughs. "Claiborne, anyone who has any influence. She makes it a point to learn our weaknesses. She knows what will levy the most pain and she holds it over our heads."

"Why are you telling me this now, Mr. Wallace?" Letty asks, her words frigid, stiff.

"I'm dying. I have maybe a week or two to live. I don't have a lot to leave my family, save my reputation in the community. Most folks have respected me. My sons have both grown up to be doctors and I'm very proud of them. I've tried hard to be a man of my word and never to break a promise. I eased my conscience about the dog tags with the idea that everyone believed James Cotton was guilty anyway, what difference did it make? But it was wrong. I knew this and I couldn't fix it. Then Helen came to see me and I was no longer bound by a promise I made twenty-five years ago."

Letty and I exchange another look. The man has lost us.

"You see," he explained, his voice growing thinner, audibly wearier, "it wasn't my honor on the line. But Helen urged me to do the right thing no matter what Lorraine said or did so that's what I'm doing."

"Are you saying you were willing to lie about the dog tags to somehow protect my mother?" It hit me then. "You had an affair."

"You'll have to talk to your mother about that." He looked to Letty. "Sheriff Cotton, I've made an official statement and signed it. You'll find it in the folder lying on the dresser over there. My secretary typed it up and brought it in. She witnessed it and Reba from over at the bank notarized it. Your father was wearing his dog tags at the time of his death. I allowed your mother to take them from his body before we carried him away. The dog tags were splattered with his blood. I witnessed her wiping it off the best she could with the hem of her dress."

I watch tears slip down Letty's cheeks.

Wallace exhales a burst of air that sounds more like a death rattle than a breath.

"However," he says, his words too soft, too thin, "those

dog tags got into that cave, your daddy did not put them there or lose them there."

34

I wait for Letty to meet my gaze and then I ask, "You think they'll go for it?"

"We didn't give them a lot of choice."

This is true. Letty called Lorraine and I called Heather. We each said basically the same thing: I have evidence your husband/father was involved in Natalie's and Stacy's deaths. I'll be waiting for you on Indian Creek Road."

We tossed around the idea of going to Claiborne but Letty worried he would give Lorraine a heads up. In the end we decided on the ABI. Special Agent Jimmy Watwood and his partner were standing by.

"We should call the mothers," I suggest.

"And say what? That we're doing exactly what you asked us not to do? Rattling the lion's cage?"

Also true. I stare out the window of Letty's Jeep to the extravagant estate perched on the hillside on the opposite side of the road. I wonder if this was the last view Natalie and Stacy saw before they closed their eyes for the final time? I know they must have been terrified. Having a teacher—a man they trusted—take their lives was almost as bad as a family member doing so. I think about Ginny's story and how Beaumont cried and claimed to have loved Natalie.

How could he have believed Natalie would be happy starting a life with him? I can't disprove the suggestion that she was flirting with the man. It's possible. Natalie was a blossoming young woman accustomed to being lavished with attention. Of course it's possible that she found herself caught up in the titillating trap of flirting with an older, married man.

I cannot see her agreeing to run away with him under any circumstances.

The sound of a car coming carries through the open windows. I crane my neck to see. A black SUV comes into view.

"That's Heather's Tahoe," Letty says.

As the vehicle draws closer I see Lorraine in the passenger seat. The women glance at us before turning down the long drive that leads to the Jackson home place. Letty starts her Jeep and follows.

Lorraine and Heather emerge from the Tahoe as Letty brakes to a stop. A tall man dressed in a suit steps out of the back seat.

"Who the hell is that?" I don't recognize the man. Sixtyish, distinguished looking.

"The family attorney." Letty blows out a burst of air.

My belly cramps. We should have expected as much.

"Son of a bitch."

I turn to Letty and she's staring at the rearview mirror. I turn around and spot another SUV, this one belonging to the Jackson Falls Police Department. My throat goes bone dry.

"It's Claiborne," Letty says.

"Send Watwood the signal." Why beat around the bush? Obviously we need backup.

Letty sends the text and reaches for her door. We climb out and move to the front of her Jeep. Heather and her mother remain near the Tahoe.

Claiborne gets out and storms up to where we stand.

"What the hell is going on here, Letty?" Claiborne demands.

"Chief, this is a private matter." She glances at Lorraine. "Unless, Mrs. Beaumont and Mrs. Turner want to make it police business."

Letty clutches the file folder in her hand. My heart is pounding so hard I can hardly hear myself think.

Claiborne glares at her for ten full seconds before Lorraine says, "Give us a moment, Chief."

Claiborne backs off. Letty waits until he's leaning against the driver's side door of his SUV before she speaks. "I have a number of official statements." She lifts the manila folder for all to see.

"Sheriff Cotton," the attorney says, "my name is—"

"I know who you are," Letty says with enough of a sneer for him to know what she thinks of him.

"Good. To be clear, I have advised my clients not to answer any questions you may have. Whatever you have in that folder you should discuss it with me."

"Here are your choices," Letty says, looking from Lorraine to Heather and back, "you hear Emma and me out—just the four of us; or, we leave now and take what we have to the media."

The attorney laughs. "I suggest you—"

"Go wait with the chief," Lorraine says.

The attorney opens his bought and paid for mouth but she stops him cold with a single look. Like a dog with his tail tucked between his legs, he strides off to wait with Claiborne.

"There's no reason for my daughter to be a part of this," Lorraine says.

"Mother," Heather protests. "I want to be a part of it."

Letty shakes her head. "You both stay or we leave."

"Talk," Lorraine snaps.

Letty passes the file to Heather. "You'll find a statement

from Mr. Niles Brewer about an incident he witnessed between Natalie and your father. You'll also find statements from both Kellie Pike and Clare Tubbs about the time of your father's accident and the subsequent request by Chief Claiborne for the time on the report to be changed."

"This is ludicrous," Lorraine rants.

Heather opens the folder and reviews the contents.

"Finally," Letty says, "you'll find a statement from Glenn Wallace, the county coroner, stating that James Cotton was wearing his dog tags when he took his life. Mr. Wallace witnessed my mother removing those dog tags. There is no way they ended up in that cave by his hand."

"Do you realize how desperate you sound?" Lorraine laughs. "Obviously," she turns her haughty glare on me, "you don't know your mother very well, Emma. Glenn Wallace would do anything for her. And you," she turns back to Letty, "your behavior is pathetic and utterly unprofessional. You should have come to terms with what your father did long ago."

I want to punch the woman. I realize I would likely be charged with elder abuse but I want it bad.

"What's this?" Heather holds up a photo of Natalie and my fury dies an instant death.

"That's the photo Natalie's parents gave the police during the original investigation," Letty explains. "That photo ran on all the media outlets and in the newspapers."

Heather studies the photo as if she is still confused.

"The necklace," I say. "That's the necklace she wore every day. She was wearing it the day she went missing."

Lorraine stops her grumbling and stares at the photo.

"You see," Letty says to Heather, "your father made a mistake when he disposed of the bodies—"

"Stop right there," Lorraine demands.

Letty doesn't stop. She recounts the story her mom told us last night, down to the last, grisly detail.

"That's not possible," Heather says and yet her tone belies her words almost as if she remembers something that causes her to doubt her conviction.

Letty nods. "What I just told you happened. Whether it was your father who killed Natalie and Stacy, I can't be sure, but if it wasn't him, then it was Mark, or maybe it was your mother."

"Leave my son out of this." Lorraine goes toe to toe with Letty. "I will not allow you to drag my children into this twisted fantasy your mothers have concocted."

A silent standoff lasts a pulse pounding half a minute.

Lorraine breaks first. "What do you want?" she growls.

"Your consent to an official search of your entire property—"

"Lorraine!" The attorney storms forward. "This has gone far enough."

"And you'll what?" Lorraine demands, her gaze locked with Letty's.

"If we find nothing, we let this go."

My jaw drops. We did not discuss letting it go. "Jesus, Letty."

"I have your word on that," Lorraine says, the gleam in her eyes indicative of her confidence that she has already won this battle.

"You have my word, but," Letty counters, "I select the search team."

The Beaumont matriarch hesitates, but only for a moment. "All right."

The chief joins the huddle and both men rant at Lorraine and Letty. Heather and I stand on the outside, staring at them and then at each other. She looks away first. In that instant I understand that my gut instinct was right.

She knows something.

∾

IT TAKES an hour to assemble the search team. Letty has set aside her personal time off for the day and directs the troops. The team consists of Agent Watwood and his partner, Letty's three most trusted deputies, including O'Neal, two forensic techs from the lab in Huntsville, as well as the county's K-9 Unit.

And me.

Once again, to keep things official, Letty deputizes me.

"How long do you expect me to put up with this?" Lorraine demands.

"As long as it takes." Letty walks away from her.

The attorney just shakes his head. Claiborne and three of his men stay near the house. Lorraine and the attorney join them.

Heather sits on the front porch. She has called Brad and told him to keep the kids away from grandma's house. Mark and Marshall haven't shown. I surmise that mommy dearest called and ordered the two to steer clear as well.

Letty motions for me to join her in the backyard.

"I want you to think 'underground'," she says. "Call my Mom and ask her if there are any specific places you should look. Helen is on the way with the pajama's Natalie slept in the night before she disappeared. She's had them packed away but it's been twenty-five years. Who knows if the dogs can get the scent, but we have to try."

I think of how Natalie's closet still smells like her. "It might just work." I hesitate. "What if we don't find anything?"

She nods. "We will. Beaumont was obsessed. I'm betting the farm on the idea that the necklace isn't the only thing he kept and that Natalie wasn't the only object of his obsession." She shrugs. "Worst case scenario, we don't find anything here, I'll interview every student Matthew Beaumont ever had. I'll find someone who'll talk."

Letty hustles off to coordinate the team while I make the

call to Ginny. We talk about the well house, the cellar under the house and the storm cellar built into the hillside at the tree line where the driveway ends.

I start with the old storm cellar. It's a fair distance from the house and judging by how difficult it is to force the door inward it hasn't been used in a while. This is where Beaumont claimed to have left Natalie and Stacy. Old wooden ladder-back chairs hang from the walls. Cobwebs and boxes of junk. With gloves protecting my hands as well as any evidence I stumble upon, I pick through the junk a piece at a time. It sickens me to think that this place may be where Natalie and Stacy took their last breaths. I force the thought away and keep looking.

Nothing.

I hear the dogs in the distance.

My chest feels tight but at the same time my pulse is pounding. I refuse to get my hopes up that we will finally know the whole truth.

I move on to the well house. It's a larger well house with both a hand drawn well and a newer state of the art pump system. The well house is cleaner. I pick through the storage boxes and wooden boxes of tools.

Nothing here either.

I head for the house, the front door stands open and techs are going in. Lorraine looks furious but Heather looks forlorn. I kick myself for feeling even a sliver of sympathy for her.

The cellar doors open fairly easily once they're unlocked by the attorney. Lorraine refuses to come near anyone involved in the search. Fine by me.

The cellar steps are sound. Luckily there's a working over-head light. As I reach the final step at the bottom I see that it's the typical old-fashioned cellar in these style houses. Brick walls and stone floors. Rough-hewn wood shelving lines one wall while more modern metal shelving lines the rest.

I start with the cardboard and wood boxes since they're older. I go through the boxes on the lower shelves first. I'll get a ladder to reach the top after I've finished the reachable ones. The task takes considerable time. As I grab the ladder from the corner behind the steps, I hear the dogs going crazy outside. I assume that means Helen has arrived with Natalie's pajamas.

Once I'm on the ladder, I can make out the faded writing on the cardboard boxes on the top shelf. *Classroom Supplies.*

I bring the first box down. Inside are beakers, test tubes and vials wrapped carefully in paper. I decide to leave these boxes on the floor until I'm finished. I do not want to accidentally knock one off while retrieving another.

Second box, same as the first. Third box, grade books. I pull down the fourth box, the last on this particular shelf. More grade books.

Damn it. I grab the first of the four and ascend the ladder once more. One by one I place them back on the shelf. Frustrated, I move on to the next set of shelves. These are the newer ones. I start at the bottom and look through the plastic tubs. School papers for Heather and her brothers. School awards. All sorts of artwork brought home from school and church that likely hung on the fridge until finding its way here.

I move to the third shelf, about even with my waist, and remove the plastic tubs and place them on the floor. These shelves are stacked two containers deep. It's easier to remove them all and then put them back as I go through each one.

Outside one of the dogs raises hell. Anticipation roars inside me but I try to focus on my goal, getting through the contents of the cellar. Letty has things outside under control. My full attention is needed on my part of this monumental task. As I remove the last tub on this shelf a lopsided row of bricks in the wall behind the shelving unit snags my attention. A frown nags at my brow as I place the tub with the others. It's not unusual in these old houses for things to be crooked or unlevel. Still, curiosity gets the better of me and I return to the shelf, reach across it and touch one of the bricks. It moves. I push at it again, this time with a little more effort. It disappears into the wall.

Pulse speeding up, I remove all the bins and tubs from the shelving unit and then drag it from the wall. I start pulling the bricks free, allowing them to fall to the stone floor where I shove them to the side with my foot. Dust flies. Dank air fills my lungs. An opening about three or so feet high by three feet wide bares itself to me. I can now see the wooden lintel that supports the brick above the opening, perhaps there was once a door.

Beyond the opening it's black as pitch. I need a flashlight.

I start up the stairs to ask one of the cops to borrow a flashlight when an animal barrels past me, almost knocking me down the steps.

Dog.

The dog disappears into the hole I've uncovered.

"Sorry, ma'am." A deputy hustles down the steps. "I was headed to the well house and when we walked by the cellar door he tore loose from me."

"No problem. I need your flashlight." I hold out my hand even as my gaze drifts over to the hole where from within those dark depths the dog yelps once, twice.

"Yes, ma'am."

The flashlight lands in my palm.

"He's young," the deputy explains. "This is his first time in an official search like this, but it sounds like he's picked up on something."

"I'll have a look," I say as I navigate my way through the maze of bins, tubs and bricks. I crouch down at the opening and turn on the flashlight.

Beyond the dog who has started to whimper and paw at the ground, the first thing I see is pink.

I can no longer drag air into my lungs. My heart shudders

in my chest. I tell myself that this could be some of Heather's things. Maybe she had a secret playhouse. Still, I tremble as I crawl on hands and knees into the space.

There are boxes and a stool. A table. Photos or something like that lie on the table. But it's the pink backpack that I need to reach. As I draw closer, I see the hearts and stars drawn in black marker all over the front of it and I catch my breath.

The dog gives a sharp yelp and paws at the backpack. Behind me I'm aware the handler has called out to him, but I cannot speak or move.

Reluctantly, the dog obeys and trots away.

When I am alone, I place the flashlight on the floor and, hands shaking, open the backpack. Books and spiral notepads are stuffed inside. I remove one of the notepads and open the front cover.

Natalie Graves.

I start to cry.

IT TAKES hours for all the evidence to be processed for removal from the scene. I standby, Helen at my side, and watch the dozens of trips made in and out of the cellar by the forensic tech. Letty keeps us filled in.

Matthew Beaumont collected photos of dozens of girls during his career as a teacher. Many of the photos show girls completely nude. Others only partially. There are two photos of Stacy, but none of Natalie. I recognize several of the girls, one in particular—Mallory Carlisle Jacobs.

Bracelets, including one belonging to Stacy Yarbrough, rings and earrings comprise his collection of souvenirs.

Lorraine and her family have lawyered up.

No one is talking.

But my mother and I now know the truth. Matthew Beaumont killed our perfect Natalie and her best friend Stacy.

I am weak with relief, overwhelmed with emotion.
But the mystery isn't completely solved yet.
Fury burns through my body.
Someone helped him bury the bodies.

35

THE SEARCH FOR EVIDENCE ON THE BEAUMONT PROPERTY IS ongoing even as darkness falls. Since one other girl disappeared twelve years prior to Natalie and Stacy and her photo was found among the ones in Beaumont's hidden playroom, the police are now searching for her remains as well.

At the Jackson Falls Police Department Agent Watwood, his partner and one of the agents from the FBI are interviewing Lorraine and Mark Beaumont. Heather and the youngest Beaumont have been left out of the questioning since she was only eight and he was only three at the time Natalie and Stacy disappeared.

Mallory isn't answering her cell and isn't at home. I guess she has already heard about the photos and knows hers is among them. She's probably embarrassed and doesn't want to talk about it. At some point she'll have to. Letty says they'll issue a BOLO if they can't find Mallory soon.

Someone leaked to Lila Lawson about the photos and souvenirs. The tip hotline is on fire with women calling in to tell their stories about how they were sexually harassed and/or abused by Matthew Beaumont. Reporters have practically surrounded the building.

Chief Claiborne is retiring. He is also in one of the interview rooms being interrogated. Pike and Brewer have been sequestered as well. The county district attorney says he is happy to recuse himself and allow the feds to handle this one since he is a longtime friend of Lorraine Jackson Beaumont.

Who's surprised with that one?

The mothers have been stashed away in the former chief's office. Letty doesn't want them out there for the reporters to hound. I wander the halls of the department, feeling oddly restless. I need a shower after crawling around in that cellar. According to Lorraine the hidden room in the cellar was a hiding place for confederate soldiers back in the day. Her family, she claims, rescued numerous soldiers. Hoping to spin the story, she weaves a tale about her great-grandmother who was originally from New York using the hiding place as a part of the Underground Railroad.

Somehow I doubt the latter since she would have been touting that connection to history for the past few decades. Anything to draw the right kind of attention to the Jackson family name.

It's clear to all involved that she didn't know how her late husband had used the forgotten room. All that evidence would have been long gone if she'd had a clue.

I walk into the chief's office, closing the door behind me. Helen smiles at me. Beyond the smile I see the weariness. This has been a difficult time for her and for Ginny, who looks equally exhausted. The nightmare is nearly over for the Cotton family. And though there is no happy ending for the Graves family, the not-knowing is mostly over. I am hoping that Lorraine and Mark Beaumont will confess to burying the bodies. Someone besides the killer did and I want to know who that someone was.

"You guys need anything?"

Helen reaches for my hand. She smiles and I go to her. She pulls me down into the chair next to her. "How about you? How are you holding up?" She smiles at her old friend. "Letty was in here a few minutes ago. She seems to be in her element."

Ginny nods. "You two did what all those others couldn't. I am so thankful."

I hug them both.

"I think I'm going to try sneaking out of here." I sniff my tee shirt. "I need a shower and a change of clothes."

Mother hugs me and makes me promise to come right back as soon as I've scrubbed the Jackson-Beaumont stench off my skin.

I look for Letty then. I'm hoping I can hitch a ride home with a cop. Delbert Yarbrough sits on the bench in the lobby. He sees me about the same time I see him. Letty told me that the district attorney is still working out the details of whether or not he will be charged for how he helped the Shepherd girl and the Baldwin girl hide. The parents were initially furious and demanding that he be charged with kidnapping but they have changed their minds. Their daughters have persuaded them to see that Mr. Yarbrough actually protected them because they initially intended to simply hide in the woods.

Personally I believe he meant well. If anything, I feel he needs counseling. I am only now realizing how badly I need to get serious about my own counseling.

I sit down beside him. "Are you doing okay, Mr. Yarbrough?"

"It's difficult to fathom the idea that my little girl was just up the road before her body was dragged into that cave." He shrugs. "I feel like I failed her."

I pull him into a hug, can't help myself, and we cry together for a few moments. Then I say the only thing I can. "We all did what we could."

Eventually I find Letty and she arranges a ride home for me.

Since all the reporters are camped out at City Hall and

none are hanging around my house, the cruiser stops out front. I thank him for the ride and hurry inside. If any neighbors are peeking out their windows, I have no desire for visitors.

I unlock the front door and step inside. Though I haven't lived in this house in fifteen years it feels good to be...*home*. I feel as if a giant weight has been lifted from my chest. In my back pocket my cell vibrates. I drag it out and stare at the screen. Dangerous. I smile. Jake, my priest. I let the call go to voicemail. I'll call him after my shower. I flip the lock and hurry to the stairs.

"Emma."

I trip on the first step, stumble and bang my shin against the second one. "Shit."

Mallory steps from behind the staircase. "I didn't mean to startle you."

I straighten, rubbing my shin. "Mallory, you haven't been answering your phone."

She hugs herself. "I couldn't bear to talk about it to anyone." Her gaze rests on me. "Except you. I can talk to you."

"Okay." I gesture toward the kitchen behind her. "You want some coffee or tea?"

The idea that she likely knows at least a few of Lorraine's secrets has my instincts humming. If I can get her talking, maybe we'll learn the rest of the story.

"Tea would be good."

We walk into the kitchen together. She goes to the bank of windows beyond the table to look out over the backyard while I set the flame under the kettle.

"Your mother has always had a green thumb. Her yard wins an award every year, did you know that?"

I reach for the cups. "That's Helen. She loves her flowers."

As a child I used to think she loved her flowers more than me. I realize now the flowers became her way of coping. I refuse to allow the insinuated affair with the coroner to enter my thoughts. If that story is true, it's Helen's business not mine.

I remove the lid from her tea chest. "What kind of tea would you like? She has Earl Grey and—"

"You shouldn't have come back, Emma."

I turn around, surprised as much by her tone as by the words. My mouth opens to ask what she means but my gaze zeros in on the gun in her hand so my tongue fails me.

"If you hadn't come back none of this would have happened."

I find my voice. "I'm sorry you feel that way, Mallory."

"I understood him. No one had ever loved me the way he did."

I feel sick to my stomach at her words. "He used you, Mallory. He was a serial pedophile."

"No!" Her hand—the one holding the gun—shakes. "Your damned sister ruined him."

Every part of me stills, grows eerily quiet. "What do you mean?"

Tears flow down her cheeks as she moves closer. I stay very still.

"He loved me. I was his special girl. We were going to be together forever until Stacy started flaunting herself around him. She let him touch her. He got all wrapped up in her and all I could do was watch. I hated her. Hated Natalie for being her friend."

I recognize I have only one option to keep her talking and to stay alive—give her what she wants. "Stacy was a whore," I say. "I hated her, too."

Surprise flares in her eyes.

"She fooled Natalie."

Fury tightens her mouth. "Natalie was no better than Stacy," she snarls.

I nod. "You would know better than me. I was just a stupid kid."

"When Matt realized what Stacy was and turned back to me I thought he had learned his lesson. Especially since Stacy kept acting all depressed and shit. She could have ruined him."

"I remember. It was around the holidays," I say as if I am commiserating with her. "Thanksgiving and Christmas."

"I hoped the stupid little bitch would just kill herself and be done with it, but, of course she didn't. She had Natalie helping her."

She stands only three feet away now, her backside braced against the table, the weapon still aimed at my chest. The kettle shrieks behind me.

I swallow back the fear. "Natalie was selfish."

"She started flirting with Matt. I warned him it was probably a trap, but he wouldn't listen. He went crazy over Natalie." Her voice rises with each word. "It was like I no longer existed. She was all he talked about, all he wanted." She laughed. "And it was different with Natalie. He actually thought she was going to run away with him. He had everything planned out. Fool."

"Did Natalie trick him?" I venture. "Or was it Stacy?"

She grasped the weapon with both hands, her entire body shaking with emotion. "Your damned sister told him to pick her up at the farm after school and they would runaway together. Of course you know what happened that day. Matt found her and Stacy walking away from the bus crash. They were all panicked and worried about the bus driver and you. Matt told them he would take them for help but they didn't trust him so he used this gun" she tilts the weapon in her hand to draw my attention there "to force them into the trunk."

"I'm sure he knew by then that you were right."

"Damn straight he did. I was waiting for him at his house. It was Tuesday. You see, every Tuesday Lorraine took Heather to Nashville for voice lessons. She wouldn't be home for hours. When Matt got to his house he wasn't too happy to see me but if it hadn't been for me Natalie would have gotten away. When he opened the trunk she tried to run. She knew he wouldn't shoot her. And she was right. But I caught her and dragged her back to him."

Agony bursts inside me. On top of that agony is outrage. I want to kill this woman.

"I helped him tie them up and gag them with duct tape. Then he locked them in the storm cellar. He was beside himself but I was there to comfort him. Then his piece of shit son called. Mark's coach found pills in his locker. The idiot got himself hooked on painkillers. So of course Daddy rushed to take care of his precious boy."

Something else Lorraine tried to cover up all these years.

"But all was not lost. I figured Matt and I could use his plan for ourselves. After all, he realized that Natalie didn't really love him. She was just trying to set him up. She and Stacy were going to record his visit to the farm. But I took care of that for him." She smiled at me. "While he went off to save Mark, I took the dumbass's baseball bat, retrieved the key from above the storm cellar door and went inside and made sure he never had to worry about Natalie and Stacy again. They tried to scream but the tape on their mouths kept the sounds from escaping. Three whacks to the head each. Then I locked the door and waited."

I no longer care about the gun in her hand. My rage roars inside me. Steals my breath.

I am going to kill her.

"Then I heard the sirens," she says, delaying my move. "It was Matt. He'd had the accident and he was hurt bad."

The tears in her voice make me smile. "I wish it had killed him."

She jams the muzzle of the gun in my chest. "What did you say?"

"I said I wished the accident had killed him."

One endless second of nothing but the high-pitched whistle of the kettle hangs in the air between us.

"Mallory."

The male voice—one I would recognize anywhere—snaps my attention across the room.

Jake.

The priest is standing just inside the backdoor. Where did he come from?

"Father Barnes," Mallory says, the pressure of the muzzle against my chest lessening ever so slightly as she stares at him, goggle-eyed.

"Mallory, the police are on the way," he says gently. "You should give me the gun now so we can clear all this up without any trouble."

She blinks, once, twice and the muzzle draws away an inch.

I duck, simultaneously shoving her arms upward.

The weapon discharges.

I hit the floor.

Another bullet explodes from the gun.

Mallory is screaming, a macabre harmony with the kettle's screeching.

I dare to move.

Jake has her pinned to the floor. The gun is lying in the middle of the room.

"Unlock the front door," Jake orders. "The police will be here any second."

I do as he asks. When I return to the kitchen. He and Mallory are sitting in the floor. She is curled in a fetal position against the cabinets, he sits at an angle in front of her, ensuring she doesn't try to take off, I presume. I turn off the stove, the whistling kettle fizzles out.

I pick up the gun and crouch down in front of them. I

hold it, muzzle down, but I want Mallory to see that I have it. "Who buried their bodies?"

She stares at the floor, bawling like a cow.

I look Jake in the eye. "Go watch for the police."

"Emma, you're upset, you're not thinking clearly."

"Go to the freaking porch and wait," I shout.

He shakes his head. "No."

"Then watch." I ram the muzzle of the gun into her chest. She grunts and whimpers some more. "What happened to Natalie and Stacy after you hit them on the head with the goddamned baseball bat?"

She lifts her watery gaze to mine. "I went to visit them a few times. Took their backpacks to Matt's secret place. I knew that's what he would want me to do. Eventually, I knew Lorraine would figure it all out because they started to stink."

Every ounce of willpower I possess is necessary to keep me from pulling the trigger.

"I hid in the woods every day after school to watch so I could tell Matt what his bitch wife did. I knew he would need me more than ever when he came home."

"What did you see?" My body starts to shake and I struggle to hold my position. I am grateful Jake keeps his mouth shut. I cannot bring myself to look at him.

"Lorraine and Mark stuffed them into plastic bags and loaded them into the truck the grounds keeper used. I didn't know where they went from there until those cavers found the bones."

I hear the sirens outside. I stand and walk to the front door, the weapon hanging from my hand.

Letty is the first to reach the door. She takes the weapon from me and I collapse against her. "It was Mallory. She used a baseball bat," I say. "Lorraine and Mark buried the bodies."

Letty hugs me hard then turns me over to Jake.

I watch as Mallory is escorted from the house.

When I can speak without sobbing, I look up at this priest

my mother adores and who shares many of my own struggles. "I won't ask how you knew to come but thank you. Things might have ended very differently if you hadn't shown up."

He smiles and I understand at that moment why Helen adores him. He really is a good man and a good priest.

"I promised I'd be watching out for you."

I nod. "I guess my mother was right."

"How's that?"

"She said I had a guardian angel."

36

MONDAY, MAY 21

THE FUNERAL MASS WAS BEAUTIFUL. IF I HEARD THE statement once, I heard it a hundred times. Jake's eulogy was perfect. The gathering of friends after the burial was long and I am exhausted. Letty and her mother refuse to go home until they've cleaned everything up. They insisted Helen and I get out of their way. So we sit on the porch swing listening to the quiet of the evening.

"As soon as Lorraine heard Mallory had been found she was ready to cut a deal." Helen sighs. "She's taking the brunt of the charges so her son gets off a little easier. He's back in rehab anyway. You would have loved seeing Ginny in action. We had decided to go home when they came out of that interrogation room. Letty had already told us Lorraine had confessed to taking James's dog tags and all the rest. I guess the good Lord wanted Ginny to have a little revenge because we were suddenly all in the corridor together. Ginny slapped Lorraine's face. Smack! Then we walked away."

"Good for her."

I feel relief and an odd sort of sadness. We know the whole truth now. My nightmares have disappeared. I feel stronger than I have in ages. There's nothing left to do but get back to my life.

But I do have a couple of questions for Helen.

"Mom, I…" It doesn't seem fair to question her actions or her motives so I shut my mouth.

She looks at me. "Ask whatever you like."

"You had an affair with Mr. Wallace."

She nods. "It was an accident. A one-time thing. I was utterly heartbroken and Andrew was completely focused on helping you deal with the loss of your sister. I was obsessed with getting posters out there hoping that someone had seen the girls. It felt like Andrew and I were miles apart. I needed to be supportive of Ginny and yet I couldn't be the friend I should be any more than I could be a proper wife to Andrew or a good mother to you."

She stares off into the distance for a moment. "Glenn's wife was going through the change and was suddenly uninterested in intimacy. We were just both in a bad place. I went to him, hoping he could tell me what more I could do to try and find Natalie. Claiborne had long since run out of patience with me. It was a moment—a single moment and a painful mistake. I asked Glenn to keep our secret and he did. The last thing I wanted was for it to get around town and hurt my family."

She falls silent, shakes her head. I wait for her to continue.

"I had no idea Lorraine had spies everywhere even then. Apparently, someone had seen us together that one time. Lorraine tucked the information away and then held it over Glenn's head when the dog tags were found in that cave. He never said a word to me, but after he signed that statement for Claiborne, I knew something was wrong. Glenn was an honorable man, so I went to him for an explanation. He told me what Lorraine had threatened, and I released him from the promise he made me all those years ago."

Wow. "Did Dad ever know?"

"I could never keep that from him." She smiles sadly. "When you love someone as much as your father and I loved each other, you share everything. I told Andrew and he forgave me."

"You never told me about the baby."

She doesn't look surprised that I figured out her secret. "It was too painful to talk about on top of everything else. I didn't want you to have to deal with anything more. I've spent years wondering if God punished me for not having faith."

"Mother."

"I know." She nods. "I was not in a good place."

I drape my arm around her. "Who would've been? You showed amazing strength considering."

She smiles at me. Takes my hand in hers and squeezes. "I'm not the only strong woman in this family."

"I don't know if I'm as strong as you think." I sigh. It's time to come clean. "I had a little meltdown about three weeks ago."

"I know."

I turn to her. "You do? How?" I am certain Letty would never betray my confidence.

"The hospital called me. I rushed to Boston but the doctor explained that you didn't want anyone to know so I came home. I figured when you were ready to tell me, you would."

Guilt piles on my shoulders. "I hope that didn't have anything to do with your heart attack?"

"Please." She pooh-poohs the idea. "Bad genes. My mother had at least three heart attacks before she checked out. So don't worry, I've got a couple to go."

I shake my head. "You are a mess, do you know that?"

We laugh and sit quietly for a moment. The breeze feels good and the lull of the slowly moving swing is so relaxing. I could sit right here forever.

"I wish Dad had lived to be here." My heart aches that he isn't. "To know the truth and to see justice done."

"The night he died," Helen says, "I told him the secret I had kept for Ginny. I didn't want him to go to his grave not knowing the truth."

"He understood?" Toward the end his lucid moments were few and far between.

"He did. He told me to thank Ginny for whatever part she played in that bastard Matthew Beaumont getting his."

A smile stretches across my lips. "Good."

Letty and her mom appear wielding a tray of lemonade and tea cakes. Letty places the tray on the table between the chairs facing the swing.

"It's my grandmother's recipe," Ginny explains. She passes each of us a napkin and then a fluffy palm size cake. "The way tea cakes were meant to be."

Letty pours the lemonade. "And this," she says as she passes each of us a glass, "is Helen's secret recipe." She winks. "It was already prepared and waiting in the back of the fridge."

We laugh and enjoy the sweet cakes and the pungent sour of the lemonade.

In all my years away I have forgotten how calming and serene it is to simply sit on the porch swing and enjoy a home-made treat and good friends. Somehow in the past fifteen years I lost my ability to touch this place inside me—this special place I remember as a child.

I think of Natalie dancing around on the front porch at the farm as we all sipped sweet tea or lemonade and applauded. I wanted to be just like her. She was beautiful and perfect and the kind of person all young women should aspire to be. She lost her life trying to help her friend and to save other girls from what Stacy and so many others had suffered. My sister died a hero.

Tears well in my eyes and I blink them away.

I lift my glass. "To Natalie."

"To Natalie," the others repeat as our glasses clink.

Helen lifts her glass. "And to the strongest women I know."

"Hear, hear," I agree and tap my glass to hers.

I look around me at the beautiful and stunningly strong women I love so deeply and I realize how very lucky I am.

For a time we enjoy the quiet and the feeling of contentment.

"I spoke to Judge Gaines before he left this evening," Letty says. "You remember him, Emma? Albert Gaines? We went to school with his son Allen."

"Yes, I remember him. Allen was the big basketball star during high school."

Letty grins. "He's a lawyer in Birmingham now. Making the big bucks from what I hear."

"I hear he has a husband," Helen says. "A very handsome husband."

"Good for him," I say.

"Anyway," Letty goes on, "Judge Gaines asked if I had any recommendations for Wallace's replacement."

Helen says, "The coroner's position is an elected position, isn't it?"

"Sure is," Ginny agrees, "but when a sitting coroner has to vacate his office in the middle of a term, the judge can appoint a replacement to fulfill the term."

I smell a set-up. "What're you three up to?"

"I recommended you," Letty says.

"Letty." I am torn between being honored and wholly frustrated.

"You seem to be undecided about where you want to go career wise at the moment. I figure you can fill in here until you decide what you want to do next."

"I could use the company," Helen adds, "after my heart attack and all."

"Right." I roll my eyes. "I think you're doing just fine, Mother."

"Maybe you can help Letty find a husband and make me some grandbabies."

Letty glares at her mother.

I laugh. "I'm afraid that would be like the blind leading the blind, Ginny."

"Will you stay for a while, Emma?" Letty asks.

I meet my dear friend's gaze. The truth is I don't know what I want to do next. Boston has sort of lost its appeal for me.

Why the hell not?

I turn to Mother. "Do you actually believe you can put up with me? I can be a pain in the ass sometimes. I like my solitude and I've been known to be grumpy."

"I would love having you home for however long you want to stay."

How can I say no? I look to Letty. "I accept."

Helen kisses my cheek, and for the first time in a very long time I am so glad to be right here.

I hate to sound cliché, but there truly is no place like home.

ABOUT THE AUTHOR

I hope you enjoyed my story! Please follow me on Amazon!

DEBRA WEBB is the USA Today bestselling author of more than 150 novels, including reader favorites the Faces of Evil, the Colby Agency and the Shades of Death series. She is the recipient of the prestigious Romantic Times Career Achievement Award for Romantic Suspense as well as numerous Reviewers Choice Awards. In 2012 Debra was honored as the first recipient of the esteemed L. A. Banks Warrior Woman Award for her courage, strength, and grace in the face of adversity. Recently Debra was awarded the distinguished Centennial Award for having achieved publication of her 100th novel. With this award Debra joined the ranks of a handful of authors like Nora Roberts and Carole Mortimer.

With more than four million books sold in numerous languages and countries, Debra's love of storytelling goes back to her childhood when her mother bought her an old typewriter in a tag sale. Born in Alabama, Debra grew up on a farm and spent every available hour exploring the world around her and creating her stories. She wrote her first story at age nine and her first romance at thirteen. It wasn't until she spent three years working for the Commanding General of the US Army in Berlin behind the Iron Curtain and a five-year stint in NASA's Shuttle Program that she realized her true calling. A collision course between suspense and romance was set. Since then she has expanded her work into some of the darkest places the human psyche dares to go. Visit Debra at www.debrawebb.com.

Made in the USA
Middletown, DE
27 April 2021